Larentina

Myth, Legend, Legacy

Linda D. Coker

iUniverse, Inc.
Bloomington

All characters in this story are fictional; any resemblance to actual persons, living or dead, is purely coincidental, with the exception of historical figures who were mentioned in this fictional account.
The views and opinions presented in this story are those of the author, who does not speak in an official capacity for the US military or the Department of Defense. References to political figures, biblical theology, Greek mythology, and other myths are the author's personal opinions and imagination.

iUniverse books may be ordered through booksellers or by contacting:

iUniverse
1663 Liberty Drive
Bloomington, IN 47403
www.iuniverse.com
1-800-Authors (1-800-288-4677)

ISBN: 978-1-4502-7934-5 (sc)
ISBN: 978-1-4502-7935-2 (hc)
ISBN: 978-1-4502-7936-9 (ebook)

Library of Congress Control Number: 2010919126

Printed in the United States of America

iUniverse rev. date: 01/05/2011

Dedication

I dedicate this tale to the American Armed Forces and to my family for instilling in me the curiosity for biblical theology and Greek mythology.

In loving memory of my grandmothers
Alice Virginia Swann

(July 5, 1916 - August 31, 2007)

&

Martha Frances Gibson

(February 17, 1917 – February 12, 1994)

Acknowledgments

I would like to thank Andy Forward for providing me with the audio sounds of a horse. I used these sounds when writing descriptions of the sounds made by Celeris. Writing a description of a sound is much easier if you have the sound readily accessible. You can visit his website at www.horsepresence.com/shop/SoundsHome.html.

I would like to give thanks to Denise Howard Long of FirstEditing. Denise and her editing team are the greatest. I truly enjoyed working with these professionals, and I consider them part of my team.

I would like to give great thanks to Ailia Athena for introducing me to Howard David Johnson. You can visit her website at www.paleothea.com.

Finally, I would like to give great thanks to Howard David Johnson for his fantastic illustrations. You must check out his website at www.howarddavidjohnson.com.

Prelude

American soldiers join the army to serve their God, their country, and their family. They define themselves through honor, duty, loyalty, and personal sacrifice so that our civilians may bask in honor, glory, freedom, and liberty, and more easily grasp the American dream. An American soldier is prepared not only to spill blood, but also to die for these simple beliefs, just as many great military forces have sacrificed throughout the ages for their own beliefs.

Very little historical documentation exists to explain why Spartan women experienced greater freedom than women in other Greek city-states. Only a few Spartan women became famous throughout the ages. Theories and opinions abound regarding how their liberties were embraced by their culture, but my research failed to uncover any concrete facts. Throughout time, Spartan women have been defined as strong and noble, but men who feared these women because they could not understand them also described them as whores.

Spartan women proved they were good for more than simply giving birth to strong Spartan warriors. They also could be trusted to protect their city-state while their men were off in battle.

In Roman mythology, the Romans depicted Larentina as the she wolf from whom the twins, Romulus and Remus, suckled as infants. These babes who fed from the breasts of a She Wolf grew to become the founders of the Roman Empire.

The Greeks knew Aphrodite as the goddess of love. The Egyptians knew her as the goddess of war; she was called Isis, Hesiri, and Hathor. Throughout the ages, she has been known by hundreds of names, and myths about her have been told throughout the Middle East, Greece, Europe, and even Russia.

Aphrodite's mortal names were Semiramis, Astarte, and Ishtar, which means gift of the sea, and also from the land she came from. Semiramis was the wife of Noah's great-great-great… grandson, Nimrod, the king of Babylon. The biblical words describe her as an abomination.

THE CONCEPTION STORY OF LARENTINA AND LYCURGUS

ANCIENT SPARTA

Queen Agape, the wife of King Karpos and the twin sister of Queen Alexis, was bathing in a small lake located in the forest less than a mile from her home. It was a beautiful sunny day, and she was enjoying the solitude from her normally busy life.

Agape would visit the lake whenever she had a chance. It had a small grassy embankment surrounded by thick green foliage. Agape watched as two deer timidly drank the water on the other side of the lake. She could hear the birds chirping as she relaxed in the cool water.

As Agape walked up the embankment, she noticed a large group of multicolored wildflowers on the edge of the clearing. She could not resist and bent down, smelling their sweet scent. She picked several of them before she lay upon the soft grass, continuing to breathe in their sweetness.

Her husband, King Karpos, was off in battle, and she was looking forward to his safe return. Agape had learned from her sister that King Alcaeus, the other Spartan king, was preparing to relieve King Karpos from the battlefield.

According to Spartan law, only one king ruled the military legions on the battlefield at a time. The kings had been best of friends since childhood. Because they were such close friends, they always shared the glory of victory and took turns leading the battle.

As Agape rested on the grassy embankment, enjoying the warmth of the sun on her lean, naked body, she let her thoughts wander pleasantly back to when she and her sister first met their husbands.

* * *

Agape had met King Alcaeus by chance almost three years ago, while picking wildflowers close to her family home. It had been an embarrassing moment because Alcaeus was relieving himself behind a tree, and he did not notice Agape nearby until he heard her gasp. He peeked from behind the tree and blushed as Agape's round cheeks turned red, and she nervously giggled as she lowered her gaze from him.

Agape's skin was golden brown from the sun. Her eyes were emerald green, and her hair was a shiny, light brown. She wore one thick braid down her back, and her face was framed in curls. Her full, red lips and small, pert nose made her even more beautiful, and atop her head, she was wearing a crown of wildflowers that she had made. The tunic she wore was a soft, light pink cotton, and it flowed to her knees. The gold belt cinched at her waist accentuated how tiny she was, and her feet were bare on the ground. In Alcaeus's estimation, she could not have been any older than seventeen.

Alcaeus was still a prince and was not crowned yet, but for the last two years his father had become increasingly weak and frail. Alcaeus had already been leading the battles as king because of this and the increasing responsibilities of the king were being put upon his broad shoulders. His father was dying from some unknown sickness and he prayed to the gods to make his father strong and healthy again because he loved his father very much, and he did not want the chains of responsibility that would come with the crown. Alcaeus was a man of duty and honor and if this was the will of the gods so be it. He would enjoy what little bit of freedom he had left.

Prince Alcaeus's skin was also a golden tan from the sun, and he stood at least six feet tall. His eyes were a deep brown, and he had a manly nose. The sun had bleached highlights into his wavy light brown hair, which came down just past his shoulders, but he had it pulled back into a ponytail.

Alcaeus was wearing a headband of thick, twisted leather tied in a knot at the back of his head. His face was unshaven, but he did not wear a beard. His body was broad and muscular. He was a very handsome and strong young man. Although bare from the waist up, he was wearing brown suede pants and riding boots.

After he had finished his business, Alcaeus slowly walked toward Agape; he bent down, picked a flower, and handed it to her as he sat down beside her. He flashed a boyish smile and seductively apologized as he moved his face within an inch of hers, "Please forgive me, my fair maiden, for I did not see your beauty among the flowers that you are kneeling upon. I am Prince Alcaeus of the house of Agiad. Did the gods send you to me?

You are one of the most beautiful maidens I have ever laid my eyes upon. I must know your name."

Before Agape could answer, her sister Alexis called her name, running across the creek separating the forest and the small grassy clearing where Alcaeus and Agape stood.

Alexis and Agape were identical twins. The only thing distinguishing them at present was the crown of wildflowers upon Agape's head, and the ensemble Alexis was wearing—pants and an old shirt belonging to the girls' father, both of which were completely inappropriate for a girl to be wearing.

Alexis's hair was pulled back in a pair of braids, and you could smell the sweet smell of honey on her skin. She had been collecting honey from a beehive before being sent out to retrieve her sister.

Out of breath, Alexis began barking orders disapprovingly. "Agape, Mother is looking for you. She is very displeased that you wandered off like this. You must come home now! Who is this handsome young man? What are you doing here in the forest alone with a stranger? When Mother discovers this, she will not be pleased, not pleased at all. You know we both must—" She stopped scolding her sister because she suddenly realized the stranger was likely going to take advantage of her twin.

Before Agape knew it, her sister lunged toward Alcaeus and punched him squarely in the nose. Alcaeus fell to the ground with Alexis on top of him as she continued to punch and smack him, and she screeched at him, "How dare you, you nasty monster! I will kill you for trying to take advantage of my sister! You are nothing more than a nasty cretin! Oooh! You do not deserve to live!"

Alcaeus merely laughed as Alexis continued to assault him. He was intrigued with this feisty young woman. She had shown no fear of him at all. She displayed courage, a trait that he found most admirable. She was like no other woman he had ever met.

Agape was stunned, but she mustered some courage and pulled her crazed sister off the handsome stranger, commanding, "Sister, enough! He is the prince of the Agiad house! Leave him be before you bring us both trouble! We can be executed for this!"

As Agape tried to pull her sister off of Prince Alcaeus, another handsome young man arrived on horseback. She could only imagine what this other man thought as he approached the scene.

The man chuckled at the young prince while dismounting from his horse. He asked, "What is this, Alcaeus? We have a few moments of freedom, and you have already snared not one, but two, lovely maidens! You know the rules—you must share the spoils of war!"

Karpos had been crowned king a few years prior after his father was killed in battle. Karpos prayed to the gods that his death would be as noble as his father's was. He was a man of honor and glory and considered dieing on the battlefield the most glorious death of all.

King Karpos was completely different from Prince Alcaeus. He was a few years older than the young prince and also a few inches taller. His thick straight hair was pitch black and fell loosely past his shoulders. His hair was still wet from a swim in a nearby lake. His black beard was short, unlike the typical Spartan custom. His eyes were bright blue, like a cloudless day, and his thick eyebrows were the same black as his hair. His nose was straight and strong, like a Spartan warrior. Karpos's arms and legs were composed of solid, sinewy muscle, and his chest could be seen through his open tunic. Quite simply, he was a strong and handsome man.

Karpos wore a soft cotton tunic that fell to the top of his bare feet. The tunic was a solid maroon with white trim, held in place by a wide brown leather belt tightly fastened around his waist. His sword was strapped in its leather sheath, loosely draped around his shoulder and waist. He tossed the sheath to the ground and plucked Agape off Alexis and Alcaeus as if she were a rag doll. He held her from behind by her waist as her feet dangled above the ground. Agape pulled at the stranger's arms and hands, trying to free herself, punching and scratching at his arms, but it did her no good.

She commanded him angrily, "Let go of me, you swine! You beast of a man, my father is going to kill you for touching me! Let go! Let go this instant! My sister is beating on the prince of the Agiad house, and we are surely going to be executed for this! Let me go!"

Karpos let Agape loose and guffawed teasingly. "Oh my, what shall we do? Two lovely virgins attacking a Spartan prince. Surely, the two of you shall be executed for treason! But for you to beat on a Spartan king, you will be spanked instead!"

Karpos found himself fascinated with this young woman's fiery attitude; he enjoyed the strength she demonstrated. She was lively, whereas his first wife had been somewhat boring and docile. She had bore him a son, Androcles, and she died in child birth. While he had loved his first wife dearly, this young woman was completely different.

Agape became furious with this stranger and lunged at him, beating him with her fists as hard as she could. "You lie, you nasty beast! You have no clue of the Spartan ways! My sister was protecting my honor; she does not believe he is a prince! My father surely will kill you for this!"

Alcaeus was still laughing at Alexis, as she continued beating on him.

She angrily yelled at Agape, "This man is not a prince, Sister! A Spartan prince would not try to defile a virgin maiden from his own kingdom! Neither one is wearing a Spartan uniform!"

Undisturbed by her assault, Alcaeus playfully asked, "Karpos, do you think these beautiful twins will ever tire out?"

Karpos laughed as he answered, "I do not believe so! They must be Spartans! I want this one! We should marry them! They will give us strong and healthy sons! We do not want our people thinking we run about the countryside defiling lovely Spartan virgin maidens!"

Both twins screamed in unison, "Never!"

From there, things progressed quickly. The next thing Agape realized, King Karpos and Prince Alcaeus were eating supper with her parents. Several months later, King Karpos and Prince Alcaeus were asking permission to marry Agape and Alexis.

* * *

Agape found herself thinking about how blessed she was to have captured the heart of a king. She truly loved her strong and powerful husband. She had been blessed by the gods for reasons she would never understand. She truly was happy and content. She could not wait to feel the touch of her husband again. She longed to give him strong and healthy sons.

Agape thought of the last time she had seen her husband. They made passionate love the night before he left for battle.

The next morning, he kissed her and said, "Do not worry, Wife, for I will be in your arms once again."

After King Karpos mounted his steed, Agape rubbed his horse's neck, looked up at her husband, and said with conviction, "Spartan Warrior, either come back with your shield or on it."

King Karpos smiled with pride and galloped away.

* * *

King Karpos had given Commander Nikephoros direct orders to check on Queen Agape. The commander was becoming irritated with both kings because their minds always seemed focused on the beautiful twins rather than the battlefield. Even though he completely understood that the kings were obsessed with the strongest and most beautiful women in all of Sparta, it showed weakness in them, and Nikephoros did not like this. He did not approve one bit, because if the kings were weak, Sparta was weak.

As Nikephoros and his soldiers approached the borders of Sparta, he ordered his men to go to King Alcaeus's home. They would leave at first light in the morning because he had to check on Queen Agape before escorting King Alcaeus to the battlefield. He couldn't help but feel like a helot when he had to do these domestic chores for the kings, but nonetheless, he loved both of them as if they were his brothers. They were noble and good men, and he had grown up with them in agoge.

Despite Commander Nikephoros's feelings that these tasks were degrading, he followed his orders obediently. He slowly led his horse toward the home of King Karpos and decided to rest at the lake, where the horse could drink before he completed his menial task.

Commander Nikephoros was not handsome like the Spartan kings, and he was a couple of years older as well. He had been born into a wealthy noble family. His thin straight hair was a dark brown and pulled back into a long braid, which revealed the receding hairline at his temples. He had a clean-shaven face, as was customary for a Spartan soldier, although not mandatory.

His eyes were small, light gray, and slanted slightly downward, as were his thin eyebrows. His nose was long, straight, and pointed with a bump on the ridge where it had not mended properly after being broken in battle. In addition, he was covered by scars from wounds of previous battles. He was muscular from head to toe and much stronger than his kings; he could fight in battle like no other. In fact, he was much stronger and more cunning than any other soldier. He was considered one of the greatest champions of Sparta, but the kings were considered greater because of their place in the kingdom. He worshiped the kings as gods and would have gladly given his life to protect them.

He wore the standard Spartan military garb and rode a horse issued to him from the state because of his high status.

Commander Nikephoros came upon Agape while she lay sleeping in the afternoon sun, completely naked. He had to admit that she was very beautiful and appealing. He then shook his lustful thoughts from his mind. She belonged to another man, and that man was his king.

* * *

For two years, Aphrodite had despised Alexis and Agape, because the twins had spoiled her plans to start a civil war between Alcaeus and Karpos. She had lain with both men in the hopes that typical male jealousy would result in a war over her, but instead, she discovered that these twins had somehow captured their hearts. She felt that the Spartan twins did not deserve the kings. Even though both kings were strong and skilled lovers, Aphrodite felt it was she who had taught them these skills; after all, she was the goddess of love.

Aphrodite thought she had their hearts to play with, but instead they married these beautiful twins and spoiled her plans. She had been patiently watching and waiting for an opportunity to use the twins to her advantage. Finally, the opportunity presented itself.

This day, she had her faithful companion Cupid with her. Cupid had red curly hair, and freckles covered his face and nose. He looked like a boy barely the age of ten, but he was actually thousands of years old. He feared Aphrodite because her magic was much stronger than his magic, and he obeyed her for fear of the consequences.

Aphrodite whispered in Cupid's ear, "Use your most potent arrow, my friend. Aim carefully so that you do not miss the heart of our young Nikephoros."

Cupid hesitated as he gazed at his mistress with a puzzled expression, but he did not dare to question her. He took careful aim, and his arrow struck Nikephoros in his chest as he was turning toward them.

Nikephoros felt a sharp pain in his heart. When he looked down at his chest, he saw something quickly turn to ash, but it blew away with the soft breeze before he could see what it was.

He shrugged his shoulders as he gazed at Agape once more, as if he was shrugging off the lustful thoughts in his mind. He mounted his horse and shook his head again, as the overwhelming urge of lust for Agape coursed through his entire body.

Nikephoros was a well-disciplined soldier. He suspected that Cupid's arrow had just struck him, but it would take much stronger magic than that for him to dishonor himself and his king. As he slowly rode his horse, he said to himself, *I would never dishonor my king's house; never. If I can find Cupid, I will break his little neck for doing this.* The more Nikephoros thought about what happened, the angrier he became.

Out of the corner of his eye, Nikephoros saw the wicked cherub, who had been hiding behind a tree, running away from him. Nikephoros quickly dismounted his horse and ran after him, calling out angrily, "Come back here, Cupid! Come back here so I can break your scrawny little neck. I know what you did. Now remove this spell! Now! You better not force me to chase you! So be it!"

Nikephoros caught Cupid and smacked him with so much force, he fell to the ground. Nikephoros put his sandaled foot atop him and grabbed his bow and arrows. He snapped them all at once in one bundle and angrily tossed the pieces to the ground.

Cupid was scared by the soldier's anger and confessed in a quivering voice, "My mistress—my mistress made me do it. I swear it. I cannot remove the spell; my arrow only intensifies the heart's desire; nothing more. Please let me go."

Nikephoros commanded, "Where is your mistress Aphrodite? I command you, Aphrodite, to appear before me!"

Nikephoros could not see her, but he could hear her say, "I will not. You must pray to me, and then I might appear to you."

Nikephoros breathed heavily and said, "Then I pray to Aphrodite to appear before me."

Aphrodite came into view and walked seductively toward him, saying, "All I wanted was to give you a gift for being such a strong and brave warrior. I know your heart's desire, and you would give anything to be Karpos for just one day."

As Nikephoros watched Aphrodite walk toward him, he realized that the stories about her were true. Her skin was fairer than the skin of any Spartan woman. Her eyes were the blue of the sky on a clear day, and her hair was of the purest gold. Golden curls cascaded down her back and framed her face. Her face was long and oval with a small pert nose that made her even more beautiful. She had small, red lips and just a touch of pink in her cheeks. A diamond-encrusted tiara was perched in her hair. She wore a pale purple tunic that came to her ankles, and the sheerness of the fabric allowed Nikephoros to see through it. The tunic was cinched around her tiny waist with a wide golden belt bearing gemstones, and it accentuated her perfect figure. She was wearing golden sandals and large golden bracelets; a golden necklace with a green crystal pendant rested in the cleavage of her full, round breasts.

She walked around Nikephoros, letting her hand slide down his arm. She took his hand and held it in both of hers. She looked at his palm, as if she were studying it. With the tip of her index finger, she followed the patterns of the wrinkles on his palm. Aphrodite looked up at him and softly asked, "Is it not your heart's desire to be Karpos for one day? To possess the heart of Agape as Karpos does?"

Nikephoros jerked his hand from Aphrodite. He looked down at her and, with conviction, protested, "I would never betray my king and friend."

Aphrodite smiled softly at him and responded, "Yes, you will. The only way to break Cupid's spell is to fulfill your heart's desire. I can help you do this. I can transform you into Karpos for just this day. Just ask and I will grant you this wish. If you become Karpos, no one will know. Agape will never know. You will lose nothing."

Aphrodite touched her green crystal pendant, and Nikephoros could not fight her strong and potent magic. The lust for Agape suddenly devoured him completely. He became obsessed. He found himself begging Aphrodite, "Yes, I would like to be Karpos for one day and to make Agape mine. I will give you anything for this."

Aphrodite had received the response she wanted, and at that, she transformed Nikephoros into Karpos. As she started to fade into thin air, she commanded, "Now take her."

Nikephoros, now completely crazed with lust, mounted his stallion quickly and galloped back to where he had seen Agape. He dismounted his horse just as she was stirring from her sleep.

Agape rose quickly and started putting her clothes back on. As she reached for her garments, she said, "My husband, I did not expect you to return …"

Before Agape could finish her thoughts, Nikephoros, who had been transformed into Karpos's likeness, forcefully grabbed her by the waist and passionately kissed her. With a fervent intensity, he took her right there at that moment. Later, he helped her to dress and mounted her onto his horse, still not uttering a word.

Agape was confused. Something had happened, because her husband was silent. Something was different about him. He did not seem like the same man.

Once they arrived in the courtyard of King Karpos's home, Nikephoros dismounted and helped Agape down. As he was doing so, Bion arrived. Bion, a member of the gerousia council, tried to speak with the king, but Nikephoros ignored him, picked up Agape, and carried her across the threshold. Bion called Karpos's name three times, but again, he was completely ignored.

Nikephoros made love to Agape many more times throughout the night. Just before midnight, Nikephoros took Agape one last time. At the stroke of midnight, Aphrodite appeared before Nikephoros and transformed him back into himself. Only Nikephoros could see Aphrodite. As Agape watched her husband's figure transform into Nikephoros, she heard a woman giggling wickedly.

When Agape realized who she had been with, she screamed in horror, "How could you? My husband will kill you for this! You tricked me! You have defiled me!" Agape smacked and kicked him as she screamed, "Get off me! Get off me!"

As Aphrodite continued to giggle, Nikephoros scrambled for his clothing. Now that the spell had been broken, he had nothing but remorse in his heart for the vile way he had betrayed his queen and his king. He glared at Aphrodite and bellowed angrily, "You lied! You promised no one would know!"

Aphrodite just laughed at him as she disappeared.

Agape continued screaming at Nikephoros. Suddenly, Bion opened the door and asked, "What has happened here?"

Bion had already dismissed the servants, so he was the only witness that night. He realized immediately that the man before him was not his king, and he asked in a strangely calm voice, "Commander Nikephoros, what are you doing here? Where is our king?"

Nikephoros, now fully dressed, said nothing and tried to walk past Bion, who stood almost six feet tall. Bion grabbed Nikephoros by his forearm and said, with concern in his voice, "I know not what you have done, but we will talk. Go to my home and wait for me there. We will discuss this matter when I return."

Commander Nikephoros bent his head in shame; he silently left the bedroom chamber.

Nikephoros was ashamed that he had been tricked by Aphrodite; he would never trust another woman again. He felt that all women, both mortals and goddesses, should be caged like wild animals—they used men up and discarded them. His shame could only be blamed on the actions of Aphrodite and Agape. They were at fault, not he.

Bion turned his attention to Agape, who was now curled up in a fetal position on the floor. She was sobbing in total shock, but her spirit returned, as she said, "I command you to arrest that cretin now! He has defiled the queen! I demand justice! My husband will kill him immediately!"

Bion had no sympathy for Agape; he commanded her viciously, "Shut up, whore! You are the one who defiled a great warrior! Remember, you are the second wife of King Karpos, not the first. If she had not died in childbirth with his first son, you would not be here! You are nothing but another possession to the king. Can you comprehend that, whore? The only reason I am not arresting you and having you stoned to death is because your sister is married to King Alcaeus. I will not have a civil war erupt between the kings over you women! You gave yourself willingly to the commander, and you seduced him somehow. That is what I saw. If you tell King Karpos, know this: he will kill you himself! Now cover yourself!" Bion walked out and slammed the door behind him.

Agape was in complete shock that this baboon would dare speak to her in such a manner, but he was right. How could she have been so foolish as to think her husband would even consider her feelings? He would react just as Bion had reacted. She hated them all, but she had nowhere else to go. Would her sister shun her too? She just wanted to run away.

Agape rubbed her stomach. She knew she was now pregnant with Nikephoros's child, as she could feel the warmth of conception fill her body. She hated her sister for having happiness. She hated Karpos, Alcaeus, Nikephoros, and Bion. At this moment, she hated all of Sparta!

She dressed quickly and ran as fast as her legs could take her back to the small lake where she had been earlier. She took off her clothes and threw them onto the ground. She ran into the cool water and scrubbed her skin as hard as she could, trying to remove the stench of Nikephoros from her body.

THE CONCEPTION OF AN AMERICAN SOLDIER

1979

BELINDA D. BISHOP ENLISTS AND DEPARTS

Chapter I

It is the middle of October; it is cold and raining as I board the train at the Snobville, Virginia terminal. I am leaving my home and all that is familiar to me as I'm heading toward the unknown—Fort Jackson, South Carolina.

I had just settled into my seat and I am staring out the train window when I hear the train conductor yell, "All aboard!"

I thought to myself, *Belinda, what have you gotten yourself into?* Then I let my mind wander back three months to the decision that had sealed my fate.

I had been out drinking and getting stoned with several of my girlfriends. We were all either college students or nurses. I was the latter, a nurse. I had graduated high school when I was sixteen years old. I had lived with my grandmother until the day after my eighteenth birthday, when I moved into my own apartment.

I was used to being the youngest in my group of friends. It had been that way most of my teenage years. I never told my friends how old I actually was, and they just assumed I was the same age as they were. My family and friends of my parents had always told me I was very mature for my age, and I felt more comfortable around people who were older than I was.

As we were partying, I told my friends that I had recently heard the Women's Army Corps (WAC), Women Air Force Service Pilots (WASP), and other female military branches were being disassembled and integrated into what we call the "Men's Military Forces." It took some talking, but I was finally able to convince them all to join the Air Force with me.

The next morning, after staying up all night planning, we all went to the Air Force recruiter's office. In our town, each branch of the military had their recruiters on the same block, downtown. We told him what we wanted, and he simply said, "Well, the first thing you have to do is fill out these forms." He handed each one of us a file folder filled with forms. He then pointed to a table where we could sit and fill them out. We all finished about the same time and handed them in. He reviewed them and continued, "Everything looks like it's in order now. The next thing you guys have to do is take a test. Do you guys have the time to go ahead and take this test today?"

We all shrugged our shoulders and told him we could take the test; little did we know it was going to take us the rest of the day.

He instructed us to follow him to another building located on the corner of what was commonly called Military Row. We were greeted by a sailor in Navy whites. After the first recruiter left, the Navy recruiter told us to follow him into a large classroom filled with desks in six uniform rows of ten. He motioned for us to sit in the front row.

Once we were settled in our chairs, he stated professionally, "The test you will be taking today is called Armed Services Vocational Aptitude Battery, known as the ASVAB test. This test will be the first step in determining if you are even eligible to be accepted into any military branch. We have four types of these tests. The one you will be taking today is basically an overall, general one."

After several grueling hours, we finally finished the test. I had a headache from hell. From the looks on each of my friends' faces, they were experiencing one also. To me, the test basically consisted of commonsense questions. I thought it was very easy, especially the math section. It seemed to me that a child could have easily passed it, but little did I know that was not the case at all.

After we had finished taking the test, the sailor instructed us, "Okay, ladies, I need you to wait here for a few minutes so we can get your results. Your recruiter will be here to take you back to his office, so he can go over the results with each of you individually."

The Air Force recruiter was smiling from ear to ear when he greeted us again, and we followed him back to his building.

After we were back in the front office of the building, he took each of my friends separately back into a smaller office and closed the door. My first friend came out crying and sobbing, "I wasn't accepted! Apparently, my test score didn't meet the minimum requirements. He told me I could come back later and retake it. I'm going home to bed. This was a stupid idea anyway, Belinda."

That was the last time I ever saw her.

My remaining friends and I looked at each other in shock. I had always considered my friends smarter and wiser than I was, so I thought for sure we must have all failed the ASVAB.

Then my second friend was called into the recruiter's office, and he closed the door again. She came out crying also; because of this experience, I guess, she never spoke to me again either. The same thing happened with my third friend.

Then it was just two of us left, Patty and me. I was surprised when Patty came out smiling from ear to ear; she proclaimed excitedly, "I made it with an average score."

I replied, "It's about damn time one of us passed this stupid test."

Next, I heard the recruiter call, "Miss Bishop." I got up from my chair and walked into the open doorway as he watched me. He closed the door behind us and said, "Please have a seat." He motioned to a chair in front of his desk. I sat down and eagerly waited for my results. I had no idea what to expect.

He looked through the file that was sitting on the desk in front of him, looked up at me, and commented, "Well, I always save the best for last. This is very rare, even with the men I've tested. You have an almost perfect score. We definitely want you, and I believe you will go far in the Air Force. I would like you and your friend, Patty, to join up as commissioned officers. Uum, you shouldn't have any problems since you already have a degree in medical science. We have a great educational program if you decide to go for your masters."

I responded, "But I do not want to be in the same field that I'm in now, and besides how can I be a leader if I don't earn it first?"

The recruiter looked at me with a puzzled expression and vocalized his observations. "You are definitely a unique individual, and you are absolutely right. I never looked at it quite like that before. Well, let's get your friend in here, and we will all discuss what the two of you want to do."

It turned out that the Air Force recruiter wanted us to sign up immediately and leave in a couple of days. We argued that because we had apartments, leases, utilities, pets, and personal belongings, there was no way we could leave in less than a week. We both needed at least three months to prepare. Since we were unable to work out a deal with the Air Force, we walked next door to the Navy recruiter. He looked at our test scores and also tried to get us to sign up and leave the next week. Since we could not work within those confines, we went to the Army recruiter's office next. There, the recruiter gave us the three months that we needed, so Patty and I took the oath and filled out more paperwork. We didn't sign a contract at this time because we still had to pass the physical.

The Army recruiter also wanted us to enlist as commissioned officers because I had a two-year college degree and Patty had a degree in pre-law. The Army would pay for the rest of Patty's education. In return, she would have to stay in the Army for six or more years.

Patty wanted to enlist as an officer, but I did not want the responsibility, nor did I want to be a nurse for the rest of my life. The recruiter told me that if I signed on as an officer, my Military Occupation Specialties (MOS) would be in nursing. I protested, "No, I want a different profession."

The main reason that I wanted to join the military was to have the opportunity to reinvent myself and become something more than a nurse. There is nothing wrong with being a nurse, but I already knew my life was destined for battle. I have been prepared and taught this since birth from my father's bloodline. I also wanted to be part of women's history, to make a difference. The recruiter told me that because I was already in the medical field, I would need to choose a different vocation.

With irritability showing in my voice, I said, "Fine; how about Military Intelligence (MI) or Special Operations (Special Ops) something like that?"

He simply answered, "MI will be no problem, ma'am, but women are not allowed in Special Ops. We have one slot left, but the highest rank I can give you is E-4, which includes an additional rank for coming in under the buddy program. You'll have to take more college in the field to become an officer."

I replied, "Well, we will see, but I'll take it."

* * *

A few days later I got the courage up and I told my mother I had enlisted, she flipped out! She smacked my face and yelled, "Belinda Bishop! You will not join the Army! People will think you're a freak or something. If you're thinking about your ancestors, well, forget about it. Your great grandmother and the rest of your father's family are crazy about why you were born; simply because you have special gifts that God gave you. I have never believed your gifts were to be used for some future battle between socialism and freedom. We already live in a free country. We don't need to be barbarians. You are a lady, and I'm ashamed of you for even thinking of living some kind of silly fantasy of yours and your father's family."

I angrily retorted, "Too bad, I've already joined! I would think you would be proud of me, because I will be one of the first women in our bloodline who has been allowed to join the men's Army in this country openly. Let us not forget about many, of both yours and Daddy's, women ancestors who disguised themselves as men just to serve. I thought you believed in equality for women. Isn't that how you raised me, Mommy?" Calling my parents Mommy and Daddy always works; they melt like butter; most of the time anyway.

"I'm tired of you always trying to run my life," I continued, "when it's always *me* bailing *you* out of trouble. It's always 'do my daughter's duty' with you and the rest of the family. Well, this time my daughter's duty will be for my country. You didn't really think I'd be around forever, did you, Mommy?"

My mother answered irritably, but she wasn't as angry, "Belinda Bishop! Of course, I expected you to be around forever. I raised you to be independent and free, but the Army? I never thought in my wildest dreams you would do this. I expected you to become a lawyer, politician, scholar, professor, but a soldier? Never! If you join the Army, I will constantly be worrying about your safety. You could be killed or, even worse, scarred for life. How do you think your father is going to react and the Mennonite community that you are part of, young lady? Let us not forget, Belinda, your blood will give away our secret."

I answered, with annoyance, "I didn't have to tell you anything that I am planning to do because it's none of your business. I have no intention of telling Daddy because he doesn't need to know. In fact, you are the only person I am telling because I need to store my stuff somewhere."

My mother continued fussing, as she asked, "Oh, for Pete's sake, Belinda Denise Bishop! So, now I'm just a storage unit for you and nothing more? I've done a lot for you over the years besides giving birth to you.

"I have a friend who works at JAG here in town. I went to high school with him and he owes me a favor. I'm sure he can get you out of this."

I replied angrily, "Mommy, if you even think about it—I swear I'll never speak to you again, and I mean it this time. This is my business, not yours, and if you interfere with me enlisting, I promise you will regret it."

It finally worked as my mother's anger completely melted as she responded, "You are my baby, not your father's. You came from me, not him."

She pulled me toward her as we stood in her living room. She hugged me tightly and my face was being crushed between her bosoms. My mother is a skinny lady and shorter than me, but when she does the mother thing, I always seem to find myself between her bosoms no matter my age, but I hugged her back and listened to her heart as she sobbed, "Baby, I did not want this day to come. Why can't you ask your father to have mercenaries or someone like that to teach you to be a soldier? We can't save you if they figure out who you are. You have been pampered and spoiled your entire life, Baby. What if something bad would happen and you revealed yourself? Someone would then know, who is not part of your family's pack. Remember your great-grandmother's warnings?"

I looked up into my mother's beautiful blue tear filled eyes with remorse and kissed her on the cheek as I answered her, "Momma, I think I can keep the family secret. I will blend in fine. I should have talked with you and Daddy, but this is something I have to do. To prove to myself I can do it."

She held my face in her two hands and softly smiled as she kissed me on both cheeks, "Well then, we need to go shopping and get the things you will need." I simply giggled at my mother.

* * *

The recruiter called me a couple of days later and asked me to stop by his office because he had a few more papers for me to fill out. He also wanted to give me orders to report for my physical.

I never understood why, but even Patty stopped calling me to go out. By my final day as a civilian, the day when I went to Tateville, Virginia, to take my physical and sign my contract, I did not have any contact with my closest friends. I reported for my physical alone, but even though I had been given the rank of E-4 because of the buddy program, no one realized that Patty had not reported, and I kept my E-4 status (specialist, soft stripes, also known as corporal, hard stripes). I would be a specialist.

I had embarrassed my friends, but I had no idea they would do so poorly on the test. I hadn't prepared and I had done well. They must have felt that I forced them into taking the test unprepared. I should have known better. I guess I deserved the silence because I was being selfish. I was scared to do it alone and wanted my friends with me. But in the end, I ended up alone anyway for the first time in my life. I had to admit, I was scared shitless.

At this moment, I guess, I didn't really care about losing my friends because I wanted to create my own life's history, but someday I would make it right with them. I considered this one of the final frontiers for women in this country—a way to prove that we are just as tough and brave as any man, a way to be part of something more than ourselves. It was a way to give my life meaning and become part of something greater than just myself—to die an honorable death, if need be.

If this was being selfish, so be it. I wanted to see the next generation of my gender go a step further toward true equality because of my generation's bravery and willingness to bleed, sweat, and even die to prove it. To me, that would be worth more than a thousand friends' feelings. If I'm destined to do this alone and fail, at least I can say I gave it my very best, alone or not.

Just as my ancestor Larentina persevered, so will I. I will be one of the first women openly serving in this country's military forces beside the men. It is the promise of my blood to fight for freedom, equality, and justice.

Chapter II

The physical actually turned out to be a two-day process; there were hundreds of women and men who were being evaluated. The physical exam was agonizing and extremely long. I stood in line at the first station for several hours so they could check my vitals (blood pressure and temperature). Several of the women in front of me were very short, and each one of them tried to stand on their tiptoes to pass the height requirement. But it did them no good; they were rejected because of their lack of height. I felt very sad for them. The disappointment was written on their faces.

Next, I went to a different station, where I had to stand in line again for hours for an eye exam. After that was the line for the hearing exam, and two more young women in front of me didn't pass this exam and were rejected.

I had to stand in line again to have a pap smear, pregnancy test, and tests for sexual transmitted diseases. After all those tests were completed, I had to wait for the results. These tests eliminated another forty-five women, several of whom looked very embarrassed. This was the end of the first day. Thank God, I passed everything on the first day without any issues.

After returning to the hotel from this first day, I took a leisurely hot bath and dressed. I decided to eat a small dinner and have a beer to pass the time in the hotel restaurant.

I went to the maître d' to take a number and wait for a table to become available. So many recruits were staying in this hotel that the restaurant was completely packed. She told me that it would be a two-hour wait, unless I shared a table with other diners. I told her that would be no problem because I was dining alone.

The maître d' found a seat for me with two handsome young men. One of the men—a god of masculine beauty and physical strength—rose from the table and nonchalantly wiped off my chair with his napkin before I sat. I blushed because I was unaccustomed to such gentlemanly behavior.

Then he introduced himself, saying, "Hi, my name is Captain Stephen Johnson, and this is my little brother, Patrick. My friends just call me Steve. I took a few days' leave and drove my little brother here so that he wouldn't have to take a bus. I haven't seen him in so long, and this was an opportunity for us to hang out again."

Patrick chimed in, "Yeah, I just enlisted and I have to go through this boring process—the dreaded physical. This was a long and boring day. What's your name? Is your husband or boyfriend taking the physical?"

I laughed, as I shook my head. "I'm Belinda Denise Bishop, and I am the one who is taking the physical."

Both men's eyes widened in confusion, and Steve was the first to speak. "Oh, you joined the WACs. I didn't know they took their physicals here now. Are you headed to Fort McClellan?"

I had a puzzled expression on my face because I didn't know Fort McClellan was headquarters for the WACs. "No, I'm one of the first women recruits to join the men's Army. The WACs are being disassembled and integrated into the men's military. I have no idea where I'm headed."

Both men in unison responded, "Oh."

Patrick added, "I didn't know that. So, what MOS did you choose?"

I answered, with a shrug of my shoulders, "I wanted Special Ops, but took MI."

Both men again looked shocked. Steve asked, "Special Ops? MI? Are you sure?"

I took a sip of my beer before answering, "Yeah. Why? Do you think I will have any problems? What are your MOSs?"

Steve drank down his entire beer before he answered, "I don't know if you will have any problems with Military Intelligence. I did not even know the WACs were being disassembled, but I don't pay much attention to that. I'm a chopper pilot."

Of course, I realized he said this because he didn't think I would understand or comprehend his correct MOS title and his college degree, but I let it go as Patrick answered, "That's kind of funny, because I chose Special Ops and hope to get into the sniper program."

As we ate dinner, we all talked about where we came from and our lives. We talked for close to three hours, and then I decided to head off to bed.

We all got into the elevator; Patrick got off on the third floor, but Steve said he would escort me to my room. I thought, *What a ham.*

Steve was very handsome, and I genuinely liked his personality. He was thoughtful and sweet. He was about five feet and eleven inches tall and had said earlier in the evening that he was twenty-seven years old. He had the standard short military haircut and a baby face with intense blue eyes. He was muscular from head to toe, and he was wearing a faded Van Halen t-shirt and blue jeans.

As I was unlocking my door to my room, I said, "Thank you, good night."

He said nothing, and then he suddenly kissed me passionately.

I pushed him away. "Good night," I repeated.

Steve gave a boyish smile as he replied, "Fair enough. Can I see you tomorrow?"

I blushed and smiled. "Maybe, if you can find me."

He took my hand, kissed it, and answered confidently, "I will. Good night, Belinda Denise Bishop."

I smiled and said, "Good night, Fly Boy."

He chuckled and left.

* * *

On the second day, I again had to wait in numerous lines so the physicians could rule out any problems with my heart, feet, bones, kidneys, and everything in between.

After I successfully passed all those tests, I went back to the lab and watched the lab technicians giving out numbers and taking personal information from the new recruits at each of their desks and telling the recruits to have a seat. They would have to wait until their number was called to have their blood drawn.

Undetected, I slowly walked into the room where they were drawing the blood for each recruit. I saw another lab technician come from another room and picked up the vials of blood. I walked toward that door as if I belonged, still undetected. Once I went through the other door I was caught, so I asked, "I must be lost. I am looking for the latrine. I need to go real bad. Can you direct me?"

The young woman with a white lab coat on, answered, "Well, yes, you are lost. How did you get in here without someone stopping you?"

I did not answer her, but I shrugged my shoulders as if I was confused. She simply directed me as she pointed her index finger, "Oh well, it doesn't matter. Over there you can use that bathroom."

I answered, "Thank you."

I walked immediately over to the bathroom she said I could use. I walked through the threshold of the latrine and immediately cracked the door as I peaked out of it and listened to the conversations in the large lab.

As one male lab technician was pushing a cart full of blood vials, I thought it, and tipped over the cart he was pushing, along with him; allowing him to think he tripped.

After reading the thoughts of everyone in the room I realized they were taking blood samples that they picked randomly from the recruits to freeze without their permission. They would be using these samples for new lab technicians to do other tests on. I could not allow that after I read one person's memories, who unknowingly picked my blood out to freeze, so I blew open the freezer doors on every single freezer and broke the glass of every single blood vial. After doing this, mass hysteria broke out as all the lab technicians scrambled about trying to clean up the mess. I walked quickly back to the door that I had come from. I considered this a very easy cover-up.

If I had not done this, and someone decided to test my blood for other things, they would discover my blood was not one hundred percent human or I should say, not normal. My family secret would then be revealed. My parents would have blasted me out for all eternity if I allowed my blood to get into the wrong hands.

I was directed to another location, where I sat down with a specialist to review my paperwork and MOS. Once he was satisfied that my file was completed correctly, I was sent to another room up the hall to wait. It was time to take the oath and sign the official contract. While I was waiting, the specialist who reviewed my paperwork came over to me and remarked, "Ma'am, we have a problem with your MOS."

I replied, "What?"

The specialist simply ordered, "Ma'am, you need to follow me back to my office."

I responded, "Yes, sir," and followed him back to his office.

He stated in a professional tone, "Ma'am, it looks like there is no position left in MI that allows women at this time, so we are going to have to find you another line of work because they are not allowing women in this field right now." His computer pulled up over 500 MOSs that I qualified for because of the results of the ASVAB.

I'm not sure why, but combat engineering first caught my eye. When I told him I was interested in that, he pulled out the informational videotape for this MOS and left his office while I started watching it. Halfway through the videotape, he opened his office door, walked over to the TV, shut the videotape off, and politely commented, "I'm sorry; I was just informed that this is for men only, as well. Women are not allowed to work in this MOS."

I asked, "Why?"

He answered, with agitation, "For Pete's sake, Bishop, we just allowed you guys in as it is. You'll have to pick out something else."

I irritably replied, "What are you talking about? Women were part of the military in Vietnam and World War II, so how can this be for men only?"

He arrogantly retorted, "Because that's the way it is. Women will always just play a role as support personnel; they will never serve in combat, never."

After choosing thirty more MOSs, from which I was promptly rejected because of my gender, I got so pissed off that I barked, "Just make me a fucking secretary for crying out loud, or is that for men only as well? I'm not going to work in the same field I'm already in, damn it!"

The specialist became annoyed as he responded to my outburst. "Watch your mouth, Missy. You're damn lucky that the Army, I mean the real Army, is letting you silly females into it to begin with. What did you think, just because they are integrating you freaky females, who really want to be men, into the real Army because they phased out the WACs, that you would be doing anything else but being a nurse, secretary, or some kind of paper pusher? Did you really think that we were going to allow you guys to fight and play like the men? To set the record straight, the MI and Special Ops positions are given to men, not women, and besides, you never took the test for those fields anyway. You should be married and having babies."

I had held my temper for as long as I could. I stood up from the chair and very clearly voiced my disdain. "Listen here, you freaky little bastard, I'm from a long line of female warriors, who not only fought and died alongside their male counterparts, but in some generations, fought with the pen as well.

"Women have been proving over and over again for generations that we are just as smart and every bit as brave as men. During World War II, when the men were drafted to go and fight for our country, the women quickly replaced them in all their jobs, working in the factories and running farms. Our country didn't stop functioning because the men went to war. It continued because of the women who were not afraid to step up to the plate and fill the empty shoes the men left behind.

"Vietnam is another example of women being close to the front line, even if they were nurses, so stop your stupid crap." I calmly sat back down in my chair.

Dumbstruck by my reaction, he changed my contract and the other forms. After he handed me my files, he instructed me, "Well, Missy, go back to the other area."

After reading the contract, I now knew they did not need my permission to keep my blood because I will be signing this contract giving my body, the heart that pumps it, and my mind to the people of the United States. I thought long and strong for several minutes before signing this. Even though it did not say this in laymen's words, this is what it meant. I will be giving up all my basic liberties to Uncle Sam. In other words, to the people.

As I sat there rereading this contract over and over again, a Captain who would be giving the oath came up and asked with concern in his voice, "Ma'am, do you need any help?"

I looked up at him and could not help myself, but to read his mind. I made my mind up as I answered, "No, sir." and I signed the contract without another thought.

He simply was a Vietnam hero, in every since of the word. He was spat upon when he returned, but still held his head high. This man would die without a second thought for his fellow countrymen to be safe and secure in their homes; to be free; no matter how shameful they treated him. I considered this man selfless, brave, strong, and noble. Everything I wanted to be. When I came out of the room after swearing in and signing my contract, Steve was waiting with a red long-stemmed rose. I was still very angry because I had been discriminated against openly, but his gesture was sweet and thoughtful.

He handed me the rose, and in an unexpectedly prideful tone, he said, "Congratulations, soldier. Welcome to the boys' club."

I took the rose from his hand and replied with irritation, "Thank you. But I didn't get what I wanted. You already knew, didn't you?"

Steve let out a heavy sigh and shook his head as he answered, "Honestly, Belinda, I thought your reach was … pretty far. What MOS did you end up accepting?"

I shrugged and answered, "I don't want to talk about it. I was rejected on every MOS I chose because of my gender. Nothing has changed; nothing."

Steve hugged me and kissed my cheek. "Well, you made it this far. Let me take you out to dinner, and you can tell me all about it."

I thought it was sweet of him to be so kind. "Yes, I would like that very much. Thank you."

We talked and laughed throughout most of the evening about everything and anything. We drank at least three bottles of wine before I realized how tipsy I had become, and then I said we should call it an evening.

Once again, Steve walked me to my hotel room, but this time I let him in. We made love like there was no tomorrow—because there was no tomorrow for us, but I knew I would see him again. Even though I am forbidden by my family, I glanced into his future just for a second and saw me, but I still considered this my first one-night stand, but I was okay with it.

BELINDA'S FAMILY MEMORIES
A FAMILY GATHERING
1977

Chapter III

I abruptly returned from my memories to present, as I looked from my window to the conductor as he asked me, "Ma'am, can I see your ticket?" I showed him my ticket and asked which way to the bar car. He told me it was three cars in front of this one.

Later on, in the bar car, I sipped on a bourbon as I looked out the window, and I let my mind drift back to about two years ago. I thought of the first tale that Mom-mom had told to me and my sister Christina and our mother, Jane, and to our stepmother Annabelle and our half sisters Teresa and Joan. I could almost see my beloved ancestor Larentina's face lovingly gazing back at me through the train window in her military garb.

Over the years, I have played the tape recordings of my great-grandmother's stories over and over again until I had memorized them word for word. I loved to recall the stories as I would lie in bed at night and listen to my beloved Mom-mom's voice echoing through my memories.

Mom-mom was my great-grandmother. She's my father's maternal grandmother. Longevity runs among the women in my family. My Mom-mom has outlived at least three husbands that I know of. She retired from this life several weeks after she passed the ancestral tales down to my sisters and me.

I was Mom-mom's first great-granddaughter, and she had been delighted that she was alive to see me born. When I was just learning to talk, I could not say great-grandmother, so I simply called her Mom-mom. From that moment forward, my great-grandmother would not let us call her anything other than Mom-mom.

Mom-mom still tended her small herb garden outside the kitchen of the large plantation home. When we arrived at Mom-mom's home on one particular day, that is where I had found her.

All the buildings and farm equipment always looked new and fresh. She would still bark orders to the cowboys who worked the cattle and horses and the field hands who tilled the lands for farming. She had all her faculties and still could yell louder than I ever could. At first glance, she appeared to be in her early sixties, but we all knew she was much, much older.

Mom-mom was not a Mennonite. The only reason my father was a Mennonite is because he converted from Catholicism after he and my mother married. He simply explained that one day he was reading his Bible and realized that it didn't match what he had learned in church. He did an extensive search until he found a church that taught what the Bible taught, and so he chose the Mennonite faith.

I am still amazed that my father convinced Annabelle, his current wife, to marry him, but he can be a charmer and knows how to treat the ladies.

When Christina and I lived with our father, he made sure that we learned what the Mennonites believed, and we attended the church's small school. To please our father, we joined the church and even wore the plain clothing. Then my mother decided to keep my sister and me in her world for a few years. Then my father married Annabelle. The next time I lived with my father, it was only because Christina refused to live like that again, no matter how much she loved him.

I remembered feeling as if I had stepped back in time when I first moved back in with my father and Annabelle, because there was no television or radio in my father's house. I knew this, but it was still a shock to be without them. My father expected me to continue dressing in plain clothing with the prayer cap on my head at all times. Because I respected him and his beliefs, I did so.

In only one area did she stray from her church's beliefs; she wore Mom-mom's wedding ring. Even though I knew Miss Annabelle was breaking the church rules by wearing it, I did not say anything.

As I sat there at Mom-mom's, I compared the way she, Teresa, and Joan were dressed and the way my mother, Christina, and I were dressed. By looking at us four sisters, no one would believe that we were actually sisters simply because of our clothing and makeup (or lack thereof).

Like my mother, Annabelle was a beautiful woman, but she was different in so many ways from my own mother. Mom had blonde hair and blue eyes; Annabelle had black hair and dark brown eyes. I have to admit my father married two beautiful and very strong-minded women.

I could tell my father loved and respected strong women simply based on the two women he had loved and had children with. He also raised my sisters and me to think for ourselves, and to this day, he always tests us on our knowledge of history, current affairs, and politics. I can't speak for my two youngest sisters, but I do know that he raised Christina and me by teaching us to survive in the wilderness, to hunt, to fish, to enjoy sports, and to fight to protect ourselves. Basically, he raised us like boys instead of girls, or better to say he raised us as "she wolves." To this day, I am very grateful that he raised us this way.

* * *

This gathering that I remember so vividly was at the request of Mom-mom. My father and mother had been divorced for a long time, but only Mom-mom could make such gatherings happen. After all, Mom-mom was a feisty, free-spirited, strong-willed, and opinionated lady. She was the matriarch of our family. When she passed on, my grandmother on my father's side—Mom-mom the second, as I fondly remember her—took her place, but the stories of their lives are not on my mind this time.

It had been very controversial among the Mennonite community when Annabelle and my father began dating, and even more so when they announced their engagement, because my father was divorced. The Mennonite church has very strong family values and views divorce and remarriage as a sin because it destroys a family. I remember the Mennonite community allowed him leeway by bending the rules somewhat, stating that he had to have my mother's permission, which of course she gave freely because she wanted our father to be happy.

To this day, I will never understand why they divorced to begin with; they never argued or fought. One day my mother just packed up her belongings, took half of the property, and left in a moving truck. It could have been because Daddy was converting to the Mennonite faith and my mother didn't want to live like that, but as I said, I will never know the real reasons behind their breakup. They refused to discuss it with me. All I ever got was, "He's a good man" and "She's a good woman."

I was about sixteen the summer that we all gathered at Mom-mom's. It was the summer after I graduated high school; Christina was about fourteen, Teresa was about twelve, and Joan was about ten. I remember it was a beautiful summer afternoon. We were gathered on the front porch of the old family plantation, which had been in my father's family for generations. It is located in my beloved home state of Virginia. The plantation has over a thousand acres, and the lands are still intact. It sits on the banks of the great Potomac River, near where the river empties into the Chesapeake Bay. On a clear day, you can see all the way to Smith Island and Point Lookout. Beautiful small homes could be seen sprinkled across the riverfront, which were actually built for the freed slaves our family had employed.

According to legend, our slaves were given their freedom and an opportunity to work for wages if they chose to do so. If they wanted to return to their ancestral country, a ticket, papers, and money was provided to them. This was one reason, after the Civil War, the majority of families stayed with my ancestors because they were free anyway, and they were provided a beautiful home to live in. Even though it was considered illegal, and frowned upon in general, to teach a black person about government and running the land, one of my ancestors had built a school to teach the children, and anyone else who wanted to learn, how to read and write. The government could do nothing because it was on private property, but of course, some of the other plantation owners tried to intervene. At one point, the school was torched, but no one was injured, and it was promptly rebuilt.

My family never believed that one person should own another; many of my ancestors died because of their belief that all men are created equal. America is the land of the free and home of the brave. This belief has been passed down from generation to generation in my family. It has always been understood from the beginnings of this great land. Our forefathers could not tackle the issue of slavery in their lifetime because we had only just become a free nation. They stated in our Constitution that all men are created equal, but left the issue of slavery for a future generation to resolve.

In fact, many families, black and white, rented the small homes that their families have lived in for generations. The children would go to college, come back, and for some reason, stay. Many have tried to purchase the homes with a few acres around them, but my family always refused to sell. They always offered to rent the land to them because we always have considered their families our families as well. I discovered the rent was extremely low, but no one wanted to talk about it, for fear that some government law would force them to increase the rent or impose some type of tax, if any word was leaked out about it.

Chapter IV

I remember my sisters and I at first were very uncomfortable on this particular day because we had never seen both of our mothers together, ever. But Mom-mom seemed to have an uncanny way of always taking the edge off everything. I remember her barking her orders in her husky deep voice. "Jane," she would say to my mother, and then she would say, "Annabelle," to my stepmother, "Go cut some fresh lemons up and make us some fresh lemonade. You four girls go and help them now. Oh, Jane, make me some of those yummy cucumber finger sandwiches that you used to make me when you and Joshua were visiting. I just picked some fresh cucumbers and they are in the icebox. Annabelle, cut up some of that fresh bread you made so Jane can use it for her sandwiches."

My sisters and I exchanged wide-eyed looks as both women quickly and obediently responded, in unison, "Yes, ma'am." You could tell that both our mothers had nothing but respect for Mom-mom.

Daddy stayed away from the entire thing. I remember him making his excuses that he wanted to tour the homestead because it had been so long since he had visited, and he quickly disappeared off the front porch, leaving his wife, his exwife, his mother, and his daughters to deal with Mom-mom. My grandfather snuck away with Daddy so he wouldn't be involved. I remember my grandmother getting ready to protest, and Mom-mom commented to her, "Now, Victoria, mind your manners and go in there and help them. I have several long tales to tell these children, and I only have a week or so to tell them about our bloodline. I want to do this before I die because I know you won't tell the stories right anyway. I don't ask much of you. Remember, Victoria, Jane is the mother of two of your grandbabies, so be nice. I mean it."

My grandmother obediently replied, "Yes, ma'am."

After we made the lemonade and finger sandwiches in the large kitchen, which had been remodeled with all the modern conveniences yet somehow maintained its historical feel, we carried everything out to the front porch where Mom-mom was rocking herself in her white wicker chair. In fact, all the furniture on her large front porch was white wicker.

She ordered all of us to have some lemonade and finger sandwiches and settle down around her, which we all obediently did. None of us dared to defy her.

My mother pulled out her tape recorder and asked Mom-mom if she could record the stories. Of course, Mom-mom thought that was a great idea.

Then, Annabelle asked my mother, “Do you think you could make a copy for my girls as well?”

My mother replied, “Of course, I will make a copy for each of them.”

Both women started talking with each other as if they were old friends, while my mother was setting up the machine to record.

MOM-MOM'S STORY

1977

BELINDA, AGE SIXTEEN

Chapter V

After taking a sip of her lemonade and finishing off a cucumber finger sandwich, Mom-mom began the tale, "Ladies, I want to tell you about the first known ancestor of our bloodline, the first daughter. This story has been passed down from mother to daughter for thousands of years. You have a unique family tree because it's not father-to-son, but rather mother-to-daughter.

"This story is about Larentina, a Spartan princess. Larentina is a Greek name, meaning "she wolf." Throughout the ages, her true name has been forgotten, and she became simply She Wolf. This story is about bravery, strength, and the willingness to sacrifice everything for ideals, honor, and family. It's about an ancestor of yours who lived by the sword and probably died by it. It's about a woman, a daughter of a royal family, who proved she was as strong as a man was and just as capable of ruling her country. This is about the Spartan blood that runs through our veins, and so I am honored to have the privilege to pass this family tale to all of you—all the good and all the bad of her life."

Annabelle became upset with Mom-mom and voiced her concerns. "Mom-mom, this sounds like a violent tale, and I don't want my children subjected to this nonsense. Joan is too young for such stories."

She started to get my two youngest sisters up from where they were seated, when Mom-mom angrily stood up from her rocking chair and commanded, "Sit back down! Your religion has nothing but tunnel vision; this story is also about being open-minded and accepting other people's beliefs, whether you agree with it or not. So sit back down and be quiet. I don't have the time to wait any longer. This is what I was afraid of—that our legacy would be forgotten by future generations, and I will not stand for it. I thank God that I'm still alive to be able to keep this new generation from believing the way yours does. Now sit back down and be quiet."

My mother reached over and touched Annabelle's arm ever so gently, as if they were best of friends, and pleaded, "Annabelle, she is right. There are not many children left who know where they came from. I want my children to believe they don't need a man for anything. I want them to depend on a man only if they choose to and not to be limited in life simply because they are a woman. Please, Annabelle. Your daughters are my daughters' sisters. They are the future generation."

Annabelle let out a sigh after listening to what my mother said, turned her head toward Mom-mom, and in a patient, understanding tone, replied, "You're right, Mom-mom. I was being selfish, but I'm not doing this because it is what you ordered. I'm allowing this for Jane and for our children. To set the record straight, my religion is not tunneled. To me, you are the one who has tunnel vision for stating that." Annabelle sat back down in the rocking chair and allowed Mom-mom to continue.

I thought what Annabelle did for my mother was the most selfless act I had ever witnessed in my young life. She considered my mother's feelings before her own. She was a strong woman who really practiced what she believed.

Chapter VI

Mom-mom continued to tell the story. My sisters and I leaned forward with anticipation because we knew it was going to be a wonderful story. We wanted to make sure we could hear every word.

Mom-mom softly cleared her throat and began the tale.

"Throughout the ages, as men have a bad habit of doing with great women, they have taken She Wolf's name and changed it from something great into something repugnant. She Wolf is a name that means greatness because of the way that she lived and, most likely, died. Through the ages, men turned her name from a respectable warrior into a harlot, just as they did with Mary Magdalene in our biblical stories.

"The story begins somewhere around the end of the sixth century and the beginning of the fifth century BC, in a mystical land far, far away, called Sparta, also known as Lacedaemon, which was an ancient Greek city-state. It was the capital of Laconia and the most famous ancient Greek city-state.

"Sparta was located in a beautiful green valley in the foothills of Mount Taygetus. The Eurotas River ran through their valley, which was located in the southern part of Greece on a large peninsula.

"The Eurotas River began in the Taygetus Mountains and emptied into the Laconic Gulf. This is where the ancient Spartans had their port of Gytheiro. Gytheiro was about twenty or so miles away from the great city-state, so the ancient Spartans mostly used this river as a means of transportation, rather than hiking through the mountains.

"These mountains were also where the Spartans executed criminals and disposed of the newborns considered weak or deformed. There was no room for imperfection in their society. They were warriors who lived for the thrill of battle.

"It was a beautiful and a rich land. The mountains were breathtaking, and the soil was rich and red, very similar to our Virginia soil because it was so rich in minerals. The passes leading into the Evrótas valley were easily defendable, so there was no need for walls around their great city-state.

"Even though this was a great ancient city-state, it was actually just a group of five or so villages with simple houses and a few public buildings and statues. The grand public buildings were made of marble, and the statues appeared to be either bronze or marble. Sparta didn't have the grandeur of Athens. Remember, Athens had great temples and statues, and it was inhabited by scientists, poets, and philosophers. Although Spartans enjoyed music, stories, and poetry, their pursuits were strictly militaristic. A Spartan lived and died by the sword.

"Sparta had three classes of people, similar to our society today, but our classes are the poor, middle class, and the wealthy, while Sparta's classes were the spartiate, perioikoi, and helot.

"The word *helot* literally means 'captive,' and they were the Spartan slaves. According to legend, the helots were the original inhabitants of Sparta. They were conquered and enslaved by the Dorians of that territory. They didn't belong to an individual spartiate; instead, they belonged to the state. The helots were allowed to marry and even own a limited amount of personal property, but on the downside, they were humiliated constantly by the spartiates. Spartan law stated that citizens could not murder a helot, so just about every year the gerousia council or the kings would declare war on the helots, so that they could kill them, without it being considered murder, and keep the population down.

"The middle class was made up of skilled laborers, who were called the perioikoi. Literally translated, this means 'those who live round about.' These people were not allowed to live within the Spartan cities, but in many ways, they had more freedoms than the Spartan citizens themselves did. They were allowed to leave the city-state whenever they wanted, but a Spartan citizen needed to have permission to do so. By law, Spartan citizens could not even be involved in their own economics, but they could own land. Meanwhile, the perioikois could not own land, but they were forced to farm it along with the helots. The perioikois were also required to give a certain amount of their crops to the state; in fact, most of their crops went to the state.

"Legend also states that a perioikoi might have once been a Spartan citizen, who had not passed the rigorous agoge training. If one could not pass the training to become a Spartan, they were forced into the perioikoi class for the rest of their life. On the other hand, if a Spartan citizen adopted a perioikoi, he could then go through the agoge training and become a soldier.

"The wealthier Spartan citizens, who were called spartiate, lived in large homes made primarily of wood; they consisted of a courtyard, several rooms, and a kitchen area. Of course, the kings and their families lived in much larger and more luxurious homes than the Spartan citizens did. The lower class citizens were also allowed to live in smaller apartments.

"The Spartans spoke a language called Doric Greek, and they also participated in the ancient Olympics. Back then, the Olympics were for men only. Women were not even allowed in the arena during the Olympic Games, but there were rare exceptions to that rule. Women had been allowed in the city during the games only a handful of times, and occasionally unmarried women, who were known to be virgins, were allowed to watch the games.

"Spartan men and women dressed like the Athenians did. Both men and women wore loose-fitting tunics with a belt at the waist. Their tunics came in a variety of colors, and there were many styles of belts. During warm weather, they wore sandals on their feet, but when the weather turned cooler, they would wear boots. They were also known to wear pants and warm cloaks to keep away the chill of winter. Contrary to popular belief, most Greeks hated wearing any type of footwear. As the legends go, give a Greek a chance and they will do everything with bare feet.

"All men, with the exception of soldiers, wore beards. The wealthier men had them trimmed and shaped. The wealthier spartiate women, and even some perioikoi women, wore jewelry made of gold, silver, and beautiful gemstones of many colors and shapes.

"Sparta wasn't a country, but rather a city-state. This meant that Sparta controlled and ruled most of the surrounding areas. Most of ancient Greece was made up of city-states. Spartans were fiercely loyal to Sparta, and they would eagerly spill their blood to protect its borders, politics, and beliefs, just as we do today for our own country.

"Sparta was one of the first known democratic republic states, and their form of government was called timocracy. According to Plato, timocracy was the most preferable form of government and was very close to the ideal society.

"In a timocratic government, one must own property in order to run for public office, and a person must believe in honor as their ruling drive. This ancient government had elements that our forefathers incorporated into our own government, such as patriotism and honor. Despite the similarities, current American government is vastly superior over timocratic government, because in democracy, the people decide by majority vote, without hindrance."

* * *

Here, I interrupted Mom-mom and asked, "But Mom-mom, wasn't Plato born in the fourth century BC? So how could he have an opinion based on She Wolf's society if he wasn't born yet? Didn't their society advance and become more equal by the time Plato gave his opinion?"

Mom-mom knowledgeably answered, "Even though most of the original scrolls that were incorporated in the Bible were written long after Jesus had died, don't you still believe that he is real, that he was born and lived as a common Jew, that he died and was resurrected? Don't you believe the stories that were written about him? Just because something is ancient history does not mean that it is not relevant now. To answer your question, Belinda, I don't think that Sparta ever really advanced to equality by the time Plato was born."

I answered Mom-mom, "Well, yes, I believe the Bible, but it seems to me that men seem to distort the stories to suit their own purpose throughout the ages. Men have been to busy killing each other trying to force another to believe the way they do. To me they use their religion to control and take away God's gifts of free will and freedom of choice from others.

"To be quite honest, Mom-mom, I do not understand, throughout the ages, why men fear strong, educated, and noble women. I have never understood this. Why would you put down your women? Not educate them as your equal and treat them as such? I just do not understand this, but this is not the same thing as She Wolf's society."

Mom-mom patiently replied, "Belinda, that was an almost perfect answer. But, yes, it is, but after your great answer you are correct, my reasons are Plato gave his opinion of the Spartan government centuries later, and I used Plato to establish the opinion of others regarding the government and society that she was born and lived in. Now where was I? Oh, yes …

"Spartan women had full citizenship but were not allowed to vote or run for public office, although they had more freedoms than most women in other parts of Greece, or the known world for that matter. They were allowed to inherit and own land; they had the freedom to live their lives pretty much as they wished. Even though women were not allowed to go through military training, they were required to go through similar physical education because Sparta had great respect for strong women; they were believed to give birth to strong, healthy children. Spartans believed that the stronger the mother, the stronger the children she would produce. But if a Spartan woman gave birth too many times to children who were weak or deformed, it was rumored that the woman would be punished or even killed because she was considered weak. She Wolf's life would change the way the Spartan men thought of women, and because of her, Spartan women experienced greater freedoms and equality than other women during that time period.

"Contemporary women have come a long way in the fight for equality and freedom, and it has taken us centuries to do so. We have advanced this far because women from many different cultures and backgrounds chose to put aside their differences and join together to fight for their beliefs. Today women in other countries are still treated as property, instead of human beings.

"Sparta was jointly ruled by two kings, one from the Agiad family and the other from the Eurypontids family. Both families were supposedly direct descendants of Hercules.

"According to legend, both families were equal in authority, so that one could not act against the other regarding a veto or a change in law. The duties of the kings were primarily religious, judicial, and militaristic. They were not just the heads of the military, but they also were the religious leaders.

"Anyone in the Spartan government—including the kings—could be tried for treason, just as our government today can try government officials for treason.

"The Spartan kings were also responsible for communication with the Delian League, which always exercised great influence in Sparta, similar to the United Nations."

"The Delian League was an association of many Greek city-states, including Sparta, and they were headquartered in Athens. They would meet frequently on the island of Delos, and according to Thucydides, an ancient philosopher, the main purpose of the League was to avenge the wrongs that one of its members suffered. They did this by ravaging the territory of the king who wronged one of the League's members, and then they divided the spoils of war according to a pre-established agreement.

"League members swore their allegiance to one another and agreed to have the same allies and enemies. After reaching an agreement, they would drop ingots of iron into the sea to symbolize their allegiance. Iron was their currency because ancient laws stated that Spartan citizens could not possess gold or silver currency; instead, they used worthless iron ingots.

"In many ways, the Delian League was similar to the United Nations, but instead of city-states, the United Nations supposedly unites countries across the globe. Each member of the United Nations has made a vow to come to the aid when a member is attacked. The United Nations was created after World War II to avoid another world war, but this has not been the case; I consider the United Nations a joke and a waste of money.

"Sparta had a senate, but it was much, much different from ours, and it was called *gerousia* (council of elders). It consisted of thirty members, including the two kings. Many of the council members were also royalty. Members were elected for life. All of the members had to have successfully completed the Spartan military training program known as the *agoge*. Officially, any male Spartan citizen around the age of sixty could stand, but in actuality, members were picked from the most important aristocratic families. Most of the time, they were much younger than sixty. It was rumored that the elections were often fixed, and the results were questionable.

"The gerousia council was created by the Spartan lawgiver Lycurgus, who lived around the first part of the seventh century BC. He introduced the gerousia in his Great Rhetra, which was similar to a constitution. According to Lycurgus's biographer, Plutarch, the gerousia was the first significant constitutional instrument.

"The gerousia would prepare motions, also called the rhetra, and then pass them on to the Spartan citizen assembly, which was called the apella, who would then vote on them. This is similar to our process wherein a bill is created in the House of Representatives or Senate, voted on, then passed to the other house, where it again is voted on, and then finally given to our president, who either vetoes or ratifies it.

"The apella consisted of all Spartan male citizens thirteen or older. The gerousia could also veto motions passed by the apella, and the ephors would consult it regarding the interpretation of the law. It was similar to our Supreme Court. It could even try the kings for crimes, just as our government can try the president for crimes."

* * *

Out of the corner of my eye, I saw Teresa's hand waving in the air. Mom-mom stopped her tale and smiled at her. Teresa had a puzzled expression on her face as she asked, "Mom-mom, what is treason?"

"Treason, my dear, is when the president, or other members of our government, breaks their vow to uphold the Constitution. They do this by sharing national secrets or battle plans, taking away freedom of speech, freedom of choice, taking away free market by government control, and so forth. This could even be done by an everyday American citizen who has access to our classified materials or even an American soldier. In my opinion, the majority of our elected officials are traitors to the people because they are taxing us to death, which I think is the same as stealing. They are telling us what we can do with our own property, and they are creating laws that violate our individual liberties instead of protecting our borders and interests. A traitor is someone who takes from the American people; these officials are slowly taking our backbone of wealth and giving it to other nations, as well as taking our God-given liberties from us."

* * *

"The gerousia also had power like our Supreme Court. They had the final say as to what was or was not lawful. In essence, it was the highest part of the political basis in the Spartan constitution because it could override any decision by any other part in the Spartan political machine.

"Earlier I mentioned the ephors. An ephor was an official of ancient Sparta who oversaw and swore to uphold the rules of the two Spartan kings, and in turn, the kings swore to uphold the laws of Sparta. Five ephors were elected each year. According to legend—"

* * *

Christina interrupted Mom-mom and asked, "Mom-mom, what does our government and Sparta have to with our ancestor, She Wolf? It seems to me you are getting sidetracked with your own personal beliefs of our own government. When are you going to get to She Wolf?"

Mom-mom patiently answered, "You need to know what kind of world She Wolf was born into to understand her upbringing, beliefs, and some of what she fought for and who she was. I'm not going to deny I am old and get sidetracked from time to time, and it is your God-given right to choose what you believe or not, but I do ask that you look at the real history books without opinions on what has been rewritten before making any conclusions. The real history of our nation would be from books written before the 1920s, and even some of those could be erroneous as well. I ask that you pay close attention to our governmental representatives and make your own conclusions because when someone has the truth revealed to them, they will come to the same conclusions that I have. This is just one point of your God-given liberties that men will try to take from you by sugarcoating history and outright lying about it.

"Now I'm not going to deny that some of my information regarding the general basis of the society she lived in is not totally factual, because my memory isn't what it used to be. In fact, I will admit that some of it may be off, and you must know that there will be a lot of mythology in it as well. I'm doing my best to give you a clear understanding of why She Wolf's life is so important to us. Because of this legend, many of our ancestors chose to fight for what they believed in. Now that doesn't mean they all fought with a sword, but these legends I will tell in due time."

I looked around, and all of us were nodding our heads in agreement and understanding with Mom-mom.

Mom-mom stopped talking and took a sip of her lemonade. She picked up one of the sandwiches and ate it, while we all watched her impatiently.

LARENTINA'S STORY

Chapter VII

After Mom-mom finished her finger sandwich and took another sip of her lemonade, she put the glass down on the table and resumed her story.

"It was a windy, cold, full-mooned night when Queen Alexis went in labor. At the same time, her identical twin sister, Agape, who lived just a few miles from the palace, went into labor as well.

"Alexis had changed since becoming a queen. Responsibility, duty, and honor toward her king and country had become her ruling drive. She truly loved being a Spartan queen and all the grandeur that came with it.

"Queen Alexis's home was located on the outer edge of Sparta. The two-story building was made of white marble, and its perfectly square structure boasted a very large courtyard in the center. Both the outer and inner walls of the palace had large carved columns that seemed to stretch for miles. The courtyard and the outer grounds were filled with beautiful marble and bronze statues, flower gardens, and elegantly designed topiaries. The entrance to the courtyard was flanked with two large statues of Spartan warriors carved in marble.

"Agape was a Spartan by birth but chose to relinquish her privileges to marry the man she loved, a perioikoi named Erasmus. The ruling members and royal families were not happy regarding Agape marrying beneath her class, but it was eventually accepted because Alexis had already married the king.

"Agape's husband was not a Spartan; he was born in the lands around the city-state. As a rule, perioikois were not allowed to be soldiers, but an exception can be found for every rule, and Erasmus became a warrior. This was allowed because the king had begged his father when they were both young men to allow Erasmus to train with him; and Alcaeus loved him as if he was his own brother. King Alcaeus was only a few years older than Erasmus was, and they were best friends. They had sworn their loyalty to each other and sealed it with their own blood. How the two young men met was a mystery, and neither would discuss it. The only people who knew this secret were the twin sisters.

* * *

"When Alcaeus went into the wilderness to prove himself as a warrior when he was about thirteen years old, he had tripped and had fallen off the side of a mountain cliff into the below river with rapid waters. He was uncouncious as the rapid waters swiftly carried him down the river.

"Erasmus was hunting for food and saw Alcaeus fall. He ran down the river embankment and dove into the fast moving waters and saved the young prince.

"Alcaeus asked Erasmus, 'What do you wish for your reward, and I shall grant it?'

"Erasmus shared his heart's desire to become a Spartan warrior. After returning to agoge camp, Alcaeus immediately requested an adieance with his father and was granted it. His father refused to adpot Erasmus, but he made it law that Erasmus could train with Alcaeus. Alcaeus's father never revealed the secret because he did not need to give his reasons.

* * *

"According to Spartan law, King Alcaeus always had to have two ephors by his side every time he went into battle. Only one king could lead the army at a time because that was the Spartan law as well. For these reasons, King Alcaeus requested that Erasmus be by his side in battle. He trusted no other. As a result, both husbands were off in battle far away from Sparta on this cold, windy night when their wives were delivering their children.

"After many painful hours of labor, both women gave birth to twins: each set had a girl and a boy. Queen Alexis's twins were stillborn, whereas Agape's twins were born strong and perfectly healthy, according to the rigid examination that followed the next day. Members of the gerousia, who oversaw Spartan laws, would examine newborn Spartan boys to determine their perfection and strength. The girls were examined as well, but they were not subjected to the same tests that the boys were. Of course, this law would not pertain to the queen's sister because she had married a perioikoi. It was a peculiar law because technically, perioikois were also considered spartiates. The perioikois were mainly used as a class between the helots and the Spartan citizens because the helots outnumbered the Spartans at least tenfold."

* * *

Annabelle interrupted Mom-mom nervously, "Mom-mom, I am very sorry, but I just cannot allow Teresa and Joan to hear this. They are too young, and this story will give them nightmares."

My mother jumped in before Mom-mom had a chance to respond to Annabelle; she said, "Mom-mom, I'm recording this, so when Joan and Teresa get older, they will be able to listen to your stories."

Annabelle looked at my mother and gratefully murmured, "Thank you."

Mom-mom agreed. "All right, you're both right. Teresa and Joan can go inside and play."

Teresa became upset and cried out, "No, I'm not too young! I want to hear the stories now with my sisters, Christina and Belinda."

Annabelle asked her daughter, "Are you sure, Teresa?"

Teresa responded, with conviction, "Yes, Momma, I'm sure. I will not have nightmares. I want to hear about my ancestors directly from Mom-mom and not a machine. I want to stay with Belinda."

Annabelle relented and said, "Okay, then."

After Annabelle and Joan disappeared into the house, Mom-mom began the tale again, "Now where was I? Oh, yes. I remember …

"Queen Alexis and Agape had a very strong bond and often knew what the other was doing even when they were miles apart. Alexis knew her sister was also giving birth at the same moment, and when she saw that her babies were dead, she knew she would have to trade her children for Agape's children. This was the third time she had given birth to substandard babies, and she knew she would either be banished or killed. She would be considered dishonored for lacking the ability to give birth to strong and healthy children for Sparta. Her first child was stillborn, and the other time she had given birth to twin boys who did not meet the Spartan requirements of strength and perfection.

"King Alcaeus himself had taken each boy baby and threw him off the mountain of Taygetus because each was considered deformed and weak. Queen Alexis knew her sister would help her by giving her children to her to keep honor among the families at all costs. After all, to the young queen, her sister was still a Spartan.

"Queen Alexis immediately rose from the bed, cleaned herself, dressed, and then put on a hooded cloak. This took a tremendous amount of effort, for the queen was still weak from giving birth, and several times she doubled over in pain. As she was standing near the door, with her hand on her stomach and her face contorted with pain, she pointed her right index finger to a young helot girl named Corinna and ordered, 'You there, go and harness two horses to an old wagon. Fill the wagon with hay. Do not let anyone see you, and tell no one what you are doing. I will meet you outside shortly!'

"The young helot girl immediately obeyed her queen's orders and ran toward the stable.

"After watching Corinna leave the room, Queen Alexis turned to Doris, an older helot, who was a skilled midwife and wet nurse. Spartans frequently relied on helot women as wet nurses and midwives. The queen spouted orders to Doris, 'Clean up these babes, and bundle them in clean linens; now!'

"The woman immediately obeyed her queen and started cleaning the small stillborn babies, wrapping their tiny bodies in clean linens.

"Queen Alexis scowled at Doris with narrowed eyes and a furrowed brow, producing the deadliest glare she could muster amid the pain of just giving birth. In a deadly tone, she commanded, 'If you ever discuss what has happened this night, I swear to Apollo, even Zeus himself, that I will cut your tongue out and make you eat it! Do you understand?'

"Doris looked into her queen's face and recoiled at what she saw. She promptly lowered her head and focused her gaze on the floor. Her voice quivered, as she answered, 'Yes, my queen.'

"Doris gathered the small bodies wrapped in linens, carefully holding one in each arm as Queen Alexis watched her. The queen ordered, 'Go now and take the children to the wagon. I will be there shortly.'

"Once Doris left the room, Queen Alexis moved quickly to her dresser and pulled a dagger from the drawer. She hid the dagger in the pocket of her cloak, and then pulled the hood over her head, carefully concealing her face. She walked hurriedly outside to where the wagon and her helots were waiting for her.

"Relief spread over Queen Alexis as she settled into the wagon; no one had detected them. She felt that she was being blessed by the gods, because it was shortly past midnight and most of Sparta was sleeping on this bright, cold, windy night.

"Agape's home was a typical farmhouse, but it had two floors with several outhouses and barns surrounding it. The roof was made of straw, and the house itself was made of stones. The wheat and corn fields that surrounded the farmhouse seemed endless.

"When they arrived at Agape's home, they quietly snuck into the house, undetected. The three women entered Agape's bedroom quietly.

"Agape's furnishings, as well as the interior style, were very similar to Queen Alexis's home except they were not nearly as grand. The Spartans had copied many of the furnishings of the Egyptians in this time, but Spartans didn't believe in cluttering their homes with too many objects.

"Queen Alexis saw her sister lying on the bed, sleeping quietly with a newborn in each arm. Then the queen, as well as the helots, gasped because they saw a white wolf with a puppy lying quietly beside the girl baby. The wolf was licking the girl baby's face, and then, in turn, was licking its own puppy.

"Agape was awakened by the gasps of her sister and her companions. As the young mother shook the sleep from her eyes and became aware of her surroundings, she smiled at Queen Alexis, and then looked to her side where her newborn baby girl was sleeping in her arm. She, too, gasped at the sight of the wild wolf lying beside her, licking her baby girl. She looked at Queen Alexis in fear and asked in a calm but shaky voice, 'What do I do?'

"The queen answered, 'You have been blessed. It's a sign from Zeus. Your daughter must be the daughter of Zeus himself. I do not think the wild wolf is going to hurt you or your child. It appears she is protecting the girl child as well as her own puppy. I have never seen this before. How did the wolf get into your house?'

"Before Agape could answer, the queen walked toward the bed where Agape was laying very still, so as not to agitate the wolf, and the wolf began to growl at the queen. Queen Alexis continued toward the bed with great caution.

"Agape laid her baby boy on the bed cautiously as she watched every move of the wolf. She then slowly moved her baby girl and laid the girl beside her brother. Then, she slowly moved the puppy and laid it by the mother wolf. The mother wolf started licking Agape as well. Agape then patted the wolf and rubbed the wolf's head. By then, the queen was sitting on the side of the bed beside the wolf, and she too started petting the mother wolf. Then, the wolf licked Queen Alexis's hand, accepting her as well as Agape. Both sisters looked at each other in amazement. Agape then answered her sister, 'I do not know how, or why, this strange wolf is here. She appears to have the attitude of a tamed dog.'

"Queen Alexis told her sister what had happened to her children. Both sisters silently nodded their heads in agreement to an unspoken plan. The queen turned, still sitting on the side of the bed, and rubbed the wolf's head, looking at her helots, and asked in a soft tone, 'Could you please go and bring us some food: soup, cheese, bread, and some wine?'

"Doris looked at her queen with a questioning expression because she still was holding the queen's stillborns. Queen Alexis simply instructed Doris; 'Please lay them here,' as she pointed to the other corner of the bed.

"The queen then looked at her sister after they both watched the helots leave the room as she frantically begged her sister, 'I must have your babies, for you know what will happen to me if I do not.'

"Agape responded, 'Zeus has done this to me; he impregnated me with this girl child, making her half god. I think this is why he has taken your children from you because he wants me to give my boy child and his girl child to you, because they are royal blood and belong with you. If the gerousia discovers this, they will kill us because what we will do is against the law.'

"Queen Alexis agreed, 'You are right, my sister, but we have no other choice. Zeus must have been drunk with wine and confused you with me. Because of this, he has become jealous and has taken my children. I too agree that he wanted you to give me your children in place of them because he wants his girl child to be of royal blood.

"'This is truly a sign. The girl shall be named Larentina, which means she wolf. The boy shall be named Lycurgus, which means deed of wolf, as he will be named after the great lawgiver, Lycurgus, who was also the deed of wolf. The wolf was sent to protect her, and I have a feeling Apollo is a part of Zeus's plan for this girl child. We will let the world know that she is the daughter of Zeus and must be protected.'

"The two sisters talked and planned more so that no one would ever know who the real mother was. They agreed to announce publicly that the boy child was the son of King Alcaeus and the girl child was the daughter of Zeus. It would be explained that this was a great honor bestowed upon the king because the queen not only gave him a strong son, but a daughter of the greatest god of all, Zeus. The king would be given the honor to raise her and protect her as the king's ward.

"As they ate the food that was brought to them, they planned more for the future of Agape's children. Both sisters solemnly vowed to each other that they would never again speak of this night, and they would go to their graves with this secret.

"The house was quiet in the dark of the night, but the four women all looked at each other with their eyes wide because they heard a door open and close. Queen Alexis walked to the door and stood with her ear pressed hard against the wall. She pulled her dagger from her cloak pocket, raised it over her head with the blade pointed forward, and froze in that position. The helots moved quickly and sat on Agape's bed opposite the wolf and puppy. They all watched the closed door, in terror of being discovered.

"The door slowly opened and revealed Andreas, one of the members of the gerousia council. A strong wind started blowing all through the room. Small lightning bolts appeared, and objects flew around the room. Andreas did not know his queen was on the other side of the door. He surveyed the room and asked, 'What is going on here?' as he dodged an object.

"He continued speaking in a fearful and frantic tone, asking, 'What god have you angered, Agape? I just came from Queen Alexis's home and her bed was covered in blood, but she is nowhere to be found. Is she here? What is this before me? There are four babies lying on your bed. It appears ...'

"Before he could finish speaking, the queen pushed the door so hard it knocked Andreas off balance. Before the older man had a chance to react, the queen lunged toward him, using the force of her body to bury the dagger deep in his chest. Swiftly, the mother wolf jumped down from the bed and joined in the attack, as she tore at his arms and legs with her sharp teeth. Unable to regain his balance, Andreas fell to his knees; he looked up at Queen Alexis with shock and horror on his face, as a flying object hit him in the head. The queen stared down at him with hatred in her eyes, pulled the dagger from his chest, and continued stabbing him as the wolf tore at his flesh. As the life slowly faded from his eyes, Queen Alexis said in a strong, calm, but deadly voice, 'This is a good night to die and a noble one, old man!' Andreas took his last breath, and the room become calm again.

"Queen Alexis trembled with remorse from killing another human being, but she knew it had to be done to protect her sister, her sister's children, and herself. She stood staring at the lifeless body of the gerousia.

"Agape yelled at Queen Alexis, 'Enough!' The mother wolf continued attacking the slain gerousia member, and Agape commanded the wild wolf, 'Wolf! Enough!' forgetting that it was a wild animal. Amazingly, the wolf heeded her order. She stopped her attack, walked back and jumped onto the bed where Agape was sitting, and began licking the blood from her fur. She stopped for a second to lick the hand of Agape and then resumed licking her fur.

"The queen immediately stopped and looked over at her sister and the two living babies, and her eyes grew wide at what she discovered. Agape followed the path of her sister's gaze and saw Larentina's eyes. They had turned to a deep maroon color with lightning bolts in her irises. She was completely covered in Andreas's blood, but her brother, who was lying next to her, remained untouched, without a single drop of blood. The boy child was crying, but Larentina just lay there.

"The sisters were amazed and murmured in unison, 'It's another sign.'

"They looked at each other once again, bewildered. To them, this was an unworldly sight to see because they could not comprehend or understand what telekinesis and telepathy were.

"Queen Alexis ordered the helots to help her remove Andreas's body and bury it. Agape immediately left the bed to help the queen and the other two women. They moved very quickly, but to the queen it seemed an eternity; nonetheless, they had no problem moving the body to the wagon.

"The sisters each picked up one of Agape's babies, while Doris and Corinna covered each of the stillborns with white linens. Then, each helot picked up one of the small bodies on Agape's bed, and the four women climbed into the wagon. The queen and her companions rode a few miles until they were safely at the base of the mountains. There, they dug a deep hole and buried the gerousia member and the twins Alexis had delivered. They returned to Agape's home, where they bathed themselves, put on fresh tunics, and burned the soiled ones in the fireplace in the main room.

"The two twin sisters stood in front of the large stone fireplace, watching their clothing burn, and each was indistinguishable from the other. They both had thick, light brown hair that stretched to the lower part of their waists. They both had beautiful green eyes and tanned skin. Their slender bodies featured voluminous bosoms and strong, powerful legs and arms.

"The twins turned toward each other and, for a moment, gazed into each other's eyes before embracing tightly. They began to cry and held each other for many more moments until Alexis could bear it no longer.

"Alexis sobbed, 'Agape, please forgive me. We have been distant these past many months. I do not know what I have done to prevent you from coming to me when all this happened to you. You have blocked your feelings, so I could not feel them. I did not know that Zeus had taken you in this manner. All that I knew was that you were with Erasmus, and now I understand why. Promise you will not keep secrets from me ever again. I hope that you know I will die to protect you.'

"As tears flowed steadily from Agape's eyes, she clung harder to her sister Alexis. She sadly replied, 'I forgive you, my sister, my friend, but you must forgive me as well. I cannot help but continue to hate you for this. I should have been with Alcaeus, and you should have been with Karpos. You are stronger than I, and what happened to me—you are right—should have happened to you. I do not wish to speak of this further.'

"The two women continued to watch the fire; after they had sent the helots to the bedroom to attend to the children's needs, Agape changed the subject. She whispered to her sister, 'If our murderous deception is discovered, we will both be dishonored and killed.'

"The queen looked at her sister with a serious expression and said simply, 'I do indeed agree. That is why they must never discover this. Do you think we should kill the helots?'

"Agape answered her sister, 'No, there has been enough blood spilt this night. They will not dare speak of this, for they know they would be executed beside us.'

"The young queen nodded her head in agreement as she commented, 'We must protect Zeus's daughter and her brother with our very lives.'

"Agape replied, 'Then this matter is settled. They are my children as well as the seed of Zeus and my husband. If anything should happen to them, I will hold you fully responsible.

"'Promise me one thing, Alexis. I want my daughter to become the symbol of women's strength, and we deserve to be treated as equals to men. She will be our hand of justice for all who have persecuted me! She will even teach the gods a lesson or two as well. She will be the one who will change the way men treat mortal woman and even goddesses!

"'I want my son to learn to treat Larentina and all women as equals and to protect her. With these values instilled in my son, when he becomes king, he will replant the seed of all that my daughter will do for Spartan women.'

"Queen Alexis responded, 'I swear it with my own life! And I know if I fail you and the gods, I surely will deserve your wrath as well as theirs. We are blood, and your children are my blood as well.'

"Queen Alexis collected the healthy babies to return to her home; the wolf gently picked up her pup in her mouth, jumped into the wagon, and rode with them to Queen Alexis's home. When Queen Alexis and her babies were settled into the freshly cleaned bed, the wolf jumped on the bed with her pup and lay protectively next to Larentina. They all fell into an exhausted sleep.

"As Agape watched her sister leave, she began to tremble and quickly sat at the large eating table located in the middle of the room. She stared at the fire as she relived the night.

"Agape thought back to the conception of Larentina and Lycurgus. She said aloud to herself, 'Was Zeus under all the layers of the men's faces? Was I deceived by a god as well as a man? Who or what type of woman did I hear laughing that night? What have I done—I gave up the daughter of Zeus to my sister. Or did I?' Agape began to sob uncontrollably. If she had not shared her sister's feelings, she would have killed the newborns. Remorse swept through her heart. Her emotions changed again as she became stronger.

"Agape said, 'My daughter will determine this unseen truth, and if I ask when my daughter becomes of age, my daughter may seek vengeance for me and also change Sparta at its very core with the help of my son. After all, my daughter truly is half god, even if I lied and wanted my sister to think this. My daughter has proven she possesses something unearthly. Only my daughter will have the strength and cunning to kill all of them and shake Sparta's very foundation. I hope my daughter will become as strong as Zeus is and punish the goddess who was part of this. I know she will not be as strong as the king of the gods, but I hope she breaks his heart as he has broken mine.'

"Agape smiled as strength and conviction encompassed her soul. She would ensure her daughter's success with the help of her sister. She may not be able to be present in Larentina and Lycurgus's life, but she will be there in the background. The nightmare of her children's conception, however, will always fill Agape's heart because she does not know the entire truth of what happened to her."

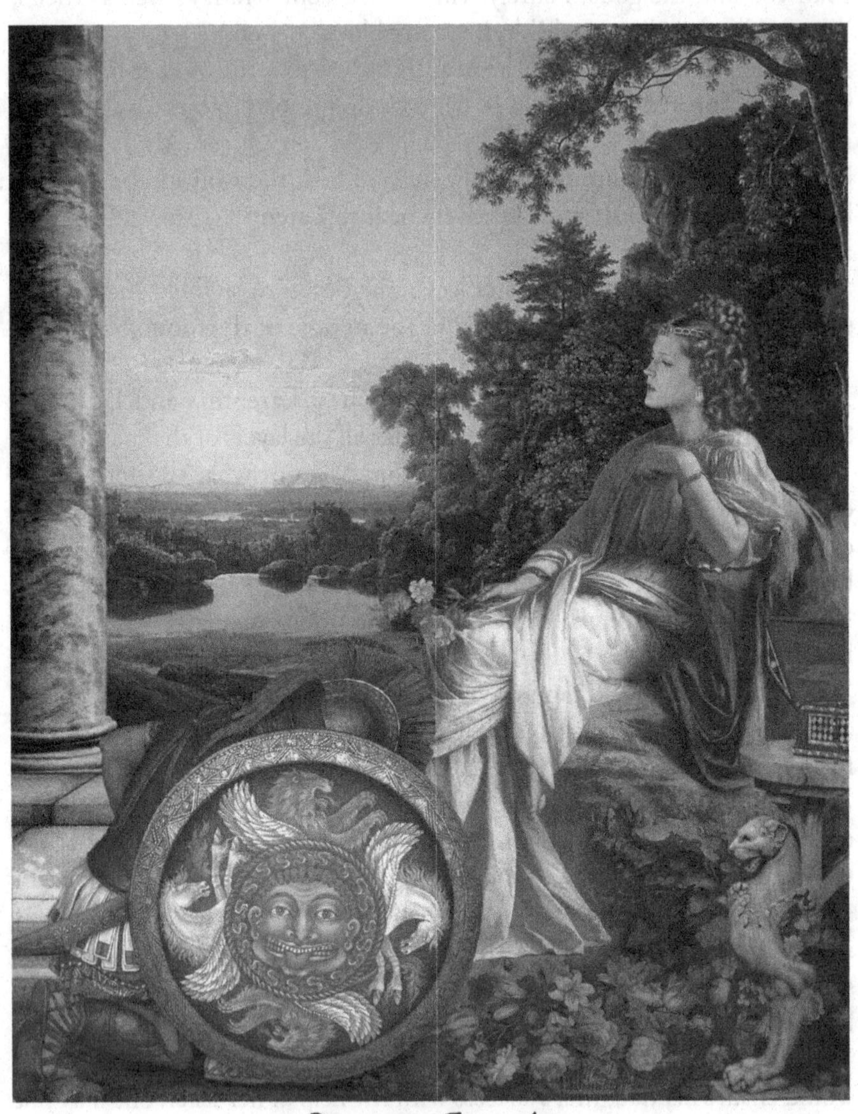

Queen Alexis

Chapter VIII

"The following morning, Doris woke Queen Alexis by lightly shaking her shoulder; she said in a scared and frantic voice, 'My queen, the gerousia are here.'

"Queen Alexis shook the sleep from her eyes and immediately had Doris begin feeding the babies. Corinna had entered the room as well, so the queen ordered, 'Fetch me warm water so that I can bathe, and you can bathe my children. Tell the gerousia members that I will be ready within a few moments.'

"After she and her children were bathed and wearing fresh clothing, Queen Alexis met with the gerousia members in the large gathering room of her home. As she left her bedroom carrying a babe in each arm, the wild wolf picked up her pup and carried the pup in her mouth, following the queen. Once they reached the large room, Hesiodos and Hygieinos took the children from the queen's arms. The third gerousia member, Bion, asked, 'Where did that wolf come from?'

"Queen Alexis proudly informed the three gerousia members that the wolf was a gift from Apollo to Zeus's daughter, Larentina. She explained to them how Zeus was the father of her daughter and King Alcaeus was the father of her son, Lycurgus. She told the entire tale of what transpired during the birth of her two children. She told them every detail that she and Agape had agreed on during the dark hours of the night.

"After the gerousia members examined the babies to make sure that they were healthy and not deformed in anyway, Hesiodos took Lycurgus to a large wooden bucket that had been filled with wine for this event, and he bathed the child in the wine.

"Queen Alexis proudly asked, 'Why do you not test the strength of the girl child since she is the daughter of Zeus?'

"The gerousia members exchanged glances and nodded their heads in agreement. Another bucket was filled with wine, and Hygieinos placed Larentina in the bucket alongside her brother.

"The boy child started to cry, but Larentina reached out her small little hand and touched her brother's arm, and then Lycurgus stopped crying. None of the three gerousia members had ever witnessed such an event, but then they had never tested a boy child and girl child at the same time. It had always been just a boy. They hastened to agree that this girl child was, beyond a doubt, a half goddess because it was only through divine intervention that this girl could provide such strength to the boy. Both children survived the wine test, which showed they were strong; after Larentina touched her brother, neither of them cried throughout the remainder of the tests.

"After all the gerousia members agreed, they approved the health and strength of both children, and Bion told the queen that her twin sister's children had been stillborn, and they too had been twins.

"Hesiodos declared, 'Agape deserves to be cursed for marrying a perioikoi and betraying King Karpos.'

"An ephor entered the room earlier. He had come from the battlefield by orders of King Alcaeus. The ephor was there to ensure King Alcaeus had a reliable source to relay that his boy child was healthy, but the king did not know that his wife had given birth to twins and did not know about his girl child.

"Before Bion had a chance to scold Hesiodos for his remarks, the ephor glared at him and warned, 'The king has made allowances in this situation because, after all, the perioikoi was adopted by the king. You must heed your tongue and not slander his adopted son in such a manner.'

"Hesiodos immediately replied in a sarcastic tone, 'Pardon me; I should have minded my words. Please forgive my rash statement.'

"During the next week, numerous questions arose regarding the disappearance of Andreas, the gerousia member who had gone to check on the queen the night the babies were born. Both the queen and her sister kept to their story that he had never arrived at either home that night, and soon the fate of Andreas was but a distant memory.

"A few weeks later, King Alcaeus returned from a victorious battle and was honored by the Spartan people. He was even more honored by the birth of his two children, because not only had he received a strong, healthy son, he had also received Larentina as a gift from Zeus. He would find himself being told the tale of his children's birth over and over again, not only by his wife and her sister, but also by Spartan citizens who had not even witnessed it, but yet claimed they had been there. Neither sister disputed their claims. In their opinion, the more witnesses to the great event of Larentina and Lycurgus's birth, the more it would be ingrained in people's minds that Larentina was indeed the daughter of Zeus. The tale continued to grow, until people were saying that they had witnessed Zeus himself appear in the room and bestow strength on his daughter, just as he had bestowed strength to his son, the great Hercules himself.

"Before Larentina's first birthday, everyone truly believed she was the daughter of Zeus and that Apollo was her guardian. The news of her birth spread throughout the lands, and the tale became even more embellished than when King Alcaeus had first returned home.

"The tale became so stretched that King Alcaeus was beginning to wonder about its validity, and he considered seeking the wisdom and knowledge from the Oracle of Delphi.

"King Alcaeus still could not truly believe that Zeus was the father of his daughter; he did not know why the god had given her gifts and protection, instead of his son Lycurgus. He did not understand Zeus's plans regarding the girl's destiny. After all, she was just a girl and could never be as powerful as his son.

"The mother wolf disappeared a few months after the birth of Larentina, but she left her female puppy with Larentina. Queen Alexis named the young pup Lambda, which simply means 'wolf.'

"There would be many such pups throughout Larentina's life, as each wolf begat pups and chose to leave a female pup with her. Larentina simply called each one Lambda. Each pup looked identical to its mother, who was pure white. When people around Larentina saw the wolf with her, they would tell her life's story: 'The wolf would turn to ash and be reborn again, like the mystical Phoenix, to serve and protect Larentina. The wolf never died, but was always reborn to her.' This, in turn, served to enforce the belief that she and the wolf came from the gods. The wolf and the wolf's pack will protect her throughout her life."

King Alcaeus

Chapter IX

Mom-mom cleared her throat, took a sip of lemonade, and smiled at us. She continued.

"King Alcaeus finally decided to seek the wisdom and foresight of the Oracle of Delphi, but he wanted to first confer with King Karpos. The next morning, he rode to the home of King Karpos. When he arrived, he was promptly greeted by a male helot, who offered to take his horse. King Alcaeus dismounted and walked into the courtyard and waited for King Karpos.

"King Karpos's home was located closer to the great city of Sparta. It was a single-story home, a complete circle of marble with carved columns placed evenly within the courtyard walls and the outer walls of the palace. Two large bronze sphinxes appeared on either side of the main entrance to the courtyard, which was filled with beautiful flower gardens.

"It had been many years since he had discussed personal matters with his old friend. The last time had been when King Alcaeus was courting Alexis. He trusted his friend to provide sound advice, especially because this matter regarding his daughter could affect the both of them, as well as their beloved Sparta.

"Even though King Karpos and King Alcaeus did not consider themselves superstitious, in reality, they both were very much so. Both kings worshiped the same gods: Zeus, Apollo, Poseidon, and Hades. Both kings considered these gods the strongest and bravest.

"King Alcaeus was different in so many ways from King Karpos. King Alcaeus was considered easygoing and mostly patient; he loved his wife more than life itself and considered her his equal. He never displayed this in public, but in private, he often sought her advice and wisdom regarding matters of the state. He was a man of duty and honor, but he thought before he took action. He truly longed for peace and freedom. He did not care for the responsibilities that came with being a king. He considered himself a man chained and bound by Spartan customs, politics, and responsibility to the people.

"King Alcaeus even adopted Erasmus because he loved his wife so much, he did not want to lose her heart and it was the only way to protect his long time friend and Alexis's sister. He knew Alexis would never forgive him if he did nothing to protect Agape and he would never forgive himself if Erasmus was killed by Karpos.

"All King Alcaeus knew was Erasmus did not report to him. All he knew was after he received word from his wife that Agape ran off with Erasmus and King Karpos had discovered this and was seeking justice for this betrayal. Alcaeus did not blame his friend, Karpos at all, but Agape was Alexis's sister and he had to protect Agape and Erasmus no matter how wrong they both were.

"On the other hand, King Karpos possessed a bad temper and reacted before thinking. He loved being a king and was proud to be a Spartan. He enjoyed life as it came to him and lived for battle and glory. Once he trusted someone, as he trusted Alcaeus, he had no problem relying wholeheartedly on that person's word, which is how he felt in regard to Alcaeus.

"Karpos's voice was deep and strong, unlike that of Alcaeus. Karpos's voice alone put fear in men's hearts. Everyone liked Alcaeus and did not fear him as they feared Karpos. Beyond the rough exterior of King Karpos, however, he was a man who not only fought hard, he loved and played hard as well. Most who encountered him knew him to be a noble and strong man, and he was sincerely liked.

"Unlike Alcaeus, Karpos's heart had been hardened when Agape left him without a word; the wound remained deep and fresh. The next thing Karpos knew, she was with Erasmus. After he discovered where Agape was, he did not even think. He planned on killing both of them for their betrayal, but Alcaeus somehow learned of his plan, returned from the battlefield, and had stood at the entrance of Karpos's home, sword in hand, to stop him.

"Alcaeus told Karpos that he had adopted Erasmus, and he was prepared to defend his house's honor. Karpos became enraged with Alcaeus for preventing his retribution of this betrayal. Nonetheless, Alcaeus convinced him to forgive Agape and let her live the rest of her life in peace. Even though there were so many unanswered questions, Karpos did the unthinkable and put the matter to rest, but he had not forgotten. His heart still bled from the dagger of betrayal his beloved wife had thrust through his chest for reasons he still did not understand.

"Karpos possessed women, whereas Alcaeus honored and respected them. Karpos had seen and felt something that had changed his mind, while Alcaeus simply must feel it within his heart to change his mind. These were just a few of the differences between the kings.

"After Alcaeus convinced Karpos to allow Agape to live in peace, Karpos wanted to show Agape that she could easily be replaced, and he married Irene.

"Bion had introduced King Karpos to Irene. She was beautiful and fair-skinned; she did not speak until she was spoken to. In many ways, she was dull and boring like Karpos's first wife, Androcles's mother, had been, but it did not matter. Karpos did not even court Irene; he simply took her as his wife. Irene's father was a wealthy Spartan merchant, and she assumed that King Karpos fell in love with her the moment he saw her. She felt blessed to be beautiful enough to catch a king's eye. She truly loved being King Karpos's wife, but she was disappointed because he showed no love toward her. He would take her and leave her, without so much as a word.

"King Karpos greeted his friend, King Alcaeus, in his courtyard as if everything was forgotten. 'Well, what a nice surprise, old friend. I think I know why you are here. It's regarding your daughter, Larentina. You know news travels fast in Sparta.'

"King Alcaeus acknowledged his friend as Queen Irene entered the courtyard.

"She greeted King Alcaeus with a hug and kissed both cheeks. With a soft smile, she said, 'Come and break bread with us, so the two of you can talk.'

"King Alcaeus replied, 'I would like that very much, but I need to speak with Karpos alone.'

"Queen Irene immediately responded, before her husband had a chance to say a word, 'I will make that so.'

"Both kings followed the queen into the house. Queen Irene even helped the helots to set the table, and she instructed the helots to close all the entrances to the large eating room. As Queen Irene closed the two main doors, she smiled at the two kings and commented, 'My kings, eat and drink well.' She then bowed and left the room.

"As King Karpos poured wine into their goblets, he asked, 'Please, old friend, tell me what troubles you?'

"As they ate and drank, King Alcaeus began the tale. 'Well, Karpos, you know it is reported that my daughter is the daughter of Zeus. There is no doubt that she has exceptional strength for a girl, as I have tested

Larentina numerous times along with her brother, Lycurgus. In addition to her physical strength, she possesses a strange power over her brother. Each time he begins to cry, she will touch him, and he somehow becomes stronger and instantly stops crying. I have never witnessed such a sight in my life. I have never even heard of such a thing. She is the most beautiful baby I have ever seen, and it's becoming harder not to hold and love her. I just can't explain it in words. She has a power over me unlike the pride I feel toward her brother, my son. Not to mention this mysterious wild wolf that remains with her at all times and follows wherever Larentina goes. No one can explain where the mother wolf came from or where she went. This wild wolf acts as a housedog. Now, the mother wolf has gone and left her puppy to protect Larentina. My wife has even named it. She calls it Lambda.

"'My wife still has not explained to me or anyone how this came to be, because she sincerely does not remember. She claims she only remembers my touch that night and no other.

"'There is also the fact that Andreas, one of the gerousia members, is still missing. His own wife claims that he left their home in the wee morning hours to check on Alexis, per my instructions before I left, but my wife claims he never came. I do not understand what has happened. This is why I'm here. I feel I need to seek guidance from the Oracle of Delphi in this matter. That much I do know. If this is truly the will of the gods, I need to know for sure and for what purpose.'

"King Karpos took another sip of his wine after listening to his friend and responded, 'Alcaeus, I truly believe your daughter, Larentina, is the daughter of Zeus. Not only because of what you have just told me, but Hesiodos, Hygieinos, and Bion have also announced this to be true. I know all three of these men very well, as do you, and I do not believe they are superstitious. In fact, Bion himself told me, "I would not have believed this, if I had not seen it myself." In fact, all three of them claim it to be true because they witnessed it. You have confessed you have been bewitched by a girl babe's power.

"'It is not ours to understand the acts of the gods or why they create beings such as your daughter. You know when Zeus wants something, he takes it. You have no doubt that our own ancestor, Hercules, was made by the gods, do you?'

"King Alcaeus, slightly irritated, answered King Karpos, 'That is different.'

"King Karpos bluntly asked, 'Why do you say that?'

"King Alcaeus became irritated with his friend and answered him, after taking another sip of wine, 'Simply, Hercules was a half-mortal man, not a half-mortal woman with these types of strengths. Zeus has fathered hundreds of children, but he has chosen to interfere in the destinies of only a few of his half-mortal children. Less than a handful of them have inherited any of his godly powers, and those that have are all men. He has never taken an interest in any of his mortal daughters, to my knowledge. Granted, he has fathered goddesses from other Olympian deities and has always favored them, but as I have said, he has never taken an interest in mortal girl children who he has fathered. These facts, in and of themselves, speak volumes. Why would he now change and decide to give his girl child, Larentina, godly powers of this nature? Better yet, how did she even inherit some of his powers, when no other mortal girl has inherited these gifts? Why would she be any different?

"'To be quite honest, I am totally angry that Zeus, god or not, seduced my wife by disguising himself as me. If he were a mortal man, I would have killed him. How can this be an honor, to raise another man's child? Nothing further needs to be said.'

"King Karpos sighed and answered his friend, 'Yes, more does need to be said. I would be angry as well. You know my past history, and you interfered. Zeus is not a mortal, and that is the difference. Our people worship him as they worship us. Neither you nor I could best the king of the gods. If we even dared to try, he could kill us and our entire kingdom.

"'I agree that we need to seek guidance from the Oracle because we must protect this girl child, or there will be a heavy price to pay to the gods. You know this. The point you have made is valid. Why did he give such strength to a woman child and not a man? How did she inherit godly powers from Zeus to begin with? It does not make sense, but I do not question the gods as you have.'

"King Alcaeus responded to this new insight. 'Yes, Karpos, I believe you speak the truth. We must protect Larentina, at all costs. I will try not to question the gods again, but we do need to understand this so that we make the right decisions regarding this unique situation.'

"King Karpos replied, 'We will meet with the gerousia council at first light, provide instructions to the ephors, and promptly leave.'

"King Alcaeus was surprised. 'We? This is my quest, not yours.'

"King Karpos retorted, 'Did you actually think I was going to let you go alone? This will affect both of us, because I want your word of honor that your daughter will not marry anyone other than my firstborn son. This will ensure we are still united.'

"King Alcaeus became agitated. 'Now that my eyes are opened with your reason, you would like to know that it is true as well. Did you ever think that perhaps your son is not strong enough for my daughter?'

"King Karpos argued, 'I swear to Apollo, where did that come from? Of course, I want your daughter for my son because, if you stop to think, you would realize that she might be the only princess in the lands strong enough for my son. Now let us stop this petty bickering. We need to work together on this matter.'

"King Alcaeus nodded his head in agreement and drank the rest of the wine from his goblet. He reached for the wine flask to pour himself more. King Karpos put out his goblet for King Alcaeus to fill his as well. Both men looked at each other and chuckled, because not only were they bickering like two old hags, they were also waiting on each other like helots. They guffawed even harder as King Alcaeus remarked, 'If the Spartan citizens saw us now, what would they think? Kings? Old hags? Or helots?' Both kings laughed even harder because their entire behavior seemed so humorous to them.

"After a few minutes, they both became serious again and began planning the quest before them."

Chapter X

"The following morning, the kings called a special meeting with the gerousia council and ordered all the ephors there as well.

"After several hours of arguing with the gerousia council, which wanted a military escort to accompany the kings to Delphi, King Alcaeus protested, 'This need not be a state affair, for this is merely a personal matter to me; I do not need a military escort. In fact, this entire matter has been blown out of proportion. I am quite capable of protecting myself, although I completely understand your concern.' After a long debate, both kings finally agreed to allow a military escort to accompany them along with three gerousia members.

"The council members agreed that the kings needed to seek the Oracle's wisdom and knowledge regarding this matter, but they firmly suggested that the kings wait to leave until the following morning, so that every detail could be worked out sufficiently. The council wanted to leave nothing to chance when it came to their kings.

"Bion's statement reflected the thoughts of all present: 'After all, this entire matter is unprecedented, but I too agree. Understanding this girl child who Zeus has given us truly requires more explanation because we are just mortal men and not gods ourselves.' The room became very noisy as the council members argued amongst themselves for several minutes, but it was finally agreed that the two kings should go together.

"The kings decided to give the Oracle six stallions, three white from King Alcaeus's herd and three black from King Karpos's herd, along with a chest full of gemstones. The kings personally selected the best young goats and lambs to sacrifice as offerings to Apollo.

"The following morning, King Karpos, several of the gerousia members, and six soldiers met at King Alcaeus's home. Several hundred Spartan citizens had rallied outside. They began cheering for all the men mounted on their horses, as King Alcaeus mounted his steed as well. After several last-minute details, they started their long quest for the advice and wisdom of the Oracle.

"It only took a few days for them to reach the slopes of Mount Parnassus. The Sanctuary of Apollo, the site of the Oracle, was located on a semicircular spur, a plateau that was known as Phaedriades. This beautiful sanctuary overlooked the most breathtaking view of the Pleistos Valley.

"Whenever King Alcaeus came to this area for the Pythian Games, to attend the theater, or to worship Apollo, he always stopped and stared in awe at the beauty of the surrounding landscape that the gods had discovered.

"He completely understood why Zeus himself had sent two ravens to find this place and why Zeus and the other gods considered this the navel of not only the earth but also the universe. He knew why Apollo chose this sacred land to allow mortal men to speak to him and ask him questions.

"King Alcaeus knew that he could not speak directly to the gods, and he understood why he would have to speak to Apollo through the Oracle, which was something he had not done before. To his knowledge, King Karpos had not done so either, despite it being a normal practice among all the Greek city-states.

"They decided to make camp in the valley where the two kings could register and pay their fees as they awaited their appointment.

"The valley was completely surrounded by mountains. Above the thick treetops, large waterfalls could be seen from a distance, and the dark green trees seemed to reach the clouds.

"The valley was full of hundreds of pilgrims seeking the advice and wisdom of the Oracle of Delphi. Some journeyed a great distance just to gaze at the beauty of Pythia, Apollo's priestess. Many merchants camped in the valley as well, making a living off the pilgrims. The scent of fresh bread and spices could be smelled from miles away.

"A pilgrim's status and wealth dictated where they set up camp. Naturally, the kings chose the outer edge of the valley, away from the crowds of people who had come before them.

"The kings washed in a bathing trough adjacent to the Castalian spring. This ritual was necessary so that they could purify themselves before seeing the Oracle. The male helots waited for them, guarding the gifts for the Oracle along with the goats and lambs that would be used for sacrifice.

"The two kings then proceeded up the hill along the sacred path, a narrow zigzagging flagstone trail that ended outside the temple. As the two kings walked the sacred path, they both marveled at the beautiful statues and small shrines spread about on both sides of the path.

"When they reached the temple, they were greeted by two priests. The kings immediately sacrificed a lamb and goat, which the two priests then examined for omens.

"King Alcaeus asked the priests, 'Since we are both kings of Sparta and our questions pertain to the future of Sparta, may we both enter at the same time to ask our questions of the Oracle?'

"The older of the two priests answered, 'No, only one pilgrim may enter at a time.'

"Both kings became irritated but held their tempers. King Karpos gestured for his helot to bring the three stallions as an additional gift. King Karpos presented his gift to the priests and said, 'Here, these I give to the Oracle of Delphi to make this allowance because our urgency is great.'

"The older priest shook his head and responded, 'This gift is acceptable, but we will allow only an additional question to Pythia, the priestess of Apollo.'

"In turn, King Alcaeus proceeded to give his three stallions as a gift and pleaded, 'Here, I too give three stallions to the Oracle of Delphi to grant both kings of Sparta entrance at the same time and to ask as many questions as needed.'

"Again, the older priest graciously accepted the gift from King Alcaeus and said, 'This gift is acceptable, but you—and you alone—may ask an additional question of Pythia. Only one pilgrim may enter at a time.'

"The kings silently exchanged glances and nodded their heads in agreement; King Alcaeus ordered the helots, 'Go, and bring us the chest.'

"The helots quickly obeyed his command and walked to the mules. They had great difficulty removing the heavy chest from the mule's back, but after several attempts, they managed to do so without causing injury to the mule or themselves. They carried it to the entrance of the temple and set it between the two kings.

"King Karpos pointed to one of the helots and commanded, 'Open this chest.' The helot bent over without looking the kings in the eyes, quickly opened the chest, and moved away. The eyes of the priests grew wide as they viewed the enormous chest, which was full of rubies, diamonds, and every other precious stone known to the priests.

"*A very large treasure indeed*, the older priest thought to himself.

"The older priest then ordered in an excited tone, 'Wait here, I must speak with Pythia, the priestess of Apollo, because she—and she alone—

can make this allowance.' Both priests then walked into the temple and closed the large doors behind them.

"As the two kings impatiently waited—"

* * *

Mom-mom broke her story to add, "Remember my dears, they were royalty and not used to waiting for anything."

* * *

"King Karpos, annoyed, asked King Alcaeus, 'What in the name of the gods are we doing? We should have brought the women here to do our bartering. I'm used to just taking what I want. This is totally degrading.'

"King Alcaeus warned, 'This is a test by Apollo, I'm sure. Be careful what you say, friend, because Apollo is listening.'

"King Karpos responded, in a bewildered tone, 'Yes, indeed, you are right. If they do not allow this, I do not even know what two questions to ask. We must discuss our questions if we cannot enter together. I'm only interested in the future of Sparta.'

"King Alcaeus commented with conviction, 'I'm also interested in the gods' destiny for my daughter, as well as my son. They both reflect on the future of Sparta as well.'

"Both men argued over what questions to ask and finally agreed to most of them. After a long wait, the two priests emerged from the temple. The older priest again graciously accepted the gifts from the kings and said, 'Your gifts have been accepted. You both may enter at the same time. You may ask Pythia, the priestess of Apollo, as many questions as needed. Please follow us.'

"The kings exchanged triumphant glances and followed the two priests into the temple. After entering the temple, the kings stood in awe of the beautiful statues and treasures that surrounded them, and the hestia, the inner hearth where the eternal flame was burning in the center of the large room where they stood.

"They were led through a large hallway that gradually sloped down into the temple. As they walked into the room, Pythia was sitting on a golden tripod with the three legs ending in lion's paws. The kings thought it odd that the stool was placed closer to the wall rather than in the center of the room.

"They briefly met the gaze of Pythia, and then quickly broke their gaze to look around at the intricate gold-leafed carvings on the doors and walls.

"Busts of many of the gods sat in carved-out niches evenly placed around the entire circular room. Statues of the gods lined the wall as well. The mosaic floor showed beautiful scenes, but a deep crack in the floor ran through it for one or two feet. Pythia appeared to be sitting almost directly over the middle of the larger crack, and smoky vapor poured out of it, filling the room.

"Then, the kings looked at Pythia herself. Even though Pythia was well older than he was, King Karpos thought she was the most beautiful woman he had ever laid eyes on, with the exception of Alexis and Agape. Although Irene was beautiful, her beauty could not compare to the twin sisters.

"Pythia had skin fairer than any Spartan woman. Her eyes were the blue of the sky on a clear day, and her hair was of the purest gold. It was pinned in such a way that golden curls cascaded down her back, and her face, framed in curls, was round and full with a small pert nose that made her even more beautiful. She had full red lips and just a touch of pink in her cheeks. She wore a gem-encrusted tiara in her hair that pointed downward in the middle of her forehead.

"She was wearing a deep red cloak, and as the kings watched, she pulled the hood over her golden tresses, leaving her face visible. The cloak was fastened with one button at the base of her neck, and as it fell away from her body, it revealed a light blue silk tunic beneath that came to her ankles. A slit on each side of the tunic revealed her creamy white legs. The tunic was cinched around her tiny waist with a wide golden belt bearing gemstones in the center and throughout the belt, which accentuated her perfect figure. She was wearing golden sandals that laced up to her knees. She was wearing large golden bracelets with a large eagle carved in them and a large gold necklace, which accentuated her full, round breasts.

"A priestess entered the room, and Pythia removed her red cloak and handed it to her. After the young priestess took the cloak from Pythia, she handed Pythia a freshly cut laurel branch, full and still bearing all its leaves."

* * *

I interrupted Mom-mom and asked, "Mom-mom, what is a laurel?"

Mom-mom answered, "We know it as a bay tree. If you remember, Belinda, during the ancient Olympics, the winner received a crown made of bay leaves."

I remembered, "Oh, that's right, so that's what a laurel branch would look like."

Mom-mom agreed, "Yes, that's right. Now where was I? Oh, yes, I remember."

* * *

"The kings began to feel lightheaded, and the feeling increased the longer they breathed in the vapor that filled the room. They both made an effort to remain focused and to keep their wits about them.

"King Karpos still felt jilted because King Alcaeus had won the hand of Alexis, and her twin sister, Agape, had married a perioikoi named Erasmus. The bitterness crept back into his heart, and he thought how wonderful it would be to have the beautiful Pythia as his own. It would be the perfect revenge to see his ally, Alcaeus, jealous.

"King Alcaeus took his gaze from the beautiful Pythia and looked at King Karpos, who in turned glared at Alcaeus with a furrowed brow. King Alcaeus knew exactly what his companion was thinking. King Alcaeus's thoughts had returned to the day when he had to adopt Erasmus because Karpos was going to kill Erasmus and Agape. Agape had betrayed Karpos by falling in love with a perioikoi. King Alcaeus honestly understood how his friend had felt; after all, they were kings, and the twin sisters were the most beautiful women in all of Sparta. He had no other choice but to adopt Erasmus to protect Alexis's sister. That was the only way he could keep the affections of Alexis, who he truly loved and would die to protect. To Alcaeus, Pythia was only the second most beautiful woman in the world. His beloved wife would always be number one in his heart and mind.

"Pythia studied the movements and facial expressions of the two young kings. Prior to their entrance, she had been told their names, their titles, where they came from, and all relevant information.

"She decided from all the information she'd received that she did not like King Karpos at all. Her source regarding Larentina had been reliable in the past, and she believed without any doubt that Larentina did indeed possess some of the gods' powers. The conclusion she reached was that the story must be true. Larentina was indeed the daughter of Zeus.

"She knew the twin sisters were close from the information she had received, and she knew about the story of King Alcaeus, who adopted the perioikoi to protect Agape from the wrath of Karpos. She adored King Alcaeus because of this story, and she believed he adopted the perioikoi because of his love for his queen; he would go to great lengths to protect his queen's blood. Furthermore, Apollo had visited Pythia in a dream the night before and confessed that he had sent the wolf spirit to Larentina.

"She also discovered another lesser known story about Agape, and she believed it as well. She believed the girl child somehow would transform Sparta, but Pythia did not know if it would be for better or for worse. She believed Larentina would seek some type of vengeance against Karpos from the stories she had been told about Agape. She also wanted to believe that this demigoddess would fight for women's freedom, like her brothers Hercules and Perseus fought for men's freedom. After all, Larentina seemed to possess some of the same physical strength that they did.

"Unknown to Pythia, she would become a part of the fight for equality among not only women, but also the goddesses. She did not realize that she unwittingly would be playing an important role in Agape's plans for vengeance as well.

"She coolly waited for several minutes as they absorbed their surroundings and inhaled the vapors. Then she softly spoke. 'I know why you are here, Alcaeus, but I do not understand why you brought Karpos with you. Even so, Apollo will still answer his questions as well.

"'You are here, Alcaeus, to know if it is actually true that your daughter, Larentina, is the daughter of Zeus. You want to know what this means regarding your son, Lycurgus, and the future of Sparta.'

"King Alcaeus was amazed by Pythia's knowledge and responded, 'Yes, wise Pythia!'

"Pythia turned her attention to King Karpos and acknowledged his presence. 'You are only here to know the future of Sparta and for your personal benefit. You seek redemption.' King Karpos was amazed at her ability to read the thoughts he had kept hidden from all others, but he was still skeptical as he softly responded, 'Yes, Oracle of Delphi.'

"The vapors pouring out of the crack in the room were now affecting the kings. They became unable to focus and formulate their thoughts. Their vision had grown fuzzier, and the objects in the room had begun to move and come alive.

"Pythia picked up the laurel branch resting on her lap and began fanning the vapors toward her face. She deeply inhaled the vapors and held them in her lungs before exhaling again. She started to convulse as she sat on her tripod stool. Her eyes rolled back, leaving only the whites visible; her head went backward and the stool began to shake violently as her body convulsed. Four priests, who had entered the room a few moments earlier, quickly grabbed the tripod stool before it tilted over. The kings' eyes widened from the shocking sight before them.

"Within moments, Pythia spoke. 'The girl child is indeed the daughter of Zeus. He chose Queen Alexis because she was not only one of the most beautiful women in the land, but the strongest woman of Spartan blood. He simply could not resist her since he knew he could not have her because of her love for you. He came to her in your form to seduce her. The twin children cannot survive without each other; Larentina was jealous of your son, Lycurgus, in the womb because he was a boy. Therefore, she took his strength and will, only returning it when he begged her for it. She has more power and strength in many different forms than Hercules himself did. Larentina is the daughter goddess of duty to her god, country, family, as three equal parts.

"'If the girl child discovers the truth, you, Karpos, will die a dishonorable death by her own hand. She will shake the very foundations of Mount Olympus. She will even defy Zeus himself, and he will bow down before her.

"'It was not Zeus who gave the wolf spirit to Larentina as a guardian. Apollo bestowed this gift to her because Zeus's wife, Hera, and Apollo have been battling for many centuries. Apollo orders you, on this day, to protect this girl child with all your strength. You must also protect your son because it will be your son who saves her and helps her fulfill her destiny.

"'Apollo has claimed this child named Larentina to join him in the future as he takes up arms against Hera, because Zeus will not. Apollo is positive that Zeus will take down Hera or at least punish her if Apollo has Larentina, Zeus's newest daughter, by his side. Larentina is special to Zeus because she is the first mortal daughter of his who has inherited a portion of his godly powers, and that is why he will interfere in her life someday. As we all know, however, Zeus is a god who sometimes does not keep his word. I feel he has made a promise to Apollo, but I do not know what that promise is. All I know is that the future depends on the promise that Zeus has made to Apollo. Be warned young Spartan kings, a war between the gods is brewing and Larentina will be our only hope to survive it because she will be the key that will start this unrest between the Olympian deities.

"'Your son will do what you did not do: cherish all women, not just mothers of Sparta, and treat them as equals, not as property.

"'By obeying Zeus and the gods, your beloved Sparta will one day be protected by Larentina from Hera's wrath. This is the future of Sparta. She must change her ways or be destroyed. You cannot make beasts out of man without paying the consequences. There must be reason, love, and respect for all people, including women. Without this, Sparta shall indeed fall.'

"Pythia violently gasped for air and then began to speak to King Karpos. 'Karpos, your jealousies and greed will be your downfall. You must protect the girl child, as well as her brother, at all costs, because they are the future of Sparta. One of your children will join them in their quest, and together the three shall usher in a new era in Sparta.'

"During Pythia's revelations and prophesies, King Alcaeus began hallucinating, but he did not realize it. Two large ravens pulled his spirit from his body and took it to Zeus, and he found himself kneeling in front of Zeus as he sat on his marble throne. Apollo stood at the base of the throne on one side of Zeus, and Hera stood on the other side of the throne. Zeus leaned forward with both elbows resting on his thighs, his right fist held up his head, as he was looking at Alcaeus. Zeus said nothing, neither did Apollo or Hera. All King Alcaeus could hear was Pythia's voice.

"King Karpos was angry at the stupid nonsense that spewed from Pythia's mouth. He didn't fear her at all because she was just a woman—a very beautiful woman, but still just a woman. He had no fear now, but he knew in his heart that he would have to obey the gods. He was shocked, however, that his favored god, Apollo, was involved in this as well. Like most Spartans, Karpos favored Apollo, second only to Zeus.

"As the two kings left the temple and walked back down the sacred path, neither of them spoke. They were both recovering from breathing the vapors in the Oracle's chamber. Neither one understood what had just happened to them. They both knew it was the gods, but Alcaeus was still unclear of what he had just experienced.

"King Karpos grew increasingly bitter and could not shake his increasing jealously toward his friend. He silently prayed to Apollo to rid him of these strong feelings.

"As they approached their camp, Hesiodos, Hygieinos, and Bion were impatiently pacing around the fire, awaiting the return of their two kings. Bion was the first to look up from the large fire at the center of their camp and saw the two kings approaching in the dark.

"Bion proclaimed, 'Our kings! Our kings have returned!'

"Bion was in his late forties, much older than the Spartan kings. Nevertheless, he was young for a gerousia member. He was never questioned when an older gerousia member had appeared to have died by natural causes, but it was Bion himself who poisoned him. To replace the fallen member, Bion bribed other members to vote him into the council.

"His thin hair was dark brown, but had mostly turned gray, and it barely touched his shoulders. His hair was straight with a receding hairline at his temples. His beard also was sprinkled with gray and was shaped into a narrow triangle. His dark brown eyes were small and slanted slightly downward. His thick eyebrows were slanted downward as well. His nose was long, straight, and pointed. He was no longer as strong as the Spartan kings, but he still possessed somewhat muscular arms and legs.

"He wore a tunic of soft, thick cotton that fell to his knees. It was a solid white with gold trim. His wide brown leather belt was tightly fastened around his waist. He wore dark blue cotton fabric draped over his shoulder to his waist. The entire gerousia council wore the same style of tunics. On Bion's wrists were large gold bands. These gold bands were worn by the gerousia council and most Spartan soldiers and civilian men and women, as well.

"Hesiodos approached the kings and asked curiously, 'Have your questions been answered?'

"The kings exchanged a look as they simultaneously reached their hands toward the fire to warm them. King Alcaeus solemnly answered, 'Yes. Sparta's questions have been answered.'

"King Karpos angrily retorted, 'The woman talks in riddles and makes no sense.' He glared at King Alcaeus as he spoke.

"Hygieinos impatiently said, 'Please, my kings, tells us what Pythia said.'

"King Alcaeus chose his words very carefully so as not to offend King Karpos. 'Pythia proclaimed Larentina as the daughter of Zeus. The twin children cannot survive without each other. Larentina is the daughter of duty to her god, country, and family, as three equal parts, and she will protect Sparta.

"'There will be a great war between the gods someday, and only Larentina will be able to protect us from the gods who are enemies of Zeus and Apollo. Zeus did not give the wolf spirit to Larentina as a guardian. Apollo bestowed the gift; Alexis was right. Sparta must now protect both my children because my son will save Larentina, so she is able to fulfill her destiny. They, and one of Karpos's children, are the future of Sparta.'

"King Karpos was grateful that King Alcaeus left out all the prophesy about his jealousy and greed.

"The three gerousia turned their gaze from King Alcaeus toward King Karpos, who nodded in affirmation. 'Yes, this is what Pythia prophesized.'

"Both kings stood in front of the fire with their hands stretched toward the warmth of the flames. They looked at each other with an unspoken acceptance of what Alcaeus said.

"Bion inquired, 'Did Pythia give the names of the gods who are the enemies of Zeus and Apollo?'

"King Karpos solemnly answered, 'No. She did not.'

"With a puzzled expression, Hesiodos asked, 'How did Zeus impregnate Queen Alexis to form only the girl child, but not the boy?'

"King Alcaeus answered, with increasing anger regarding this matter, 'Zeus came disguised as me and seduced her. Alexis said she remembers my touch twice that night, even though I only visited her bed once. I do not know why one is Zeus's child and not the other.'

"Hygieinos, with a hint of anxiety in his tone, asked, 'How can a girl be our protector?'

"King Karpos answered with anger, 'Because she is half god! It makes perfect sense to me! Do you have no shame? How would you feel if another man had seduced your woman in the way that Zeus did? Drop the subject and respect King Alcaeus!'

"Hygieinos ignored King Karpos as he shared his thoughts, saying, 'But she is just a girl.'

"Hesiodos angrily retorted, 'That is why we have to protect her, because she is the daughter goddess of duty! Being a girl is not the point; she is the seed of Zeus, idiot!'

"Before long, all three gerousia members were arguing over the interpretations of Pythia's wisdom and prophesy. Both kings broke into laughter, because the gerousia members were acting like children. King Karpos barked to a nearby helot, 'Go, and bring us some wine.'

"King Karpos looked at King Alcaeus's disapproving expression; still being flippant, Karpos said, 'What? We have much to celebrate this night! And besides, I'm very thirsty.'

"King Alcaeus's head hurt, and he was tired of listening to the gerousia arguing, so he shouted, 'Shut up! You are all squabbling like a bunch of old hags. You are making my head hurt from all the cackling!'

"King Alcaeus retired with a headache. King Karpos drank several cups of wine before retiring because he too was tired of listening to the stupid arguing.

"The following morning, they packed the camp and headed home; the gerousia members continued to debate their interpretations of Pythia's statements and prophesies.

"King Karpos grew weary of this insufferable bickering and commanded, 'Shut up! Just shut up!'

"Bion pleaded, 'But my Lord, this does affect Sparta's future. The meanings of the Oracle's prophesy need to be agreed upon.'

"King Alcaeus simply commanded, 'You can bicker over this on your own time, not ours. So simply do as Karpos has commanded and silence yourselves, or I will cut your tongues out.'

"In fear of having their tongues slashed, all three gerousia members became silent for the remainder of the journey to Sparta."

Chapter XI

"Over the next six and a half years, Larentina and Lycurgus lived a good childhood. They were loved, spoiled, and received much attention and adoration from their parents. Spartan royal children were raised differently. They were primarily raised by the wet nurses, teachers, young soldiers, and numerous other people who spoiled them rotten. The twins received affection, nurturing, and anything their little royal hearts desired.

"No one knew that Queen Alexis and Agape would trade places frequently for several hours throughout the first year of Larentina and Lycurgus's lives. They would meet in the forest between their two homes and change clothing. As long as Agape and Alexis did not speak, no one could tell the difference. Agape's voice was softer and of a higher pitch than Alexis's voice; that was the only noticeable difference between them.

"Alexis felt nothing but remorse for what had happened to Agape, and to make matters worse, Alexis had taken her children from her. Alexis would do anything to make things whole again between them. She truly loved her sister very much. Agape was grateful that Alexis shared her life with her, but she still harbored jealousy and contempt for her twin. Agape enjoyed every minute breastfeeding her children and nurturing them. To experience that joy, she put aside her ill feelings for her sister. Sadly, it was becoming more dangerous and risky for the two sisters to continue their secret 'switches'; if caught, they would be executed immediately, as well as the children.

"Larentina and Lycurgus were both very intelligent and learned how to read, write, and perform basic math, a practice that was not normally taught in the Spartan society, royalty or not (which is the likely reason there was very little written records of their society, and why very few written records exist today).

"They learned not only how to speak several languages fluently, but also how to read and write them. They also learned the stories of the gods.

They learned the tales of their father's battles and bravery along with the tales of their ancestors. They learned basic politics and how their city-state was run.

"In addition, they learned how to hunt using a bow and arrow, which Larentina excelled at, as well as the use of many other weapons of that age. She Wolf was unquestionably a tomboy by nature and quickly mastered each weapon. Few of these subjects were taught to boys Lycurgus's age, and they were never taught to girls, but the queen's sister requested it because she wanted them to have a head start in life and to receive a better education than most Spartan children.

"After all, the queen's sister did not think like a normal spartiate; she had not only married for love but she also had married beneath her status. Queen Alexis agreed wholeheartedly with her sister's request, because this was the only opportunity to use Larentina's status to encourage the Spartan men to begin teaching the girls of Sparta along with the boys. Each year, Queen Alexis began to vary the teachings and trainings, hoping not to be noticed by the king and other spartiates.

"On one of the rare times when the twins were allowed to swim without supervision, something unexpected occurred. Larentina went too deep into the river. There had been a heavy rainstorm the previous night, and the current was very strong that day. Although she was able to swim, she was unable to fight the current, and exhausted, she began to drown. She never once cried out to her brother for help, but Lambda sensed her mistress was in danger and swam out and saved her.

"Lambda and Larentina were very close and always knew what the other was thinking. Even though meat was scarce, Larentina always made sure Lambda had plenty to eat, a practice that she picked up from her mother, Queen Alexis.

"Even though she was very young, Larentina's near-drowning caused her to doubt the stories told to her by her father, mother, and others regarding Zeus being her true father. As she sat eating dinner with her family, feeding Lambda scraps of meat from the stew and silently contemplating the events of the day, she felt that she was not immortal, nor did she have the strength of Hercules, her ancestor, as she had always been told. She also realized that she could never let anyone else know this revelation, not even her brother. Larentina also vowed to excel at swimming, because she never again wanted to experience the terror she had felt that day.

"She knew that she would have to work even harder to give the illusion of being strong so that no one would ever question her being the daughter of Zeus. She sensed something was not quite right about the stories that were being told to her. At the end of her thoughts, she did the best she could to shrug the doubts away.

"Larentina had a bad habit of sneaking into her brother's room late at night. If she had a nightmare, she would curl up beside him because she felt safer with him.

"On the twins' seventh birthday, Queen Alexis woke Lycurgus up and told him to dress. Then, she proudly declared to him, 'This is a glorious day because you are going into agoge training. You will learn how to fight; you will increase in strength and knowledge and then become a Spartan warrior. I am proud to be a Spartan mother this day. Hurry, my son, for they are waiting for you downstairs.'

"Lycurgus began to cry. With panic in his voice, he said, 'Oh, Mother, please do not make me go. Let me stay here with my sister.'

"Queen Alexis became angry; she struck Lycurgus hard across the face and replied in a firm tone, 'Do not dare cry and show you are weak! You are acting like a spoiled child. You are acting worse than a woman. This is an honor bestowed upon you by the gods. Now get dressed and do not shed another tear. You are a prince, not a coward!'

"Alexis felt remorse, but it had to be done because that was the Spartan way. She continued her tough love demeanor toward Lycurgus.

"Even though Lycurgus had stopped crying, he looked at his mother with wide, scared eyes, and she slapped him hard across the face again. The force from her hand was so great that he fell to the ground. He did not dare cry, and he obediently dressed. Lycurgus timidly asked his mother, 'Can my sister at least go with me?'

"Queen Alexis softly answered her son, 'No, she cannot because she is just a girl. Thank the gods that you were blessed to have been born as a man. Now come.'

"Larentina, after hearing those words from her own mother, felt tears form in her eyes, but instead she told herself, *Swallow it, and turn it into something else.* Therefore, she swallowed the hurt of losing her beloved twin brother and hearing that she was not as valuable because she was a girl. The only person she believed truly loved her, as she loved him, was her brother. She quickly got out of her bed and ran to her brother before he reached the main entrance to their home. She turned him around, wrapped both arms around him tightly, and kissed him on his lips.

"She pulled back slightly and said, with conviction, 'I give you strength, my brother. I give you wisdom to overcome.' She spoke in Latin because she knew her mother could not understand. As she looked deeply into the eyes that were a mirror of her own, Larentina could tell that her other half was trying to hold back the tears, so she said, in Latin, 'Swallow it, my brother, and turn it into something else.' As Larentina watched her brother's face, he did just that, and his eyes turned from hurt to coldness. Then suddenly, before Larentina knew what was happening, they took her brother from her.

"The next day, Lambda disappeared. Larentina searched everywhere she could think of for her beloved wolf, but it did her no good. In just two days, Larentina had lost the only two things in her life that she loved and that loved her in return: her brother and her beloved wolf. She quietly cried every night but maintained her strong attitude during the day.

"Larentina began her training in gymnastics, dance, wrestling, and boxing, and continued her studies in politics, math, reading, and writing. She continued to become fluent in all known languages. Queen Alexis supervised all the extra studies and had numerous arguments with her husband, because he thought it was a waste of time and money to teach a girl child. King Alcaeus firmly gave his reasoning, saying, 'Alexis, the state does not even waste this type of teachings on the sons of Sparta. She is just a girl and is not worth this.'

"Nonetheless, the queen's will always prevailed; each time she would remind him that Larentina was the daughter of Zeus. 'My king, my husband, must I always remind you that she is the daughter of Zeus, and you have been honored to be her ward? She is half goddess and must be provided the very best for her destiny.' Queen Alexis would always give him a long kiss after their arguments and persuade him even further by making passionate love to him.

"After being swayed by the queen, Alcaeus would approach the gerousia council to obtain permission for the extra studies to appease his queen. Once the name of Zeus was uttered, no one dared to argue.

"Whenever Larentina had a spare moment to herself, she would continue her practices in archery. Queen Alexis managed to import the most skilled and talented experts to teach her daughter. Masters in the ancient Chinese martial arts also came to teach Larentina. Egyptian princesses taught her ancient Egyptian fighting skills. Greek scientists, poets, and philosophers taught her as well.

"One night, almost seven months after Lycurgus left for agoge training, Larentina awoke to the feeling of warm wetness on her face. When she opened her eyes, she saw Lambda standing over her, licking her face. Larentina was ecstatic to have her wolf back. While she was petting Lambda, she could feel scabs from wounds that apparently had been suffered in fights with other wolves.

"Lambda nuzzled Larentina and then picked up a pup that was resting beside her and laid it on Larentina's chest. Lambda licked the pup and then licked Larentina, gesturing that Lambda was giving her pup to Larentina. Larentina, Lambda, and Lambda's puppy finally settled down and fell asleep after the excitement of being reunited.

"During the early morning hours, before the sun had risen, Larentina awoke as Lambda jumped off the bed and trotted out of the house. Larentina followed her until they reached the woods, and there Larentina discovered Lambda's wolf pack.

"Larentina realized that Lambda had fought for the position of alpha female in the pack of wolves. Larentina spotted the other puppies that were being protected by another female wolf in the pack. Larentina was welcomed with whines, howling, and licks of affection from the other wolves. Now, Larentina fully understood why Lambda had given her the pup. She knew it was time to release Lambda as her friend and protector, so that she could live with her own pack and be free again. She gratefully accepted Lambda's gift of her first female pup."

Chapter XII

"For five years, while Larentina's brother was training, she had continuously felt hungry. No matter how much she ate, she was never without pangs of hunger. She knew deep down in her heart that it was her brother who was actually starving or not eating well.

"She frequently awoke during the night from nightmares about her brother, but she never could quite put her finger on what was wrong. She never remembered the nightmare, just the feeling of it. She concluded that it was just her imagination playing tricks on her because she missed her brother so very much.

"The day of her twelfth birthday was a routine day for Larentina. There was no celebration of her birth, because that was not part of their culture. On this day, she went to sleep early, before the sun went down. The sun was still setting when she woke up screaming from pain. Each time she screamed, Lambda would howl and begin pacing around her mistress. Larentina's screams were so loud that Queen Alexis ran to her room, with King Alcaeus close on her heels. They both entered Larentina's room with still a hint of sunlight remaining in the day.

"Larentina jumped from her bed, screaming as each wave of pain assaulted her. She ran into her mother's arms. Queen Alexis hugged her and fearfully asked, 'What has happened, my child?'

"Larentina let go of her mother and screamed again as her body convulsed with pain. Queen Alexis looked at her hands, which had been on her daughter's back, and saw that they were covered in blood. She looked at her husband, her eyes full of unspoken questions, as she asked him, 'What magic is this? My husband, do something! Make it stop! This is killing her.'

"King Alcaeus grabbed his daughter by the upper arm and turned her around so that he could see her back. He ripped open the back of her nightshirt to see where the blood was coming from. In shock, the queen and king watched as a whip mark suddenly appeared on her back as Larentina screamed again. Blood oozed from the fresh wound and poured down her back.

"King Alcaeus suddenly realized what was going on. He was taken back to his own childhood days, when he had been whipped numerous times during his first few years of the agoge training. He knew his son, Lycurgus, was being lashed for something. It was a common practice used to make a boy stronger. The king knew he had no choice but to stop the beating. He realized Lycurgus was somehow transferring his pain to his sister. King Alcaeus knew that even though Larentina was half a god, she was still a little girl and could not handle the type of pain his son was being trained to manage.

"He said nothing to Queen Alexis, but quickly left the room and yelled at the first male helot he saw, 'You there! Go and fetch my horse—now!' Within a few minutes, the helot led King Alcaeus's stallion to the courtyard, where the king was waiting. He mounted and galloped as fast as the horse could go to the barracks on the outskirts of the city.

"Agoge training was not pleasant. The barracks were a single-story building crudely made of wood, with only eight small window openings per building. Thick wool was their only means to cover the windows during the bitter winter months. The roofs were made of hay and in need of constant repair. Basic maintenance on the buildings was time-consuming and never-ending.

"Each building had a dirt floor, and agoges slept on hay as their bedding. There were two large stone fireplaces on either end of the building for heat during the winter months. Small buildings were placed sporadically throughout the training grounds to be used for human waste, and the waste was burned daily. The smell was unbearable, but with time, the agoges grew used to it. Other buildings were used for the boys to wash themselves.

"When he reached the barracks, King Alcaeus jumped off his horse before it had stopped and ran to where his son was tied to a pole; he had passed out from being lashed. He grabbed the whip from the trainer's hand and hit him with his fist, knocking the man to the ground.

"King Alcaeus yelled at two soldiers standing nearby, 'Cut down my son, now! You are killing my daughter!'

"As the first soldier shook his head, trying to shake off the dizziness of the blow, he stood up with great effort and angrily asked, 'My king, what is the matter with you? You know this is part of his training. You know that you are not supposed to have any contact with Lycurgus. Have you no shame?'

"King Alcaeus bluntly responded, 'You are killing my daughter! Each lash you lay upon the back of my son is also received by my daughter. There must be another way to do this. Do you want the gods' wrath upon us for hurting Zeus's daughter? Come with me now. I'm taking my son with us, and I will show you my daughter so you can see with your own eyes! The Oracle was right; one cannot survive without the other.'

"He looked at the other two trainers, one of whom was an eirena, which is an older boy in charge of helping to train the younger boys. King Alcaeus then watched as a younger soldier untied Lycurgus from the pole. King Alcaeus saw the scorn in their eyes, but he picked up his unconscious son and carried him toward his horse. He ordered to all the others who witnessed this, 'Go and assemble the gerousia council and gather all the ephors. Tell them to come quickly to my home now! Go and summon King Karpos as well. Do it quickly!'

"The older soldier promptly mounted a nearby horse without delay as King Alcaeus put Lycurgus, who was beginning to awaken, onto his horse. The king mounted his horse, and they swiftly galloped to the king's home.

"As they entered the main room with a large fireplace, they saw the queen washing Larentina's back, trying to stop the bleeding. The older soldier's eyes grew wide as he turned Lycurgus around so he could see his back. He moved Lycurgus closer to his sister, who was by the hearth, so he could compare the wounds on the twins' backs. He could not hold back a gasp as he saw that Larentina had the exact same whip marks on her back as her brother. The soldier could not understand this and was bewildered; he tried to formulate his questions: 'In the name of the gods—what does this mean? How can this be? I was disciplining Lycurgus, not his sister, yet she has the same wounds. I would have never believed this if I had not seen it with my own eyes. No wonder he was able to handle more lashes than any other before passing out. He did not even let out one scream.'

"The king didn't say anything. He went to the eating room, poured some wine, and started drinking it. He had no idea what to do. He only knew that the Oracle had spoken the truth, and now he wholeheartedly believed it."

Chapter XIII

"Within a few hours, the entire gerousia council, all five ephors, and King Karpos were waiting for King Alcaeus to explain his dishonorable actions. The helots had already set a large fire in the middle of the courtyard, as was the custom whenever King Alcaeus had a large gathering at his home.

"King Alcaeus emerged through the main double doors and slowly walked down the six wide steps with the twins walking on either side of him. Everyone watched their descent; neither Larentina nor Lycurgus uttered a sound.

"King Alcaeus turned his children so that everyone could see their backs. He ripped Lycurgus's tunic down the middle of his back from neck to waist, did the same with Larentina's tunic, and bellowed so everyone could hear him, 'As you can see, when Lycurgus is hurt, so is Larentina. With my own eyes, I saw the lash marks appear on Larentina as her brother was being whipped during agoge training. See for yourselves, the marks are identical. Did we not make a vow to Zeus that we would watch over and protect his daughter? What should we do so my son, Lycurgus, can finish his training? What is the solution?'

"The courtyard filled with noise as each gerousia member examined both children thoroughly and exclaimed to the others what he saw. They were all in awe and shock at the sight.

"After much talk and argument, Bion declared, 'There is only one solution. Princess Larentina must go through the agoge training with her brother, Lycurgus. This way if one is lashed, then technically, they both will be lashed, and Larentina can learn to deal with the pain as well as Lycurgus.

"'If her destiny is to protect us, it does make logical sense for us to make her even stronger and learn the art of warfare for our protection against our enemies. She will only make us stronger as a state because of the powers that she has inherited from her father, Zeus.'

"Much argument and debate ensued. Eventually, Hygieinos voiced his opinion. 'There has never been such a thing. She is a girl child, and this is not permitted. It is the law.'

"Hesiodos responded, 'Larentina is also Zeus's daughter, making her a half god, and there is nothing in the laws stating that a goddess cannot go through the training.'

"Most of the council agreed with Bion's statement, allowing Larentina to participate in agoge training with her brother. They discussed amongst themselves and then loudly reached a decision, 'We agree.' Nevertheless, opposition remained, and the argument continued.

"Bion bellowed, 'The daughter of Zeus must be allowed to go through the training for the future of Sparta. The laws do not deny her of this right and privilege, because she is not just a girl, but she is also a goddess. There are no laws forbidding this.'

"After debating for the majority of the night, the gerousia council members finally agreed that Larentina must go through the training with her brother.

"When the agreement was reached, King Karpos spoke. 'How are we going to train her and yet keep her separated from the boys? She has already missed five years of important training. Alcaeus, are you sure? After all, she is still half mortal. How will she be able to survive?'

"King Alcaeus said with total conviction, 'At first I did not believe she was strong enough, but now I have changed my mind; she will keep up. Do not forget, Karpos, she is also half god. She will be joined with Lycurgus's pack and her wolf shall accompany her to protect her. For bathing and the basic rituals of women, she will be given privacy or separated from the rest of the pack.' Everyone agreed again after much argument and discussions.

"Queen Alexis timidly spoke, 'I do not mean to offend by speaking, but what preparations will be made when she turns into a woman?'

"King Alcaeus answered his wife with a twinge of bashfulness and embarrassment regarding the needs of a woman. 'Well, ah …' After a few moments, the king regained his wits and commanded, 'Then during that one week of each month, she will be separated from her brother's pack during the nights, and you may assign a female helot to provide for her needs during that time, but she will stay a virgin until she becomes of age.'

"Queen Alexis kneeled as she took her husband's hand, kissed it, and humbly murmured as she looked up at him, 'May the gods bless you, my husband, my king.'

"Bion was totally disgusted by the entire conversation. Bion blamed Agape and Alexis for making his kings look weak. This would work out perfectly, he thought, because he believed that Larentina would not survive agoge. In fact, his thoughts were, *She will die within a week's time after entering the training camps.* He was pleased how this seemed to be working out for him. There was still hope that the two kings would become strong again once these pathetic women were out of their lives, but he did not show it as he simply declared, 'Good. Everything has been arranged. We will allow your children to stay with you until they have healed so that we can make arrangements for the girl child to enter agoge and be somewhat separated from her pack. Then, they both must return to agoge training. One last request, my kings: Larentina will not be allowed to use her divine gifts during training.'

"Queen Alexis knew that if Larentina was unable to protect herself with her divine powers, she surely would fail, and Alexis would have to face her sister. Alexis owed her very life to Agape for all that Agape had sacrificed. She did not care if she needed to humble herself further to protect her sister's children.

"Queen Alexis, who was still kneeling in front of her husband, pleaded and sobbed, 'Please, my husband, her powers must be enhanced for the good of Sparta. She should at least be allowed to use her powers to protect herself and her pack. Please, my husband, my king, you cannot command her not to use her powers, because they are a part of her.'

"Bion begun to protest but was stopped when King Karpos raised his hand, gesturing for silence.

"All eyes were on King Alcaeus as he lovingly gazed at his wife. He looked over to King Karpos, who nodded his head once, agreeing to whatever decision King Alcaeus would make.

"King Alcaeus deeply sighed. 'Your request is partly denied. Larentina will be allowed to use her divine powers to protect herself and her pack, but when it involves cases of simple training, it would not be fair for her to use her powers against her fellow agoges. Therefore, she will not be allowed to use her powers against them. These rules will have an exception, however. She can use her powers for any reason if her eirena commands her to do so against anyone or for any purpose that he deems necessary. For this eirena to have such power over my daughter, he will also carry the burden of teaching her to control and use these divine gifts for the good of her pack as well as for Sparta; given that Zeus himself will not teach her how to control these powers. When she is older, she will be able to follow orders without hesitation from her chain of command.'

"King Alcaeus winked at King Karpos, who acknowledged King Alcaeus and nodded his head in agreement.

"Jason, an ephor from the house of Agiad, asked, 'Should she serve the state until she is thirty as well? Bion, tell everyone what the Oracle told you.'

"Bion grew annoyed; he believed that she would not live that long, with or without divine powers. He provided a terse reply to appease all present: 'No, for she is a goddess and should only be trained until she is twenty and serve longer only if she desires to.

"'I did not want it known I also sought the advice of the Oracle,' Bion continued, 'but since you mentioned it, I will relay what she told me. It is true that our princess is a goddess and daughter of duty for her god, country, and family, as three equal parts, because the Oracle has stated this. Everything she has foretold is becoming a reality regarding Princess Larentina. I'm sure many of you have sought her wisdom and advice as well.'

"Many of the gerousia members spoke up and admitted the Oracle had told them the same prophesies, and arguments arose once again regarding the interpretations of the meanings from the statements from the Oracle of Delphi. Finally, everyone once again agreed Larentina would go through the remainder of the agoge training. They continued debating many other issues regarding Larentina until finally everyone wearily left and went back to their homes.

"King Karpos lingered after everyone had left. He patted King Alcaeus on the back and stated his pleasure. 'Thank you, Alcaeus. Now my son will have a fighting chance to win your daughter's affections.'

"King Alcaeus responded, with a smirk, 'I thought it fitting to give you a chance to prove that your son truly is a strong heir to your throne.' Both kings arrogantly guffawed because they knew they had outsmarted the gerousia once again. Lycurgus was in the same pack as King Karpos's son, Androcles, who was the eirena; Karpos's son would watch over Larentina.

"Once King Karpos left, the courtyard was completely empty. King Alcaeus walked up to the steps of his home, where his children were sitting on the top step. He let out a sigh as Queen Alexis walked toward them.

Both Lycurgus and Larentina stood up and wrapped their arms around their father's waist, as he reached his hands out toward them. Queen Alexis joined in the family hug, and King Alcaeus irritably remarked to his children, 'Larentina, you will be the death of me yet, as well as your brother. Lycurgus, never give your pain to your sister again. What you did today was dishonorable. You must learn to deal with pain and stop expecting your sister to handle it for you. You cheated this day, and you know it. How long has this been going on between you? No, it is better that I do not know. I am tempted to lash both of you for your dishonorable actions this day.'

"King Alcaeus looked down at his daughter, and she looked up at him as he commanded her, 'Larentina, give your brother's strength back to him so that he can deal with his own pain. I know what you did when you were in your mother's womb, because the Oracle told me. You do not need to be jealous of your brother any longer. As you can see, you will be treated as an equal from this day forward, so just give his strength back now because you will not survive without him.'

"Larentina hesitated as King Alcaeus looked down upon her young face, which reminded him so much of Alexis's face. His voice changed to a softer tone as he knelt down and gave his daughter a fatherly hug. Simultaneously, he reached for his son, giving him a hug as well, whispering to both of them, 'Fear not, little ones, for Larentina is already changing Spartan customs.' He stood back up and watched Larentina.

"Larentina touched her brother's arm and timidly confessed to her father, 'It is done. I have returned his strength.' Larentina did not understand why her father believed such silly things, but she made the gesture to show she loved him.

"King Alcaeus simply replied to his daughter, 'Good. Now off to bed.

"'Lycurgus,' he continued, 'you know damn well you are lucky this night, and the gods have favored you because the gerousia council broke the rules to allow you to recover here because of your sister. Remember, son, work together because the two of you are truly one.' Lycurgus looked at his father, nodded his head in agreement, and ran up the steps to catch his sister.

"King Alcaeus watched his children disappear into his home and turned to his wife, Queen Alexis. He looked deep into her beautiful green eyes and lovingly murmured, 'When you gave birth to those two, you made sure you made up for the others before them. I guess you did that to prove to me you are the strongest Spartan mother of all.' He chuckled ever so lightly and passionately kissed his wife. With a soft smile on his face, he commented, 'May the gods have mercy on my soul, for I am still madly in love with you.' He kissed her again.

"Tears were streaming down her cheeks as Queen Alexis kissed her husband. She knew the truth, and she would never tell him otherwise. Everything that Agape and Alexis had planned that night, everything they both had hoped for, more freedoms for all Spartan women, was just beginning. She knew that Larentina was truly changing the world, as Queen Alexis had hoped. The taste of a little bit of freedom was worth more than the love she had for her husband. It felt so good to speak freely among the men and not to be chastised for it."

Chapter XIV

"After the rest of the household was asleep, Larentina snuck into her brother's room and quietly crawled under the covers with him. As she turned to face him, before she could utter a word, Lycurgus whispered to her, 'Sister, I'm sorry for causing you such pain. I do not even know how I did it, or if I will be able to stop it next time. I'm also afraid you will not be able to survive agoge training, because I'm barely making it. You may be half goddess, but you are still a girl child, and I do not want to lose you.'

"As they stared into each other's identical, beautiful, light-brown eyes, Larentina whispered, 'The gods will protect me, and they will protect you as well. We will survive because I will not let anything else happen to us, I swear it, Brother. I love you as if you were me.'

"Lycurgus whispered back, 'I too love you as if you were me. Did you give me my strength back or did you just play a trick with our father?'

"Larentina whispered, 'What do you mean? Of course, I gave it back because he ordered me to do so. Why would I play such trickery on you or our father? You are my brother and you are my blood, as I'm your blood.'

"Lycurgus kissed his sister on her cheek and whispered to her, 'I'm sorry, but I had to be sure. I believe you, but I still do not think the gods are going to protect you, because I think that burden will fall upon me. Father will kill me if I allow you to die in just agoge. You must survive if I'm to survive.'

"Larentina thoughtfully responded, 'That may be true, Brother, but instead, let us each depend upon ourselves and protect one another. Turn over, Brother, and let me heal your wounds.'

"Lycurgus excitedly asked, 'Larentina? You can do that?' He turned his back to her.

"Larentina whispered her answer with uncertainty. 'Well, I've healed Lambda once or twice, but it seems to work better with my herbs and potions. I still would like to try.' She touched her brother's back, but it took her at least twelve attempts and scabs remained that would turn to large scars on Lycurgus's back.

"With excitement, Lycurgus murmured, 'You did it, Larentina! It does not hurt any longer.' He turned to face her, and in the dim moonlight, he saw that her eyes were still full of lightning bolts, and they were wide as if she had done something bad. Lycurgus grew irritated and asked, 'What did you do, Larentina?'

"Larentina was completely filled with guilt as her voice quivered, 'Well … Oh … Well …' She then grew indignant, and it showed in her voice: 'Lycurgus, I told you I am not very good at this. In fact, you are my first victim.'

"Lycurgus became angry and asked, 'What did you do, Larentina?' as he tried to feel his back.

"Larentina became upset and sobbed, 'I did the best I could.' With those words, she rolled over. As she was beginning to drift off to sleep, she felt her brother put his arm around her waist.

"He softly whispered in her ear, 'I know you did. I'm grateful you have these strange gifts. I love you, Sister, now go to sleep.'

"She snuggled closer to him and succumbed to slumber.

"As Lycurgus allowed sleep to overtake him, he thought of how happy he was to be sleeping in a warm bed. He finally felt safe and secure now that his sister was sleeping right next to him. Even though she was just a girl and he believed she gave him his strength back, he partly felt that when he returned to the barracks, everything would be much easier because he had his strong and powerful sister with him. Even though she hadn't mastered healing powers, her gifts were good enough for him. She was still an advantage to him and his agoge pack."

Chapter XV

"The remainder of their time at home flew by, and before Larentina and Lycurgus knew it, their wounds had healed, and they were back in the living underworld of Hades; agoge training. Every day they ran for miles, trained in wrestling and boxing, and performed rigorous exercises.

"They had built a wall in one of the barracks and made a room for Larentina on one side with a fireplace. They designated one small outhouse for her exclusive use. She would be given fifteen minutes in a bathing building each day.

"They practiced their fighting skills with thick wooden sticks and wooden swords. Larentina suffered many bruises and even fractured a rib, but she healed very quickly. Her years of training in gymnastics and the martial arts helped her stand her ground against the older boys, who were stronger than she was. She never went down without making the other agoge fight hard for it.

"She felt blessed because she already had some training in martial arts and many other types of fighting skills. She was aware that she still had much to learn, but it was becoming increasingly easier to best her male counterparts. Even at this young age, Larentina knew in her heart the only way to protect herself was with cleverness and deceit. She knew the only way she could win a fight against a man was to use her weaknesses as her weapon. She let her enemy underestimate her—simply because she was a girl—and it worked to her advantage.

"She promised herself that if she survived this, she would learn every style of fighting known to man. She even won skirmishes against Lycurgus on many occasions, because she had learned moves that were very different from what Lycurgus was taught. He could not help but underestimate her, just as everyone else did.

"Larentina had to adjust to sleeping outside on the ground. She was informed that she would have to do this for a year. They were not allowed to wear shoes and were only given two tunics, one for the winter and another for the summer. They were not even given knives or any type of weapons. They had to make their own beds out of straw and weeds that they scavenged from the riverbanks.

"Most nights, they went to bed hungry. The only thing they were fed was a thin, foul-smelling broth, and they were given just enough to prevent starvation. They were encouraged to steal or do whatever was necessary to eat, but they could not be caught.

"After many months of agoge training, Larentina had enough of being hungry. Since she had no weapons, she decided to steal food. She knew her mother's sister lived a few miles from the military barracks, and so she decided to obtain food, one way or another. She knew Lambda was also hungry. It made her sad to see the protruding ribs and hips of her poor wolf. Larentina was honestly surprised that Lambda never left her to go back to the wild.

"Larentina had never been to her Aunt Agape's home. She found an open window and quietly snuck into the kitchen. She quickly went to work, gathering cheese, bread, and even a flask of wine. When she looked up, she was shocked to see Agape standing by the window in the full moonlight.

"Agape stood in front of the open window with her arms folded across her chest, tapping her bare foot on the floor. She angrily whispered, 'Larentina, what do you think you are doing? You are not to be caught. I would think by now you would have mastered this simple skill. You must now try and kill me because I have discovered you.'

"Larentina dropped all the food that she was carrying and retorted, 'Why would I kill someone in order to steal food? That is totally beneath me. I may be trained to do this, but I do not believe in doing it. You are my blood. Why would I kill you?'

"Agape answered her daughter, 'Because you are not supposed to steal from Spartan citizens to begin with, young lady. You may steal from anyone else but a Spartan citizen.'

"Larentina sharply replied, 'But you are no longer a Spartan citizen. That is why I'm stealing from you.' Larentina was never told the story of her father, King Alcaeus, adopting Erasmus.

"Agape looked down at the floor, saddened, and before she realized what she was saying, the truth slipped out, as she whispered angrily, 'If that is what you believe than neither are you; you are a fraud. You will need to be told the story of King Alcaeus adopting my husband.'

"Larentina became angry and could barely control her volume as she answered, 'By all the gods, how can you accuse me of such a thing? I'm the daughter of our queen, Alexis. I should kill you for that statement.'

"Agape walked closer to her daughter and in a deadly murmur proclaimed, 'You are not a woman, not yet. You can't even steal for food to survive. You pretend to be a man, but you are still just a girl. You talk a big game, but you are not what you say you are. The only thing that is true about you is that you are the daughter of Zeus. Now take the food you came for, and from now on, at this very window through which you entered my home, I will leave food for you to steal every night. It is your choice to take it or leave it. I do not care. All I care about is that you survive this because you are the first and the only symbol the Spartan women have to prove we are much more than second class citizens and slaves to men.'

"Agape walked into the kitchen, leaving Larentina standing by the window, stunned. Within minutes, Agape returned with meat left over from their dinner. She handed it to Larentina as she solemnly commented, 'I'm sure your wolf is starving; feed her and yourself. Cheese and bread is good to fill you, but meat makes you stronger. Now go, before I completely lose my temper and hurt you for just being naive.'

"Larentina knew that her aunt was right in what she implied. There was no way she could take down a strong, full-grown Spartan woman like Agape. Larentina had fought mostly boys who were her own age and not much bigger or stronger than she was, and she had lost more fights than she had won. Agape was correct in stating that men underestimated the Spartan women, because if a Spartan woman wanted to hurt you, she very easily could, and Larentina knew this all too well.

"Larentina could not understand why her aunt had implied she was a fraud. She wondered why Agape would say something like that and then turn around to help her. Larentina was very confused over the entire incident, but she quickly forgot about it as she began to devour the bread, cheese, and meat that her aunt had given her. As she was eating, she watched Lambda quickly devour the large portion of meat Larentina had given her. After Larentina and Lambda ate their fill, Larentina put the remaining food onto the branch of a tree near their camp.

"She silently crept toward her brother, who was sleeping in the straw and dirt close to the fire. She gently shook him until his eyes opened. She then lay beside him and whispered in his ear, 'Brother, I've stolen food for us. Come and I will give some to you.'

"Lycurgus immediately rose from his sleep and excitedly asked, 'Where is it? Show me.'

"Larentina took him to where she had hidden it. Lycurgus gulped down every last bite of it and then asked, 'Oh, I'm sorry. I hope you ate some before me?'

"Larentina girlishly giggled at her brother as she teased him, 'Of course; I knew better than to tell you before I ate.'

"They both laughed at their gluttony.

"For several months, Larentina snuck out of the camp almost every night to take the food that was provided by her aunt. As promised, every night there were large amounts of food waiting on the windowsill. In addition to the bread, cheese, and wine, her aunt would frequently leave legs of lamb or pots of thick stews filled with meat and vegetables. No one noticed Larentina return the pot from where it came. There was so much food that the twins had enough to share with the twelve other boys in their pack. Even Lambda started gaining weight again. Not even Androcles, the young eirena who supervised her pack, questioned Larentina as to how she came upon such a rich, plentiful feast every night.

"Androcles was a few years older than the twins. He had been selected to supervise and protect her pack because he was the strongest and bravest of his own class. Larentina thought he was a very handsome lad. Even though he was tough on her and her brother, she genuinely liked him.

"It had been an older soldier who lashed her brother that fateful night, not Androcles. Although she knew the soldier had just been doing his job, she despised him and looked at him with hate-filled eyes whenever she encountered him."

Agape, a Spartan mother Defending her Child

Chapter XVI

"Bion had been certain that Larentina would not survive agoge. She should have perished in the first week. Because she had survived agoge this far, he decided to take matters into his own hands. He was a very impatient man regarding Larentina. He met with a soldier who had vowed his allegiance to Bion and instructed him to make sure Larentina did not survive much longer. Bion also instructed the soldier to keep these plans secret. The soldier vowed that he would take care of the problem. Even though he did not understand why a mere girl was such a threat to Bion, he followed his orders without hesitation.

"Larentina had established a routine of sneaking out of camp at the same time every night to retrieve the food from her aunt. As she ran with Lambda by her side, she was stopped by six older agoges from another pack, who were about nineteen years old.

"Larentina stopped as the older agoges surrounded her and Lambda. She did not realize that they meant her great harm. She irritably yelled at them, 'Get out of my way!' Lambda began to growl and snarl at the older agoges, trying to protect her mistress.

"The older agoges surrounded Larentina and wickedly antagonized her; one of the agoges said sarcastically, 'Well, well; what do we have here? Not one, but two little wild bitches: the almighty She Wolf, a freak of nature, trying to be the alpha male. I do not think so. You are no goddess, nor are you agoge. You are nothing but a pretty little beast, and it's time to put you in your place. You do not even possess any of the Olympian deities' powers, for none of us have seen it. Kneel before me, like a good little dog obeying its master.'

"Larentina was not only angry but also scared for her life as well. She could not even use her powers against these pompous asses because her father had commanded it; they all were threatening her as they laughed at her.

"Before Larentina knew it, one of the older agoges had pushed her, and she frantically pushed back. The moment he raised his fist to hit Larentina, Lambda swiftly jumped and bit down hard on the older agoge's arm with her razor-sharp teeth. The older agoge wailed in pain as he wrestled with Lambda and threw her to the ground. All the other agoges began to push Larentina and call her vile, nasty names.

"Larentina was scared to death. She didn't know what to do but pray to the gods to help her find a way out of this.

"Suddenly, they all began hitting her, grabbing her, and blasting at her. Larentina fought hard with her bare fists and kicked with her bare feet while Lambda attacked as many of the agoges as she was able to, but the two were no match against six older agoges. They beat Lambda severely and stabbed her with a sharp-edged branch from a tree.

"As Larentina fell to the ground, she heard her poor Lambda howling with immense pain. The tears slowly fell from the corners of Larentina's eyes, but her spirit was not broken—not yet. The older agoges began tearing her tunic while kicking her and piercing her flesh with sharp sticks. She screamed out for help as the pain swiftly rippled through her body.

"Fearing for her life and panicking, Larentina suddenly screamed so loudly that it awakened many in the camp a mile or so away. She continued to scream with such intensity that it hurt the ears of the older agoges who were beating her.

"Larentina still clung to her spirit, as she continued hitting, kicking, and biting anything she could make contact with. She also continued screaming, which was enhanced by her telepathic abilities, but she did not know or understand this.

"Lycurgus and the rest of her pack began running with any type of weapon within reach toward the sound of her screams. Everyone who was touched by Larentina's mind considered it an honor because she had chosen them.

"Agape awakened with tears streaming down her cheeks, and fear and hatred in her heart, because her daughter had unknowingly touched her mind with her piercing screams. Agape did not even dress herself; she instinctively grabbed her husband's bow and arrows as she quietly snuck out of her home, running toward Larentina. The adrenaline coursed through her veins as the natural instinct of a mother protecting her daughter took over her entire being. She knew she could not let anyone see her because of the ramifications that would follow regarding her sister, Queen Alexis, and her children if anyone suspected she was Larentina's mother. She ran faster and faster to get to Larentina to protect her before her child suffered any further; if necessary, she would kill anyone who got in her way. She would sacrifice her own life to protect her daughter.

"King Alcaeus and Queen Alexis were awakened with the same feelings because Larentina had unknowingly touched their minds as well. They too headed toward her.

"Lambda's pack began howling loudly as they ran toward the wolf's cries of pain and Larentina's deafening screams.

"Zeus himself heard her as well. Within seconds, he was standing at the edge of the small clearing. He had to know what type of being possessed such power. He was concealed in the dark shadows of the forest's foliage with his sword in hand. Right before he revealed himself, he saw a young boy running from another edge of the clearing, and he stopped to watch this mere boy. Zeus was puzzled; it appeared to him that the boy was about to sacrifice his own life for this little girl who possessed godly powers.

"Androcles came out of the woods into the small clearing, yelling at the top of his lungs because he sensed this pack was up to no good, and he ran to protect Larentina. He threw rocks at the older agoges as he ran to Larentina, trying to save her from the wicked beasts. Androcles had taken this mission because if Larentina succeeded in completing agoge, all the glory would be his and his alone. No other eirena had turned a girl into a warrior—what an accomplishment this would be for Androcles.

"Androcles thought, *I'll be damned if this cute little girl is going to die here and now. What a waste of life and a dishonorable death.*

"The six older agoges turned their attention from Larentina and began fighting Androcles. They fought Androcles in unison within a foot of where Larentina lay. As she painfully sat up, she saw Androcles heroically fighting the nasty beasts as they slowly beat him to the ground. Tears streamed down her face because this boy was willing to sacrifice himself for her.

"Larentina painfully made it to her feet, as she frantically yelled to Androcles, 'Androcles, give me permission to use my magic!'

"Androcles was barely audible, but she heard him give her permission.

"Hatred and contempt coursed through Larentina's entire body as her irises turned dark maroon and the lightning bolts illuminated them. She would never be able to control her telekinesis completely, because she truly did not know the depth of her skills. The winds started whining through the edges of the small clearing and grew stronger and faster all around them. Haphazard lightning bolts cascaded around them. Larentina's long hair blew in the wind. Her hands were opened wide and slightly stretched out from her sides. Objects began lifting into the wind and swirling all around the older agoges.

"Rocks and rotten logs, as well as many other objects that were swirling in the winds, started hitting the older agoges with striking force. Wolves came running out of the forest's edge and began attacking the older agoges.

"Androcles was amazed by Larentina's powers, and he now believed that she truly was the daughter of Zeus. To him, there was no other explanation. He was more determined to be the one to transform her into a Spartan warrior.

"The older agoges were fearful, but they held their ground. Several of them dropped to their knees before Larentina, but it was too late. Once Larentina started, it was hard for her to stop; this was the first time she had used these types of power.

"Zeus was totally amazed because he could see this girl child possessing the qualities of the Olympian deities. One of the gods must have fathered her, but who? Zeus could see she had his power over lightning, and he could actually see small lightning bolts charging through her eyes, mimicking those in the air around her. She definitely controlled the winds, because he had just witnessed this ability. She also seemed to have some kind of power over beasts. Where did this Spartan child obtain such powers? Zeus thought she might well indeed be his own child, because he had heard the rumors from other Olympian deities that he had fathered a Spartan daughter.

"Zeus considered himself a good father. If a woman claimed her child to be his, most of the time, he had no problem with it. He only would insert himself into the child's life if they demonstrated the gifts of the Olympian deities, or if he just could not resist interfering in their destiny. He was very well impressed; no other being could reach his ears the way Larentina had done. He admitted to himself that he was bewildered. He could not recall any other child of his who had been conceived by a mortal and yet displayed these types of powers.

"Zeus's attention was then captured by a beautiful woman standing at the edge of the forest, but she did not see him because he was invisible to all mortal eyes at that moment. He watched her as she aimed carefully with her bow and arrow, with tears trickling down her cheeks. The arrow struck her victim, and the young man fell to the ground. The young woman did not fear the chaos and power the girl child was demonstrating. The young woman was not even surprised or shocked by it. Zeus knew this woman had seen this girl child use these Olympian powers before.

"As he looked at her, he realized that she had to be the girl child's mother, because she acted like a mother protecting her child, but what Zeus did not understand was why she stayed hidden. This was just one quality Zeus loved about women. This intriguing and courageous woman had caught his eye again, or so he thought. He was still confused how he could have forgotten her so easily.

"After Agape was sure no one saw her, she watched her daughter looking around to see where the arrow had come from. She knew her daughter was safe now, and she returned to the darkness of the woods undetected (or so she thought). As Agape ran to her home, immense sorrow and regret overcame her because of the promise she had made to her sister, Queen Alexis. Somehow through her thoughts she convinced herself that Larentina truly was the daughter of Zeus and she could finally put part of the nightmare of the past behind her. Agape truly regretted not being able to display her motherly love for her daughter, but she had made a vow to her sister, and she was going to try and honor it.

"Larentina commanded the wolves to stop their attack, and they obeyed, running back into the woods.

"The young agoges now completely feared Larentina. One older agoge removed the arrow from the shoulder of the wounded agoge and helped him to escape from Larentina's wrath. But Larentina was still filled with rage, and the winds lifted the agoge who first pushed her into the air, as an unknown force started pulling his arms and legs from his body.

"Androcles calmly commanded, 'Larentina, stop. This is not necessary. They will be punished.' Larentina obeyed Androcles's orders, and everything around them became calm once more. The older agoge immediately fell to the ground and moaned in pain from the impact. Two of his comrades helped him up from the ground, and they all quickly disappeared into the forest.

"Androcles slowly stood up and put his hand on his side, hoping that doing so would alleviate his pain. He looked into Larentina's eyes as he softly pushed back a strand of her hair. He slowly smiled as he gave her new permanent orders: 'Larentina, I give you permission to use your gifts to protect yourself against anyone or anything from this day forward. I do not wish this to happen again.' He nervously chuckled as he remarked,

'Because I do not know if I will be able to protect you next time and survive it.'

"Androcles was boyishly cute with thick, curly, sandy blond hair. He kept it cut short because of the thick curls. He had startlingly blue eyes, and his skin had a golden suntan. He had a boyish nose with freckles, and he seemed to be much taller and stronger than most of the boys his age.

"Larentina just smiled sadly back at him. She would never forget what Androcles did for her this night. She did not understand it because she was so young, but she loved him because he was willing to sacrifice his life for her, and she now trusted him immensely. Trust was something Larentina did not give freely. Larentina then remembered her wolf and fearfully called out, 'Lambda!'

"Larentina hobbled over to her beloved Lambda and cried as she softly rubbed her wolf. Tears trickled down her cheeks as she sobbed, 'Lambda, you know I'm not very good at this, but I'm going to try to heal you.' Larentina tried three times, but she was unable to heal the deep wound well enough for Lambda to survive.

"Androcles was on his knees as well and petted the wolf to help console her somehow, but his actions were mainly for Larentina's comfort. He said nothing as he watched Larentina try to heal the wolf.

"Finally, Androcles softly took Larentina's hands in his as he tried to comfort her. 'Larentina, there is nothing more you can do. You are still learning how to use your powers. Your wolf will be reborn to you. I have heard the stories of your wolf.'

"Zeus could not stand to see this little girl lose her wolf after what she had just been through. He watched with empathy in his heart as Larentina frantically tried to heal her beloved Lambda. He was proud that she displayed other Olympian powers, but she was too young and did not know how to use her gifts this way. With a snap of his fingers and a pleasant smile upon his lips, he healed Lambda and then disappeared.

"Lambda immediately rose up, completely healed, and excitedly began to lick her mistress. Larentina jubilantly hugged her Lambda and cried, 'In all the heavens, Lambda! Did you heal yourself? For I did not!'

"Androcles smiled with delight that Larentina quickly recovered from the assault; he boyishly smiled and said, 'Well, my young goddess, do you think you can walk back to camp with me, now that your wolf is healed? I do not want us to be caught. You know the rules.' Larentina shyly nodded yes.

"They helped each other up. Lambda's tail wagged furiously with joy. All three were truly relieved that they had survived.

"As they were walking through the forest, Androcles painfully reached down for a large tree branch he had seen in the bright moonlight. He pulled the smaller branches from it.

"'What are you doing, Androcles?' Larentina asked.

"Androcles smiled at his companion. 'Before we continue home, I would like to teach you a few maneuvers to protect yourself from more than one bully at a time. You will be able to turn anything near you into a weapon. I want you to be able to protect yourself as a mortal would as well.'

"Although they were both in pain, Androcles taught her how to push most of the pain to the back of her mind. He explained, 'Always do your best not to show your enemy you have been wounded, because they will attack you in the same area to destroy you.'

"Androcles stood behind Larentina and showed her how to hold the large branch in her hands. He showed her how to use it as a multipurpose weapon. Lambda playfully pulled the branch from Larentina's firm grip. After Lambda had grabbed the branch several times, with practice, it soon became impossible for Lambda, or Androcles, to remove the branch from her strengthening grip.

"In fact, Androcles found himself forcefully knocked from his feet repeatedly. As he lay on the forest ground, he refused to show his pain, laughing as he teased Larentina, 'Well done, my princess, you learn the mortal ways quickly.'

"As Larentina tried to help him to his feet, Androcles pulled her down. They lightly wrestled for a few moments; he stopped while he was on top of her, gazing into her eyes. He said plainly, 'Larentina, let me see your eyes light up once more.'

"Larentina bashfully obliged him and said nothing. Androcles was in awe as he softly expressed his feelings, 'Your eyes amaze me. You possess your father's lightning bolts in your eyes. You are going to be a strong and beautiful woman when you grow up. You truly are the daughter of Zeus, but you must learn men's ways first, and I would consider it a great honor to be the one that helps to transform you into the powerful warrior I know you will become.' He awkwardly bent down closer to her face and tried to kiss her lips.

"Larentina abruptly pushed him off as irritation took over. 'If my father knew of this, he would kill you for touching me.'

"Androcles became embarrassed, for he did not understand his own feelings. He stumbled for words. 'Forgive me, Princess, but I'm just a mortal boy.'

"Larentina became indignant. 'You are forgiven, but do not try this with me again, or you will find my eyes can be just as destructive.'

"Androcles had a boyish smile upon his lips once again. 'I do indeed know of what you speak.'

"As they slowly and painfully walked through the forest again, they were met by Lycurgus, who had just seen Androcles lying on top of his sister on the ground. He was overcome with rage.

"Lycurgus was out of breath, because he had been running; he knocked Androcles to the ground and jumped on him, unmercifully hitting him with rage. He yelled, 'How dare you attack my sister! Have you no shame, you cretin?'

"Larentina angrily commanded Lycurgus, 'Stop, Brother! Stop!' She aggressively pulled Lycurgus off Androcles and declared, 'It was Androcles who saved me! He was my champion! It was not you, Brother, not this time. If it was not for Androcles, I surely would have perished!'

"Lycurgus stood up and offered his hand to Androcles. Androcles accepted the help. Lycurgus, now knowing the truth, was totally embarrassed for assuming Androcles had been Larentina's assailant. 'I'm sorry, my eirena, for suspecting it was you.'

"Androcles, who at first was totally confused, now became grateful and extended his hand. 'I would have drawn the same conclusions if it had been my sister.'

"The agoges and soldiers whose minds were touched by Larentina were just seconds behind Lycurgus and witnessed this.

"The young commander asserted his authority and ordered, 'All right, all right. Break it up, and return to camp. The excitement of this night is over. Androcles, I want you to report to me at first light, and I want a detailed account of what happened.'

"Androcles answered nervously, 'Yes, Commander.'

"There was not one sound as everyone quickly went back to camp in silence.

"When Larentina hobbled back into camp, Queen Alexis and King Alcaeus had just arrived. Queen Alexis ran to her daughter and hugged her tightly. She thoroughly examined her daughter as King Alcaeus observed with fatherly concern. The queen was relieved that her daughter was all right, except for some cuts and bruises. As concern slowly left King

Alcaeus's face, anger replaced it, and he barked commands at Androcles, Lycurgus, and the commander to tell him what had happened. All three gave a short version as King Alcaeus listened patiently. If the king was emotional, he did not show it.

"All six of the agoges who had attacked Larentina were punished severely the following morning. Larentina felt justified when she watched each one of them being lashed three times. She felt confident after everyone saw this that no agoge would dare lay another hand upon her, for fear of the consequences.

"Within just a couple of short months, the entire incident was forgotten, and everything became a routine once again."

Chapter XVII

"One of the eirenas from another pack was becoming increasingly jealous of Androcles's pack, which seemed to be blessed by the gods for having Larentina among them. When this eirena was approached by a high-ranking officer, offering him a deal to carry out a secret mission to follow Larentina and report back to him, the eirena did not hesitate, accepting it for his own agenda. Even though rumors throughout the agoge community implied that she was stealing food, everyone believed she used magic to produce such great feasts, because of the stories told by the agoges who had assaulted her.

"This particular eirena believed that her presence, not the fact that she was stealing food, kept Androcles's pack healthier and stronger than all the others. He believed that Larentina's presence made the gods favor Androcles and made Androcles's job much easier than his. It seemed to this eirena that their training sessions were less demanding than they were for his pack.

"He could not understand how she was obtaining such great amounts of food because he knew how hard it was to steal just a loaf of bread. She was coming back with feasts fit for a king. He decided to follow her to see if magic really did play a part in the matter or if she was cheating somehow. Even if she was using magic, that would be considered cheating as well.

"Because she had been undetected for so long, Larentina had become careless again when she went for food. Instead of cautiously sneaking to her aunt's house, she would run as fast as the wind, with Lambda by her side. She even used the same route to her aunt's house each night, because she was confident that no one would dare follow her because they would be lashed. On this particular night, as girl and wolf ran toward Agape's house, Lambda stopped and started growling at something. Larentina did not give it a second thought; even when she heard a branch break, as if someone was running behind her, she did not slow down or turn around.

If she would have, the full moon would have most likely revealed a figure in the distance. Instead, she went right to her aunt's window and retrieved the food that was waiting for her. By the time she realized she had been followed, it was too late.

"Agape appeared from the dark shadows of her home and sternly whispered, 'Larentina, you are becoming careless again. I thought you would have learned your lesson because of what happened to you just a few short months ago. Someone is behind you at the edge of the woods.' She passed a dagger to her daughter. 'Here, my child. You must kill him, so that we will not be discovered.' Larentina reached for the food, but Agape stopped her. 'There is no time for this. Go. Kill him before he discovers what is happening.' Larentina simply nodded her head in agreement, as she obeyed her aunt's command.

"Larentina pretended that she did not know there was someone behind her, and she casually patted Lambda on the head. She then commanded to her wolf, 'Attack!' Larentina and Lambda ran as fast as they could across the small field that separated the woods from her aunt's house.

"Before the eirena realized what was happening, he saw the small shadow of Larentina coming toward him at full speed. He did not even suspect that Larentina knew of his presence. He just assumed she was running back to camp with her bounty, and she was not even being subtle about it.

"He wickedly snickered, having discovered Larentina's secret—a perioikoi was helping her. *There is no magic*, he thought. *She is not even stealing.* He could not wait to report her as he watched her run across the field toward him. She would be lashed severely, maybe even expelled from training. He snickered aloud again and thought, *This just proves that a girl cannot follow the rules and does not belong in a man's world.*

"He failed to notice the wolf until Lambda leaped at him from the side. She attacked his forearm and bit his flesh with all the strength her jaws could muster. As the shocked and defenseless eirena attempted to fight the wolf, Larentina ran toward him with the dagger in hand and all the confidence in the world.

"Larentina's eyes already had turned to maroon, and the lightning bolts appeared in her irises. When the eirena saw this, fear burst into his eyes. Rocks and large tree branches began swirling around him, hitting him all over his body.

"She held the handle of the dagger in her hand, with the blade held along her wrist pointing toward her elbow. When she reached the eirena, she ran and leapt upon him, using the eirena's own knees to support her, with the dagger's blade still pointed toward her elbow, resting tightly along her wrist. Suddenly, she slit his throat with a long horizontal slash that almost severed his head from his neck. He fell to the ground as Larentina kept her balance on his body.

"She looked down at the young eirena, who made gurgling noises as the last bit of life seeped from his body. She yelled at the top of her lungs to the eirena, 'It is a good night to die!'

"Larentina knew this eirena had underestimated her because not only was she smaller than he, but she was also a girl, and he probably thought she was not a threat to him. Larentina realized that this eirena's behavior reinforced her belief it was in her best interest to always allow her enemies to underestimate her because of her size and her gender. She already knew this, but now she knew how to use it.

"Agape had already reached Larentina and stood catching her breath after running across the field as she witnessed her daughter use her magical powers against this boy. As she looked upon her daughter with pride bursting from her heart, she decided to break the vow she made to her sister when Larentina was born. It was time to tell her daughter the truth, because she could not stand the secret she carried any longer. If this was being selfish, Agape did not care any longer. She wanted Larentina to know her strength and cunningness came from her, not Alexis.

"Agape ordered to her daughter, 'Come, my child, and let us drink before we are discovered. Leave the body; I will bury it after you leave. We must talk now. I must tell you the truth.'

"Larentina and Agape walked silently across the field and back into Agape's home. Agape lit two large candles on a large wooden table in the eating room, because the large fireplace did not provide adequate lighting for her to look on her daughter's face and body. Agape took out two goblets and filled them with wine.

"Once again, Larentina's face was covered in blood, reminiscent of the night she had been born. Even though Agape took this as an omen, she said nothing to Larentina about it. As Larentina sat at the table, Agape calmly removed the dagger Larentina was still clutching and laid it down on the table. She took her daughter's two hands in hers, stretched her arms out, and proudly gazed at her beautiful face and lean body. She noticed Larentina had turned into a woman before her very own eyes, and she proudly stated her observations. 'Look, my princess, you have turned into a woman this night. We must clean the blood from your face and body, and I will tell you about your womanhood.'

"Agape gently cleaned her daughter from head to foot as if she were a helot. Not a word was spoken. Agape gave Larentina an old tunic that was identical to the one she had been wearing earlier. Larentina was confused by the actions of her aunt but still said nothing and waited for her to explain herself.

"The mother and daughter sat back down at the table. Agape solemnly watched as her daughter ate the stew that she placed on the table. Larentina picked up the goblet full of wine and took just a small sip, because she did not want to feel the effects the following day. She then looked at her aunt and asked, 'Why do you do these things? You owe me nothing.'

"Agape then told Larentina about her womanhood and part of the truth mixed with lies of the birth of Larentina and Lycurgus. Larentina listened to her aunt but became angry after hearing the tale. 'You lie! Why would you lie so? If it is so, why did you break your vow to my mother, your sister?'

"As Agape answered her daughter with another question, her voice was full of love and patience. 'What would you have done? If it was not for my sister, Queen Alexis, I would have been killed by Karpos, and you would not be here today. I owed my sister two lives, and I paid for it dearly.'

"Agape wanted her daughter to kill Karpos first because Agape loved Karpos and because of what Bion had told her; she felt betrayed by Karpos for she knew he would have killed her instead of being her champion. She could not tell her daughter about Nikephoros so she continued the lie to convince her daughter to seek vengeance against Karpos first when she got older. Agape deliberately left out the part that she was actually Karpos's wife before she married Erasmus.

"Agape told how Karpos forced his advances upon her. She told Larentina she could not get away from him, and he had assaulted her viciously and repeatedly. She told Larentina that he was a cruel and vile man. Although Erasmus was a perioikoi, he had saved her from another attack from Karpos. Agape continued, 'When I discovered that I was with child as a result of the assaults, Erasmus married me. Thank the gods that the babe died before anyone discovered that I was with child. Zeus was drunk and he came to me, not Alexis, disguised as Erasmus. I owed my sister the greatest gift I could give her—you and your brother. If it were not for her, King Alcaeus would not have adopted my husband, which provided my husband and me protection from the wrath of Karpos. It was a life for a life, and I owed Alexis two lives. Do you understand now?'

"Larentina had tears in her eyes after listening to the nightmare her real mother had lived. She had even sacrificed her own children to obtain freedom from this tyrant, King Karpos. This woman had suffered greatly. Larentina spoke harshly, but with a touch of empathy toward her true mother. 'Why do you speak the truth to me now? After all, Mother, you yourself told me I was still a girl. It is not right for you to put this burden upon my shoulders, for I'm not the fraud, you are. How do you expect me to continue living this lie? What do I do regarding my brother? Should I tell him the truth or keep it secret? Am I truly a daughter goddess of duty and honor? If so, what does this really mean? You proclaimed that I am the daughter of Zeus, but you and Alexis lied to the world about everything else. How can I believe anything?'

"Agape could not hold back the tears any longer, as she felt the pain and confusion of the past and the pain Larentina must be feeling. Agape had to continue lying to Larentina because it was the only way to have her blood seek vengeance against all who wronged her.

"As Agape started to speak, Erasmus appeared from the darkness of the open doorway. Agape let out a gasp, stood up from the table, and asked, 'My husband, how long have you been there?'

"Erasmus answered quietly, 'Long enough.' He gently took his wife into his arms and kissed her. He looked over at Larentina, who was still sitting, and said, 'Please, Larentina, stand so that I may look upon you.' He looked at her with pride in his eyes for he believed she was his daughter not Zeus's. 'You and your brother were a large price to pay to Alexis.' He walked toward his daughter, hugged her, and kissed her cheek. 'I never knew. You and Lycurgus are a secret Agape kept from me.'

"Agape asked Erasmus, 'Are you angry with me, my husband?'

"Erasmus answered, 'No, but I should be. I completely understand it had to be done. I just wished you had told me the truth instead of allowing me to believe Alexis's lifeless children were mine. Larentina and Lycurgus have a chance to change Sparta. It may not be in our lifetime, it may not even last, but I truly believe the gods gave us Larentina and Lycurgus to change the world's views.

"'Look at what Larentina has accomplished already—the first girl allowed into agoge training. What a coup! She has already changed the way our Spartan government views women. I hope to live long enough to see what other accomplishments she will achieve, along with her brother.'

"The three of them talked for a while longer before Larentina finally left the table, saying, 'I must go. I haven't decided yet whether to tell my brother. I love you both for the sacrifices that you have made for us and for Sparta. I am glad that I now know the truth.'

"Agape quickly rose from the table and ran outside to catch her daughter. As Larentina turned around, Agape grabbed her and hugged her tightly. Larentina could not help but return the hug. Larentina could truly feel this woman loved her deeply.

"Agape held her daughter's face in her hands and kissed her forehead, both cheeks, and her mouth. Agape gazed softly into her daughter's beautiful eyes and spoke. 'When the time comes, my beloved daughter, you will seek the truth, and when it reveals itself, you will honor your blood.

"'I pray to the gods that you punish all Spartan men for disrespecting us, who are simple women, and you instill fear in their hearts when they do so. Fear and humiliation are the answer, Daughter, to make men change their hearts toward us. Now go before I begin to weep.'

"As Larentina walked quickly back to camp, she began to feel remorse for killing the young eirena, but she eased it from her mind because it was her duty to protect herself and her family. There was no other way. She had never killed anyone before, and she knew life was very precious, but again her training kicked in: 'Kill or be killed.'"

Chapter XVIII

"After that night, Larentina never returned to Agape's house for food, for fear that she would be discovered again. Nonetheless, she did visit with Agape and her true family sporadically throughout her teenage years, and she formed a deep and meaningful relation with them. She loved them as she loved her royal family, if not more. Larentina considered this a great secret of her blood and her family.

"Many months passed following that fateful night, and the twins' thirteenth birthday drew near. Upon turning thirteen, they were expected to undergo the rite of passage to become men. Even though Larentina was a girl, she would have to go through it as well.

"By now, Larentina was again tired of being hungry. Since the night at the home of her biological mother, she had begun to forage for their food. She picked fruit whenever she saw it, stole corn and other vegetables from surrounding farms, and occasionally caught a fish, but she continued to yearn for meat. Meat in Sparta was scarce to begin with, and it was nearly impossible to obtain without weapons. Larentina decided it was time for her brother to help.

"Larentina waited until everyone was asleep and then quietly walked over to Lycurgus's straw bed and lay down beside him. She playfully squeezed his nostrils shut until he began stirring, and then she released his nose until he completely woke up. He looked at her with anger in his eyes. Larentina then whispered to him, 'I'm hungry, and I'm tired of being hungry. No one said we could not hunt for our food. Come, let us hunt, so we can fill our bellies.'

"Lycurgus sarcastically whispered to his sister, 'Yes, but you are still a pain in my ass. Pray, Sister, how are we going to hunt without any weapons? Oh, shall we use our bare hands to catch and gut an animal?'

"Larentina picked up her bow and arrows, which she had retrieved earlier from her hiding place, revealing them to her brother. Corinna, the helot who was assigned to attend to Larentina's womanly needs, had snuck them into camp per Larentina's command.

"As Lycurgus stood there in amazement with his mouth half opened, he leaned toward his sister and whispered in her ear, 'Larentina, how in the gods' names did you get that? If we get another lashing because you have gotten caught again, I'm going to lash you myself.'

"Larentina teasingly giggled softly. 'Well, then, I can't tell you. Now can I?'

"Lycurgus shook his head in bewilderment. With disappointment in his voice, he whispered, 'Damn it, Larentina, damn it.' He grabbed his sister by her forearm. 'This is not funny. Do you really want to be lashed again? I can't prove it, but I think you had something to do with the disappearance of the eirena, whose pack was constantly goading us into fights. It is kind of strange how you stopped bringing back feasts for us the same night he disappeared.'

"Larentina ignored him and didn't answer. She simply commanded, 'Let us go and get us something to eat.'

"Lycurgus shrugged his shoulders and followed his sister into the woods.

"Once they were out of hearing range of the camp, he grabbed her forearm as he lost his patience, saying, 'Larentina, stop! I'm not finished discussing this matter with you. You did not answer me. How did you come about your childhood bow and arrows? Answer me now and stop playing games with me. We are not babes anymore.'

"Larentina looked at her brother in the darkness, studying his face for a moment, and voiced her observations. 'If I tell you, you will be angry with me again.'

"Lycurgus impatiently sighed. 'I promise I will not be angry with you. Will you also tell me about the other eirena? Please?'

"*Please* was a word that Lycurgus never used, but he used it with his sister because she could be so stubborn.

"Larentina paused for a few moments as she studied her twin. She then answered, 'As you wish. Corinna snuck it into the barracks several weeks ago.'

"Lycurgus was persistent. 'Very well; now tell me if you were involved in the disappearance of the other eirena.'

"Larentina let out a fearful sigh. 'But I am not ready to tell you.'

"Lycurgus became angry. 'What? So you were involved! Damn it, Larentina! You tell me right now what you have done! I mean it! How can

I protect you from something stupid you may have done if you do not tell me?'

"Larentina just could not tell her brother—not yet anyway. She was just not ready to tell the truth about that night, so she simply hugged her brother. 'Please, Brother, do not ask this of me yet. I'm just not ready to tell you the truth. I promise I will tell you when I'm strong enough to do so.'

"Lycurgus truly did not know how to handle this with his sister. She had never begged him for anything before. He let out a sigh. 'Very well, Sister, I will let this go for now, but I expect you to tell me the truth as soon as you have the strength.'

"Larentina smiled and kissed her brother on the cheek, her demeanor and tone girlish. 'May the gods bless you, Brother; now let us hunt for something to eat. I am starving.'

"Lycurgus let out another irritable sigh. 'But I do not have a weapon, and you have only your old childhood bow and arrows.'

"Larentina replied cleverly, 'My bow and arrows may be old, Brother, but I can still hit and kill just about anything with them. Also, here is a dagger I stole from one of the older soldiers.' Larentina giggled as she victoriously passed the dagger to her brother and whispered, 'The sorry donkey's ass is still looking for it.'

"Lycurgus could not help but chuckle with his sister after realizing that she had stolen the dagger from the same soldier who had first lashed him right before Larentina was enlisted into agoge. Larentina confessed to her brother, 'I will never forget the lashing from that soldier, so for my revenge, I stole his dagger.' They both laughed louder.

"Lambda started growling at a figure in the distance. A goat had been separated from someone's herd; Larentina aimed carefully and released the arrow. They could barely see in the darkness as the figure fell to the ground, but they both knew it had been hit.

"Lycurgus, Larentina, and Lambda all ran to the fallen goat, and Lycurgus proudly declared, 'We will eat well this night!'

"Lycurgus quickly gutted the animal with the dagger, and Lambda ate the animal's inner organs. After Lambda ate her fill, she quickly caught up to Lycurgus and Larentina as they carried the goat's carcass between them, strung up on a large, thick branch. They had used long vines that were growing in the trees near the kill to secure the legs of the goat to the branch.

"Before they reached camp, Larentina requested, 'Brother, give me the dagger so that I may hide it with my bow and arrows.' Larentina quickly hid the dagger as her brother watched.

"After the weapons were hidden, they picked up the goat's carcass and proudly carried it into the camp. In a loud voice, Lycurgus asked, 'Is any one of you hungry for meat this night?' It seemed like the entire pack was instantly awake. Larentina surveyed their pack: everyone's eyes were wide with hunger. They all eagerly helped Larentina and Lycurgus put the entire goat's carcass on two large sticks that had a vee shape in them, which one of them had found near camp.

"Larentina gazed upon Androcles's face; he looked back at her and said with a smile, 'You two still amaze me. How in the gods' names did you kill that goat? No, no, I do not want to know. You two are truly becoming great soldiers.'

"Lycurgus smiled with pride at that statement. Larentina just blushed."

Chapter XIX

"The following day, Corinna was sent to take care of Larentina's womanly needs, as had been the process for several months. Instead of just staying with her at night, the way her mortal father had commanded, Corinna stayed with Larentina in the barracks room all day and all night for the entire week. Corinna and Larentina were developing a close bond and friendship that would last throughout their lives.

"Corinna was an Israelite and had a heavy accent. When she became upset or excited, she would speak so quickly that Larentina could not understand her. The last time Corinna stayed with Larentina, she had asked her friend to teach her to speak Hebrew so she could understand her.

"Larentina asked, 'Corinna, do you have a favorite god?'

"A puzzled expression crossed Corinna's face, but she was careful to answer. 'Yes, my mistress.'

"Larentina asked, 'Since you do, please pray to your god to give me strength and wisdom because I can use all the prayers possible to survive agoge.'

"Corinna did not speak, but she acknowledged Larentina by nodding her head.

"Larentina did not have any close friends who were girls. The only other women who were a part of her life were her mother and Agape. She did not have any contact with girls her own age because she was being raised in a man's world.

"To pass the time, Larentina asked Corinna about her God. Corinna hesitated before answering. 'But my mistress, I fear I will be punished because my God is an enemy of your gods.'

"Larentina was curious, which made her persistent. 'No one will hear you. Who would care? I beg you; I truly would like to hear the stories.'

“Corinna agreed and began telling her a story of her God. She told her the story about Adam and Eve. Unfortunately for Corinna, someone else was listening, someone who did care. Unknown to Larentina, she and Corinna had been overheard by a soldier who had been ordered by General Nikephoros to keep a close eye on Corinna when the girl helot was with Larentina.

“He had been instructed to use any information he discovered as a reason to either kill the young helot or severely punish Larentina. The ultimate goal was to force Larentina from agoge training. As the young soldier understood his task, he was to pursue this plan so that life in agoge could return to normal in Larentina’s absence.

“Hidden from sight, he was standing outside one of Larentina’s small windows behind the barracks. He had done the same each month, but this time he caught the helot telling stories about a god who was an enemy of the Spartan’s gods. He did not need to hear another word, because her story was treason in itself.

“He kicked open the door to Larentina’s room and snatched the helot, saying, ‘You will be publicly executed, traitor.’

“He dragged Corinna out of the room as she begged for her life.

“She cried out, ‘Larentina! Larentina, save me!’

“The soldier became infuriated by the helot’s audacity to call the princess by her name. He growled, ‘Shut your insolent mouth, helot. You are speaking to your princess and mistress. You will call her by her rightful title. You will be executed for this crime as well!’

“Larentina was shocked and confused. Why had a Spartan warrior been listening in on her conversation? Why was he taking her only girlfriend to be executed over a simple tale? Larentina found herself all alone again, without the protection of her brother and Androcles. Somehow, she had to prevent Corinna from being killed. Larentina became enraged and ran after the soldier. Larentina pulled and hit at him as she screamed commands. ‘Stop! Stop! Corinna is not a traitor! Kill me instead, because I commanded her to tell me the stories! Stop!’

“They were in the center of the camp and everyone could hear the commotion. One of the commanders asked the soldier, ‘What is this? The helot is supposed to be here for the girl agoge; that is the king’s law! You must obey it!’

“The soldier had a solemn expression on his face as he answered, ‘I am obeying orders, and I caught this helot telling traitor’s stories to the princess. The helot was also too familiar with the girl agoge by calling her by name instead of her title.'

"While the commander and the young soldier—who still had a tight grip on a struggling Corinna—continued discussing the matter, Larentina saw an opportunity. She commanded Lambda to attack, and the wolf obeyed her mistress, attacking the soldier and setting Corinna free.

"Corinna ran to Larentina with fear in her eyes. Larentina grabbed Corinna's wrist and stepped in front of her. Larentina's irises began to change to a dark reddish brown as lightning bolts formed within them; as she stretched out her hands, the winds began to pick up all around the commander and the young soldier. Larentina commanded, 'Lambda, return!' The wolf obeyed without hesitation and stood fearlessly in front of Larentina while continuing to growl at the commander and the soldier.

"Before the young soldier knew what was happening, a piece of firewood that was swirling in the winds struck him in the head. Larentina yelled at the soldier, 'You will not kill my helot! She belongs to me! If anyone will be executed, it will be me!'

"The commander angrily barked orders to Larentina, 'She Wolf, halt, now! I command it!'

"Larentina immediately stopped, and everything became calm once more.

"The wise commander calmly said, 'There will be no execution this day, but because the girl agoge claims she is responsible, she shall be punished severely. The helot will not be killed, because I do not believe she is a traitor to Sparta. Heed my warning, girl agoge, if you are discovered just once more listening to stories of a god we do not worship, you will die.'

"The commander ordered the soldier, 'Since General Nikephoros ordered this, you will be the one to lash her. I will not anger Zeus or our king.' The soldier had no problem doing so. He grabbed Larentina and tied her to the whipping post.

"Corinna was crying as she watched her dearest friend being punished in her place for telling a simple story. Corinna had never witnessed such a selfless act in her entire young life. She had heard stories of people who had sacrificed themselves for others, but this was the first time she had ever witnessed it with her own eyes.

"As Larentina waited for the lashings, she wondered why a general would take such an interest in her and her helot. She realized that if she cried out for help, her mortal father would remove her from training. She would be disgraced and would not fulfill her mother's dreams of freedom for Spartan women. She refused to allow the general to win this one.

"She felt the first painful lash, and the next, and so on, as Lambda growled. That unmerciful soldier would have whipped her to death, but after the eighth lash, the commander ordered that enough had been done. Larentina had passed out after the fourth lash. She screamed each time the whip made contact with her flesh, but she refused to allow her telepathy to reach anyone else's mind.

"The moment the soldier walked away, Corinna and Lambda ran to their mistress. Corinna quickly untied Larentina, and Lambda carefully licked her unconscious face. None of the soldiers in camp lifted a finger to help. They simply went back to what they were doing as if nothing had happened.

"No one, not even Zeus, found out what happened this day.

"Corinna took Larentina's limp arm, wrapped it around her shoulders, and dragged her inside to tend to the wounds."

Chapter XX

"The following morning, Larentina was jolted awake. She touched the wounds on her back and was relieved to find that her body had almost healed them. She found both Corinna and Lambda sleeping next to her. As Corinna awakened, Larentina giggled.

"Corinna knew her mistress was up to something and feared she had not learned any lesson from the previous day's lashing. 'No, my mistress, whatever it is, no. We almost were killed yesterday; remember the commander's warning.'

"Larentina did not understand why she had to stay in this dark, dusty room for a week out of the month anyway. As far as she was concerned, the requirement brought them trouble to begin with. She was restless to seek vengeance in some form. Larentina decided that the time had come to use her gifts for the good of womankind.

"She said, 'That is true, Corinna, but no one said I could not teach the Spartan men a lesson. I may not be able to punish the general, but I can punish Spartan citizens as long as I am not caught. I need you to pretend that I am still here with you if someone should ask.'

"Corinna became fearful. 'But Mistress, I will be lashed if you are discovered missing, and I cannot lie for you. We can never talk about my God ever again. I do not want to die. You cannot leave, especially after what happened yesterday.'

"Larentina gave Corinna a childish pout, and Corinna succumbed to the facial expression because she was indebted to Larentina for her life.

"Larentina joyfully hugged Corinna, kissing her on her cheek, and whispered in her ear, 'Thank you. I will never forget this.'

"Corinna whispered back, 'I still will not break my God's law, "Thou shall not lie," but if you tell me you are going to bathe yourself, then I can truthfully tell anyone who asks that is where you are.'

*   *   *

"Larentina hid in the shadows of a dark alley and peeked from the corner of a building on a busy street in Sparta.

"The smell of fresh bread, meats, and other delicious foods surrounded her, and she breathed in deeply. *What I would not give for just a piece of bread*, she thought.

"She watched as the men walked a few feet in front of their women, and the women never said a word. She saw a wealthy merchant smack a young girl across the face, knocking her to the ground. He picked her up and punched her in the face. He angrily yelled, 'You stupid helot! You burned the bread and now it is no good. The only thing you are good for is on your back.' He continued beating her.

"Naturally, Larentina had no idea what 'on your back' meant. All she knew was that it did not sound pleasant. Larentina became angry, and after many months of learning from Androcles how to control and focus her powers, she decided to teach the man a lesson.

"Her irises changed to a dark reddish brown as lightning bolts charged through them. She saw a piece of firewood on the street. She focused on the log, lifted it into the air, and caused it to carve itself into a paddle. She moved the paddle through the air toward the wretched merchant and tapped him on the shoulder with it. The merchant irritably turned around, and the paddle smacked him across the face, knocking him to the ground. The merchant screamed as he was lifted into the air and flipped around several times; the paddle spanked him repeatedly on his backside. There was panic and chaos throughout the street as people saw what was happening. Merchants' canopies tumbled, and food and other goods began to spill throughout the streets.

"Larentina had learned to throw her voice, and she took advantage of this well-practiced skill. Suddenly, her voice took on the deep tone of a man's voice and sounded from all around the street, saying, 'Hear me, you fat old man! If you lay another hand on the girl, I will feed you to the wolves. If I find her on her back, I will put you on your back for all eternity!'

"Lambda ran toward the merchant, growling and snarling at him, and then quickly returned to her mistress's side.

"The merchant was so scared he urinated on himself as he soiled his tunic. Now on his knees with soiled clothing, with his hands together as if he were praying yells up toward the heavens scared to death as his voice quivered, "Please, please almighty one, do not punish me for I will do as you command. Please do not kill me!"

"It seemed as if time had stopped because the people froze in place and all were frantically looking all around them and toward the heavens to see if they could see which god was angry at them. Most dropped to their knees and continued searching all around them to see if they could get just a glimpse of the angry god.

"With the snap of her wrist and her index finger pointing toward the busy street, so to give her aim without hurting anyone, she shot large lightning bolts toward the feet of many men. Smoke rose from the street where the lightning bolts hit and the people ran in all directions in fear they would be struck. It appeared to the people that Zeus himself was shooting lightning bolts from the heavens.

"Larentina continued, 'If I find another Spartan woman walking behind a Spartan man, I will come back and kill all of you! I am a powerful god, and I will destroy you all if you do not start treating your women with respect. They should be seen as equals!'

"Larentina had no idea what she was saying, but she enjoyed the reaction to her words immensely. She quickly covered her mouth so no one would hear her giggling. She knew that if she did not leave soon, she would be discovered and punished. She ran back down the dark alley, headed out of the city, and returned to the forest. She ran as quickly as she could back to the camp, slipping into the barracks before anyone discovered she was missing."

* * *

"As a coincidence, Agape was trading goods in Sparta that very day and watched these events unfold. She smiled to herself as she saw Larentina peeking from around the building. Pride filled Agape for Larentina's actions, but she also realized they were childish. She would have to contact Queen Alexis regarding the matter because it was dangerous for all involved. Nevertheless, she realized that Larentina had taken her advice to heart because her daughter was now instilling fear in the men of Sparta."

* * *

"Like Larentina's mother, Zeus had a habit of peeking in on his daughter's activities every chance he was able. He had to be very careful not to be caught by his wife, Hera. After watching Larentina display more control over her powers, he was pleased. He thought to himself, *Why not have a daughter champion instead of a son?* He had many daughters from mortal women, and he loved them. Granted, some of them inherited a few traits of the Olympian deities, but none had demonstrated as many of these powers as Larentina had displayed.

"Zeus knew Larentina was going to start some type of war between the Spartan women and men because of her mother's influence, but he was delighted watching it unfold. She was growing more powerful than Athena, one of his favorite daughters. He realized, however, that Larentina was not self-absorbed and spoiled like the goddess Athena was.

"What Zeus did not completely understand was that Larentina was not just fighting about small freedoms for Spartan women, but about vengeance, justice, punishment, and freedom of many different types."

* * *

"That was the day Larentina began to transform Spartan society by instilling fear and chaos throughout the great city-state. She knew that if she were caught, the gerousia council and the apella would execute not only her, but Agape, Alexis, and Corinna as well. Despite this risk, the following day, Larentina snuck out of camp again, but this time she went to visit Agape, which she enjoyed deeply. Lambda, as always, ran beside Larentina through the woods to Agape's home.

"Of course, this time was different because Agape, a concerned mother, scolded Larentina for displaying her powers in the open. She reminded Larentina that if she were caught, she would be punished severely or even killed. Agape warned Larentina to be very careful not to be caught.

"Agape told Larentina that she had spoken with Alexis, but Alexis could not visit her in secret. She feared she would be caught and killed. Agape and Alexis also agreed that it was in the best interest of all concerned for Larentina to stop sneaking out of camp to visit Agape and the queen. Most importantly, they warned Larentina to stop playing with Spartan citizens because of the dangers her actions were causing for others.

"Despite these warnings, Larentina did not stop visiting Agape and Alexis in secret, but she did limit the frequency of her visits. She also continued spanking Spartan men in public every chance she had."

Chapter XXI

"A few months after the twins' thirteenth birthday, their pack was once again allowed to sleep in the barracks. They had survived a long year without shelter and adequate food. As a result, going forward, they had earned these basic luxuries and would advance to the next level of agoge training. They started every morning standing in formation for inspection by Androcles. On this particular morning, their eirena was joined by a general and several older soldiers. As they stood at attention, Androcles gave a speech with pride. 'This day is a glorious day! This day is a rite of passage. You will be tested on your strength, your will to survive, and all the other trainings you have received in order to become great Spartan soldiers!'

"General Nikephoros, in his full Spartan uniform, then spoke in a deep, loud voice. 'Androcles indeed speaks truthfully. You all will be sent into the wilderness this day for one week to test your skills. Some of you will never return. For those of you that do return, you will be even stronger than before. You must go alone, each and every one of you, and prove to the gods that you are worthy to serve your great country, Sparta. You must go alone. You may not pair up. If you do, and you are caught, I will lash you myself. Now go and prove you are men! Uh, and a woman!' General Nikephoros turned a little red in the face because he had forgotten momentarily that he was also speaking to Larentina, and he was not used to including a girl in his speeches. He thought to himself, *Training Larentina to become a Spartan warrior was a ridiculous waste of time and money*, but he did not verbalize his thoughts.

"On hearing those words, the packs in formation let out a battle cry of excitement and ran off in many different directions, except for Larentina and Lycurgus. They both ran into the woods toward the mountains, but when they realized what they were doing, they stopped. General Nikephoros, Androcles, and the other soldiers, who had been watching them, noticed this instantly. Androcles feared that the general may lash them for staying together; he immediately yelled at the twins, 'I know that you two think as one, but this time, you must complete your fates alone! Now, go!'

"Larentina and Lycurgus looked at Androcles as he yelled his orders to them. The twins then turned and ran into the woods in different directions.

"When she reached the woods, Larentina stopped and hid in the foliage so that she could see what was about to unfold.

"General Nikephoros looked at Androcles and said, with much anger in his voice, 'You have spoiled those twins. They should have been lashed for hesitating like that and disobeying my orders. For this insubordination, you will take their lashing for them.'

"Androcles defiantly retorted, 'I will take the lashing eagerly, for I did no wrong regarding my goddess and her brother. I will die if need be to protect Larentina, even her brother, because he will be a king someday!'

"As Androcles walked toward the whipping post, General Nikephoros, with a facetious tone, asked, '*Your* goddess?'

"Androcles continued to walk toward the whipping post in silence; he was not going to be goaded by this old fool. Androcles picked up the whip, walked back to where General Nikephoros was standing, and handed it to him. General Nikephoros was astounded at Androcles's behavior and his remarks. He gave Androcles two strong lashes, and the young eirena did not flinch or make a sound.

"General Nikephoros confessed, 'I must admit, Androcles, that your behavior regarding these twins amazes me. You may be right regarding allegiance to Lycurgus, but to the girl, Larentina? I honestly believe you would die for him, but for the girl child? Enough! Go. You have been punished enough this day.'

"Androcles's back was screaming in pain from the lashes his general had given him, but it was well worth it to keep Larentina from failing the training. Androcles finally admitted to himself that he genuinely loved Larentina, even though she was still a child. She had some kind of magical spell over him, and he feared that he might be too weak to fight it.

"Larentina saw what Androcles had done for her and her brother. Her heart was filled with admiration, because he had always sacrificed himself for her without fear or hesitation. She did not understand why he did it, but she was grateful he was her eirena and no other. She trusted him blindly because of this, and she was developing warm feelings toward him as well.

He treated her as an equal and had no shame in doing so, like her brother did. She quickly dismissed these thoughts and ran into the forest."

Lycurgus's Dream

Chapter XXII

"After the first day and night of scavenging for food and trying to find shelter from the intolerable nonstop rain, Larentina stumbled upon a hidden waterfall at the base of one of the mountains.

"She discovered a beautiful waterfall surrounded by so much foliage that it provided perfect shelter. There were fruit bushes and trees that seemed to reach all the way to the heavens. The waterfall dropped into a deep pool of water and then spilled out in higher ground, turning into a small creek. It was a paradise that seemed untouched by man.

"Larentina picked fruit and ate until her belly was satisfied. She then looked down and noticed that she was covered in mud from running in the rain-soaked forest. As she looked at the beautiful scenery in front of her, she realized that Zeus must have created this secret haven to make her rite of passage easier. She gladly accepted this gift from her father. Larentina thought for sure that she had been wrong in not believing she was half goddess, and she decided Zeus must be her father after all. Her next thought was, *Be damned these mortal men for making me suffer so. My father will protect and provide for me. To Hades with them all!*

"She first washed her dirty tunic and then jumped into the fresh clean water. She looked up and discovered a large, flat rock right under the small waterfall. She stood on the rock as the clean water poured over her body. It was very relaxing. She felt like she never wanted to leave this place.

"Larentina swam back to the other side of the pool, climbed onto the soft grassy embankment, and found a nice dry area beside the trunk of a large tree. She found some hay near the area and made herself a bed, and then she built a fire to keep herself warm. She fell asleep instantly.

"She was immediately awoken by a nightmare that she could not remember, similar to the ones she had experienced when she was much younger. She realized then that she had not only slept through the day, but the night as well, and most of the new day.

"She felt sadness and pain. She instinctively knew that her brother was screaming for her. She had to find him this second. She swam back to the bank where she had left her tunic hanging on a tree. She put it on quickly and ran back into the woods, looking for her brother."

* * *

"Lycurgus, on the other hand, had not been faring as well as his twin. He had stumbled upon a mother bear and her cub. The mother bear charged at him, and before Lycurgus could react, she had smacked him with her powerful paw. In a daze from the powerful blow, he managed to flee, and the bear stopped chasing him.

"He had found himself stuck in thorns and briars. After fighting through them for unending hours, he looked up to see that he could go no further. There was a solid rock ledge going straight up for at least a hundred feet in front of him and a large dark cave off to the side.

"Cuts and bruises covered his entire body from pushing his way through the thorns, and he had suffered deep wounds from the claws of the bear on his shoulder and chest. He hadn't eaten for the entire time since leaving the barracks, and he was starving and thirsty from all the energy he had been using. He thought his sister must have perished by now, because she did not answer him after he tried reaching out to her with his thoughts. He knew he had somehow entered the underworld of Hades. Lycurgus knew he had to find his sister before Hades took hold of her.

"He started hallucinating, but to Lycurgus it was all too real. He found himself walking through a vast field of soft wheat, and as he walked toward the edge of the field, he saw the large dark cave.

"Lycurgus saw his sister at the entrance of the dark cave. She had on a soft red tunic with a golden rope belt and golden sandals that laced over her feet and up her calves. Upon her head, she wore a solid gold headband, and her curly hair was pulled back into a ponytail that cascaded down her back. She was singing and laughing as she picked the wildflowers that surrounded the mouth of the cave.

"Lycurgus was overcome with happiness. As he smiled broadly at the sight of his sister, Hades suddenly emerged from the darkness of the cave. He looked down at Larentina and smiled as he picked a wildflower and handed it to her. He looked up and stared at Lycurgus.

"Hades's skin was an even light gray, and he stood about twelve feet tall. His thin hair was pitch black and pulled back into a ponytail that revealed the receding hairline at his temples. He was wearing a headband of thick, twisted, gold rope and large gold hoop earrings in both ears. His black beard was shaped into a narrow triangle. His small, pitch-black eyes slanted slightly downward. His thin eyebrows were also black and slanted downward as well. His nose was long, straight, and pointed. Hades's arms were solid muscle, and one of his arms would have equaled four of Lycurgus's legs. Likewise, his legs were also of solid muscle, and he had muscular thighs that seemed to stretch for miles. His bare chest was large and muscular, as was the rest of his body.

"He wore a tunic of soft, thick wool that fell from his waist to the top of his feet. It was a solid purple and had gold trim with a black G shape woven into the gold trim. He wore a wide bronze belt tightly fastened around his waist, holding his tunic in place.

"On his wrists were large gold bands with large, black Gs around the top and bottom. In his right hand was a large sword that was longer than Lycurgus was tall. The ivory handle was comprised of the face and horn of a ram. Draped across his left shoulder was the pelt of a ram with the face and horns still attached and resting on his shoulder.

"Hades lightly touched the back of Larentina's head with his left hand. Larentina looked up at Hades and smiled as she turned her head to look at Lycurgus, still smiling. Lycurgus ran toward Hades to fight him and save his sister from the underworld. As Lycurgus was running toward them, Hades threw his head back and laughed. His deep, loud laugh reverberated throughout the rocky cliffs surrounding the field. Hades yelled at him, 'Boy, I can't believe that you would even think about fighting me. Stop, boy! Come inside my house and drink with me, so that we may talk.' The three of them entered Hades's house.

"After the souls of the damned served the two of them wine, Hades declared, 'If you do not ensure that Larentina fulfills her destiny, you will stay here, for I will not allow Larentina to leave unless she begins the battle between Hera and all the other wicked gods and goddesses. If she does not follow her destiny, then I will take her as my bride. She will rule with me, and she will never see the sun again.

"'I will use you to entrap her, and I will seduce her in front of you. I will have both your souls, and you can do nothing about it. You will belong to me, and I will torture both your souls for all of eternity. This will be my revenge to Zeus, my brother, for not cleaning up his house. I will take his daughter, of whom he is so very proud.'

"Lycurgus angrily bellowed, 'You will not take her, for I will fight you! You do not have my soul to judge me yet, Hades, not yet, not this day!'

"Hades's voice resonated with laughter. 'Today is not the day to be judged, boy, because you are not a hero yet, not this day. You must earn that privilege. Now go to your sister and protect her so that she can start the battle in the heavens. If she does this, I swear I will unite with Zeus to take down our enemies.'

"Lycurgus woke up as he heard his sister's soft voice calling, 'Come back to me, Lycurgus, come back!' Lycurgus opened his eyes and saw his sister looking down at him and smiling.

"Larentina softly commanded, 'Eat this, Brother, for it will make you strong again.' She handed him some fruit and rubbed some herbs on his wounds as he lay in the thorns.

"Lycurgus asked Larentina, as he put his arms around her, 'Are you real or just a trick of Hades?'

"Larentina answered, in a soft and loving tone, 'Brother, it's me and all my herbs. I even brought you some fruit. Are you strong enough to follow me to the paradise that Zeus has given to me? Hades will never tempt you again.'

"As Larentina led him to her small paradise, Lycurgus announced, 'The battle between the gods is beginning, Larentina. Hades wants you and me to start the war.'

"Larentina said nothing as they reached her paradise.

"After her brother absorbed the scene's beauty, Larentina commented, 'Hades will never tempt you again, Brother. Zeus, my father, is punishing him right now for trying to take you from me. Come eat as much fruit as you desire, and we will plan our future together. Give me your tunic, so that I may wash it for you.'

"Lycurgus obeyed his sister. He removed his torn and dirty tunic for her to clean as he continued to eat.

"After Lycurgus had eaten his fill, he jumped into the pool of water and started to bathe himself. Larentina, thinking nothing of it, hung her tunic by her brother's on the tree, and jumped in with him. She washed the dirt from her brother's neck and back. Then, she saw his scars again—not from just the first lashing, but from several since, because he had taken blame for her failures. She had never again felt the pain that her brother endured for her.

"In a sad voice, Larentina confessed her feelings to her brother. 'I'm truly sorry for all the pain I have caused you, Brother. I love you so much. You are all I have in this world.'

"Lycurgus turned, faced his sister, and with a smile on his face confessed, 'As our father has said numerous times, you will be the death of me, but you are all I have as well, Sister. If it were not for you, this day I would be in the underworld forever. I will gladly take pain and anything else the gods may dish out to protect you. I am honored this day to call you Sister. I said it before, and I will say it again: I love you as if you were myself, because you are. Now stop all this girlish stuff.' Then, Lycurgus dunked his sister playfully.

"They swam and played in the large pool of water until their skin shriveled up like prunes. They climbed onto the bank, now that the sun was out, to warm themselves. They started talking and planning for their return. As they both lay on the bank enjoying the warmth of the sun, Lycurgus said, 'Now Larentina, we will have to go different paths back to the training grounds to make sure we arrive at different times. If we are discovered together, you know that we both will be lashed. No one must ever know you rescued me from the underworld. Do you understand?'

"Larentina answered, 'Yes, my brother. I will do as you tell me.'

"They enjoyed the small paradise for one more night and day before returning to the barracks. It was decided that Lycurgus would go first, and Larentina would wait two hours before taking another path back. As she neared the camp, Lamda and her pack rejoined her.

"Several agoges had already returned by the time Larentina got back. Six boys had not returned yet. In fact, they never would return. As happens with agoge training, no one ever knew their fates.

"Androcles's face lit up with pride when he saw Larentina walking lazily through the wooded edgeway. General Nikephoros stood up and was in total shock by what he saw.

"Larentina stopped at the edge of the woods as she let the entire wolf pack jump up on her as if they were trying to hug her. They were all wagging their tails as they licked her face, saying good-bye. Lambda's pack had come for her, and Larentina knew it was time for her wolf to go back to the wild. She hoped that she would see her beloved wolf once more with a gift to give her.

"After Lambda and the other wolves disappeared into the forest, Larentina walked up to General Nikephoros, who said to her, 'You truly are half god! I will never underestimate you or your brother again.'

"Larentina arrogantly replied, 'Yes, you will, and that will be your downfall.'

"General Nikephoros grew angry, but he ignored the comment and yelled, 'It's a glorious day, for you all have become men!' He then walked away, mounted his horse, and rode away.

"After the general left, Androcles told her in a half whisper, 'I'm very proud of you, Larentina. I always knew you were strong and brave.'"

Chapter XXIII

"As the years flew by, Larentina grew into the most beautiful woman in all the lands. She was even more beautiful than Queen Alexis and her sister, Agape. She was strong from all the training and could wield a sword as well as any man. In fact, she could fight better than most of the seasoned soldiers. She was truly the pride of Sparta. She had turned into a very formidable soldier, almost as formidable as her brother was.

"From being out in the sun and swimming in salt water most of their lives, the twins' hair naturally bleached to white, and their skin became a deep golden brown; to most, this made them even more god-like because blond hair was rare, and white hair was even rarer.

"Larentina grew to be five feet and seven inches tall. She did not have arms of muscles like a man, but you could still see the strength she possessed. Her legs were muscular, and she had a firm, rounded butt and full breasts. In other words, she possessed a feminine figure, which was to her advantage. Everyone underestimated her strength and battle skills because of her beauty and femininity.

"As Lycurgus grew, he no longer looked identical to his sister, even though he possessed many of her same facial qualities. He was completely masculine in every way. He kept his hair cut very short and had dark brown whiskers. He had grown to be a few inches over six feet.

"Both Lycurgus and Androcles had arms that were solid muscle, and one of their arms could equal both of Larentina's. Likewise, their solid legs had muscular thighs that seemed to stretch for miles. Their chests were large and muscular, as were the rest of their bodies. They both had many scars on their backs from being whipped throughout the years.

"Both were stronger than Larentina was, but they could not run as fast as she could. Androcles taught Larentina that if she was unable to use her magic or create any weapons to protect herself against an enemy army, then she should run away as fast as the wind.

"He would always say to her, 'It is better to retreat and live to fight another day. There is no shame in this for you, like there is for men.'

"Androcles was just an inch shorter than Lycurgus, and his hair was a curly ash. He kept his hair cut short because he did not want his curly locks to make him appear 'pretty,' a word he had hated since he was eight years old. His eyes were the bluest of blue, and gazing into his eyes was like peering at an endless horizon of sky. When he became angry, however, his eyes would turn into a deadly, stormy blue. His freckles had faded just a few years ago, and he had grown into one of the most handsome men in all of Sparta.

"Androcles was laid back and did not really take anything seriously, except for Larentina. He took pride in everything he had taught her. He only worshiped Zeus because of Larentina's presence in his life. He felt that she was just as powerful as all the other Olympian deities, and he did not fear them because he did not know any better. In many ways, Androcles was like his father with the exception that he was mostly liked and no one feared him, despite his deep voice.

"Lycurgus, on the other hand, was serious in everything he did. He always liked to have a plan of action, and he did not like the idea of acting on the spur of the moment, which he often seemed to find himself doing because of his sister. He did not fear mortal men because he knew his sister, the demigoddess, was always by his side. Nonetheless, he did not want to get into a fight with the deities who were Larentina's enemies, because he considered them more powerful than she was, and they were the only beings he feared.

"Both Larentina and Lycurgus had been hardened by the agoge training, but somehow they managed to keep intact some of their compassion for others. Maybe it was because they nurtured each other when no one else would; maybe it was because they loved and respected each other as well; or maybe it was because Larentina was more educated than most. Regardless of the reason, they didn't become as hardened as most Spartan soldiers did. It was as if their spirits were untainted to a certain degree.

"The twins were about to turn twenty, and they had just about completed their military training. For the last two years, they had been soldier cadets. They were considered to have the most beautiful, perfect bodies in all of Sparta, in addition to Androcles.

"They were practicing their sword skills when Larentina was chosen by one of the commanders to fight a cadet from another pack. This particular cadet was one of the strongest and most skilled of his own pack. Androcles stood to the side with the others to watch.

"As Androcles watched, she began to perform the strange ritual that she had started years ago before she would participate in any hand-to-hand or sword-to-sword combat. She crouched down close to the ground and slowly picked up a handful of dirt. Before she stood again, Larentina looked directly into Androcles's eyes with a belligerent gaze, rubbed the dirt between her hands, and let it slowly fall to the ground again. Androcles could not take his eyes off Larentina as she stood up. She had turned into the most beautiful woman he had ever seen.

"As she prepared for the battle, she looked directly at her combatant with a deadly stare, pulling her sword from her side. Larentina truly hated this pompous ass because he was always harassing her and had called her nasty names for years, but this time Larentina was determined to kill him.

"It only took Larentina a few minutes to accomplish her goal; she did the same thing she had done many years ago with her first kill. She ran straight toward her opponent, leaped upon the young man's knees, and thrust her sword directly into his neck. As his body fell backward, she kept her balance by standing on the falling body as if she was riding a wave of water, pulling her sword from the neck and shoulder of the young cadet.

"Androcles could not help himself and cheered loudly for the stunning feat. He was so proud that he was the one who had trained her and molded her into an almost perfect Spartan warrior. She bowed triumphantly for her bloodthirsty audience, and as she was about to return into the barracks, she turned and saw the crowd clear a path for someone she still could not see because of the crowd.

"Little did the young Spartan agoges know that this had been a test for Larentina, and Larentina alone. General Nikephoros had been hidden behind the audience watching the entire fight. Once again he was disappointed that she had not been killed, but at the same time he was amazed by Larentina's quick assault, and she did not hesitate to kill the young cadet. He admitted that she truly was a she wolf of the Olympian deities, and it was becoming harder to have the will to kill her. For just a moment, he felt some strange connection with Larentina and even with her brother. He quickly shrugged it away.

"The crowd moved, creating a pathway for the general to walk toward Larentina. She watched the general approach. She was puzzled as to why he was here. General Nikephoros uttered in a loud, powerful voice, 'Larentina, you have done well, for you have won the honor of your pack to fight as warriors in battle with the Spartan legions. If you had not won this fight this day, your entire pack would have been dishonored.'

"General Nikephoros turned and began speaking to the entire agoge audience. 'You all know we have been at war for several weeks now; we have been summoned by the Delian League to fight against the barbarian, Kutir-Nahhunte, and his army. He has invaded Thebes without provocation and has proclaimed himself ruler. We have made a pact, and we are honoring it.

"'King Karpos has already led us into battle, and he has requested his son to join him at this time. Because Larentina is in his son's pack, the gerousia requested a test of Larentina's skills, given that she has only been used in past battles as a healer and an archer. Nonetheless, Larentina, this day, has proven that she is not a weak link, and the honor to fight in the ranks and prove themselves as future warriors has been bestowed on King Karpos's son's pack. Androcles, go and prepare your pack, for we leave at first light.' He mounted his horse and left the campgrounds.

"Larentina felt like a fool, for she had never been told the name of the prince of the Eurypontids house. In fact, she didn't know the names of any of King Karpos's children. During agoge training, no one was ever called by their true title. Talking about your family was also forbidden, because you would be considered weak for discussing your parents.

"She never knew one of her pack members was the son of Karpos, and the general did not even mention his name, and Larentina still had no idea who he is. There was no way she was going to embarrass herself by asking her brother, who might not know anyway. She just shrugged it off because she knew that one day, she would find out the name of Karpos's son."

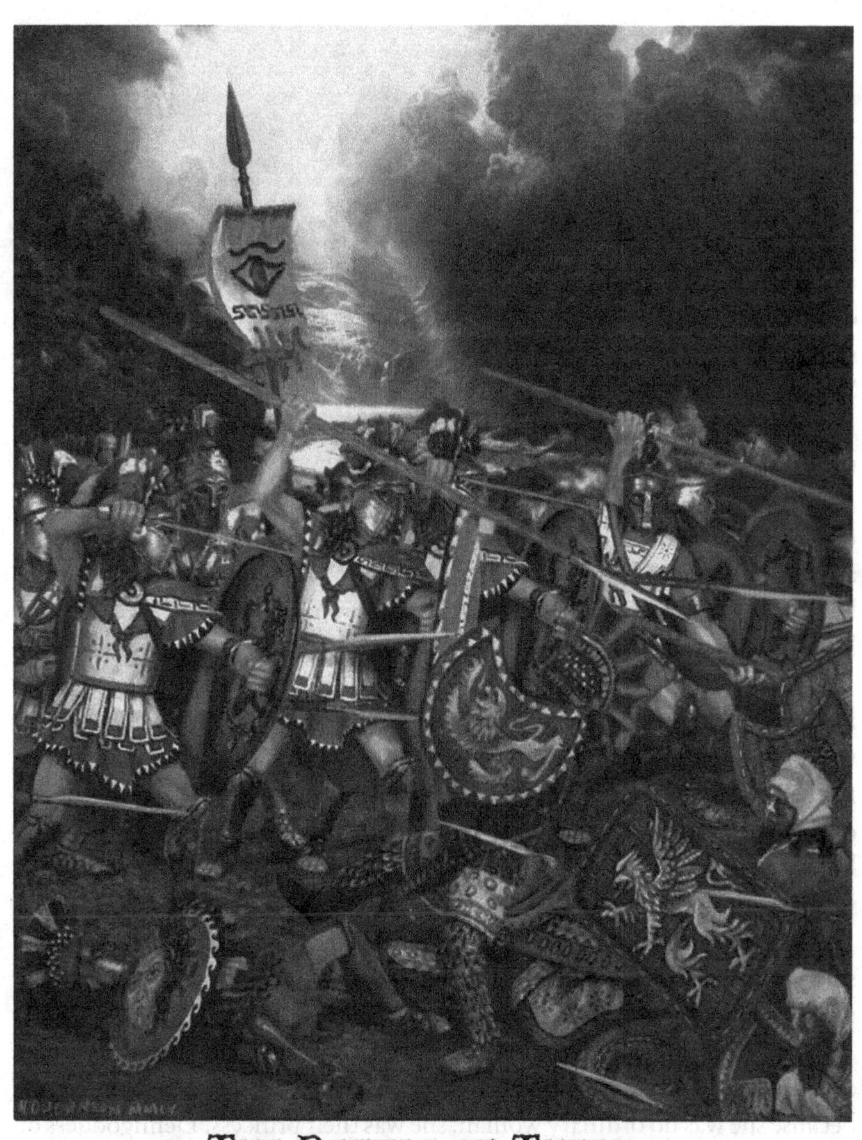

THE BATTLE OF THEBES

Chapter XXIV

"When Larentina and her pack arrived at the battlefield, the smell of death overcame her. There were hundreds of slaughtered bodies across the sloping fields, and they were not just those of the enemy, but many were Spartan warriors. In fact, there were too many losses for Sparta.

"Larentina had to cover her mouth and nose to prevent from vomiting; the stench of death was revolting. She had never witnessed such a large slaughter before. The times that she had been allowed into battle, she was far from the actual fighting and had been allowed in the ranks of the archers only once. Those times, the physical fights only lasted a few hours before the enemies of Sparta surrendered. Larentina had never seen Sparta lose so many of her warriors in her young life.

"This time, Larentina's country was fighting barbarians who had no honor about how they fought. It had taken Sparta weeks to become close to reclaiming the city-state. She saw hundreds of Spartan Hoplite Phalanx formations as they slowly pushed the enemy backward. Larentina heard one of the commanders yelling orders to Androcles. The next thing she knew, she was being told to help the fallen warriors, and she obeyed without question.

"She opened her pouch of herbs and potions and helped the wounded soldiers as best she could. She was angry that she was not allowed to fight with the men, but she understood why.

"She knew Spartan warriors were not accustomed to having a woman among them, and they would make mistakes simply because of her presence because she was no ordinary woman; she was their princess. Demigoddess or not, they would make mistakes because she was considered more beautiful above all Spartan women. She did not want anyone dying because of her presence, no matter how much she wanted to prove herself. This shows just how unselfish Larentina truly was, no matter how arrogant she portrayed herself to others, but like all women in her bloodline before her, when she looses her tempter she will protect her own no matter the cost.

"After several weeks of fighting, Larentina was disgusted by how many fallen soldiers that her beloved Sparta had suffered. She decided to take matters in her own hands, because they would not allow her to fight. She was tired of battle and did not like it, not one little bit. She had also grown weary of death and wanted peace for Sparta again.

"Larentina watched as Androcles, Lycurgus, and the rest of her pack fought for their very lives on the battlefield, and tears welled in her eyes. She could no longer bear the feeling of being weak and cowardly. She quickly picked up a sword from a fallen Spartan warrior and retrieved his shield as well. She gently removed his helmet, which had a black and red plume. She put it on and ran full force to another warrior who had just been slaughtered, a member of her own agoge pack; Lambda was by her side as she ran.

"The same barbarian who had just killed her friend and member of her pack was preparing to stab her brother in the back with his spear. Tears flowed down Larentina's cheeks, and then her eyes lit up. You could see the lightning bolts flowing from her irises from a distance. She was an unnatural sight to see. She screamed a battle cry like no other, as she charged toward the barbarian without fear or thought of the deadly consequences.

"Androcles, Lycurgus, and the rest her agoge pack looked in the direction of her deadly cry, but they were engaged in bloody sword fights. Androcles and Lycurgus had prepared themselves to fight in unison for many years; they were trained to fight as one with their pack, but they practiced together as one so they would always be in front of Larentina to protect her. Unfortunately, this day had come. They quickly glanced at each other as they fought the enemy, thinking the same thoughts.

"Lambda was the first to meet the barbarian; as she leaped into the air, her powerful jaws caught the barbarian's arm between her teeth. As he fought off the wolf, Larentina leaped into the air as well, landing on the barbarian's kneecaps as Lambda released her grip. Larentina quickly thrust her sword deep into the barbarian's flesh at the base of his neck, and she twisted her sword. As he fell, Larentina pulled her sword from his neck and attacked another barbarian soldier. Lambda bit at the barbarian's leg, and once she had a firm hold, she did not let go. As the soldier tried to thrust his sword into the wolf's flesh, Larentina stabbed her sword into his rib cage, and he fell to the ground.

"As Larentina turned once again, another enemy soldier charged toward her; he was met by Androcles and Lycurgus's swords crossing each other, forming an X. They stabbed the barbarian in unison. Within moments, Larentina's pack had formed a circle around her instead of a Hoplite Phalanx formation, fighting the enemy from all directions to protect her. Lycurgus was on one side, and Androcles was on the other side of her. Larentina had caused the winds to encircle them, with spears, swords, shields, and even the lifeless bodies of fallen comrades being blown into the enemy. From a distance, it looked like a tornado with the young agoge pack fighting in the eye of it.

"The barbarian soldiers initially began retreating, but they courageously started fighting the dead bodies that would strike at their swords in the winds. Many barbarians dropped to the ground after being attacked by the objects that swirled in the winds, and they attacked them as well from the funnel of wind. They would jab in the winds hoping to pierce the flesh of one of the Spartans within the funnel walls, but it did them no good.

"As spears fell to the ground in front of each agoge, Larentina thunderously commanded, 'Pick the spears up I have given you; as I command "attack," thrust your spears, with your shields close to your body to protect you, into the wind and fight the barbarians; when I command "retreat," pull your spears back from the wall of wind.'

"Larentina would calm the winds six inches in width per each man within the circle so that they could step forward and step backward, killing each barbarian who just happened to be directly in front of them. She kept all the objects floating in the air within these openings as the rest of the funnel swirled all around between each brief and small opening. At the same time, she read the enemy's minds to anticipate where each barbarian would attack.

"Larentina commanded, 'Attack!' And no more than a fraction of a second later, she commanded, 'Retreat!' All the well-trained agoges obeyed her commands without hesitation repeatedly. Piles of lifeless barbarian soldiers formed all around the outer wall of the funnel of wind and lightning bolts.

King Karpos saw this; General Nikephoros saw this; everyone on the battlefield saw this; even Zeus himself was watching. The Spartan legions fought more intensely because they knew their She Wolf was on the battlefield now, and they all fought harder because they knew she could not fight this battle alone, no matter how powerful of a being she was, but Zeus did not see this. He just assumed his daughter was fighting the

Spartans' war alone. This was all he saw in his mind's eye as he watched the battle.

"Larentina was increasingly becoming weaker from all the energy she was using, both mentally and physically. She could not sustain the chaos much longer. She just could not fight so many barbarians at once like this, but her life, as well as the lives of the Spartan legions, depended on her. The barbarians just kept coming, wave after wave.

"After four full hours, Larentina made a mistake. She did not keep her shield directly in front of her, leaving her left side partly open, and she was stabbed with a spear that went completely through her side, narrowly missing her vital organs. Immediately, the tornado and all the objects within it fell to the ground as the winds became calm again.

"Larentina looked down at the spear after softly making a painful groan and used what little bit of physical strength she had left to grab the spear. But the barbarian continued pushing the spear, and it went completely through her body. Her expression was shock as she looked into the barbarian's eyes. She slowly dropped to her knees and, with one last burst of mental energy, pushed him several feet away. Lambda howled into the sky and ran toward the barbarian, ferociously attacking him and knocking him to the ground. The barbarian's eyes grew wide with fear as the frenzied wolf continued attacking, trying to reach his neck and kill the cretin who had mortally wounded her mistress.

"Larentina's entire pack bellowed, 'Larentina! She Wolf!' after seeing their demigoddess dropped to her knees. The young agoges attacked the barbarians with a burst of merciless rage.

"Larentina may have been a pain to most of her pack, but they all truly loved her spirit, her courage, her gentleness, and her sacrifice just to feed them more. She healed them, and because of her, they survived. She touched all of their lives like no other, and they all were willing to die for her.

"King Karpos and the others watched as the tornado disappeared and everything within it dropped to the ground. King Karpos felt pain and sorrow like he had never felt before for his closest friend, Alcaeus. He knew Alcaeus had loved this child from the moment he held her in his arms when she was just a few months old. He knew Alcaeus would kill him for not protecting his baby girl, and King Karpos knew he would deserve to be killed! King Karpos also knew that Alcaeus did not care if she was the daughter of Zeus, and he feared that if Zeus felt this way toward her as well, then all of Sparta would be punished. He knew Alcaeus loved his son, but he loved his daughter because she was a part of his wife, and he knew how that felt because of the love he still harbored for Agape.

"For the first time in King Karpos's life, tears formed in his eyes as he struggled to suppress these strange feelings. He felt his son had failed, as well as Alcaeus's son. He just could not help himself as he mourned and bellowed, 'Larentina! Larentina!'

"Even General Nikephoros experienced mixed feelings. He had prayed for the day that Larentina would die, but now that the day was here, he felt remorse. He could not even explain his own feelings to himself. She was a Spartan and should have died by a Spartan's hand, not a barbarian, and he considered this a dishonorable death. He became angry all over again. Larentina should not have died this way."

*   *   *

"Zeus was furious, enraged, mournful, and vengeful; he was feeling so many emotions at once that he could not even articulate exactly what he was feeling. This was not fun any longer for him. Why did the Spartans think a demigoddess could fight an entire army by herself? What was Larentina thinking? Only a few gods could fight entire legions, not any goddesses. Only his brothers and a few other gods could produce energy in this manner. The Olympian goddesses created creatures and put curses upon mortals, but none had ever tried this before, because they were not strong enough.

"He shook his head in disappointment and cascaded lightning bolts down on the barbarian legions. As he bellowed, Mount Olympus and the ground shook. 'Larentina! You are not invincible, like me!'

"Zeus failed to realize what the Spartans knew perfectly well—Larentina was incapable of such a task. She was being protected by the Spartans because she was ordered to heal, not fight. The Spartans had completely mixed feelings regarding Larentina being among the warriors at all. Both armies immediately stopped fighting on both sides and started running away for fear of Zeus's wrath. Soon the entire battlefield was deserted and became deadly calm. The barbarian legions were completely confused, as was their king. The barbarian king did not know who or what Larentina was, nor did he understand why Zeus was involved.

"Zeus appeared in the middle of the battlefield; he stood one hundred feet tall in his military garb with fists on his hips. He was furious that anyone would dare wound one of his favorite daughters, who had captured his heart in such a short period of time. He was livid and also angry with his own child. He had never felt like this in his entire life, and his head ached as well as his heart."

* * *

"The Spartans began to cheer. Zeus had come to rescue his daughter, and they all knew without a doubt that she was truly Zeus's child. King Karpos and General Nikephoros stood side by side as the god they worshiped appeared before their own eyes. Not only was Larentina truly the daughter of an Olympian god, she was the daughter of the king of the gods. Neither King Karpos nor General Nikephoros could help themselves, as proud smiles formed on their faces. General Nikephoros no longer wanted to kill the She Wolf, but he still wanted to remove her from his army. She was nothing but chaos to him, but a warm spot formed in his heart for her, just for a moment.

"King Karpos knew he could never allow Larentina on the battlefield again, to keep Zeus from destroying all of Sparta."

* * *

"Zeus shrunk to six feet and ran to his daughter's side. Androcles and Lycurgus knelt by Larentina and tried to remove the spear from her side. Lambda licked her mistress's wounds as Zeus watched the two mortal warriors trying to save her. He watched as Lycurgus knelt with Larentina's head in his lap, lovingly combing her hair with his fingertips, trying to comfort her.

"He softly spoke to her. 'Larentina, do not leave me, I need you. You are part of me always and forever. Demigoddesses do not die.' Tears were streaming down the cheeks of this strong and brave Spartan warrior.

"Suddenly, Larentina jolted into a sitting position and cried out, 'Mothers, I have failed you! Mothers, I have failed you!' She fell backward as Lycurgus caught the back of her head. Lycurgus and Androcles just looked at each other with puzzled expressions.

"Zeus did not think much of Larentina's outburst as he continued observing. Androcles said calmly, 'Lycurgus, hold her steady. I am going to try and break the spear close to her flesh, and then we need to turn her, so that I can remove the spear from her back as quickly as I can.'

"Lycurgus nodded his head in agreement.

"Androcles winced as he broke the spear; Larentina moaned in pain as both young men turned her to her side. Androcles removed the spear as quickly as he could, and then he tore two long strips from his tunic sleeve. He put the cloths on the entry and exit wounds.

"Zeus looked all around him; he had never seen so many warriors with tears flowing down their cheeks. These Spartans were a strong and ruthless race, but they were showing compassion and love toward his daughter. He looked around as every Spartan warrior had removed their helmets, and even the Spartan king had removed his helmet and was now standing beside his son.

"Zeus became livid once again and he yelled, 'Which parasite did this?'

"At this point, Zeus did not give a damn that he was about to change history.

"Androcles and Lycurgus, without uttering a word, in unison pointed toward the barbarian, who was already half dead from Lambda's attack. Lambda howled toward the heavens.

"The onlookers watched with shock as Zeus's irises turned from a light gray to a dark reddish brown as lightning bolts charged through them. He snapped his wrist with his index finger pointed toward the barbarian.

"Larentina opened her eyes as she looked at Zeus, and her eyes changed as well. As she looked at Zeus, she murmured, 'Father?' and her eyes closed again.

"The barbarian soldier was lifted into the air as Zeus's magic ripped him apart slowly. The soldier screamed in agonizing pain. The barbarian screamed, 'Forgive me, Zeus, the god I worship, for I did not know she was your daughter!' He pleaded for his life as Zeus tortured him slowly by pulling at his arms and legs. Zeus had no mercy; everyone heard a loud pop and the barbarian's body became nothing but pieces of flesh as it fell to the ground. The only thing that remained intact was the barbarian's head. The barbarian army retreated as they tried to run from Zeus's wrath.

"Zeus stretched out his arm, waved his hand in the air, and killed at least two hundred barbarians that were nearby. He killed them in so many ways, words just could not describe the bloody sight, and he did not even touch them physically.

"Zeus angrily commanded, 'Get away from my daughter!'

"But Androcles and Lycurgus stayed and refused to move.

"Zeus commanded again as he pushed Androcles and Lycurgus away from Larentina with just one thought. 'Move aside, only I can heal her. She belongs to me, not you. I allowed her to live among you because of the love her mother felt toward her, but you have failed to protect her.'

"Naturally, all the Spartans thought Zeus was speaking of Queen Alexis, but he was referring to Agape.

"Zeus bent down and gently picked up his daughter; she shivered and made a soft, painful moan. As Zeus held her in his arms, he kissed her forehead. He murmured in Larentina's ear, 'Daughter, the lengths you will go to for just a moment of my attention.' He smiled sadly at his most beautiful daughter."

* * *

"General Nikephoros, whose feelings regarding Larentina had not changed, shocked himself as the words and emotions came from his own lips. He wielded his sword and commanded Zeus, 'Halt, king of the gods! She is Sparta! When Larentina bleeds, Sparta bleeds! As we worship you and must endure you, so we do for her! We have become accustomed to her presence, her mischievousness, her chaos; without her wildness, we would have no life; Sparta loves her; Sparta hates her; Sparta fears her; Sparta shall kill her; Sparta shall give her life; Sparta needs her because she was made from Sparta, not you, king of the gods! She is and always has been a Spartan wolf, and we will not return her to you because she belongs to us; we will fight and die to keep her!'

"Everyone who heard these words from the general, even King Karpos, nodded their heads in agreement; the warriors slowly removed their swords from their sheaths, preparing to die to keep their She Wolf.

"Zeus just looked at this Spartan general with disdain. He truly did not know how to react to such a brave man who tried to defy him. Nevertheless, Larentina was his and no one else's, so he said nothing as he carried her toward the setting of the sun, with Lambda by his side. They slowly disappeared from sight of the Spartans. Zeus heard Androcles as he faded into the last rays of the sun.

"Androcles dropped to his knees as his sword slipped through his fingers and fell to the ground; he cried, 'Damn you, Zeus! Damn you! I will come for her, somehow. One day!'

"Even though the general and Androcles gave such a passionate plea, Zeus disappeared without saying a word."

* * *

"King Karpos wiped his face with his hand and looked down as General Nikephoros watched him. General Nikephoros, like any great leader, was prepared to take the blame. He said, 'I have failed you, my king, and I have failed Sparta. I am prepared to relinquish my command and all titles. You may execute me if you see fit, my lord.'

"King Karpos put his hand on General Nikephoros's shoulder and said sadly, 'I did not know you felt this way toward our She Wolf. I have heard from many that you disliked her and have on many occasions wished that she did not exist; fear not, for you have not failed, Nikephoros. Zeus entrusted us with his strongest and most beautiful mortal daughter, and we have failed him. As I have said in the past to Alcaeus, it is not our duty to question the gods.

"'I am the one who has truly failed because of the pride I harbored for my son. I fear Alcaeus will never forgive me, but I have fought with demons of vengeance against Alcaeus for so long, and now that justice seems to have found its way, I feel loss and sorrow for my friend.'

"Nikephoros's heart broke after hearing this confession from his king. He knew it was he who had caused Agape to run from King Karpos. He had carried this burden of shame upon his shoulders for so long, but he never realized until now just how much he had hurt his king and friend because of the love Karpos felt toward Agape. He shrugged off these emotions.

"General Nikephoros voiced his thoughts on the matter without showing his true emotions to King Karpos, who did not know of this. 'I still feel mostly the same regarding our presumed She Wolf, but now I have mixed feelings because I did not realize just how much her presence had influenced our customs and the Spartan people. She symbolizes something, but I just do not know what that is.'"

* * *

"Zeus returned to his own bedroom chamber in Mount Olympus and lay his daughter gently on his bed. She was feverish and in and out of consciousness. He examined her wounds as his irises turned maroon with electric static charging through them. He put his palm on her head, and just moments before he touched her wounds to heal them, he watched in amazement as Larentina began healing the wounds herself.

"Zeus gently opened Larentina's eyelids and saw the lightning bolts in her eyes. He saw just how much energy her soul could produce. He was bewildered; she had to be an Olympian to do this. Larentina jolted into a sitting position as she cried out, 'Mothers, I have failed you!' She fell back into unconsciousness.

"Zeus was baffled as Larentina repeated the same outburst. Zeus tried to read her thoughts, but he could not. 'What is happening?' he asked. 'What or who is this being before me? What or who are her mothers?'

"Zeus stood up quickly as Hera abruptly opened the door to his bedroom chamber, yelling, 'How dare you! You have gone too far, Husband! You have the audacity to flaunt your infidelities before me! Do not dare trifle with me!'

"Zeus became angry. 'Get out, Hera; this is not your concern! She is my daughter! If you dare come before me with your jealousies in this manner again, you will pay severely! Now get out!'

"Hera was furious; she threw her head back indignantly and slammed the door behind her."

* * *

"Agape was skinning a rabbit for dinner, and Queen Alexis was tending to her gardens when they both heard Larentina's outcry from the battlefield. Instinctively, both women stopped what they were doing.

"Agape ran toward her sister's home. Queen Alexis pulled a helot from one of her husband's horses and mounted it as fast as she could. Her long tunic was in the way, and she tore it to her knees.

"The sisters met each other within a half hour of Larentina's first cry. Alexis jumped off her horse before it had even stopped. They ran into each other's arms as tears flowed down their cheeks.

"Agape, now angry, screamed at her sister, 'Alexis, you promised me! Where is my daughter? Where is she?'

"Alexis and Agape looked at one another for several moments, and then Alexis cried out, 'She is on the battlefield!'

"Agape screamed, 'In all the heavens; she has been mortally wounded. I see what happened. Do you see, Alexis?'

"Alexis sobbed, 'Yes,' dropping to her knees and trembling. Alexis continued, as excitement crept into her voice, 'Zeus, Zeus has her. Wait, he was going to heal her, but Larentina has astonished him because she is healing herself.'

"Agape paced back and forth between the trees. Both women feared Zeus would discover the truth. Agape kept trying to see and feel Larentina's thoughts, but they were so mixed. 'Wait, she opened her eyes. She is in Zeus's own bedroom chamber, and she felt his thoughts, wait. Oh, um, he doubts …'

"Alexis impatiently asked, 'What is it, Sister? What do you see? How can he doubt she is his daughter?'

"Agape tried to touch Larentina and answered, 'He is questioning what we are!'

"Alexis's voice quivered as she asked, 'What … What … do you mean?'

"Agape let out a frustrated sigh as she answered, 'I do not know. We can only read each other's thoughts and feelings, nothing more.' Agape grew angry and yelled, 'She is not his! She is mine! Sister, he plans on keeping her. What can we do?'

"Alexis contemplated and then spoke her thoughts out loud: 'Agape, let us first calm down, now that we know she will be safe again. All I wanted was for your daughter to change Spartan customs toward its women, to grant us some type of freedom. I love your daughter for all that she has sacrificed for us and this unspoken battle. She has already changed so much. I can walk down the street with my head held high and speak in public with another woman. I walk beside the king instead of behind him. I have even been speaking among the men. Many Spartan women are reaping these rewards since she started mischievously spanking men in public when they continued the old ways with their women. She has not failed us. We can call the forces of nature to help us summon Zeus.'

"Agape looked at her sister with a smirk. 'Yes. We can do that. Do you remember the words of the spell?'

"Alexis smiled back at her sister as she answered, 'Yes. Let us try.'

"Agape quickly made a small fire. Alexis grabbed the goat skin flask that was filled with water. Agape pulled a dagger from her boot as Alexis pulled a dagger from her saddlebag.

"Alexis fearfully commented, 'Agape, we have not done this since we were children.'

"Agape did not reply but just began the incantation: 'Mother earth, hear us. We seek all energy of light from us and all around us to summon and bring before us Zeus, king of the Olympian gods.'

"Agape took her dagger and drew blood from the palm of her hand. Likewise, Alexis did the same. They locked their hands together and dripped their mingled blood first into the small fire and then onto the soil that surrounded it. Alexis sprinkled water into the fire and all around it. The soil quickly drank their blood and the water. In unison, they continued, 'Our blood, which is the energy of life, light, and the water within it, we mingle with soil and fire to become as one. We call the South, North, East, and West winds to mingle with all the energy we have to offer to summon before us Zeus, the king of the Olympian gods.'

"The winds picked up as the fire continued to burn. The soil around the fire began to bubble, and a bright light of energy hovered over the fire in the shape of a circular cage. Slowly, Zeus appeared inside the cage, and he was furious. 'How did you witches do this? I knew something was amiss because Larentina was too strong. Now I know what she is—she is half witch, not half mortal. Now I understand why she has such strong powers. I command you to let me out of here now!'

"Agape lost all her fear and screamed at Zeus, 'Give me back my daughter! I do not care what you think we are, but we are not witches. We are mere mortal women, protecting my child. We only summoned you here to return my daughter to Sparta. You tricked me before, but I am thankful you gave me Larentina. However, you will not take her from me!'

"Naturally, it only took Zeus a moment to break free from the cage of energy that Alexis and Agape created. His anger melted away as he gazed upon the beautiful twins. He said calmly, 'Agape and Alexis, I do know what the two of you are up to, as long as you keep your war of the sexes in your own country. Are you sure you are not witches? Explain to me how my daughter possesses so much energy.'

"Alexis answered, 'We are not witches. We are simply daughters of energy from light, nothing more. We cannot explain why Larentina has so many gifts. We were hoping you would give us the answer. Please forgive us, almighty Zeus, for your daughter is a handful, but she belongs with us. We sympathize with Hera's plight, but we do not want her to destroy Agape's daughter. This is just one reason why she belongs with us; you must put her back on the battlefield, so she can continue her life's journey.'

"Zeus chuckled as he shook his head from side to side. 'I must admit all of you Spartan women can be a handful. I only return her because of you, Agape, and you, Alexis. I will be keeping a closer eye on Larentina, and I will also give her advice to prevent her from trying to take on armies by herself. Do not go against my will regarding this matter. She has proven her courage, but her powers are not strong enough to defeat entire legions, trying to prove herself to mortal men.

"'One last thought to both of you: if you ever summon me in this manner again, the punishment will be severe.'

"Both women fearfully looked to the ground as they acknowledged Zeus's command, saying, 'Yes, my lord.'

"With that, Zeus disappeared."

* * *

"Zeus sat beside Larentina as she slept on his bed. He gazed at his daughter, shaking his head from side to side, and murmured, 'What am I going to do with you, my child? My wife now knows of your existence. I fear your mother is right. There is so much I need to teach you, but for your own protection, you must stay in your mother's realm, and I cannot be with you as your father. I hope someday you will forgive me.'

"Zeus kissed his daughter on her forehead and healed her. Larentina slowly opened her eyes.

"Zeus smiled as he softly spoke. 'Larentina, to kill the beast, you must sever its head first. Its embodiment will always scatter. If not, then remove each of its limbs.' Zeus kissed her on the forehead once more, and with one thought, he sent her back to the Spartans."

* * *

"Unfortunately for Larentina, she only remembered Zeus's last words, which she thought was a dream. She found herself lying by a campfire. As she tried to shake off the confusion, Lycurgus turned over from where he was trying to sleep. He jolted up as he rejoiced, 'Sister! Zeus returned you! What happened?'

"Lycurgus did not even give Larentina a chance to respond as he excitedly grabbed her and stood her on her feet. He held her face between his hands and kissed her all over her face. He hugged her tightly. 'Praise Zeus for returning you to me!'

"All the young agoges around the fire excitedly rose and hugged Larentina. Finally, Androcles grabbed her and, without thinking, kissed her full on the mouth. Androcles looked into Larentina's eyes with a broad smile and teased, 'Praise the gods, Larentina. Did Zeus himself grow weary of you so quickly?'

"The young warriors guffawed at the joke.

"Larentina rolled her eyes with a smile on her face and asked everyone, 'What are you talking about? I do not remember. Was my father Zeus here? Tell me, what has happened? How did I get here?' She looked down at her side as she remembered being wounded. She exclaimed, 'I'm healed? Did Zeus do this? Where is he?'

"All the young agoges told the story of Zeus and his almighty fury. After listening to the heroic deeds of Zeus, Larentina became very upset. For the first time in her life, Zeus had made his presence known, but she couldn't remember it. At that moment, she felt that Zeus was a coward who did not want to face her, and she was very disappointed.

"She did not understand General Nikephoros's actions and words at all, because she knew he did not care for her and wanted her dead. Nothing made sense, and nothing had been accomplished. She had proven nothing, she had failed, but she remembered the words from Zeus and the war continued."

Chapter XXV

"It was only one day later when Larentina found herself healed and alive instead of being in the underworld. Naturally, her Lambda was with her. As she softly rubbed Lambda, Larentina whispered in her ear, 'Go and get your pack. Do not let anyone see you, for I have a plan to kill the barbarian king.' Lambda instinctively understood Larentina and ran off into the darkness of the night.

"Three nights later, Lambda returned and softly nuzzled her mistress to awaken her by the campfire. Larentina quietly awoke and looked to Androcles, who was on guard duty. Androcles said nothing as he watched Larentina follow Lambda into the wooded area.

"At first Androcles thought nothing of Larentina's actions, but after she did not return in a few minutes, he realized she was up to something dangerous. He quietly walked over to Lycurgus and shook him awake. When Lycurgus opened his eyes, Androcles leaned over and murmured, 'I think it is nothing, but Larentina has left the camp with her wolf and has not yet returned.'

"Lycurgus rose to his feet and quickly grabbed his sword.

"Lycurgus did not care who heard him, as he voiced his concerns to Androcles: 'Your suspicions are correct, Androcles. She is up to something. I am sure she is very angry that she has not been allowed to fight with us, but it is for her own good. She may try to finish this war somehow. We must follow her and provide her protection. Whatever she is planning just may end it.'

"By then, several other members of their pack woke up and declared that they were coming to protect their Spartan She Wolf. Of course, Androcles and Lycurgus could do nothing to stop the others from following them.

"Larentina and Lambda's wolf pack found the camp of the barbarian king, Kutir-Nahhunte, on the outskirts of the city, several miles from the battlefield. Larentina quickly and quietly, in the darkness of the woods, removed all her clothing. Since Lambda was solid white, and Larentina had white hair, her plan was to use illusion as her first weapon. She figured that these barbarians were just as superstitious as her own people were.

"Lambda and her pack instinctively knew what Larentina was planning and ran into the camp with no fear of the campfire. They attacked the sleeping men before the soldier standing guard could utter a word.

"King Kutir-Nahhunte was a big man who stood well over six feet tall and weighed at least 350 pounds. His entire body was firm and muscular. His hair was long and pitch black; his beard was black as well; and his eyes were black and slanted. The king as well as the men around him had not bathed in weeks, and the stench of their bodies was unbearable. Their body armor was stained with Spartan blood, as were their spear tips.

"Larentina silently watched in the cover of the darkness as the wolves began fighting the men. After several wolves were killed by the blades of the barbarians, Larentina broke a twig as a signal for the wolf pack to disengage, leaving her white Lambda standing and snarling at the king before she ran into the edge of the darkness behind Larentina.

"Larentina's eyes had already changed as she stooped with both hands on the ground; the men could just barely see her eyes glowing from the light of their fire. She slowly moved her head from left to right, giving the appearance of a wolf's eyes glowing in the darkness. She stood and walked slowly toward King Kutir-Nahhunte in the soft light, as the fire illuminated her figure. The strong wind was already swirling objects around them. Several of the barbarians ran in different directions into the woods because they thought she was some kind of goddess, able to change from a wolf into a woman.

"Larentina heard the screams of the barbarians as the wolves attacked them in the dark woods, but she did not know that her own pack of men were also in the woods, working together with the wolves to kill the barbarians in the darkness.

"Only King Kutir-Nahhunte and six of his men were left standing in the camp. The barbarian king's eyes were wide, and he thought Larentina must be a goddess because she was the most beautiful women he had ever seen. They truly believed that she was the white wolf that had attacked them. The king was scared of her but did not show it; he asked, 'Who are you? What are you? Are you the daughter of Zeus? Are you on the Spartan's side? If so, is Zeus on the Spartan side as well? Was it you that summoned Zeus?'

"Larentina answered him, in a authoritative voice, 'I am Larentina, the She Wolf of the Olympian gods, and daughter of Zeus himself.'

"All six of the king's men immediately kneeled before Larentina, but King Kutir-Nahhunte still stood, looking all around him as if he expected Zeus to appear again. He decided he had better take this She Wolf at her word and knelt before her, asking, 'What do you want of me, Daughter of Zeus?'

"Larentina quickly looked at a sword that had been dropped by one of his men, and it flew into her hand. As she thrust her sword into his chest, she bellowed, 'Die, for slaughtering Spartans!'

"The six barbarian soldiers all stood and began to fight Larentina after seeing their leader killed. The objects that had been swirling around them started hitting them with full force. Lycurgus, Androcles, and the rest of the pack came out of the darkness and met the barbarians' blades before any of them had a chance to touch Larentina.

"Lycurgus struck the blade of the first barbarian who attacked Larentina; he threw her clothes to her as he fought with the barbarian and yelled, 'Sister, have you no shame? Put your clothes on and fight with us!' Lycurgus laughed heartily at his sister. As far as he was concerned, after what he just witnessed, she had earned her place by his side in battle.

"Larentina casually put her clothing back on and laced up her sandals, yelling to her brother, 'I could have handled this myself, thank you very much!' Lycurgus and the rest of the pack guffawed at Larentina's statement, as they continued to fight the barbarians.

"After the last barbarian had fallen, Androcles stabbed him with his sword one more time. He looked over at Larentina, who stood with her hands angrily on her hips. As Androcles playfully shook his head from side to side, he smiled broadly and pointed out, 'My young She Wolf, from what I could tell, you and your wolves needed a little help. I know that I have trained you well, but pray tell me how you were going to fight six men by yourself, and completely naked to boot, after killing their king? I do not think you could have won this battle without us. I fear you have not learned your lesson. Remember, Daughter of Zeus, he is watching you ever so closely. I will not have him take you from us again.'

"Larentina ignored Androcles's flippant comments; still with her hands on her hips, she sarcastically proclaimed to every Spartan man standing there, 'And it took a woman to stop a war! Ha! Not the daughter of Zeus!' In a more serious tone, she continued, 'I do not wish the glory. I want my brother to be the one, for what I did was shameful, but necessary. You all must never tell the true tale of this night!

"'If you plan to join me,' she added, 'prepare yourselves, for this night is not over. We must sever more heads to be truly victorious for Sparta.'

"Through the night, they did the same trickery and killed five of the king's generals.

"After the last killing, there was much talk; all present agreed, even though the true glory of the night belonged to Larentina, that what she had done would be looked upon as shameful, and everyone involved in helping her would be dishonored, so it was Lycurgus and Androcles who brought the heads of King Kutir-Nahhunte and his generals to King Karpos.

"The following morning, King Karpos, General Nikephoros, two other great generals, Androcles, and Lycurgus carried the barbarians' heads on their spears as they led the Spartan legions onto the battlefield. There was already much confusion in the barbarians' army, but after King Karpos threw their king's head toward them, and the other heads followed, they scattered across the land and surrendered. Thebes was reclaimed by the rightful heir."

Chapter XXVI

"The cadets returned to the agoge camp, and after some time, the excitement settled down. Once again, life became somewhat routine. Larentina had started another ritual of going to her paradise every chance she had. She bathed herself by climbing onto the flat rock and letting the cool water spill down over her body. It was very relaxing, and she felt it had magical powers of some sort, because she always felt better after this ritual. She found that swimming in the small, deep pool of water was relaxing as well.

"Unknown to Larentina, Androcles had been falling deeper in love with her as he watched her slowly complete her metamorphosis from a little girl into the most beautiful woman he had ever seen. But he continuously battled with himself regarding his true feelings, a conflict that was with him for a very long time. He would proclaim his love for her and then deny it to himself, but he did his best to conceal it. Androcles was only interested in one woman: Larentina. He didn't need to know any other. He knew she was half goddess and a very strong-willed individual, and he was not the only man in the Spartan military who had his eye on her.

"He had many conversations with many soldiers—not just the young, but older ones as well—joking and laughing about taking her and being done with it. But most of them had the same reasoning: 'Not only is she a princess, but a goddess, daughter of duty. I shall not lay a hand on her in fear the gods would come down on all of us. Zeus made her so perfect because he is testing us as mortal men. Let her enjoy her innocence for as long as we can bear it.'

"Androcles had been in numerous fistfights with many of the other young cadets and young soldiers who were disrespectful toward Larentina. They just did not know her as he did. On many occasions, he found himself allowing her to win a fight or outwit him, but after returning from battle, and being a keeper of her secret, he knew that she did not need to be coddled any longer.

“Androcles had to admit to himself that his pack, for which he had been responsible, was suffering from a lack of discipline because of her presence. Goddess or not, men do stupid things around such beauty, and he had witnessed it firsthand.

“Numerous times, he had lost his focus when she was close to him; he found himself taking deeper breaths just so he could smell the sweet fragrance of wildflowers on her. The temptation was too much for him to bear, and he decided to follow her and see if he could speak with her alone. He wanted to tell her his true feelings because time was running out. The twins would complete their training in a few weeks and become warriors, and he feared he might never have another chance. It was time for him to be completely honest with himself and to stop fighting his own feelings.

“Androcles had to be very careful following Larentina. In addition to her heightened senses, she also had her wolf with her at all times, and that made it even more difficult to go undetected.

“Late one afternoon on a very hot summer day, he saw her walking with a bundle in her hands and Lambda close beside her. He followed her as she slowly walked from the training grounds. No one really paid any attention to her; she was always given this type of freedom, unlike the men in training. He never understood why she was allowed this type of solitude. There never was any type of pattern to her wandering off alone. He acted like he didn’t notice either and waited until he could not see her any longer before following in the direction she went.

“He was very lucky because he had been downwind as he followed Larentina, and her wolf did not detect him. He stayed far away from them, and momentarily, he lost Larentina’s trail, but he rediscovered it again when he heard her singing.

“He pushed back some of the heavy foliage to see where Larentina’s voice was coming from; when he looked up, he saw her beautiful, naked body standing under a waterfall with a pool of water surrounding it. He did not see Lambda, but he could not take his eyes from the demigoddess. He let out a soft sigh as he took in her beauty. He thought, *No wonder the barbarian king and his men thought she was a goddess, because she is so beautiful and strong.*

“All of sudden, he heard growling and looked to his side, where Lambda was standing. The wolf started barking and growling at him, but Androcles stood his ground in front of the wolf.

"Larentina yelled, 'Who's there?'

"Androcles answered her by calling out, 'It's me, Androcles!'

"Larentina dove into the water and swam toward him as he watched. Lambda continued growling at him. Larentina reached the bank where Androcles was standing and commanded, 'Lambda, enough!' The wolf obediently stopped growling and ran off.

"Larentina looked up at Androcles and asked in a soft voice, 'Why did you follow me? This is my secret place.'

"Androcles shyly answered, 'Princess Larentina, I had to seek you out so that I may tell you my feelings.'

"With a puzzled expression on her face, Larentina said, 'Well, then join me and we will talk.'

"Androcles quickly stripped off his clothing and jumped into the water; by this time Larentina had swum out to the middle of the water, closer to the waterfall. He swam around in circles, closer to her.

"Larentina smiled and felt unusually warm, because his naked body was so close to her. She had felt this before when she had stood close to him, but this time they were both naked in the water.

"He was so close to her that she started to feel uncomfortable about having him join her. In a soft voice that she had never heard him use before, Androcles said, 'I love you, Larentina, I always have. You have bewitched me. I want you to be my queen and bear my children.'

"Before Larentina could respond, he kissed her gently, yet passionately. Larentina found herself accepting his advances; she responded to his passionate kiss, as he wrapped his arms around her waist. She wrapped her arms around his neck for a moment.

"Larentina quickly pushed him away. 'But I do not really know anything about you, Androcles.'

"Androcles asked, 'What do you want to know?'

"Larentina nervously and shyly murmured, 'Well, I have never asked who your family is, because that has been the rule.'

"Androcles asked, 'We have been living together for years, and you never asked anyone, not even your brother?'

"Larentina blushed as she answered, 'Well, no. I was too busy training and never really thought about it. I never heard anyone call you by a title because that has been the rule; so no, I do not know anything about you.'

"Androcles softly chuckled as he swam close to her, and he kissed her again. Larentina could not help but return the passionate kiss. After a few moments, Larentina came back to her senses and again gently pushed Androcles away from her. She asked again, 'You did not answer my question. How can I answer your question if I do not know anything about you?'

"Androcles swam close to her again and answered her in a seductive voice. 'I gave you a hint earlier when I asked you to be my queen. I'm the firstborn son of King Karpos.' Then, he leaned closer to kiss Larentina again.

"This time, Larentina pushed Androcles away from her with force, swam back to the bank, and quickly put her clothing back on.

"Androcles was very confused and yelled, 'What? What have I done?'

"Larentina angrily answered, 'It is not what you have done, it's who you are—the son of Karpos!' She took off running and left Androcles there.

"Androcles was confused. The way she had returned his kisses led him to believe that she was going to give herself to him this very day. What had his father done to Larentina for her to hate him so? He was completely bewildered regarding the entire incident. Any other woman would have been pleased to discover he was a prince and heir to the throne. It would figure a half goddess would react as a mortal woman, but she acted so strangely over something they should be proud of. He would never understand Larentina—never.

"Larentina started crying as she ran back to the training grounds. The entire time, she wondered how she could have feelings of love for the son of a tyrant, the son of a donkey's ass. As far as she was concerned, she would never have anything else to do with Androcles—never.

"It was time to tell her brother the truth, so he would protect her from this son of a beast, because she did not trust her own decisions any longer regarding Androcles. He was so handsome and charming. He had sacrificed so much for her and had always treated her as an equal. How could he be the son of Karpos? Androcles appeared to be so different!"

Chapter XXVII

"Androcles had to find out the truth, so as soon as he arrived back at the training grounds, he asked for a few days' leave. Of course, he was granted his request because he was, after all, an honored cadet.

"He immediately jumped on his horse and rode to his father's home. Upon arrival, he went straight into the king's eating room where his father, his father's wife, a few members of the gerousia council, some ephors, and his younger siblings were all gathered around the large table, drinking, eating, and having a merry old time.

"They all looked up in surprise as Androcles came in and angrily demanded, 'Father, I must speak to you in private, immediately.'

"King Karpos responded, in an irritated voice, 'What is this? How dare you interrupt me? As you can see, we are eating. What are you doing here anyway? What is so urgent that you speak to me with that tone?'

"Androcles realized he had offended his father and humbly answered, in a calmer tone, 'My father, my king, I apologize for disrespecting you so, but I urgently need to speak with you regarding something important.'

"King Karpos let out an irritated sigh, as he decided to give an audience to his son. 'You are forgiven, my son; come and we will walk out into the courtyard.'

"King Karpos then commanded the male helot, 'You there, pour my son a goblet of wine.' Androcles took the goblet, gulped the contents, and held it out for a refill, which he was promptly given. After Androcles received the second goblet of wine, King Karpos gestured for his son to follow him into the courtyard.

"When they were standing in the middle of the courtyard, King Karpos stopped, turned to face his firstborn, and asked, 'Now what is so important that you had to come home and speak with me?'

"Androcles chose his words carefully before speaking because he did not want to anger his father. 'My father, my king, I am deeply in love with the most beautiful, strongest goddess in all the lands, and I asked her to be my queen, but when she discovered I was your son, she ran from me without giving me an answer.'

"King Karpos immediately became angry, and his voice showed it. 'So what?' he yelled. 'Just take her! What kind of man are you? She may be a goddess, but she is still a half-mortal woman and is nothing more than property! Just take her and be done with it!'

"Androcles became indignant and said angrily, 'Not only do I love this woman, I worship her as a goddess. After all, she is the daughter of Zeus! If you were any other man, Father … How dare you? She is not property, but a proud, strong Spartan warrior! She has proven herself repeatedly! She is not just a woman! You have no idea who I speak of!'

"King Karpos retorted in an angrier and even louder voice, 'Yes, I know exactly who you mean! There is no other woman that fits that description except for the daughter of the Agiad house! Besides, it has already been arranged that you will marry her when she becomes of age! How can you tremble to a mere woman? She must be a witch as well, to have such a strong spell on my son.'

"Androcles, still angry, argued, 'That may be true, Father, but I do not care. I have seen her powers! I am now not good enough for her because of you! What have you done to make her reject me so? I demand the truth from you, for I am your son!'

"King Karpos became even angrier as he bellowed, 'How dare you speak to me in this manner? I answer to no one, especially my own son, who is bewitched like I was by a mere woman, especially from the house of Agiad. I do not give a damn what that Oracle said!'

"A puzzled expression came over Androcles's face as he looked at his father, and in a calmer tone he asked, 'Father, what do you mean, "what the Oracle said"?'

"King Karpos realized the wine had loosened his tongue and he had said too much, but at this point, he did not care. After all, this was his son he was speaking to, and it was time he knew some of the truth.

"King Karpos let go of his anger as he heavily breathed, 'Son, I guess it's time for you to know the truth.'

"Androcles, still bewildered, asked, 'What truth, Father?'

"King Karpos said simply, 'I need more wine.' He instructed one of the helots standing close by to go and bring more wine. Both king and son solemnly gazed at each other for a few minutes in silence. The helot returned with a flask of wine and refilled their goblets. Both men took a heavy drink.

"King Karpos ordered all the helots to leave the courtyard. After the helots disappeared into the house, King Karpos turned toward his son and confessed, 'Alcaeus and I did not relay the entire prophesy of the Oracle of Delphi after we sought her advice all those years ago. What we did not say was that if Larentina discovered the real truth, I would die a dishonorable death by her own hand.

"'We did tell part of the prophesy regarding the great battle between the gods. Larentina will become so powerful that Zeus himself will bow down before her. She will be the goddess who in essence will weaken Zeus's wife, Hera.

"'You and Lycurgus will treat women as equals and not as property. It is Lycurgus's destiny to protect Larentina. If we obey the gods and protect Larentina, she will protect Sparta from Hera's wrath. The future of Sparta rests on Larentina's shoulders, but it is also foretold that one of my children will have the burden to protect Larentina and think as she does. I did not want this for you, but now I see it is the will of the gods. I cannot fight the destiny that the gods have laid out for you. You, my son, are the future of Sparta as well. Everything the Oracle has foretold has come to pass as truth. So if it is truth you are seeking, my son, you now have it.'

"Androcles was shocked at the information his father had just given him. Everything was so focused on Larentina, he had never paid attention to the rest of the tale regarding one of King Karpos's children. Androcles had not realized that it was himself they were referring to, but why did Larentina become so angry? There was still something missing from his father's story. Therefore, he asked, 'Father, why would Larentina be angry with the entire truth of the Oracle's prophesy, which pertained to you? Why would the Oracle prophesize Larentina killing you over this? It does not make sense to me.'

"King Karpos took another sip of his wine and answered, 'I do not know. I did not understand the riddles and the ramblings of the Oracle. The gerousia council has been arguing over the Oracle's prophesies for years. All I know is that her meaning will appear right in front of us when it happens. Just look at you, my own son. We know now that the Oracle was talking about you.

"'Neither Alcaeus nor I understand what truth will appear in front of Larentina for her to kill me dishonorably. We have discussed this for years amongst the two of us. I have done nothing to my friend or his household, and he knows this. He and I still do not know what I have done to warrant such prophesy, but I do know now she has discovered some type of truth that only the gods are aware of.

"'I did not want it to be so; maybe that is why Larentina has rejected you. Only the gods can understand women, or even goddesses, for that matter.'

"Androcles did not push his father any further; he simply voiced his gratitude: 'Thank you, Father, for telling me the entire truth. I will speak with Larentina myself to understand her mixed feelings regarding me and her hatred of you.'

"Both men hugged each other; Androcles decided to stay a few days and get to know his father again."

Chapter XXVIII

"Larentina had not spoken to her brother of the truth. She brushed it off, as she has done all these years. She felt relieved that she did not have to face Androcles because when he returned to the barracks, she saw him talking with one of their commanders, and then he immediately left. She assumed he must have taken some type of leave. She did not know for sure and really did not care.

"Larentina's pack was the top pack of them all, not just because she had defeated and killed another agoge to receive the honor to go into battle, but because they were truly the strongest, and they were all loyal to Androcles and the twins.

"As they were practicing their fighting skills one morning, Androcles rode up and stopped his horse close to where Larentina was demonstrating her fighting skills with another young cadet.

"Larentina ignored Androcles, who was just sitting on his horse watching her. He commanded, 'Larentina, come here! I will speak to you now!"

"Larentina stopped practicing and looked at Androcles with a deadly stare, but she did not move toward him. She stood her ground. Androcles repeated his orders, in an even louder voice, 'Larentina, I order you to come before me!' Larentina gave him another deadly stare and refused to approach him. After dismounting his horse, Androcles yelled in anger this time, 'Larentina, you will obey me or be lashed!'

"By this time, the entire camp was watching Androcles and Larentina. She was being extremely disrespectful to her upper chain of command by ignoring Androcles's orders.

"Lycurgus could not understand why his sister was being deliberately insubordinate. Lycurgus yelled, 'Larentina, obey your superior's commands now!'

"Larentina yelled back, 'I will not, he is undeserving!'

"Lycurgus, along with the rest of the pack, stared at her in total disbelief. She had always obeyed orders without question. This was not like her at all. She had absolutely no fear of the consequences of her actions. She knew she would be lashed, and she appeared not to care.

"Androcles became so angry that he ran to the whipping post, picked up the whip, and walked quickly toward her. Larentina prepared herself to fight him as she continued to stand her ground.

"Larentina's eyes had already changed and the wind had started swirling as it picked up objects surrounding her. The body armor, helmets, swords, and spears that were resting near the barracks flew up and took the shape of a man's figure, but there was no one wearing them. The marching armor surrounded Androcles and Larentina. She threw her shield to the ground, firmly gripped her sword in one hand, and bent one leg in front of her with her other arm outstretched, preparing to catch the end of the whip.

"Androcles had only seen her use her gifts a few times like this. He did not fear her, no matter how strong her magic was. All the young agoges and cadets instinctively moved further away from this fight, in fear they would be struck by one of the flying objects. Many who witnessed this now feared her even more.

"As Androcles came within a foot of her, he simply stopped and dropped the whip to the ground. His shoulders sagged in defeat and he let out a heavy sigh, saying, 'Larentina, you will be the death of me, for I cannot lash you. I must protect you. I love you, please yield to me!'

"All the young soldiers muttered to each other in total disbelief that one of their leading cadets was actually begging, let alone to Larentina, a woman, goddess or not. What other powers did she possess over this strong leader?

"Lycurgus had to do something because Larentina was causing his eirena, Androcles, to lose the respect of his men. Lycurgus knew Larentina possessed some unknown power over men, but she still amazed him with her goddess powers.

"With sword in hand, Lycurgus ran full speed toward his sister and stopped when he was between Larentina and Androcles. Lycurgus struck at Larentina's sword, and they fought vigorously against one another. Lycurgus barked, 'You will yield to your superior now! If you cannot fight Androcles without magic, then do not fight him at all!'

"As they were fighting sword to sword, move against move, Larentina retorted angrily at her brother, 'I will not!' They fought hard and strong against one another as if they were enemies battling for their very lives.

"Lycurgus commanded his sister once again, 'Stop using magic! If you continue using magic, you are nothing but a coward.' Immediately the wind stopped, and everything dropped to the ground. Lycurgus was relieved that he still had some influence over his sister, but he realized he was losing control very quickly.

"Androcles stood there frozen for a moment, stunned. He too now realized Lycurgus and he were losing control over Larentina. Both the Spartan princes were baffled and had no idea how to regain it.

"Knowing his true destiny was to protect Larentina at all cost, he wielded his sword against Lycurgus. Lycurgus then found himself fighting between Larentina and Androcles.

"Unknown to anyone in any of the packs, General Nikephoros had been in camp for some time, watching all the soldiers as they practiced their fighting skills. Several commanders were by his side, speaking with him and giving him updates on Larentina as well as her brother.

"As the commanders moved toward the commotion, General Nikephoros wisely ordered them, 'Halt! They are the future of Sparta; we will let them fight it out.' The commanders obeyed him. If General Nikephoros had fear of the magic Larentina possessed, he did not show it.

"General Nikephoros was very pleased that this was happening because he was the soldier Bion had assigned to see Larentina did not survive agoge. He had planned two attempts and both had failed. This was delicious because who was better suited to have her kicked out of his army than the two princes of Sparta? After what had happened on the battlefield, his heart was not to see her killed, but to remove her from his army, dishonorably. Goddess or not, she had no place among warriors.

"Larentina resumed fighting against Androcles; before they knew it, all three of them were fighting each other. None of the other cadets knew who to root for, so they cheered for all three of these great warriors. No one had any idea what the fight was about to begin with.

"As all three of them were fighting against one another, Larentina angrily demanded, 'Tell the truth to my brother, Androcles! I know you went to see your father. Did he tell you the truth?'

"They continued fighting as Lycurgus chimed in, 'What truth?'

"Androcles said loudly with conviction, 'Yes, my father told me the truth of the Oracle's prophesy, the entire truth!'

"Larentina aggressively struck harder against Androcles, and he held her in abeyance with the strength of his own sword as he pushed her away. He did not want to hurt her, and he knew he could. He knew every weakness and strength of her sword skills.

"Lycurgus, now completely annoyed for being ignored, spat out, 'What entire truth? What are you talking about?'

"Androcles struck harder at Lycurgus, and Larentina struck toward him. Androcles maneuvered quickly against her blow and, with conviction once again, answered Lycurgus, 'Larentina will kill my father by her own hand, and I, the child of Karpos, will protect Larentina and help her prepare for the great battle between the gods!'

"Larentina again struck harder against Androcles, and the twins, both baffled regarding Androcles's statement, replied in unison, 'What? What are you talking about?'

"Larentina angrily replied, 'Yes, I will kill your father and see that he dies a dishonorable death! But he still did not tell you the entire truth!'

"Androcles was now completely bewildered; as they continued the heated sword fight, he yelled, 'What other truth is there? My father does not know of it!'

"Lycurgus immediately stopped fighting and threw his sword down. He glared at Larentina and then looked at the man he had admired most of his life. He scolded both of them, 'I'm disgusted with the both of you! Why hasn't the entire truth of the Oracle's prophesy been told to me?'

"Larentina continued to fight Androcles and yelled, 'That is not the truth I refer to!'

"Androcles and Larentina ignored Lycurgus and continued to fight against each other. Larentina was growing tired. Before she knew it, Androcles had tripped her; she lost her balance and fell to the ground, landing on her back. As she lay there on the ground, arms outstretched above her head, Androcles placed the point of his blade in the middle of her throat. If she moved a fraction of an inch, the sharp blade would pierce her flesh. Androcles looked down at Larentina and commanded in a deadly, firm voice, 'Woman, yield to me, now!'

"Larentina looked up at him with a deadly glower once again; she gritted her teeth in defiance and snarled, 'Never!' She grabbed a handful of sandy dirt and threw it in his face. She pushed herself up, sword in hand, and prepared to strike Androcles with all her might. Before she had a chance, Lycurgus knocked the sword out of Androcles's hand, as Androcles was wiping the grit out of his eyes with the other hand.

"Lycurgus then pointed his blade toward his sister, who was now standing and poised to kill Androcles. She stopped as her brother angrily ordered, 'Enough!' Lycurgus glowered at Androcles and swore in a very deadly tone, 'If you harm one more hair on my sister's head, I swear I will kill you here and now!'

"Androcles fell to his knees at Larentina's feet and looked up at her in defeat; he said, 'Lycurgus, then let Larentina kill me now, for I cannot bear anymore! I am bewitched by her! I just wanted her to yield to me. I would never really hurt her because I love her. I told her that, but once she discovered I was Karpos's son, she acted like I was not good enough for her.'

"Lycurgus looked at Androcles in total disbelief; he could not understand what his sister has done to this great warrior. He glared at his sister and asked, 'Why have you done this to this great warrior? He has been put on this earth to train you, protect you, and probably die for you. Why in the gods' names have you done this?'

"Larentina looked at her brother and rolled her eyes, brushing the sandy dirt from her clothes, and answered irritably, 'I did not do this to him; his father did!'

"Androcles rose to his feet, totally frustrated, and said, 'By the gods, I know not of what you speak! My father has done no wrong to your father's household.'

"Larentina angrily answered, 'It's not my household, it is our blood that he has wronged!'

"Androcles, now even more frustrated at Larentina, pleaded with her, 'In all the heavens, Goddess, how can I right a wrong that I do not know of?'

"Larentina just glowered at her brother as Lycurgus let out a frustrated sigh. He let go of his anger and calmly answered, 'I will speak with my sister. There has been enough fighting and bickering this day between the three of us. We are the future of Sparta, so that much we all agree to! We will talk later and prepare for the war that has already begun in the heavens.'

"All the cadets and soldiers, young and old, cheered. The ones holding their shields beat them with their swords at Lycurgus's statements. The three of them looked around and saw that they were not only surrounded by their fellow cadets, but several legions were watching and cheering. There must have been at least a thousand.

"General Nikephoros looked to his left and then to his right, as he stated to all the commanders around him with pride in his voice, 'See, I told you they are the future of Sparta. See how they are working it out without our interference? They will be great leaders one day.' One of the commanders almost corrected the general, but he held his tongue in fear of the consequences and just shook his head; he remembered the numerous times over the past years when General Nikephoros had commented that Larentina, goddess or not, should not be taught to fight. A woman's place should always be beneath men and giving birth to strong Spartan warriors—men, not women.

"General Nikephoros's true thoughts were that Larentina was just a mortal woman, who just happened to know some type of sorcery. He trusted her instincts regarding war and protecting the state, but he truly believed she was nothing more than a witch, and not a very strong one at that. She could very easily be the daughter of Zeus, but he felt her powers did not come from the king of the gods, and that is why he believed her to be a witch of some sort. The general truly could not make his mind up about what Larentina was, but he still didn't like the fact that she was in his army. General Nikephoros had been avoiding Bion, and he had openly disobeyed Bion's orders to have her killed.

"This fight with one woman will be told over and over again throughout the ages; Larentina had simultaneously fought two great warriors, who were destined to be the future kings of Sparta. She even had one of them on his knees before her.

"The Spartan warriors will even have images of Larentina carved or painted on their shields. Throughout the ages, the memory of her human form would fade, but the image of the wolf would replace it. The myth, the legend, the legacy had just begun!"

Chapter XXIX

"Naturally, Zeus had been observing Larentina more frequently of late because of her increasing displays of her powers, and he was becoming more proud of his child. She did not have a personality like Hercules or Perseus, but she was increasingly becoming more defiant of the natural order of things. His main concern was that she was a girl; Zeus truly did not know how to handle this in the mortal realm. She was nothing like Athena or any of his full-blooded Olympian children, who feared him.

"Zeus often forgot his promises, and he didn't even remember being with Agape, but then he had fathered hundreds of children and naturally could not remember all the women he had been with. He loved mortal women as well as goddesses.

"Zeus decided he had best not interfere in his daughter's destiny at this time, but he enjoyed checking in on her from time to time. He never knew what she would be doing, and he loved how she played with the minds and hearts of mortal men."

* * *

"Of course, Lycurgus was still angry with his sister; and that night after everyone was asleep, he snuck into Larentina's private room in the barracks and murmured, 'Larentina, meet me at your paradise. I want to speak with you immediately.'

"Larentina turned her head away from her brother because she could not look him in the eye; she murmured with apprehension, 'You do not understand, Brother, and I really do not know how to tell you the truth.'

"Lycurgus angrily whispered, 'Larentina, look at me.'

"Larentina turned her head and looked up at him. Lycurgus knelt down beside her bed and said in an agitated murmur, 'You will tell me the truth this very night; no more excuses or trickery. Do you understand?

Now get up and get dressed. I will be there shortly behind you.' Lycurgus did not say another word; he just left Larentina's room.

"Larentina quickly dressed and quietly snuck out of the barracks. When she got close to the edge of the woods, she broke into a run with Lambda close by her side.

"Androcles, who could not sleep because of the events of the day, was leaning up against the corner of the barracks in the shadows. Larentina did not notice him, but he saw her running away from the barracks and toward the forest.

"At first, Androcles was going to follow her, but something restrained him. He was glad he did not follow her, because within minutes, he saw Lycurgus walk into the woods. Androcles realized that Lycurgus was going to make his sister tell the truth and explain her actions of this day.

"Androcles desperately wanted to know what his father had done, but he decided to wait a few moments before going to Larentina's paradise, allowing the siblings time to talk first. Then maybe Lycurgus would tell him the truth before the night was over.

"It was a hot, full-moon night, and Larentina was hot and sweaty from her run, so she decided to cool off in the pool of water, as she had done with increasing frequency over the last few years. She hung her clothing on a tree branch and dove into the cool water.

"Moments later, Larentina heard her brother call, 'Larentina, I'm here!'

"She responded, 'I'm here in the water, Brother.'

"Lycurgus was also hot and sweaty and decided to join his sister, so he undressed, hung his clothing next to Larentina's, dove into the water, and swam to her.

"Lycurgus could see his sister's face in the moonlight and impatiently demanded, 'Well, Sister, tell me what all this nonsense was about today.'

"Larentina let out an apprehensive sigh, went around her brother, and then swam into the shallow water. Lycurgus followed her and asked in a softer tone, 'Well?'

"Larentina still didn't answer him. Instead, she simply got out of the water and dressed. Lycurgus followed her and dressed as well; both remained silent.

"Larentina sat down on a large rock close to the waterfall. Again, Lycurgus followed and sat down beside her; Larentina still resisted telling him the truth. Instead, she simply asked, 'Brother, do you remember asking about the eirena from the other pack that disappeared many years ago?'

"Lycurgus looked at his sister, who was staring out onto the pool of water illuminated by the moonlight, and simply answered, 'Yes.'

"Larentina continued to gaze at the water and, without looking at her brother, continued, 'Well, I killed him because he caught me taking food from Agape; that was the last feast I brought for you and our pack.'

"Lycurgus was puzzled; he wondered why his sister used the word *taking* instead of *stealing*. He still said nothing and waited for Larentina to continue.

"After a few moments of silent contemplation, Larentina let out a heavy sigh, as if a great burden had been lifted from her shoulders. As she continued to look at the water and not at her brother, she asked, 'Do you remember the stories of our birth, and the mystery of how a gerousia council member disappeared that night?'

"Lycurgus scowled at his sister before answering, 'Yes.'

"Larentina blurted out, 'Queen Alexis, whom we know as our mother, killed him that night.'

"Lycurgus leaned back, looked up to the heavens, and asked in an agitated voice, 'You believe our mother committed murder. Why would she do such a thing?'

"Larentina let out another heavy sigh, looked upon her brother's angry face, and replied sadly, 'See, Brother, you only know a small part of the truth, and you are already acting as if I lie. I do not lie and I never did. I reacted the same way when I learned the truth; this is why I did not want to tell you. This is our family secret, and you cannot tell another living soul, or both of us will be killed.'

"Lycurgus contemplated his thoughts before asking, 'Why would we be punished if it was our mother who committed such a heinous crime?'

"Larentina let out another heavy sigh. 'Brother, swear to me that you will never tell what you are about to learn.'

"Lycurgus studied his sister's face, as if he were memorizing every detail; he also let out a heavy sigh as he realized that his sister was carrying such a heavy burden on her shoulders. 'We are one, so I must know the truth that you carry alone upon your back, for it must be my burden as well. I swear it.'

"After hearing these words from her brother's own lips, she proceeded to tell him everything she had learned. Larentina began, 'I was not stealing the food; Agape was giving it to me. The eirena had followed me that night, and I was afraid he would speak the truth of what I was really doing. I had to protect our family; that is the reason I killed him.' Lycurgus tried to comprehend the magnitude of the truth that would affect their lives.

"After listening to every word of Larentina's story, Lycurgus let out another heavy sigh. 'It is much to swallow, Sister, but I believe you. I agree with our real mother that you and I belong here. As you and I are one, so Agape and Alexis are one, because they are twins also. You are the daughter of Zeus, and I am your protector no matter who really gave birth to us. You are a princess, and I will be the future king, because Alexis is our mother and King Alcaeus is our father.

"'Now regarding King Karpos, we will seek vengeance together, not just you alone. When the time is right, we will know what to do, because as of right now, you only know Agape's truth and no other's. I believe that it is the truth as she knows it, but that does not necessarily make it the complete truth, just her version of it.

"'Androcles, on the other hand, is a completely different man. He thinks the way you and I do. He treats all women and men as equals, maybe because of your presence for all these years, but he truly loves you, and it is a good match. You have just told me how you feel about him, how you want to be with him, love him, and give him some of your strength as you give me, but the decision of giving you to any man belongs to your father, Zeus, your guardian, King Alcaeus, or myself.'

"Larentina did not say anything; instead, she held her tongue. She needed neither man nor a god to give her permission as to whom she would love.

"Lycurgus finally asked the most important question: 'Why do you really feel disappointed in Androcles? I know you; it could not be simply because of his father. Why do you love him anyway? You have me; you need no other. I'm your brother and part of yourself; no other mortal man could fill that.'

"Larentina shook her head in disappointment. 'You of all should know me, but you know nothing of my heart. I simply love him because he was willing to die for me. What is so sad, Brother, is that he is still willing. He worships the ground I walk upon. Over the years, instead of leading me, he has allowed me to lead. When he confessed he was Karpos's son, he became flawed, somehow, to me. After all, I have held him on a pedestal since the night he saved me. I revered him in the highest regard, as I have you. What is my true purpose in this life? You do not even know, Brother. You are, after all, the elder of us; even if it is only by a few minutes. So should you not be the wiser? I love him, Brother, because he has been there when I needed someone the most, and you were not.

"'He defies me and he does not lead me, but instead he inspires me as you do because he truly is my match. He is everything you are not; he is the one who completes me.'

"Lycurgus was completely taken aback; he became jealous and voiced his displeasure: 'I cannot believe you would put another above your own flesh and blood! You have hurt me deeply! I am your brother! You have magic, Sister, but it is not as strong as that of the deities! You have needed, and always will need, me, and no other!'

"Larentina tried to kiss her brother on the cheek because she did not mean to hurt him, but he turned his head and raised his hand, rejecting her gesture of sisterly love.

"Larentina became exasperated. 'How dare you! I need no man, nor permission from anyone to love another. Especially permission from my own brother! I may be a thorn in your side, but you can be an arrogant, pompous ass. You do not know all the answers, but neither do I. So let this go, Brother. After all, you asked.'

"Lycurgus became defensive. 'You may have a valid point, Sister, but that is respect to King Alcaeus, Zeus, and myself. These are our customs, and you must honor them. I cannot believe you would blatantly defy them. I am jealous that you put Androcles above me.'

"The twins hugged as they forgave one another. Larentina lovingly whispered in her brother's ear, 'No man will ever be above you, Brother, but Androcles will be beside you in my heart. After all, Brother, you are the deed of wolf. I consider you both warrior gods.'

"Unknown to Larentina and Lycurgus, Androcles had arrived and overheard the last words Lycurgus and Larentina spoke. He stood silently in the foliage surrounding the large flat rock as the twins argued over him. Larentina actually put him above Lycurgus and considered both of them gods. He knew he would know the truth soon, and he knew his friend had guided Larentina back to her senses regarding him. There was hope in Androcles's heart once again that he would have Larentina's heart.

"As Androcles watched Larentina's expression in the bright moonlight, she blushed slightly as she began thinking warm thoughts about Androcles once again. Larentina smiled and softly spoke to her brother. 'You are right, my brother, I do truly love this man, for he is a strong, handsome, good, and decent man. He will give me strong and healthy children. He truly is nothing like his father, whom I consider a donkey's ass and tyrant.'

"With concern in his voice, Lycurgus responded, 'But Sister, you must tell him the truth of his father someday.'

"Larentina asnwered, 'I might someday, but not this day. I want to compete in the Olympics, Brother, and I must stay untouched by man.'

"Naturally, Lycurgus was arrogant and subconsciously considered himself far superior to Larentina. Even Larentina only allowed a few men these types of indulgences toward her because she only admired a few mortal men in her heart as mortal gods of strength, courage, honor, duty, and so much more than herself. In her heart, she knew men would be men and women would be women.

"Lycurgus leaned back and lifted his face toward the heavens as he roared in laughter at Larentina's plans. 'You are a woman! You know they do not allow women to compete in the games.'

"Larentina responded, with a devilish smile, 'But I'm also half god, you beast of a man, not to mention I am also a virgin and will remain so until I have a crown of laurel leaves placed upon my head.'

"Androcles could not bear it any longer; he emerged from his hiding place and playfully guffawed at Larentina. 'In all the heavens, my goddess, how will you accomplish such a feat?'

"Larentina demanded, 'How dare you come upon us unannounced.'

"Lycurgus became serious again and asked Androcles, 'How much did you hear standing there hidden like a thief in the night?'

"Androcles continued to smile as he sat down next to Larentina and proudly answered, 'Just the part where Larentina announced her love for me. That is enough for me; she can either tell me the truth regarding my father or not. I do not care any longer, as long as I know I have her heart. So we must decide how we can get my goddess into the Olympics.'

"Lycurgus realized that Androcles would not be so playful if he had heard anything about the twins seeking revenge against King Karpos. Lycurgus laughed at his friend and teased, 'You two are going to be the death of me yet.'

"Larentina gazed upon the beautiful smile of Androcles as he joked, 'I deny that, for it is your sister who will be the death of both of us.'

"Both young men guffawed. Larentina teased, 'No, you are both wrong. The two of *you* will be the death of *me*.'

"All three continued their comments as their anger melted away.

"Androcles, still chuckling, flippantly commented, 'May the gods have mercy on all three of us for making such fools of ourselves this past day, but seriously, if Larentina will not give herself to me until she has been crowned with laurel leaves, then it is my duty as her future husband to make this true.'

"Lycurgus replied with a chuckle, 'Pray, tell me, future brother, how will we as mere mortal men make such a thing happen?'

"Larentina simply announced, 'There are no laws that I am aware of stating that a goddess cannot compete.'

"Both men nodded their heads in agreement. Androcles added, 'Then we must find out how to make it happen. We have less than a year to prepare.'

"Larentina voiced the obvious: 'We are Spartan warriors; how much planning do we need? I only wish to compete in running and archery, and the chariot races as well.'

"Lycurgus responded, 'I would consider it a great honor to compete in the disc events; I also would enjoy competing against you in the chariot races.'

"Androcles chimed in, 'I would like to compete in the javelin competitions and chariot races as well. So it is settled, since the Agiad house is going to compete, it is only fitting that the Eurypontids house competes as well.'

"Androcles leaned into Larentina and looked at her beautiful brown eyes with a smile. Larentina blushed, smiled as she looked into his beautiful blue eyes, and said softly, 'We agree, it is only fitting.'

"Lycurgus yawned. 'Okay, okay, we will make this so, but not tonight. We will plan and talk more another day. I'm headed back to the training grounds. Larentina, come.'

"Larentina gazed at Androcles and responded, 'Go ahead; Androcles and I will return shortly; we need to speak more.'

"Androcles chimed in, 'Yes, I think Larentina and I will talk further.'

"Lycurgus solemnly stared at his sister for a moment and asked, 'Are you sure? I do not want another repeat of today.'

"Both Androcles and Larentina answered Lycurgus at the same time: 'We are sure.'

"Larentina and Androcles watched as Lycurgus faded into the woods. They turned their heads and softly gazed into each other's eyes. Androcles slowly moved his face toward Larentina's and stopped as his lips almost touched hers. Larentina closed her eyes and moved forward, touching his lips. He kissed her more passionately than he had the last time they were alone in her oasis.

"After the long, passionate kiss, Larentina suggested, 'Let us walk back to the training grounds.'

"Androcles yawned. 'Yes, let us return.'

"As they walked, they talked about competing in the Olympics someday. Before they knew it, they were back in the training camp and said good night to each other."

Chapter XXX

"Larentina woke up with mixed feelings; she was both excited and sad. Today there would be a big celebration as they completed their last day of military training. Granted, she had fought in many campaigns, but this day would show that she was a full-fledged Spartan soldier.

"All the families of the cadets would be there. Larentina thought they were indeed blessed by the gods, as it was a beautiful sunny day with just a few fluffy white clouds in the sky.

"When the sun was halfway to her summit in the sky, all the graduates gathered in the center of the barracks. They marched in formation and then had sword fights against one another to display their formidable skills in front of the audience.

"After the ceremony, Larentina gripped her brother's forearm with her right hand and hugged him with her left; she turned and did the same with Androcles. Then Lycurgus and Androcles congratulated one another.

"Larentina proudly announced, 'I can't believe we are true Spartan warriors this day.'

"Lycurgus uttered his excitement in turn, 'This is the beginning of the rest of our lives.'

"Androcles proclaimed with a bit of boyish humor, 'Finally, I not only survived agoge, but the two of you. After this, I can survive anything.'

"The three laughed at Androcles's comment and started to plan for the upcoming Olympics.

"As Larentina, Lycurgus, and Androcles were talking, King Karpos and King Alcaeus walked toward their children; their wives, Queen Irene and Queen Alexis, walked beside them. The queens stopped several feet away as the kings joined their children and displayed their pride. The queens watched their children silently, with smiles of pride on their faces.

"King Karpos and King Alcaeus greeted their sons in unison by gripping their forearms, as Larentina had done earlier, and then half hugging them. King Karpos proudly confessed to Androcles, 'I thought I would not live long enough to see my firstborn son turn into one of the greatest warriors of all of Sparta!'

"King Alcaeus uttered his pride to his son as well: 'The gods have graced me with such a powerful, strong son. I am pleased.'

"Both kings totally ignored Larentina's presence; it was as if she did not exist. She stood in silence as she watched her father talk with Lycurgus, laughing and showing pride in his great accomplishments. King Alcaeus commanded, 'Come, my son, we have a great celebration awaiting you.'

"The king and Lycurgus walked away from Larentina.

"Larentina dropped her head and looked toward the ground. She felt worthless at this moment and inferior to her brother. She even had a twinge of jealousy as she watched the queen and king celebrate Lycurgus's accomplishments, totally ignoring her.

"Larentina stood with disappointment in her eyes as the kings and the princes mounted their horses to ride back to their homes. The queens and everyone else in the entourage climbed into their wagons.

"Right before Queen Alexis's wagon drove off, she noticed her daughter and commanded, 'Come, Larentina!' Larentina looked up and glared at her mother, but she climbed up into the wagon. As Queen Alexis chattered away, Larentina looked out at the countryside in silence. Her heart was full of sadness and disappointment.

"Without warning, Larentina jumped out of the wagon and ran as fast as she could away from everyone. As she ran, she heard Queen Alexis frantically yelling, 'Larentina! Larentina! Stop, come back!' The queen's voice faded as Larentina put more and more distance between them.

"When Queen Alexis's wagon entered their courtyard, she climbed down and ran to her husband, who was standing with King Karpos, Lycurgus, Androcles, and several ephors and gerousia council members. As she tried to catch her breath, King Alcaeus demanded, 'Woman, what in the gods' names is the matter with you?'

"Queen Alexis finally answered, in a scared, shaky voice, 'My husband, my king, Larentina has taken off. I'm afraid for her.'

"King Alcaeus irritably responded, 'So what? She will return. Remember, she is like a wolf; she needs to return to the wild from time to time.'

"Lycurgus and Androcles laughed; they knew how true the king's remark was.

"Lycurgus walked toward his mother, still trying to control his laughter. 'Mother, fear not, for Androcles and I both know where she has gone. She probably went to her secret place because of all the excitement of this day. She will be fine.'

"Queen Alexis ignored the unwanted laughter and replied uncertainly, 'I hope that the gods keep her safe.'

"King Karpos tried to console Queen Alexis, 'Do not worry, woman, she will return before morning, I'm sure.'

"Within an hour, King Alcaeus stood on the steps of his great home and called out to everyone who had joined the great celebration. He yelled, 'Hear ye! Hear ye!' Everyone stopped talking and gave their total attention to the king as he began to speak.

"As helots brought out the gifts for Lycurgus, the king declared, 'I would like to present these gifts to my heir, my son, and now a Spartan warrior.'

"Lycurgus looked up at his father as King Alcaeus continued, 'I present to you, Son, a beautiful stallion along with body armor, helmet, shin guards, shield, sword, matching dagger, and a fifteen-foot-long spear.'

"King Alcaeus turned to face his son and proudly said, 'Here, my son, are gifts that will make you even greater.'

"Lycurgus gratefully accepted the gifts. 'Thank you, Father, for I will use them well in battle.'

"Then, King Karpos presented the same gifts to Androcles, saying, 'These gifts will not only make you a greater warrior, they will also protect you from Sparta's enemies.'

"Androcles also graciously accepted his father's gifts.

"Then, each king presented a fine leather pouch full of coins to the other king's son as a token of allegiance to each of their houses. Both sons accepted this gift as well.

"Everyone ate and drank through the evening in celebration of the accomplishments of these two future kings; when the subject of the fight between Larentina, Lycurgus, and Androcles finally arose, there was much confusion about why the fight began.

"One ephor said, 'Now the three of you act like best of friends again.'

"Androcles was somewhat embarrassed over the entire thing and said, with superiority in his tone, 'She had overstepped her place, but she had good reason to do so. It was our responsibility to put her back in her place.'

"Lycurgus just looked at his friend and then nodded in agreement.

"Bion sarcastically asked, 'Then why could you not just lash her a few times instead?'

"Lycurgus said, 'Because if he lashed her then, he would be lashing me; remember what happened the first time I was lashed.'

"Bion looked confused, and the same ephor stated, 'But that was not the case; you transferred your pain and wounds to her; she has never transferred any pain or wounds to you.'

"Lycurgus gave a simple explanation: 'Yes, over the years she has transferred pain to me as well. I do not think she meant to, but it has happened from time to time. I'm stronger than she is, and that is why no one has ever seen any of her wounds on my flesh.'

"Lycurgus looked at Androcles, because they knew they were both lying.

"Bion did not completely believe this, and he remarked, 'That was the whole point of Larentina being allowed to go through training with you. If one was lashed, then the other would suffer as well, together.'

"Androcles decided to change the subject, so he stood up from the table. His father, who was sitting next to him, tapped a knife against his wine goblet to attract everyone's attention. 'Hear! Hear! My son has an announcement to make.'

"After everyone became quiet, Androcles announced, 'I have chosen Princess Larentina to be my queen, not because our fathers agreed to this when she was an infant, but because I accept this greatest gift from King Alcaeus.' Everyone cheered and talked loudly about this news.

"After Androcles sat back down, he looked at his father, who nodded his head in total agreement.

"King Alcaeus stood up, raised his glass, and declared, 'The house of Agiad and Eurypontids shall become as one, but yet I am the guardian of Larentina, and there was never such agreement, but it will be considered.'

"King Karpos stood and responded, 'That is true; many years ago, I asked for this match but King Alcaeus did not answer, so I was wrong, my son.'

"Androcles was very angry to hear this information, but he never showed it. All he thought was, *Larentina must be mine. There can be no other for me.*

"The conversations continued throughout the evening and it finally returned to Larentina once again. Hesiodos told one of the other gerousia members, 'It should be put on record that Larentina has changed the way we think of our women. She has proven that women can fight and prove themselves almost as good as any man. We must provide similar training to our women as well as our men. Granted, it should not be as rigorous, but nevertheless, our women should be taught to fight just as well as we train our men, because they will need to protect our country when our men are off at war.' There was loud grumbling from many men in the courtyard and much more discussion over this.

"Hygieinos remarked, 'But don't you think that a woman is a disruption while training with men?'

"Hesiodos responded, 'Yes, you are right, my friend, so we will have women separated from the men instead of allowing them to live with the men during agoge training. We will also test them to see that they are strong when they are infants. We will have a vote soon asking this very question to the apella.' Everyone including the kings and their sons agreed to this.

"After an hour or two had passed, King Karpos rose from his seat and remarked, 'It is getting late. This has been a grand day indeed, but it is time for rest from this great celebration.' Everyone started saying their good-byes soon after. Soon there was no one left in the courtyard except for the helots cleaning up and Lycurgus and Androcles.

"Before Androcles mounted his horse to leave, he once again gripped Lycurgus's forearm and hand, then half hugged him. He knew Lycurgus was still worried because Larentina had not returned yet, and he tried to console him. 'Lycurgus, do not worry, for I am sure she will return before daybreak. She will be safe because she has Lambda by her side always.'

"Lycurgus remained very concerned. 'In all the heavens, I pray you are right, friend, but we both know how stubborn Larentina can be; what you do not know is Lambda left Larentina's side and returned to the forest several weeks ago.'

"Androcles replied, 'That does not really matter, because we both know where she is. I will never understand that goddess; as soon as I think I have her figured out, she reacts like … Well, I have said enough. I will see you back at the barracks in a few weeks.'

"Lycurgus just nodded his head in agreement. Androcles mounted his horse and rode off, as Lycurgus watched him disappear into the darkness."

Chapter XXXI

"As Androcles rode slowly to his father's house, he thought that maybe he should go find Larentina just to be sure she was all right. He had been thinking of her all night and could not understand why she sought solitude on such a day. He knew something was very wrong, but he looked up to the heavens and chuckled to himself as he said aloud, 'Women!'

"Before Androcles realized what he was doing, he noticed that he had ridden his horse through the paths in the woods toward the secret paradise. When he could not ride any farther, he dismounted, tied his stallion to a tree limb, and proceeded on foot through the woods to the hidden waterfall.

"Androcles pushed the foliage back and looked for Larentina. He saw her lying in a bed of leaves beside the pool of water. He walked quietly around the pool and approached her sleeping figure in the dim moonlight with a small fire burning close to her.

"He quietly lay down beside her and softly and playfully uttered, 'Larentina, wake up, my sleeping goddess.'

"Larentina opened her eyes, quickly got up, and uttered in a loud voice irritably at Androcles, 'How dare you? Get out! I do not want to speak to you or anyone else!'

"Patiently and softly, Androcles asked, 'Why, my love? What has happened that you do not want to be around me or your family?'

"Larentina angrily answered, 'They are not truly my family, and I am not your love. There will be great wars regarding equality between all mankind, including women, I swear it. If it takes me the rest of my life, the lives of my daughters, and their daughters, even through all the ages of my blood, I will fight all men until all women are treated as equal. Of course, you do not understand what I'm implying.

"'I will not ever be treated as property or as if I am less worthy than any man! Sparta shall indeed fall along with every great civilization because no man has the right to own another, and this also includes women!' Larentina was ready to fight Androcles physically, and she didn't care if she died, because she refused to live like this any longer.

"To Larentina's surprise, Androcles continued to lay there with his head resting on one hand; he looked up at her without anger and proclaimed in a soft voice, 'Larentina, have I not always treated you as my equal, as an equal to men? I believe your brother has also treated you this way as well. So have the majority of the cadets and soldiers. So please tell me why now, after you have accomplished so much and have even changed our own society in many ways, you still feel this way? I have just learned that the gerousia council is going to make it law for other women to be able to train in many ways as the men do.' Androcles sat up, gathered some small twigs bearing green leaves, and started making a crown.

"After hearing this, Larentina let go of her anger and sat down beside Androcles. He held the completed crown in his hands and gazed upon her face. She looked into his blue eyes and asked in a soft tone, 'Is this true?'

"Androcles smiled as he gazed upon Larentina's beautiful face. 'Yes, my love, it is true. You have already changed so much. You have stolen my heart simply because you are so strong. I will never treat you as less than my equal. I swear it.'

"Of course, Androcles only meant that he would treat her as an equal on the battlefield and in private. He knew if he did this in public, he would be looked upon as weak, but at this moment he just wanted Larentina to love him and no other, so he would say just about anything to keep her heart.

"Then he placed the crown he had made upon her head and looked at her with sincere love. He asked in a seductive tone, 'Now will you give yourself to me? Remember, you once said you would not give yourself to me until you were crowned with laurel leaves?'

"Androcles took Larentina's hand and kissed it. Larentina blushed and giggled ever so slightly as she lay down beside him; they kissed passionately. After a few moments, she softly pushed him away and said, 'Not this night, for I still dream of competing in the Olympics. I truly love you, Androcles, and from this moment forward, you will always have my heart.'

"Larentina turned away from him. As she lay there, Androcles wrapped his arm around her waist and whispered in her ear, 'You are worth the wait. I always have and always will love you. I will protect you with my dying breath.' He kissed her on her cheek and lay there beside her.

"Androcles awoke to the sounds of birds chirping. He yawned and stretched his arms, smiling because he finally had Larentina's heart, and he knew she would soon be his. He knew he could never love another woman as he loved Larentina, his future wife and queen. He sat up and realized that Larentina was no longer lying beside him. He looked around the pool of water but could not see her anywhere. Once more, she had disappeared. He would never understand her! He grimaced as he realized how frequently that thought had passed through his mind, time and time again."

Chapter XXXII

"Larentina awoke to Lambda licking her face. Without waking Androcles, Larentina quietly got up, dressed, and followed Lambda into the woods. Larentina knew it was time for a new generation of Lambda. Her life would change once again.

"Larentina followed Lambda through the woods until they reached Lambda's wolf pack, and once again, the older Lambda gave her female puppy to Larentina. Larentina played with the wolves for several hours and then decided it was time to visit her real mother, Agape.

"Larentina found herself standing at the same place the eirena had stood all those years ago, near Agape's house by the edge of the forest. She stood there silently for several moments, petting the new Lambda and staring at Agape's home, deep in thought.

"Larentina let out a heavy sigh and slowly walked through the field toward her real mother's home. She saw Agape carrying a large basket full of vegetables and fruit, walking toward the front door. Larentina thought how simple her life would have been if Agape had kept her children and let the gods deal with Queen Alexis and Sparta.

"When Agape looked up, she saw Larentina, dropped her large basket, and ran to her. When Agape reached Larentina, she jubilantly threw her arms around her daughter and the puppy, hugged them tightly, and said with pride in her voice, 'I'm so very proud of you, my daughter, my princess, my warrior. Come, let us eat and drink. We have much to discuss. I want to know everything.'

"Larentina did not speak a word, but she walked beside her mother obediently as Agape led them into her home, talking about her simple life and Larentina's other siblings.

"As Larentina walked into Agape's home, she asked, 'Where are the others?'

"Agape answered, 'Oh, they are all in the fields.'

"Larentina simply responded, 'Oh.'

"As she poured wine into three goblets, Agape announced, 'I will go get my husband.'

"Larentina reached out and grabbed her mother's forearm, stopping her, and solemnly commanded, 'No, Mother, I want to speak with you alone.'

"Agape sat back down at the table and looked at her daughter with a serious expression.

"Larentina unconsciously rubbed Lambda, who slept in her arms, and told her mother everything that had happened since the last time she visited Agape and her family.

"After hearing what her daughter had gone through, Agape let out a deep sigh and shared her wisdom. 'I can only say this, my daughter: you are not completely mortal because you have been chosen either by fate or coincidence to change our world. I do not know how or why you have been chosen, but you are part of the gods, as well as part of me. You must follow your own heart, no other. I am glad that your life has been this way. I am proud that you have accomplished so much. Your actions will determine who and what you are. You must seek your own destiny and live life the way you choose to, for this is a blessing from the gods to give you more freedoms, rights, education, and survival skills than any other woman before you. Go out, seek your father, and have him provide answers for you, because I believe he truly loves you.

"'It is time for you to know that you are from my blood, and why you are almost as strong as the gods. You are the daughter of energy that comes from light; this is what we are. You are not half witch, nor mortal, but a child from energy and nothing more.'

"Larentina let out another heavy sigh and simply agreed, 'You are right, Mother. There is more to this world than just Sparta.'

"Agape changed the subject and proudly announced, 'Zeus, your father, and his two brothers have left gifts here for you, to help prepare you and protect you in your life's destiny. He told me to give them to you this day.'

"Larentina looked puzzled but followed her birth mother to the barn. Agape led a solid auburn stallion from one of the stables. Larentina joyfully gasped because she had never seen a horse that was so beautiful and strong.

"Agape proudly announced, 'This first gift is from Zeus. Celeris is one of the offspring of Pegasus. The way we learned the legend of the birth of

Celeris's father, Pegasus, was that Perseus had cut off Medusa's head, and her blood mingled in the ocean's foam, creating Pegasus. That is not exactly correct. Medusa is still alive! It was not her, but one of her Gorgon sisters who was killed. You must seek Medusa and convince her to join you in the battle between the gods.

"'When Poseidon learned of Zeus's gift to you, he visited me in a dream and told me what his wish from you is. Athena was jealous of Medusa and turned her into a gorgon. Poseidon wants you to return his beloved Medusa to her former beauty and bring her back to him. This is all he asks of you. Celeris will be yours until you release him and give back his freedom.

"'Daughter, I know you will not understand what I am about to tell you, but please remember my words. The story of my past is very similar to what happened to Medusa. I know what I ask of you; I do not expect an answer. It must come from your heart when the truth presents itself to you. I humbly request that you seek vengeance for your blood.'

"Before Larentina could respond, Agape hugged her daughter and whispered, 'Hush, there is no need for words. Let us be happy for just this moment.'

"The beautiful auburn stallion, Celeris, nuzzled his head against Larentina, and she rubbed his forehead as her solemn expression turned into a smile of joy. Larentina excitedly shared her thoughts: 'I thought my father and his brothers didn't care about me since I was born a woman instead of a man.'

"Agape responded to her daughter with a mother's loving advice and wisdom. 'Of course your father loves you; after all, you are a part of him. Neither Zeus nor his brothers look at women the way mortal men do, that is why I told you earlier to seek him out and have your questions answered by him directly, so he can truly show you he loves you and is very proud of you. I honestly believe that he does not care whether you are a woman or man. He is very proud of you because every day that you live, you prove that you are his offspring, who was born a female child instead of a male child. You show that you are just as formidable as mortal vain men are. This is one reason he will be trying to help you throughout your journey, but you must earn it first.'

"Larentina observed the horse in front of her, as she rubbed Celeris's neck. 'I thought Celeris had wings like his father, Pegasus, but he does not.'

"Upon hearing that, Celeris briefly sucked in his breath before he made a loud whinny that echoed throughout the barn. He then shook his head up and down in disappointment with Larentina's statement and galloped out of the barn. Agape and Larentina frantically ran behind him in fear he would run off.

"Celeris stopped several feet outside of the barn and released several loud whinnies along with several nickers as he reared on his hind hoofs. Larentina and Agape then watched as flickers of light appeared around his sides and wings magically appeared before them. They let out gasps of excitement.

"Larentina instinctively ran and leaped onto Celeris's bare back, and Celeris stomped his two front hoofs one at a time into the dirt as he made outdoor whinnies and nickers with pride of himself, and took off running with her on his back.

"Larentina looked back and saw Celeris was running so fast that his hoofprints were smoking; they smoldered and went out within a few seconds. Celeris then leaped into the air and started flying as Larentina rubbed the neck of her new friend. She said with excitement, 'My cousin, I will never again doubt your abilities!'

"Celeris threw his head up and down as he flew and whinnied as if to say, 'I showed you.' Larentina giggled loudly as she threw her head back and let the wind blow into her face and through her long beautiful white hair.

"They flew so high she could see for miles. She felt as if she was finally free, and she was truly happy at this moment; words just could not describe the wonderful feeling of flying. She was scared and empowered at the same time. She felt that she was, indeed, beyond a doubt, a goddess. Why else would she have such strong magic all around her and be able to look at the earth as the gods do?"

* * *

Of course, Mom-mom was so engrossed in her story that she just now noticed that Christina, Teresa, and I were looking at her with a twinge of irritation. There was so much fiction in her story, even my mother was glaring at Mom-mom.

Mom-mom then asked, "What?" as she took another sip of lemonade with a half smile upon her face. She put down her glass and stated, "Oh, for Pete's sake, ladies, I have already stated that this is myth as well as truth. Besides, every great storyteller must bend the truth a little to keep the audience's attention. I have your attention, don't I? I'm just telling you the story the way it was told to me. After all, this story has been passed down for a couple of thousand years, and there has been a lot of stretching of it." Then she looked at us, still smiling, and ordered, "Stop looking at me like that."

Before any of us had a chance to respond, Teresa gave her opinion. "Mom-mom, you had us all going, because you had explanations for why She Wolf, her brother, and the other characters of your story believed the way they do, but this is stretching the imagination."

Mom-mom became irritated. "And how do you know they didn't have flying horses, young lady? Neither you nor I were alive then."

Christina retorted, "Mom-mom, we are not stupid. There is no such thing as a flying horse. Celeris is just a myth along with all the other gods."

Mom-mom defended her story and simply said, "But it's a true myth that was distorted by the Greeks and then the Romans! So there you go. It is up to you to find the meaning of this story. I cannot give it to you, or it will defeat the purpose. Besides, I already told you there was a lot of mythology in this story."

I finally chimed in, "Christina and Teresa are correct, but in this case a real person did turn into a legend, and the myths that Mom-mom is talking about really were written by ancient storytellers. People did believe these stories, so let Mom-mom tell the story the way she wants to. I think it's very exciting, even if there is a lot of fiction in it."

Everyone nodded their heads in agreement because, after all, Mom-mom was telling us a great story. I had to admit that she had our undivided attention. I knew there was truth and meaning all through it.

Mom-mom made one last comment: "It will be up to you to either tell the stories the way they are told to you or just simply tell the facts to your children." No one dared to say another word about it.

Aphrodite Emerging from the Sea

Chapter XXXIII

Mom-mom once again cleared her throat and resumed her tale.

"When Larentina and Celeris returned, she dismounted from Celeris, rubbed his neck with a proud smile on her face, and said, 'Cousin, that was the best ride I ever had in my life. Thank you so much for being my horse and new friend. We will have many great adventures together.

"'Mother, I want to share this with you. Let Celeris take you into the sky so you can see mother earth as the gods see it.'

"Agape blushed and replied, 'Oh, I could not, I just could not.'

"Larentina smiled at her blushing mother and commanded, 'Come, Mother, let me help you.'

"Before Agape knew it, she was on the back of Celeris, looking down at the lands below. She truly felt she was free, as Larentina had felt earlier. She thought that she was glad she had lied because her daughter had been given everything that Agape could only dream of. Agape prayed for Larentina to seek vengeance against everyone who had wronged her.

"After dismounting Celeris, Agape hugged Larentina and thanked her daughter for the experience. Celeris nuzzled Larentina and made soft nickers in response. Larentina and Agape again watched the flickering lights appear, and Celeris's wings disappeared.

"Larentina turned and jubilantly announced to her mother, 'Celeris is the greatest gift anyone has ever given me.'

"Agape smiled at her daughter as she proudly announced, 'I have many more gifts I must give you from your father's family. Follow me, for I have hidden these next gifts.' Larentina followed Agape back into the house and into her mother's bedroom. Larentina watched with anticipation, wondering what other gifts would be presented to her. Agape pulled a series of horse blankets out from under her bed; each blanket covered a treasure. After Agape laid the last item upon her bed, she uncovered each gift and folded each blanket, one by one.

"Larentina was flabbergasted; she could not restrain herself once the treasures were revealed to her. She touched each one in awe as they lay on the bed. She picked up a perfectly round, golden shield, and Agape explained its history, saying, 'These gifts are from Zeus's brother Hades, with the help of other gods. He asked Hephaestus, the blacksmith god, to construct this shield and the finest body armor, helmet, shin guards, sword, dagger, and spear. Hades also asked Ares, the god of war, to instruct Hephaestus on their shapes. Hades provided Hephaestus with the finest metals the earth could provide. Hephaestus, Ares, and Hades give these gifts to you to help protect you from our family's enemies, mortals or divine.

"'Ares said this golden shield is perfectly round, not like a Spartan shield, because the circle represents the perfection of our mother earth. It will provide better protection from the forces of evil that you will encounter.'

"Larentina gazed in awe once again at all the objects as she laid the shield back down upon the bed. She picked up each item, reverently touched it, and gently rubbed her hands over it to confirm it was real and not her imagination. Once again, she picked up the shield and gently rubbed her finger over the wolf images that were etched into the metal. On the body armor, the chest plate displayed the image of the first Lambda. Larentina gently touched it and let her fingers trace the carved etching in the metal, as she had done with the shield.

"Larentina could not keep the tears of joy from forming in her eyes; she said in a humbled voice, 'My family truly loves me, and they must be very proud of me to give me the greatest gifts in the world.'

"Agape put her arms around Larentina, hugged her daughter tightly, and murmured her pride in Larentina's ear, 'I have been blessed by the gods that they have given you to me. I have always loved you and your brother, and I am truly happy that Zeus has given you back to me.'

"Larentina picked up the sword, wheeled it, balanced it in her open hand, and smiled; it was such a perfectly balanced sword. It could not have been more perfect.

"She picked up the helmet next; it was not made like a Spartan helmet. It was shaped like a perfectly round bowl with a leather chinstrap to keep it on her head. Like all the other gifts, the metal seemed lighter, but more durable. It had a ridge at the top, and the nosepiece came directly between her eyes. As Larentina placed the helmet on her head, she thought of Androcles for a moment, and then she jumped backward quickly because a vision appeared; she could see Androcles talking with his father, as if she was really there.

"Agape asked, 'What is it, my daughter?'

"Larentina answered with excitement, 'I see Androcles talking with his father.'

"Then she thought of her other mother, Queen Alexis, and saw the worried look upon her face. Agape ordered, 'Larentina, give this to me.' Larentina obediently removed the helmet from her head and passed it to Agape.

"Agape put the helmet on her head and jumped back in horror. She quickly removed the helmet from her head and passed it back to Larentina, who asked with concern, 'Mother, what did you see?'

"Agape simply answered, 'I saw the past.'

"Larentina looked questioningly at Agape; she was sure that she had seen the present, and she asked, 'What do you mean?'

"Agape answered with a half lie: 'I saw Karpos standing over me, like he did all those years ago.'

"Agape and Larentina realized this magical helmet showed the past as well as the present.

"Agape then shrugged the past from her thoughts and said with a proud smile, 'There is more.' She pulled out one last object from under her bed and presented it to her daughter.

"Larentina opened the blanket and smiled as she gazed upon it. 'It's beautiful and so perfect.'

"Agape gazed down at the objects and looked at her daughter with pride once again. She said, 'The bow and arrows were a gift from your father, Zeus. He told me that the arrows will always be plentiful; your quiver will never run dry. This gift will keep yourself fed and dressed like the queen that you are, to protect you from physical confrontation so you may stay hidden until you are ready to fight face to face with our enemies. This is the greatest gift he could give you.'

"Larentina started to cry because this was all she really wanted, to be recognized, respected, and acknowledged by her father (or any mortal man) as an equal. To be given the affection that she had sought for most of her life was more than she could comprehend.

"Agape hugged her daughter again. 'Daughter, there is still more.'

"Larentina inquisitively asked, 'How could there be anything greater to give me?'

"Agape simply answered, 'Because these gifts are from me, the queen, and the Goddess Aphrodite. She broke her vow with Zeus not to interfere; she could not resist because she considers no other her equal in beauty and charm, only you. She wants you to use these gifts of your womanhood to beguile men and take from them as they have taken from women.'

"Larentina simply smiled at her birth mother and kissed her on her cheek, because she did not intend to use men the way men used women. Larentina believed men and women should treat each other as equals.

"Agape presented her daughter with the most beautiful multicolored chiton Larentina had ever seen, but then she was used to wearing the military-style cotton tunics. She never really paid much attention to what the queens had been wearing.

"Unknown to Agape and Larentina, Aphrodite was peering into Agape's bedroom window, watching the mother and daughter.

"Aphrodite could not stand it any longer. She had to meet this beautiful, strong mortal woman who she considered her only equal in beauty (although she arrogantly thought Larentina did not have the grace and charm that she possessed). Aphrodite knew she could teach Larentina very easily.

"She wanted to meet Larentina because she wanted to use her to seek vengeance against her husband, Hephaestus. Aphrodite also wanted to teach Zeus an embarrassing lesson because he had given Aphrodite to the ugly, beastly god. Hephaestus entrapped her with a lover, and all the gods had laughed at the sight. Aphrodite had not forgotten this. She loved young, beautiful women, and Larentina's flesh smelled very, very familiar.

"Aphrodite did not even remember that it had been her own nasty games of playing with mortal men's hearts that had caused Larentina to be conceived.

"Athena had caught Aphrodite as she had been weaving the fabrics for Agape to make the chiton, which was the most beautiful and seductive clothing. Aphrodite had just finished the last piece of fabric before Athena caught her; she yelled, 'This is my domain! How dare you! I'm going to tell Zeus that you have crossed the line!'

"Aphrodite became angry, got up from the loom, and sarcastically remarked, 'Fine, I will never lift another finger to work around here again! I thought you would be pleased with my hard labor!'

"Athena just tossed her hair over her shoulder, acting as if she were far superior to Aphrodite. 'Fine, but if I catch you again, I will see to it that

Zeus punishes you!' With those words, she turned her back to Aphrodite and left her standing there.

"As Aphrodite stood at the corner of Agape's house, contemplating how to carry out her devious plan, she thought back to when she was born. Aphrodite had deceived the Olympian deities by making them believe that she was born of Ouranos, who was the sky, and Gaia, who was mother earth. Ouranos was full of love and spread himself full upon Gaia. As the two gods were making love, Kronos, the son of Ouranos, attacked Ouranos and castrated him. After castrating his father, Kronos threw the severed genitals into the ocean. The ocean began to swirl and foam around the discarded genitals of Ouranos. From the sea foam, Aphrodite arose fully grown, and she was swept away by the currents. Technically, she was Larentina's great-aunt, because Ouranos was the grandfather of Zeus.

"Aphrodite victoriously laughed because she had fooled all the gods on Mount Olympus; she was the one who convinced Kronos to attack his own father. Aphrodite was much older than anyone knew, for she had come from many different lands and was not who she appeared to be at all. As she recalled how clever she was, she touched the green crystal pendant around her neck and wickedly laughed aloud.

"Then Aphrodite thought of the other things that Zeus had done to her, even though she knew Zeus and his brothers killed their own father, Kronos, and divided the earth between them. She did not like the idea of having to obey the gods, because she felt that she was never treated as great as the other gods were, so she decided to go ahead and use Larentina because of her family relation.

"Aphrodite decided to use this woman child as a perfect pawn. She knew she had to appear to hold the same beliefs as her mortal great-niece. Aphrodite had to convince Larentina that Aphrodite had endured the same fate that Larentina did. Aphrodite did not know what plans Zeus and his brothers were conjuring, but she didn't care. She was going to use Larentina to her advantage and protect her at any cost to change the way mortal man and the gods treated their women!

"Aphrodite laughed viciously because as long as Larentina believed that she felt this way about her and men, she would rule the world and the heavens once again.

"Aphrodite entered Agape's bedroom but remained invisible as she listened to the mother and daughter."

* * *

"As Larentina caressed the light, silky material, Agape suggested, 'Please, Daughter, let me help you put it on so I can shape it to your body.' Larentina eagerly removed her military tunic and allowed her mother to dress her. After Agape placed the last piece of jewelry on Larentina's body, she touched up a strand of her daughter's hair and turned her around to look in the full-length mirror, which was made out of silver and polished until it showed a reflection. Larentina could not believe she was staring at a woman instead of a soldier. She moved her hands down her sides, feeling the material that Agape had made this chiton from.

"There were two gold wolf heads with ruby eyes on each side of Larentina's shoulders, clasping the material in place. The neckline dipped low and revealed her ample cleavage. Her back was bare; the chiton looked like a halter-top in the front. Agape had wrapped a wide gold colored belt, made from a thicker material, around her waist. Her upper back was completely bare from the waistband up. The material that was clasped together by the wolf's heads draped down the sides of her body and was tucked in the belt. Larentina had healed from all her lashings without leaving any scars, whereas her brother's back was still covered with scars.

"The chiton was edged with gold fringe that brushed against the top of her feet. Agape had dyed the bottom half of the chiton with vegetable dyes, turning the material a turquoise blue, making the chiton even more beautiful. On Larentina's right index finger, Agape placed a wolf's head ring that matched the bangles, fashioned out of twisted gold that clasped where the two wolf heads met.

"Agape had placed a diamond headband on her daughter's head; the large diamond rested on the center of Larentina's forehead, and Agape styled her beautiful, long, curly white hair around it.

"Agape gazed in the mirror at her most beautiful daughter. 'This is to help you seduce men to do your bidding.'

"Larentina looked over at her mother in amazement and commented, 'I didn't know how seductive being feminine could be.'

"Agape smiled at her daughter and replied, 'Your womanhood is the greatest gift from the gods, because men will do stupid things to just possess such beauty.'

"Larentina giggled devilishly, and her mother joined in. Agape playfully remarked, 'And that, my child, is why men try so hard to keep us beneath them. Do you understand?'

"Larentina looked at her mother and simply nodded her head in total agreement.

"Then Agape presented Larentina with several more beautiful chitons, tunics, and pellas; several different styles of sandals and soft suede boots; suede pants and tops; and pearls and gold jewelry, including pierced earrings.

"Larentina asked, 'What kind of earrings are these? I have never seen such a wealth of jewelry before. How did you come about these treasures?'

"Agape giggled softly and answered, 'The jewelry I must admit comes from your other mother and the Goddess Aphrodite. Aphrodite even brought me the fabrics she had made and suede that she handpicked from across the lands to make you clothing fit for a queen. Come here, my child. To wear some of this jewelry, we must pierce your ears, your nostril, and your belly button. These traditions are not Spartan ways, but my sister and I agree with Aphrodite that you do not just belong to Sparta. You belong to all cultures, as you to try to persuade all of mankind to think as we do.'

"Before Larentina realized what had happened, Agape had pierced her ears, a nostril, and her belly button. Agape put a large diamond stud in her belly button, which made it appear that the diamond was her belly button. She put a diamond in her nostril and two gold loop earrings in her ears. Larentina did not even flinch while being pierced; it was not painful at all.

"Agape pulled out a golden box so small that it fit in the palm of Larentina's hand. There was a small golden key already placed in the lock; Agape turned the key and the box unfolded like a large blanket. Agape neatly placed all the clothing and jewelry on the blanket. Then she turned the key, which was now on the edge of the blanket, and it magically folded into a small golden box again. Astonished, Larentina voiced her emotions: 'By all the gods, I have never seen such great magic.'

"Agape smiled. 'I forgot to tell you that the wolf jewelry and this box are also from Aphrodite.' Then Agape put a long, thick chain through one of the small loops on the small box and placed the necklace around Larentina's neck. Agape said, 'This way, if you need a change of clothing for any occasion, you will have these things with you everywhere you go.'

"Larentina just looked at her mother with astonishment and asked, 'Are all women so vain?'

"Before Agape could answer, Aphrodite appeared in front of them, arrogantly laughing; she answered Larentina, 'If they are not, they should be; all women possess the power of seduction, not just me.'

"Larentina glared at Aphrodite and asked, 'Who are you?'

"Aphrodite answered with a question: 'Can't you tell who I am?'

"Larentina irritably answered, 'No, I do not know who or what you are.'

"Aphrodite answered, 'I am your great-aunt, Aphrodite. Do you not like my gifts?'

"Larentina rudely replied, 'They are frivolous and vain, but some of them are useful, and I thank you for them.'

"Aphrodite became insulted and irritated with the mortal woman; she snapped, 'You are still in denial that you are a very beautiful woman, and you have not yet embraced your womanhood. So therefore it is my duty to teach you.'

"Larentina grew angry. Agape sensed this and did not want Aphrodite to cause her daughter any harm, so she dropped to her knees, bowing in front of Aphrodite, and pleaded, 'My goddess Aphrodite, I truly apologize for the arrogance and ignorance of my child. My daughter and I would consider this the greatest and most honored gift you could give her, to teach her about her womanhood, to be graceful and charming.'

"Larentina became even angrier as her own mother groveled to Aphrodite; she retorted, 'I bow down to no god, goddess, or mortal man.'

"Aphrodite threw her head back, laughed loudly at Larentina, and arrogantly retorted, 'You dare defy me? You are more brazen and reckless than your father, Zeus! So therefore I should not expect anything less of you.'

"Larentina was ready to be turned into something awful by Aphrodite because of her actions; she was completely confused by this goddess's actions.

"Aphrodite studied Larentina's facial expressions for a few moments as she decided what tactics to use. 'What? Did you expect me to act like a child and do something nasty to you? I'm not as vain as most goddesses are. Then I will ask you, please come with me and let me teach you the arts of being a beautiful woman, which you truly are. After all, Larentina, you do have some of my blood running in your veins as well, since I am your great-aunt.'

"Never before had Aphrodite used the word *please.* Larentina was amazed at Aphrodite's unpredictable behavior and gratefully accepted, saying, 'I will consider this a great gift that you will give me.'

"Agape stood back up after kneeling before Aphrodite, saying, 'Oh praise the most beautiful goddess of all. Thank you, Goddess Aphrodite.'

"Aphrodite smiled triumphantly because she had convinced Larentina to be her student in the arts of love and seduction. Little did Aphrodite know Larentina would just watch her; she would never give herself to anyone other than Androcles.

"Larentina shook her head from side to side in disgust, but she had to admit she was just a little curious as to what exactly Aphrodite could teach her, because Larentina considered the sword and battle the only way to change men's minds.

"Aphrodite ordered, 'Come, Child, hold my hand, and we will travel together.'

"Larentina did not trust so easily. 'Wait, I must put my armor on, and my horse is waiting for me along with Lambda.'

"Aphrodite ordered, 'Collect your things and your wolf only. Say good-bye to Celeris, for he is no ordinary horse. Let him go, and all you have to do is call him, and he will find you wherever you may be.'

"Larentina did as she was told. She ran outside to Celeris, rubbed the neck of her horse, and said to him, 'You must go, Cousin, and enjoy your short time of freedom, but please return to me when I call.'

"Celeris nodded his head, whinnied good-bye, and galloped off into the forest.

"Larentina had sadness in her heart, but she knew she would see Celeris again soon enough. She picked up her wolf puppy and carried her in her arms.

"She returned to the house to change into her military garb, but Aphrodite commanded, 'No, you are already dressed for where we are going.'

"Larentina hesitantly did as Aphrodite said.

"Agape frantically cried, 'Wait!' as she hugged and clung to her daughter.

"As Aphrodite took her hand, the goddess and Larentina disappear right in front of Agape. She began crying because she had lost her daughter once again."

Chapter XXXIV

"It had been several months since Larentina had disappeared. Lycurgus and Androcles had been searching for her all over Sparta. The kings and their queens, the gerousia members, soldiers, ephors, and even the helots searched for Larentina. No one wanted to admit that she had touched so many hearts throughout her life.

"The helots did not need to be ordered to search for her, because they all loved her. She always treated them as equals, not as slaves; in other words, she respected everyone no matter how minute their task, and many times she even helped them with their mundane daily chores. She never ordered them to do anything; she simply asked.

"No one knew where she had gone, but they all feared that if something horrible had happened to her, they would soon feel the wrath of Zeus.

"Lycurgus heard whispers from Hera goading him to go to Erasmus's house as he laid in his bed worrying about Larentina. Finally he decided to visit Agape and Erasmus, even though he did not believe the crazy story his sister had told him. All he knew was his sister believed the story that had spewed from Agape's lying tongue.

"Lycurgus did not understand that they were whispers from Hera, he believed them to be his own thoughts and he believed Agape was jealous of his mother, Queen Alexis. He concluded that Agape must have been in love with King Alcaeus, but he had spurned her for her twin. Lycurgus believed that King Karpos loved her, but Agape did not want him because she loved King Alcaeus. Lycurgus knew something was wrong with Agape's story, and now Agape was trying to seek vengeance by using Larentina. Lycurgus was convinced that if Queen Alexis were to discover Agape's lies, she would slay her herself, but at this moment, he had to find his sister, and he knew she had believed the lies that were told to her. It was time to confront his sister's demons once and for all and bring her home to her true family.

"It was very late on a rainy, cold night when Lycurgus rode his horse into the small courtyard of Erasmus's home. He did not know that Androcles had been following him, as he had on many occasions since Larentina's disappearance.

"He dismounted his horse and shook the rainwater from his face. No one heard his arrival because they were all asleep, so Lycurgus yelled at the top of his lungs, 'Erasmus! Erasmus! Come out with your lying wife! I demand you to return my sister now!'

"Erasmus was immediately awakened, but he did not know it was Lycurgus, because he could not quite make out what Lycurgus was yelling about. He grabbed his sword lying next to his bed. He looked over at Agape; at first, both Agape and Erasmus thought it was Karpos.

"Erasmus and Agape quickly dressed. Agape followed closely behind Erasmus as he opened his front door and stood in the threshold with sword in hand. As he peered into the darkness, he realized it was Lycurgus and yelled, 'Son! What are you doing here, standing in the rain? Come inside and dry yourself. We will talk!'

"Agape tightly clutched her husband's forearm as he tried to convince Lycurgus to come in from the rain.

"Lycurgus came closer and stood on the first step to Erasmus's front door. He squinted his eyes to see Erasmus more clearly, because the rain was falling fast into his face; he disappointedly yelled at Erasmus, 'So you too are beguiled by your wife's lying tongue!'

"Erasmus became very confused as to why Lycurgus was behaving so violently toward him, and he was unclear what lies he was referring to; he simply asked, 'What is the meaning of this? What in all the gods … What do you want? Please, Son, come inside, dry off, and explain your actions this night of all nights.'

"Lycurgus grew angrier but realized after a moment that maybe Erasmus did not know the truth. In addition, Erasmus had been adopted by King Alcaeus, so Lycurgus decided to give Erasmus the benefit of the doubt. Lycurgus realized that Erasmus was also a good friend of his father, and Lycurgus trusted his father's judgment. So Lycurgus let go of his anger and accepted Erasmus's invitation.

"Erasmus led Lycurgus into his eating area; Erasmus passed Lycurgus a thick towel and said, 'Here, my son. Dry yourself.'

"Lycurgus took the towel and voiced his gratitude obnoxiously. 'Thank you, but I'm not your son.'

"At this, Erasmus did not say anything. He simply let out a disappointed sigh as he watched his wife lighting the large candles that were placed throughout the large room. Then Erasmus added more logs onto the fire.

"Lycurgus glared at Agape as she lit the candles and poured the wine for the two men. Still, all three did not speak. Both men were now sitting at the large eating table, watching Agape cut the bread and cheese. Agape looked directly at her son and said meekly, 'You are as beautiful and perfect as your sister is, but I can tell you are much stronger than she.'

"Lycurgus just glared at Agape and let out a low grunt of disgust at the comment; he said with a twinge of anger still in his voice, 'Where is my sister?'

"Erasmus sternly voiced his displeasure: 'Do not speak to my wife with such a sharp tongue, young man.'

"Agape was crushed; her own son hated her so much, and she did not even know if Larentina had told the truth to him, because she did not mention it the last time they spoke. Tears streamed down her beautiful cheeks, as Agape fearfully asked, 'Did Larentina speak with you regarding your origins?'

"Lycurgus glared at Agape with even more hatred as he answered her sharply, 'She told me the lies you charmed her into believing; I truly believe you used the same lies to beguile this poor perioikoi.'

"Erasmus grew extremely angry; he stood up, slammed his fist on the table, and uttered in a loud tone, 'Not even King Alcaeus speaks to me like that! If you were any other man, I would have cut your tongue out! I'm a Spartan warrior! I deserve your respect!'

"Lycurgus threw his head back and let out a loud sarcastic laugh as he remarked, 'My anger is not directed at you, since technically you are my adopted brother, nor do I really care about your wife's lies. They have been told and are done with. My mother will deal with Agape in her own way. I simply want to know where my sister is.'

"Agape, still sobbing, said, 'She is with the gods. She came here the day after you completed agoge. She told me how you, the king, the queen, and everyone else ignored her as if she didn't exist. Not one word from the queen and king acknowledging her for her own accomplishments, but her real family, Zeus and his brothers, and many other deities, came to me many weeks before that day, bringing godly gifts to honor her and her accomplishments, which you and your family failed to acknowledge.' Agape did not dare tell the entire truth of where Larentina went and with whom, so she held her tongue.

"Lycurgus, still silent, stared at Agape's face, looking for a sign in her expressions showing if she was lying. He saw none but still believed she was lying. Why would the gods go to her and not his father and mother, the king and queen? He voiced some of his thoughts aloud: 'You lie, woman, for why would Zeus and the deities come to you? Why would they not let the whole world know of their presence in front of Larentina, acknowledging her?'

"Agape became exasperated. 'I do not lie; I do not pretend to know the actions of the gods and why they do things.'

"Lycurgus grew furious as he stood up quickly. He slammed both fists down on the table, but before he could continue arguing with Agape, Erasmus stood up, firmly gripped Lycurgus's forearm, and said sternly, 'Enough! This is getting you nowhere. Agape has spoken the truth to you. This is all she knows. You must leave!'

"Lycurgus totally lost his temper; he heard someone whispering a command in his ear again, but he refused to obey it.

"Unknown to anyone in the room, Hera had been watching the scene, invisible from their sight. Since Lycurgus's will was stronger than she thought, she used her magic and turned him into a statue, preventing him from moving. She turned herself into a clone of Lycurgus and appeared before them.

"Lycurgus saw himself standing before him. Agape gasped in horror, and Erasmus could not believe what he saw—a frozen Lycurgus, and another Lycurgus, walking toward him and his wife.

"Lycurgus could hear and see what was happening but could not move as he watched his other self approach the awestruck perioikoi and his wife.

"The duplicated Lycurgus, who was really Hera, grabbed Lycurgus's sword from his leather sheath. With one clean stroke, the cloned Lycurgus sliced Agape's head from her body and then decapitated Erasmus as he stood there. The clone looked up and saw two of Erasmus's sons running from the darkness into the room. Lycurgus's clone decapitated them both and then searched the house and killed another son as he ran toward the cloned Lycurgus with a pitchfork.

"Lycurgus's clone walked throughout the house and came upon a little girl in a bedroom, crying as she clutched a doll in her hand. Lycurgus's clone lowered his sword and stared at the girl, who was no more than seven years old. She looked uncannily like Larentina did when she was a young girl. The clone disappeared.

"Lycurgus felt complete remorse for the actions of this clone and wished that he had never come here, but the whisper was so strong it seemed that his body was separated from his soul. It was as if he was possessed by something controlling his feelings and actions, and he created this other form of himself.

"Lycurgus saw the little girl, dropped to his knees in front of her, and begged, 'Please, forgive me, for I knew not the truth. I have been deceived by my own ambitions and greed this night.' Lycurgus stood up as he recovered his sword, which the clone had dropped when he disappeared, looked at the little girl with remorse, and left her standing in the corner of the small room.

"It was still raining, but not as hard. Lycurgus took a burning log and set fire to everything in the house, praying that the little girl would run to safety. As he was doing this, he could hear the voice whispering in his ear once again. He felt justified because, after all, he was the protector of Larentina, and whoever threatened him, threatened her.

"As he came to the front door of the house, he threw the burning log into the entrance and ran into the small courtyard. He stood with his hands and arms outstretched by his sides, with his face toward the heavens, so the rain would clean the blood from his face and body. He yelled toward the heavens, 'I've done your bloody deed. Now return my sister to me—my blood, my other half!' He then fell to his knees in total remorse. He looked toward the heavens again and yelled, 'Forgive me, my sister, for I did indeed doubt what you spoke of. May the gods have mercy upon me, for I still truly do not believe it!'

"Androcles had been watching Lycurgus from the darkness, and he was very confused by the sight of his friend yelling at the gods. He had no idea whose house this was or what had happened inside, but he was alarmed when his friend came running out of the burning building.

"He ran up toward Lycurgus and yelled, 'Lycurgus, what has happened here? Do you need my help? Did you find Princess Larentina? In all the heavens …'

"Lycurgus sadly confessed to his longtime friend, 'I have been tested by the gods this night, but for what purpose I do not know. I have failed. You must never speak of this to anyone, not even my sister.'

"Androcles was totally baffled as he answered, 'I do not understand. Of course, my friend, I will not ever speak of this, for I do not even know what has occurred. I'm sure you are justified in your actions.' He grabbed his friend's forearm, stopping Lycurgus from leaving, and firmly commanded, 'But you still must tell me what has just happened and why.'

"Lycurgus jerked his arm from the grip of his friend and mounted his horse; he looked down at Androcles and simply confessed, 'The story that you must protect your father from Larentina's wrath is nothing more than a lie. I have just destroyed it. I have no idea how I'm going to convince my sister otherwise. I will truly need your help someday, my friend, to accomplish this.'

"Androcles looked down at the ground in disappointment, shaking his head from side to side. He looked back up at Lycurgus and simply remarked, 'We must find her first.'

"Lycurgus nodded his head in agreement and facetiously remarked to his friend, "Stop following me like a jealous hag."

Androcles solemnly watched Lycurgus and his horse disappeared into the rainy night.

"Androcles turned and looked at the burning house. To his amazement, a little girl came running out of the front door, screaming. He didn't realize there had been children in the house. He ran to her, scooped her up in his arms, and sadly smiled at her. As the girl clung tightly to his neck, he asked with a deeply concerned tone, 'Now what do we have here? Are you okay?'

"He looked deeper into the child's face and saw her uncanny resemblance to Larentina. His eyes widened in amazement at how much this girl looked like his beloved Larentina. *Was this Agape's home?* he thought to himself. *How close was the family tie really?*

"Androcles kissed the little girl on the cheek and commented, 'We must get you out of the rain before you catch a nasty cold.' He kissed her once more on the cheek. She was so cute and sweet, and he felt remorse for what his friend had just done to her family, but he considered this child an innocent.

"As he was preparing to mount his horse, he saw a flicker of lights and Larentina and a goddess appeared in front of the house. Larentina screamed and ran toward the now-smoldering house. The goddess grabbed her and they both disappeared once again.

"Androcles truly believed now that Larentina was part of the gods. He had just witnessed it, but why would Larentina appear at her aunt's house? Why did Lycurgus kill the occupants and leave this one girl child? Nothing made any sense to Androcles at all. He dismissed his confusion and curiosity at the same time and simply thought of this poor helpless little girl, who reminded him so much of his one true love.

"He found a nearby farm that was occupied by a family of perioikois and ordered them to take care of the little girl as if she was their own. Then he mounted his horse and left.

"As his horse galloped away in the rain, Androcles wondered whether Larentina truly was with the gods or had she been abducted by a jealous goddess. He knew he could not speak of what he had witnessed until he found Larentina herself to answer these questions."

Chapter XXXV

"The gerousia council called a meeting the following day. Both of the kings, their sons, their queens, and all the ephors were summoned because Bion, the senior member of the gerousia council, was determined to discover where Larentina had disappeared to once and for all. Technically, Larentina still belonged to the state; they had not formally released her from service yet.

"Bion didn't want to formally accuse Larentina of being a deserter, because when she had started agoge training, it was agreed by the council and the kings that she and the gods would decide when her term of service was over. He had to admit to himself that this girl child had been a thorn in the gerousia council's side for a very long time now. On the other hand, they had also discovered that Spartan women were good for more than giving birth to strong Spartan children; they could also make very formidable soldiers. Because of this, Bion found himself with increasing opposition regarding the changes in Sparta's society, and he feared Sparta would become weaker if it allowed its women to rule even more. If need be, he would destroy the kings and rebuild if necessary.

"After everyone had gathered into the assembly hall, Bion stood up and loudly barked, 'Be seated and come to order!' The great hall instantly became quiet, and Bion surveyed everyone.

"Hygieinos immediately stood up and shouted, 'This is totally unprecedented to have women in this meeting. The queens need to be excused, at once!'

"Bion shouted back, 'Having a half goddess amongst us is what has gotten us into this mess to begin with, Hygieinos, or have your forgotten this? She is not just a mere woman; who better than the queens to help us figure out what has happened to Princess Larentina?'

"The kings and many other gerousia members yelled, 'Hear! Hear!' in agreement with Bion's statements.

"Bion looked at Queen Alexis and asked her, 'Queen Alexis, do you have any idea what has happened to your daughter?'

"Queen Alexis stood up from her seat and answered Bion in a loud voice, saying, 'I do not know! It is as if her father, Zeus, has snatched her up and has taken her from the Spartan people! His reasoning I do not know!'

"Bion then asked Queen Alexis, 'Do you believe harm has fallen upon her?'

"Queen Alexis again answered him, 'No, that I'm sure of. I believe she may have gone to Zeus to seek answers; if he did not take her, perhaps she sought him out!'

"The hall became noisy again, as the council members talked amongst themselves. Most of the members nodded their heads in agreement with Queen Alexis's insight.

"Hesiodos stood and concluded, 'Then if this is the fate of Princess Larentina, there is no action to be taken.'

"Once again, the assembly members called out in agreement, 'Hear! Hear!'

"Androcles could stay silent no longer. He could not bear the thought of never seeing Larentina again, so he stood and proclaimed, 'I must be heard! Larentina has agreed to be my consort! I must find her; I must know her fate! It is not right for Zeus to take her from me after he has given her to me!'

"King Alcaeus and Lycurgus became furious in unison and immediately stood up. With anger in his eyes, King Alcaeus furiously bellowed, 'How dare you? I did not give you my daughter!'

"Androcles angrily retorted, 'I did not need your permission because her true father, Zeus, did!'

"King Alcaeus became even angrier and raged, 'Zeus gave me his daughter to protect; she is my official ward; I am her guardian, as well as her mortal father. He would have spoken to me first, so I know you lie! If you were not the son of King Karpos, I would kill you where you stand!'

"Lycurgus became angrier and could not stand looking at the cocky Prince Androcles any longer; he lunged toward him and knocked Androcles into the other men who were seated around him. Lycurgus and Androcles fought each other fist to fist; as they wrestled on the ground, it took several minutes before the two kings could get their sons apart, because no one else dared touch either prince. King Karpos and King Alcaeus held their sons by the back of their forearms and ordered in unison, 'Enough!' Each prince stopped resisting their fathers, and the kings released them.

"King Karpos simply confessed once again to Androcles, 'I was wrong, as I explained the other night. There was no agreement, just wishful thinking on my part.'

"Androcles glowered at his father and, at that moment, considered him a coward.

"Lycurgus remained extremely furious with Androcles and voiced his disdain. 'What about the vow you made to me and my sister? Now it makes sense why you have been following me everywhere like a jealous woman!'

"Of course, Androcles knew exactly what Lycurgus was referring to and vindictively replied, 'Oh, just another pipe dream of Larentina's. In all the gods … I know you were just coddling her, as I was.'

"Lycurgus balled his fist up and hit Androcles in the side of his face, knocking him off balance. He shouted out, 'That is not true! You have been struck by an arrow of Cupid's and are acting like a love-stricken puppy! Have you forgot about the fight? Let us not forget the night that the three of us spoke. You may be correct in your assumptions, and I may agree with parts, but I know my sister; she never has been with you in that way! She would never dishonor herself or her household, you donkey's ass!'

"Androcles retorted to these statements in a bitter tone. 'I never said she did, but she gave me her heart forever. She made that vow to me. What you do not know, Lycurgus, is that after the celebration, I went to her secret place and spoke with her that very night. When I awoke the next morning, she had disappeared! And let us not forget your lies at the celebration!'

"Lycurgus raised his fist again to hit Androcles, but he was prepared this time. He grabbed Lycurgus's fist, held it at bay, and took his own fist and hit Lycurgus with all his strength in the stomach. Lycurgus bent over in pain, lunged, and grabbed at Androcles, pushing him to the ground.

"Both kings shook their heads in total disgust at their sons' behavior. They looked at each other without saying another word, agreeing to let their sons battle it out, so that they could have more insight into what this argument was truly about. Not only were the kings bewildered by the nonsense spewing from both princes, but everyone witnessing this heated argument was bewildered as well.

"As they wrestled, once again Lycurgus angrily yelled at Androcles, 'And have you forgotten the lies that you told about her that night?'

"Both princes had grown tired and were now standing. Androcles answered, with a twinge of anger still in his voice, 'I have not forgotten, so let the truth be known. You and I both know from living and fighting with her all these years that she is like no mortal woman. She has never transferred her pain to you, but you have always managed to have yourself lashed instead of her. Let us remember, Brother, the countless times she has healed our wounds and broken bones so quickly with her herbs and magic, as well as our pack. Granted, she is not very good at it because we still carry the scars on our flesh, but we may not have survived without her. Let us not forgot all the great feasts she managed to steal to keep our strength. Not to mention how she took you on secret hunts and the two of you magically returned with fresh meat. Do you think I was blind to this? We have been spoiled because of her, and we have spoiled her as well. Why is it so hard for you to accept that she considers me a mortal god and hero as well as you and King Alcaeus? The difference between you and I, Brother, is that I earned it. I trained her more than you or any other. After all, I was her eirena, no other. I have earned all the glory by proving I could transform a mere girl into a formidable warrior. She might not be as physically strong as we are, but she is very, very clever, and you know it.'

"Lycurgus let out a heavy sigh as he let go of his anger and answered, 'Nor have I forgotten, but you act as if she is less worthy. As you confessed, she was not as strong as we were, but she was much more. You know this as well, and this is the only reason you want her because you want to tame her. I will not allow it. She belongs wild and free, or you will destroy her spirit, and as we are one, you will destroy half of me. I am the deed of wolf!'

"Androcles snickered as he answered, 'You do not know of what you speak, for I do not want to tame her. I can do that with any mortal woman. I want her to give herself to me willingly, because then I have conquered her heart and soul. I know after getting her heart she will still be free and wild, and my undying love for her will be tested for all eternity. That is why I want her—the conquest will always be trying to keep her. I worship the very ground she walks upon, and I'm willing to die for her. I do not need your permission, nor that of Zeus, because her free spirit has already given me her heart. I will fight to keep it against all others.'

"Lycurgus let out another heavy sigh as the anger melted away, and he agreed with some of what Androcles was saying. 'You are bewitched, Androcles, you are blindsided, for my sister is stronger than us, but not physically. She is not as strong as she appears to be. She is still just a woman, and you have forgotten this. You may deny it, but I know myself, on many occasions, I have let her best me over the years, as well as you. Not to mention I know she has bewitched all of the Spartan legions, but that is what makes her stronger than us because she is She Wolf. She is clever; she is smarter than we are; she not only uses her weaknesses against her enemies, she destroys them because of their own knowledge of her own weaknesses. You have witnessed this, as well as I; she never uses the same trick twice, not that I'm aware of. This much I agree with.'

"Androcles let out a heavy sigh as well, letting go of his anger. 'You are right regarding this. I have been blindsided, but as soon as I believe what you speak of, magic always surrounds her.'

"Both princes guffawed at one another after they realized they were both wrong and both right at the same time. King Alcaeus could no longer stand not knowing what the two princes were arguing about. He asked both princes, 'What in Hades's name are you talking about?' King Karpos also had a puzzled expression on his face.

"Both princes became embarrassed, and Androcles simply answered, 'I made a vow to Lycurgus and I broke it.'

"Lycurgus simply nodded his head in agreement.

"Bion immediately ordered, 'Then this matter is settled, you both will go and find Larentina; bring her back to answer for her actions to the gerousia.'

"Everyone present excitedly bellowed, 'Hear! Hear!'"

Larentina's Sorrow

Chapter XXXVI

"The morning of the meeting, Larentina convinced her great-aunt, Aphrodite, to return her to Agape's home. They had already appeared there the night before, when they discovered Agape's home on fire, but then Aphrodite had snatched Larentina away from the smoldering site to protect herself from Zeus's wrath. Larentina pleaded with Aphrodite to return her to Agape's home so she could find out what had happened to her mother. Aphrodite agreed and returned her great-niece to the very spot where she had taken her from to begin with.

"Larentina just stood there, staring in total disbelief at the smoldering house. She could not comprehend why someone would commit such a heinous crime against her family. She could still smell human flesh burning in her nostrils, and she began to vomit because of the stench. She ran as fast as she could from the house with tears streaming down her cheeks, so that she could not smell the terrible odor.

"Larentina dropped to her knees in the middle of a wheatfield. She screamed aloud, trying to release her tremendous sorrow from losing her real mother, the one who had given birth to her. No matter what Agape may or may not have been, Larentina loved her for giving her life and allowing her to keep it. She screamed in agonizing pain louder and louder, trying to somehow dim the immense feeling of hurt and loss. She had never experienced sorrow like this before in her young life. She had cared for these people. Agape had always been in her life; she was Larentina's rock, and she would miss spending time with her mother and her mother's family. She had thought they would always be there for her, and now they were gone because of her. She possessed all this magic, yet she could not save her birth mother. She yelled at the top of her lungs for Celeris to return to her.

"Larentina ran back toward the house, dropped to her knees, and started sobbing because of the guilt that was slowly consuming her.

Larentina controlled her emotions, walked into the house, and discovered the bodies of her mother, Erasmus, and two of her brothers, decapitated in the eating room. She walked through the rest of the burnt house and discovered the other siblings had met the same fate as her mother, but she noticed her youngest sister's body was nowhere to be found, and she hoped the little girl was still alive. She believed that this was the doings of Karpos; there could be no other, and she was going to kill him with or without the Agiad household by her side. Her feelings of guilt, sorrow, and remorse turned to hatred and vengeance as her irises started to change.

"Larentina walked outside with tears streaming down her face; they were tears of hatred and sorrow combined. She looked at her mother's home one last time, as she was already carrying a torch in her hand, and she set fire to it all over again. She stood there for at least an hour until the house was completely engulfed in flames, once again.

"Larentina turned from the burning house and walked out into the open field with her hands open wide, touching the tops of the wheat that came to her waist as Celeris stood watching, waiting for her; the horse greeted her with a couple of nickers of true sorrow for her loss. She mounted Celeris's bare back and walked him toward the barn. Larentina dismounted Celeris; walked into the barn, and retrieved a soft, red wool horse blanket, harness, and other horse items from her mother's barn. After putting these items on Celeris, she mounted him with Lambda in her hand as tears continued to trickle down her beautiful cheeks, and she asked with the deepest sorrow in her voice, 'Please, my cousin, take me to my paradise, so that I may clean the smell of death from my body.' Celeris's wings appeared, and he flew her to her beloved waterfall.

"Larentina slowly cleansed herself underneath the waterfall. She opened the small box Aphrodite had given her to store her beautiful clothing. Larentina then put on the military-style tunic and slowly put on all her body armor, along with the leather sandals and shin guards. She slung her shield across her back and inserted her sword into the leather sheath on her side. She attached her dagger to her leg, concealing it behind her shin guard. She closed the box once again. She slowly put her bow, arrows, and spear on the side of Celeris. She picked up Lambda, mounted Celeris, and put Lambda between her legs. She had returned to the living. Her will, her very soul, and her strength had found its way back into her heart, and she was now ready to take on the world once more.

"Larentina put on her helmet and could see the gerousia's assembly taking place. She removed the helmet and hung it from her saddle. She bent down toward Celeris's ear and whispered, 'Please take me to the assembly hall as fast as you can, but land a mile or so from there, so no one knows your true nature.' Celeris's wings reappeared and off he flew; they lamded about a mile or so from the assembly hall, and he galloped like lightning, leaving a small trail of smoldering flames the rest of the way. Larentina dismounted Celeris, put her helmet back on, and walked to the large doors of the assembly hall.

"At the foot of the assembly hall's steps stood two bronze chariots with four horses in a running pose, with a statue of a Spartan king in each chariot. The assembly hall was constructed entirely of white marble. It was the largest and grandest building in all of Sparta. It had classic Greek columns, and battle scenes were carved in the base of the triangular roof around all four sides of the building. The doors were so large a giant sixty feet tall could easily have walked through them.

"Larentina opened the large doors and walked through them. As she entered the great hall, Queen Alexis was the first to see her, and she stood up and joyfully yelled, 'Daughter!' Everyone stood up as Bion turned to face the entrance. He was stunned and dropped the scrolls in his hands because of what he saw before him. Even though he had heard stories of her, he did not believe them until now; he understood why he could not kill her. He knew he would have to be more clever in order to destroy her.

"Larentina's eyes changed as winds started swirling in the hall. Few people in the hall had seen Larentina's eyes like this before. Bion knew her beautiful armor must have been a gift from the gods, for he had never seen such perfection: the chest plate was molded perfectly to her bosoms, and her bare legs were strong and muscular, as well as her arms, but at the same time she looked like a woman should.

"Androcles could not help but stare in awe at such a perfect woman warrior. He was smitten all over again by such strength and beauty. He was so proud that he had been part of her transformation into a warrior.

"Bion irritably spoke loudly to Larentina. 'What is the meaning of this? You did not have permission to leave, and you are not wearing traditional Spartan armor. All of Sparta has been searching for you. Where have you been?'

"Androcles snickered; he could not help himself. He never had cared for Bion, but he always held his tongue because of the friendship between his father and the senior gerousia. As Androcles thought more on the matter, it seemed to him that the kings also feared Bion and the gerousia because of the power they held. Now, however, the kings showed no fear of Bion.

"Androcles felt a sharp jab from Lycurgus, who had a solemn and agitated expression on his face.

"Androcles whispered, 'You take this too serious, Lycurgus. You know everywhere your sister goes, chaos and tempers flare. I know before the sun sets that she will have me confused, happy, and more than likely angry. You must learn to take things in stride.'

"Lycurgus simply responded, 'And you, Androcles, make light of almost everything. When you become king, you will find life is not so carefree.'

"Androcles just shrugged his shoulders indifferently, with a smirk still upon his lips."

* * *

"Larentina stood with her helmet in her hand. She completely ignored Bion as she furiously bellowed, 'I am here to right a wrong of the house of Agiad!'

"King Alcaeus walked toward his daughter, stood in front of her, and remarked in an angry voice, 'The house of Agiad has not been wronged, so stand down, Daughter. I command it!'

"Larentina stared at her mortal father with defiance in her eyes. 'Queen Alexis's sister, her husband Erasmus, and their entire household were murdered this past night!'

"There were loud gasps of disbelief and then loud chatter among the audience regarding Larentina's accusation. Several objects swirling in the wind forcefully struck Bion, King Karpos, and many of the gerousia. King Alcaeus became irritated with his daughter and commanded, 'Larentina, stop using magic, you are scaring everyone here! You are a Spartan. Your duty is to protect Sparta and its citizens!'

"Larentina closed her eyes and all the chaos suddenly stopped. Her eyes turned back to a hazel brown. The great hall was once again calm.

"King Alcaeus had regained some of his patience and asked, 'How can this be, Daughter? I just spoke with Erasmus yesterday.'

"Larentina stared at her father and tears trickled down her face as she spoke. 'I was there this past night with my great-aunt, the Goddess Aphrodite; I witnessed Erasmus's house burning. I believe the murderer tried to cover up his actions with the fire.'

"The audience gasped in shock at this news. Everyone now believed that Larentina was truly a demigoddess as well as a Spartan, because few had actually seen her use her divine powers. They all wanted to hear from their one and only She Wolf. She was a celebrity and everyone wanted to know everything about her.

"Bion began to ask Larentina a question, but King Alcaeus put his hand up, gesturing him not to speak. Bion bowed slightly and stepped backward from the king and his daughter.

"Both King Alcaeus and Larentina looked into each other's eyes with total seriousness. As they stood there looking at each other, Bion realized the magnitude of her accusation; he commanded in a loud authoritative voice to everyone present in the assembly hall, 'All the apella, leave immediately! All the ephors, leave immediately! Queens, leave us now! Gerousia members, leave us, with the exception of the other four senior members!'

"As everyone started to leave, King Karpos joined the small circle that was forming around King Alcaeus and Larentina. Lycurgus and Androcles instinctively stood on each side of Larentina, and the other senior members had already taken their places beside Bion and King Karpos. Queen Alexis sheepishly said in a soft voice to Bion, 'I will stay, I must.' Bion just nodded his head, giving Queen Alexis permission to stay.

"King Alcaeus became angry with Bion. His heart had been completely transformed, as were the hearts of many Spartan citizens, regarding women because Larentina was a force to be reckoned with. He wanted more than ever to put his beloved child upon a pedestal, and he had endured enough. Larentina just seemed to open men's hearts.

"King Alcaeus roared, 'How dare you presume that you have authority to command your queen to leave, and then grant her permission to stay! She does not need permission from you to stay or go! She is my wife and a Spartan queen. She rules in my absence. This is my law and shall be adhered to, or I will cut out your tongue! You disrespect my wife and you are disrespecting your king! I do not know when this became a custom, but I will not tolerate it any further. She is your queen and from henceforth, you will not speak to her until she grants you permission to speak. Kneel before her and beg for forgiveness.'

"Bion, as well as everyone else, was baffled, but the law is the law during any king's reign. When a king makes a law, it must be enforced. Bion was completely angry at this weak, foolish king, but he obeyed the command and knelt before Queen Alexis.

"'I humbly beg for your forgiveness, my queen. I did not know of this law.'

"Queen Alexis blushed, but at the same time felt empowered. 'You are forgiven. Rise, Gerousia.'"

Chapter XXXVII

"Zeus just happened to look upon his daughter on this day, as he had done on many occasions throughout her life. He stood in the middle of his throne room in front of a large, waist-high crystal basin that was filled with water. He stretched out his arm and waved his hand over the basin. The water turned to ice. He then walked lazily to his throne, sat down, and watched as the images appeared from the ice in three dimensions.

"Zeus was a very handsome deity. He looked like a mortal man in his midthirties, with muscles like his son, Hercules. His head was completely bald. His eyes were the lightest gray with a freshly shaven face. You would think he stayed out in the sun because he had the most perfectly tanned skin, like his daughter Larentina. No wonder he could have any woman he wanted, and that is probably why he has had so many. He was still not sure if he truly was with Agape, because he had forgotten so many of his conquests, but he did not care. Larentina had already proven she was his daughter like no other had done before.

"He was wearing a white tunic that flowed from his waist down to the tops of his knees, with a wide gold belt that held it in place at his waist. His chest was bare except for the soft, white material that draped over one of his shoulders, exposing part of his muscular chest. It is no wonder everyone feared him, because he not only possessed magical power, but his physical strength alone would leave men trembling.

"Zeus became increasingly angry when he learned of Larentina's activities these last few months, and you could feel the thunder when he commanded Aphrodite to appear in front of him.

"Hera was already sitting on her throne beside Zeus, watching the Spartan mortals and their foolishness, doing her very best not to giggle in front of Zeus.

"Aphrodite appeared immediately. Zeus, in a thundering voice, demanded, 'Aphrodite, did I not command you not to interfere in my daughter's journey?'

"Aphrodite, with fear in her voice, still managed to be coy and answered Zeus, 'No, my king, you only said you wished that I not interfere.'

"Zeus became even more irritated. 'My wish is always my command. Being clever with words does not excuse you!'

"Aphrodite tried her charms on him by simply stating, 'But I have caused no harm, I will always protect my new friend, my great-niece, always. She needed to learn about love as well.'

"Zeus was impressed with Aphrodite's response; he shrugged his shoulders and said, in a softer voice, 'Aphrodite, you are probably right, because Larentina holds more powers of the gods than I expected. Therefore, I forgive you, but my daughter will not become a harlot like you. Have I made myself clear on this matter?'

"Aphrodite nodded her head, acknowledging she understood, not daring to push her luck any further with Zeus.

"Zeus looked at his charge and solemnly asked, 'Do you know who murdered Larentina's mother, Agape?'

"Aphrodite slyly answered, 'No, my king. When I returned her from our travels together, we discovered Agape's home was engulfed in flames, but we arrived too late. I instinctively swept her away from the awful smell of death.'

"Zeus shook his head from side to side in disgust and waved his hand as if shooing Aphrodite away, as he commanded, 'Just go. I do not think you have caused great harm.'

"He looked over at his wife, Hera, and angrily demanded, 'Hera, what have you done?'

"In fear of being caught lying to her husband, she just simply smiled and answered him cleverly, 'You had commanded Lycurgus to be Larentina's protector. He was confronted with a threat by Erasmus and Agape, so I simply whispered in his ear to protect her.' Hera smiled triumphantly because she saw to it that her mortal rival was killed by Zeus's own daughter's brother, and that was revenge enough for her. Of course, she left out the part that she had done the slaying, disguised as the young Lycurgus.

"Zeus irritably retorted, 'I should punish you, but you are right because I did command Lycurgus to be her protector.'

"Zeus left his throne, stretched out his arm with his hand opened, and turned the ice in the basin back to water. He was angry at how clever his wife had been. He had to find a way to keep his daughter from killing her brother for his crimes against her mortal mother. After all, she was the daughter of duty, honor, and so much more.

"Zeus smiled to himself because he was truly proud of his daughter. He had not felt like this in a very, very long time regarding one of his offspring. He did not want to interfere in her journey too much; he had to admit he would not want any other woman thinking the way he had seen fit to teach Larentina, but it had been done.

"Zeus knew Larentina was becoming more than a handful because he had no other choice the last time but to interfere. If he had not intervened, Larentina would not have survived. He would have to deal with it. He had no idea that her powers would grow so strong, or was it her will, maybe her spirit? He simply shrugged these thoughts from his mind. After seeing with his own eyes the lightning bolts in Larentina's eyes and her power to command the winds, he knew she was his daughter although he did not remember being with Agape, a thought that kept returning to his mind. He saw her once all those years ago, and then the surprise of a lifetime came when Agape and her sister added natural energy to their will and summoned him to them. But that incident did make some sort of sense in view of Larentina's increasing powers. His energy mixed with Agape's naturally would create a strong and powerful being.

"He had to admit, Agape had been a very beautiful woman, strong and powerful as well. He must have been drunk from wine because he would have never forgotten a woman like that. She was a woman who could have easily captured his heart for a moment in time.

"Hera was a beautiful and older goddess. She had fiery red hair, light gray eyes, and fair skin. She had a straight nose and an oval face. Her hair was curled and pulled back neatly from her face. She was slender and wore brightly colored tunics flowing to her ankles. She loved rubies and her jewelry showed this. She was vindictive, as well as jealous, and she felt she had every right to be so because of Zeus's infidelities. She felt vindicated when she killed Agape and her family, but she still wanted to see the daughter produced by her unfaithful husband dead.

"Hera just could not understand Zeus's reasoning for taking such an interest in Larentina. He had never showed this kind of enthusiasm for any of his daughters before.

"As he was about to walk out of the throne room, Hera decided to continue playing a wicked game of chess, with the mortals as her pawns. Hera had been playing this game with him for thousands of years; she cleverly asked, 'Zeus, did you know your daughter has consented to be Androcles's consort?'

"Zeus walked quickly back to his throne, and as he sat back down, he asked, 'What do you speak of?'

"Hera, smiling at her husband, answered him softly, 'Oh, you can't blame Aphrodite for that one, because your daughter had already promised to give herself to Androcles after the Olympics. You heard it for yourself when Androcles proclaimed her as his future consort. Androcles even announced that you gave Larentina to him.'

"Zeus shrugged his shoulders, gesturing that he was indifferent to the subject, and he voiced his thoughts on the matter. 'He lies because he must have been struck by an arrow of Cupid's. I am going to have to do something with that mischievous rascal of Aphrodite's.'

"Hera giggled softly and said, 'I do not believe Cupid or Aphrodite had anything to do with it, because your daughter gave her consent freely to Androcles, not the reverse. Remember, she is your daughter, not your son.'

"Zeus responded with irritation to the cleverness of his wife, saying, 'So what? Men take women all the time. So if she takes a man, what difference does it make? What are you trying to imply anyway?'

"This wicked game Hera played with Zeus would ultimately be his downfall. After all, Hera was the goddess of marriage. And marriage was a situation that Zeus would ultimately lose because he was so often unfaithful to his own wife.

"Hera replied, 'My husband, I'm saying that she has given consent to him without permission from Alcaeus or you; by the rules of proper marriage, she must have her father's or guardian's consent to marry.'

"Zeus became more irritated with Hera and simply responded, 'It does not make her unsuited. After all, she is still a virgin and untouched by man. Even Aphrodite could not tempt Larentina to stain herself. She can love whoever she chooses, and marry whoever she chooses, because I command this.'

"Hera turned her gaze from her husband, smiling, and cleverly stated what Zeus had forgotten, 'Do you not remember you made a promise to Apollo when she became of age to marry? You promised you would give her to him as his consort; in return, he gave your daughter the power over the wolves and the wolf's spirit as her guardian and protector. He also promised from your bargain that he himself would be her guardian as well.'

"Zeus scratched his clean-shaven face as he contemplated his dilemma. He had truly forgotten that promise to Apollo, so he simply remarked, 'What I do not understand is why Apollo did not discuss his intentions to me when Larentina was born. I did not know anything of this matter until she was twelve years of age. I heard gossip but did not pay much attention to this until Larentina reached out to me then. Apollo did not mention anything until I spoke with him years ago. I believe I will speak with him further on this matter, now that I can remember many things, but until then, she has married no one, and she will choose who she pleases. Is that understood?'

"Hera just smiled at her husband and answered, 'Completely, my husband, but I believe Apollo will be very upset.'

"Hera got up, still smiling, because she had outwitted her husband this time, and she walked out of the throne room, leaving her husband to contemplate the dilemma.

"Once outside the chamber, Hera leaned up against the wall and put her hands over her mouth to muffle her giggling of triumph against her adulterous, self-righteous husband.

"Zeus could not stand it as he watched his wife leave the throne room; he quickly got up, turned the water to ice again, and stood at the well watching his daughter and the events unfold. He did not know if he would have to intervene if his daughter made a bad choice because of Hera's deliberate interference. He watched impatiently. He was not going to allow Hera to do what she did to his son, Hercules. He just was not going to allow it."

Chapter XXXVIII

"After everyone had left the hall, King Alcaeus solemnly asked his daughter, 'If this is so, then we must seek vengeance. Who do you believe is the murderer? We will seek vengeance together as one household should. We will right a wrong that has been done to our household, but Daughter, before you speak, be very careful who you accuse; you must be certain. You must have proof.'

"Larentina took her mortal father's advice and thought for a moment before answering, 'I accuse Karpos and his household, because he took Queen Alexis's sister by force and continued to abuse her; that is the main reason she married in a lower class—anything to keep him from taking her again and making her his for all time, to torture and abuse her, to be enslaved by him and his lust. This is the proof I have as to why it was Karpos. So it would be fitting for him to be killed by a woman and by Agape's own blood.'

"Bion was in total shock by this accusation; he wisely commented, 'These are just words. We were not there, and after all these years, nothing new has been discovered. If King Karpos wants to take a woman in any manner, he has the right to do so. It does not mean, after all these years, he would decide to murder her. It does not make sense why he would do this. Is this the truth to which the Oracle referred?'

"King Karpos let out an agitated sigh because of these false accusations. He was exasperated, because after all these years, he believed the Oracle had it all wrong. He voiced his dismay and defended himself. 'If I wanted her, I would have taken her as my wife, and I did just that. When she rejected me, I did seek to punish her and Erasmus, but Alcaeus interfered with my retribution by adopting Erasmus, which put her under his protection. I would never raise a hand against the Agiad household—never! If this is what the Oracle was speaking of, then you are seeking vengeance based off a lie.'

"King Alcaeus patiently explained to Larentina, 'He speaks the truth, Daughter. We all know how Agape felt toward Karpos; what you do not know is I met Agape by chance. She was the first sister. I was enchanted by her beauty, but when I met Alexis, I fell in love with Alexis's strength and will. Karpos chose Agape, but I believe Agape was furious because I chose her sister and not her; this is the reason she left Karpos. The next thing we all knew, she married Erasmus. Karpos truly loved Agape; he would have killed her and Erasmus because Agape was really Karpos's wife, and he did have the right to do so. I only adopted Erasmus because Alexis would have never forgiven me if I allowed Karpos to kill her sister. So you see, Daughter, you do not know all the sides of the truth. You only know one part. This is why I asked you to be very careful who you accuse. There truly has been no wrong committed against my household. As for the tragic fate of Agape and Erasmus, I am truly saddened that such a fate happened to them.'

"Queen Alexis gently took Larentina's hand in hers and lovingly shared her intuitive wisdom with Larentina. 'You are my daughter, and you have always been this since the night you were born. My husband and King Karpos speak the truth, Daughter. There is much you do not know of my sister. You are still young and do not know the secrets of the heart.'

"King Karpos then added to this truth, 'Larentina, I do not need to speak about my actions to you, but out of respect for my longtime friend, you must also know that Agape only hated me because I was not Alcaeus; it was very hard for me to let go of the jealousy I felt toward my friend because of this, but I valued my friendship and my country more than I valued the love I felt for Agape. I wonder, will you choose the same fate for my son: to go through life with a broken heart?'

"Larentina was very confused. Did Agape lie about being her mother? Was this truly a setup created by Agape for her to kill Karpos? Then Larentina remembered the helmet. She gently removed Lambda from her helmet and passed the wolf to her mother to hold. Larentina put the helmet on her head and thought of Agape, Alcaeus, Karpos, and Alexis. She moved backward as she saw only her past, her birth, and nothing more. All she saw was Queen Alexis killing the gerousia member. What was strange was that she thought she saw Bion in Agape's mirror. She was not sure though. When she removed her helmet and came back into the moment, Androcles was holding her and speaking to her with loving concern. 'Larentina? Larentina, what is the matter?'

"Larentina shook her head from side to side as if she was in a daze; it had been just like she was really there. The images that were before her had been so real and alive; she still did not believe King Karpos. 'You still lie!' She looked at King Alcaeus and still pleaded her case, 'Father, you have been lied to. It must be King Karpos.' Larentina then pulled her sword out and began to wield it, but her sword was met by Lycurgus's sword. Larentina passionately yelled, 'Brother, step aside, I will have justice!'

"Lycurgus firmly retorted, 'I will not.'

"Androcles wielded his sword as Larentina tried to strike down King Karpos. He retorted, as he met her sword to prevent her from striking down his father, 'Stand down! For from your own mother and father's tongues, my father has done no wrong to your household! My father was not at Erasmus's house, but I was!'

"Larentina was totally confused and shocked. She lowered her sword and said passionately, 'You lie to protect your father!'

"Androcles said with conviction, 'I do not, Princess, for I saw you and a goddess appear in front of their house. I saw you running to the front door; the beautiful goddess ran behind you, and you both disappeared in front of me. It was still raining. I had Agape's youngest daughter in my arms.'

"Larentina immediately wielded her sword to kill Androcles without a second thought, but her sword was once again met by Lycurgus. Lycurgus yelled at his sister with total conviction, 'He did not kill them …'

"Before Lycurgus had a chance to utter another word, Zeus angrily yelled from Olympus, 'Enough, Daughter!'

"Within a matter of a second, the large room filled with mist and there stood Zeus, standing tall, hands on his hips, and his legs spread apart. His facial expression was of complete anger.

"Everyone in the room dropped to their knees, and they gazed toward the ground in total fear of Zeus. Larentina was the only one who remained standing, glaring at Zeus. She angrily uttered to Zeus without fear, 'Well, Father, so after all these years, you decided to show yourself to me, instead of everyone else around me.'

"Everyone remained on their knees, as they stared at Larentina in complete horror that she would show such disrespect to a god with such power.

"Zeus looked up at the heavens and playfully guffawed at his daughter's defiance of his presence, and he said, 'Well, Child, you are definitely my seed—just as stubborn, but I will not allow you to cause a civil war among mortal men. Nor will I allow you to create another war between the sexes.

They will do this all on their own without interference by me and especially by you. I did not intend this to be your journey.'

"Before continuing, Zeus chuckled at his own joke regarding the sexes. He became serious as he continued to lecture Larentina. 'I wanted you to have a simple loving life without a care in the world, but lies and deceit have brought us down the path that was chosen for us. This was neither your choice nor mine, but what has been done is done. Learn from the mistakes of these vain and arrogant people; you lack wisdom and understanding. You will not change anything with the sword alone, my child.'

"Larentina simply said to Zeus, 'But I can try.'

"Zeus said in a patient and understanding tone, 'You may try, Daughter, but your efforts will be in vain. Being the strongest and the cleverest does not make you the most righteous. Winning a war and conquering are very different; just look at your own people, who still enslave their conquered. Through the ages, you and I will be forgotten by men; your efforts and accomplishments for your people will also be forgotten.

"'Acting upon a partial truth is still a lie. So righting a wrong will simply turn into murder. I did not want to interfere again, but you have left me no choice. I will not allow my daughter to murder her brother because she does not know the entire truth.'

"Larentina was still angry with Zeus and viciously exploited his absence in her life. 'Admit it, Father, your absence in my life was because I was a daughter and not a son. You interfered in Hercules's life, and the lives of many of your other sons as well; I do not even recall a half-mortal daughter of yours ever being mentioned. So, because I'm just a daughter and my life is less important, you confessed to me that you do not want to interfere. You also said, Father, that you wanted my life to be simple and loving, not strong and complicated like your half-mortal sons' lives were.'

"Zeus had lost some of his patience with his daughter's lack of understanding and commanded everyone in the room, 'Get out! I want to speak with my daughter alone.'

"As everyone ran from the assembly hall in fear of their lives, Zeus commanded, 'Except for you, Alexis and Lycurgus!'

"King Alcaeus was already angry with Zeus for not only tricking his wife, but for having the audacity to call Larentina 'Daughter.' Larentina was *his* daughter, and only he should have the right to call her that, but he kept his emotions to himself.

"King Alcaeus stopped, turned to face Zeus, and voiced his reservations: 'What does my family have to do with this?' Zeus had lost most of his patience with these mortals and vocalized his annoyance. 'Because, silly man, they are my daughter's family as well. Before I completely lose my temper with you, Alcaeus, I have never spoken to any of my offsprings' mortal guardians before this day, but then, I never had a daughter—or son, for that matter—who inherited my stubbornness. So for Larentina's sake, I want to commend you formally for protecting and looking after my daughter. I want to announce that you are her formal guardian, and she is your ward. You have raised her nobly, despite the fact she is not yours. You are a wise and noble king. Now get out before I punish you for disobeying me to begin with!'

"Zeus then looked at his daughter and commanded with a tender tone, 'Come before me.' Larentina hesitated for a few moments, put her sword into its sheath, and hesitantly walked toward Zeus. He hugged his daughter and whispered in her ear, 'You are right, my daughter, on many things. Please forgive me, for you are not like any other mortal daughter. I am and have always been very proud of you. You do not think like most women, but it is time you knew the entire truth of the matter before us.' He let go of Larentina and gazed deep into her eyes and humbly asked, 'Do we agree on this much at least?'

"Larentina's eyes were welling with tears, and she simply nodded her head in agreement.

"Zeus, with a proud smile upon his face, commanded, 'Good; now that it's just the four of us, I want you, Alexis, to tell the truth to Agape's children.'

"Alexis gazed down at the ground shamefully and hesitated for several moments before speaking the truth to both twins. 'I am not your mother; Agape was. Lycurgus, your real father was Erasmus. I convinced Agape to give me her babies because mine were stillborn. I was afraid I would be killed because of this.'

"Lycurgus dropped to his knees with remorse and regret because he believed he had killed his real mother and father in cold blood. He was even more ashamed because during the first and only conversation he had with his real parents, he had behaved so cruelly toward them. This would now be the only memory he would have of them, and he would have to carry it with him for the rest of his life. This also meant he was not the true heir of the throne. He was truly just a perioikoi and nothing more.

"Zeus then commanded, with empathy, 'Stand, Lycurgus, for you did not kill your parents; my wife, Hera, did; she simply used your likeness to murder Agape because I loved her for one night, and Hera wants my daughter to fail. I never wanted Alexis because she was not like Agape. I did not know that Larentina would become so strong. I thank you for this, Alexis, for you are truly a good woman and mother.

"'The truth of this matter will stay with only us. No one else need know. Lycurgus, you are still heir to the throne, and if anyone dares to state otherwise, they will feel my wrath. So fear not, young Lycurgus, because it will take a king to keep your sister safe. By becoming king, you will command legions, and hopefully that will be enough to protect her and the chaos I know she will bring. After all, Larentina is much like me.

"'I will do my best not to interfere anymore, Daughter, in your journey of life. I only did so because Hera caused this. Now go and fulfill your true destiny, for this is not it. You have been tested this day and you have failed, but I'm giving you a second chance.'

"Larentina had tears streaming down her cheeks as she hugged her father. Zeus returned a fatherly hug, kissed her on her forehead, and whispered in her ear, 'You are the apple of my eye, my pride, my joy, and sorrow, for no other child of mine has caused me so many emotions. You truly will be the death of me.' He sadly chuckled in Larentina's ear.

"Larentina looked up at her father, smiled at him, and humbly murmured, 'Thank you, Father, for saving me this day.' She still hugged him so tightly because she did not want him to leave her again. When she opened her eyes, he was gone out of her life, once again.

"After Zeus disappeared, Lycurgus and Queen Alexis both hugged Larentina as tears streamed down her cheeks. Lycurgus was completely remorseful for what had happened to his own mother and father and siblings; he sadly begged for forgiveness. 'Larentina, I'm truly sorry for what I have done. Will you ever forgive me, for I do not know if I will be able to forgive myself?'

"Larentina let go of her brother and sadly gazed into his eyes full of tears, and she answered, 'You have done nothing, Brother, to warrant my forgiveness, because it was Hera that did this. I swear here and now to you, we will seek vengeance for the wrong she has committed against our family, but if you seek forgiveness to give closure to us, then you have it.'

"Lycurgus smiled sadly toward his sister, kissed her on the forehead, and proclaimed, 'If justice is what you seek, Sister, then you shall have it. I swear to all the gods, I will not rest until Hera's head is brought to you.'

"Larentina strongly ordered, 'Enough! Let us swallow it, Brother, and turn this into something else.'

"Larentina kissed Queen Alexis and announced, 'You are our mother; you have been and always will be. Let us all make a vow, we will never let the truth of Lycurgus's and my birth divide us, again.'

"Lycurgus and Queen Alexis vowed in unison, 'I swear it.' All three of them gave each other a hug. Then they prepared themselves to face the kings and others outside the assembly hall."

Chapter XXXIX

"Queen Alexis, with Lambda in her hands, emerged from the assembly hall with Lycurgus and Larentina a few steps back, flanking both sides of her. All three of them held their heads high.

"Larentina walked with pride directly toward King Karpos and knelt on one knee. She gazed toward the ground first, looked up at him, and humbly asked, 'Please forgive me, my king, for I'm but a foolish girl.'

"King Karpos looked down at Larentina and in an authoritative voice announced for all to hear, 'Rise, Goddess, for you are forgiven. It is your nature to be of duty and honor; I completely understand this. Now let us have a celebration!' He looked at the crowd with his hands raised above his head and proclaimed to the world, 'Princess Larentina is truly a Spartan goddess of duty, honor, and courage, for she has even stood up to Zeus himself, knowing Zeus could have easily destroyed her!'

"The crowd cheered and chanted, 'She Wolf! She Wolf!' The people of Sparta picked up Queen Alexis, Lycurgus, Larentina, even Prince Androcles, and carried them several feet before putting them back down again.

"Androcles, with a broad smile, proudly yelled to the crowds, 'The three of us shall compete in this year's Olympics, to show the world that both women and men of Sparta are truly a force to reckon with!' The crowd cheered even louder at Androcles's proclamation.

"King Alcaeus and King Karpos were now standing beside Androcles, Larentina, Lycurgus, and Queen Alexis. King Alcaeus displayed his affections publicly for all to see as he passionately kissed his wife. He loudly commanded to all the Spartans, 'From this day forward, we will treat our women with respect and love and honor them most highly as the mothers of our great warriors! Our Spartan women will walk beside us as equals! Larentina has earned these freedoms for them!'

"The crowd cheered even louder. King Karpos in the heat of the moment was confused as to why Alcaeus would command this, but it did not matter to him if a woman walked beside a man or behind him. He simply agreed as he too loudly announced, 'This shall be done! Our She Wolf has earned this for our Spartan women!'

"King Karpos leaned toward King Alcaeus and whispered, 'Pray, tell me, Alcaeus why did you order this? I thought you were going to discipline Larentina for publicly spanking Spartan men for the last several years for doing as was Spartan custom among men and women.'

"Alcaeus laughed as he whispered his answer. 'It is now apparent to all who saw Zeus come before Larentina that she is a demigoddess without question. Would you not allow a mortal father to reward his daughter instead and be in her favor? Furthermore, she has already put fear in the hearts of the Spartan men for treating their women as such, for many years now. Have you not noticed almost all of Sparta has been treating women with respect? The men walk beside their women instead of having them walk behind them. We are kings and we should lead by example. I am tired of having citizens complain about Larentina, and I know you hear just as many complaints. You know our She Wolf will continue lurking in the shadows of the streets and punishing every man who makes a woman walk behind him. She has used fear and humiliation to slowly transform Sparta's ways. In the last several years, I have witnessed men leaving their property to their widows. I am tired of putting this issue off with Bion and the gerousia. You may not like this, Karpos, but you cannot deny Larentina has already changed us. To be honest, I see nothing wrong with what she is trying to accomplish.'

"King Karpos responded, as the crowd continued cheering them, 'You may be right, but I still have my reservations. Even though I have seen much divine power from Larentina, it is still hard to completely believe.'

"King Alcaeus nodded his head, agreeing, as he raised his hands in the air. 'Spartan citizens, hear me!' The crowd grew silent. King Alcaeus continued, 'Our She Wolf has not asked for much. She only wants us to treat each other, including our women, with more respect. She has already transformed us and changed the hearts of men. This is why King Karpos and I have agreed that this shall be our law for Sparta.'

"King Alcaeus turned and faced Larentina as he commanded her, 'Larentina, it is the law now. I command you to stop publicly humiliating Spartan citizens with your powers.'

"Larentina nodded her head in agreement with a smile upon her lips.

"In unison, Queen Irene and Queen Alexis jubilantly hugged Larentina as both princes shook their head from side to side in disbelief.

"Bion almost lost his balance as he stood on one of the upper steps to the assembly hall. He could not believe these stupid, foolish kings.

"King Alcaeus smiled with pride at his children and asked, with a twinge of concern, 'Now tell me, the three of you, how will you be ready to compete in the Olympics when the games begin just several months from now? None of you is prepared. Larentina, you may be half goddess, but it's still a huge challenge, because you will be competing against the world's greatest athletes.'

"Lycurgus smiled at his father and arrogantly responded, 'After all, Father, we have been training all of our lives; we will be ready; I swear it!'

"Androcles guffawed at his friend and arrogantly repeated, 'We will be ready.'

"Larentina just shook her head from side to side at how arrogant her brother and Androcles were.

"Androcles leaned into Larentina and whispered in her ear, 'Now will you be my consort?'

"Larentina slyly smiled at him as she slightly blushed when answering, "No, not this day, but maybe someday.'

"Androcles was disappointed, but voiced his patience, 'Fine. I will wait until you are ready.'

"Larentina reached over, kissed him full on the mouth, and softly murmured, 'I promise someday. Please, Androcles, be patient with me.'

"Androcles smiled and kissed Larentina once more. 'I will wait for you for all eternity if need be, my love.'

"As Androcles kissed Larentina passionately, King Alcaeus stepped between them and firmly, but still smiling, protested, 'Androcles, it is clear she is not yours, not yet. You will have to prove yourself to me.'

"Androcles chuckled and boasted, 'Forgive me, my king, but I will have her someday.'

"King Alcaeus, with a devilish smile, responded, 'That may be, but not this day.' Then he put his arm around Androcles's shoulders, patted his back, and teasingly snickered.

"Larentina mounted Celeris as her brother, Androcles, and the kings mounted their steeds; the crowd continued to cheer for them. Celeris let out a few nickers as he nodded his head up and down with the pride of his mistress.

"Queen Alexis passed Lambda up to Larentina as she was sitting on Celeris, and Larentina put her hand out for her mother to mount Celeris with her. Queen Alexis blushed and said to Larentina, as she looked up at her daughter, 'I could not.'

"Larentina playfully giggled as she announced, 'Oh yes, you can, I have a treat for you this day.' Queen Alexis grabbed her daughter's arm as Larentina helped her mount the stallion.

"After Alexis mounted Celeris and sat behind her daughter, Larentina announced to King Alcaeus, 'We will meet you later for the great celebration!'

King Alcaeus nodded his head, acknowledging Larentina and allowing his wife to go with her.

"Celeris galloped away with the two women and Lambda on his back out into the countryside. Once they were out of sight, Larentina had him stop. Larentina dismounted the great horse with Lambda. She looked up at her mother, Queen Alexis, and commanded, 'Stay! Celeris will show you mother earth as the gods see it. You have earned this for all that you have given me.'

"Alexis looked at her daughter with a puzzled expression as Larentina smacked Celeris on the rear and commanded him, 'Fly, cousin, and let my mother see mother earth!'

"Celeris made several nickers and several loud whinnies as he ran across the open field. His wings had already appeared, and he took off into the sky, leaving smoldering hoofprints below. Queen Alexis held onto his neck in fear she would fall off the great stallion's back.

"Alexis was now in the air; she saw the beauty of the lands of mother earth below her. The wind has loosened her hair from its pins, and it was now flowing behind her. Her entire body tingled because she was so high in the sky. She felt like a goddess, free with the winds. She looked up toward the fluffy, white clouds and said aloud, 'Thank you, Agape, my sister, my friend, for giving me your daughter and all the wonders of true freedom that she offers. Forgive me, Sister, as I forgive you of the past. Your death will not be in vain, for I swear to the gods before my death, somehow, some way you will be remembered as the true mother of the She Wolf, goddess of duty and honor! I swear it! I do not know how or when, but your name will be remembered throughout the ages as well as your daughter's name!'

"As Celeris flew to the ground, Alexis watched her daughter smiling up at her. Once Celeris came to a halt beside Larentina, Alexis dismounted, hugged her daughter tightly, and jubilantly expressed her gratitude to

Larentina. 'Thank you for a moment of true freedom. I will never forget what you have given me this day and the future generations of Spartan daughters.'

"Larentina proudly expressed her thoughts to her mother. 'And I will never forget it was you who made it possible for me to have more freedoms than any other woman before us. I wish my other mother, Agape, were here to see this. Now all of Sparta can walk the streets with their heads held a little higher.'

The two women hugged for several more minutes; Alexis was crying because she was so happy and so proud of Larentina.

"Larentina whispered in her mother's ear while they were hugging, 'Mother, you must not tell anyone that Celeris can fly.' She let go of her mother and rubbed Celeris's neck as she asked the stallion, 'Do you also want to compete in the Olympics, my cousin, my friend?'

"Celeris answered Larentina by shaking his head with his entire neck, up and down, as he let out a loud whinny, letting Larentina know her insight about him was correct. Larentina playfully giggled at her horse and said to Queen Alexis, 'So, you see, Mother, no one must know who Celeris truly is because he wants to compete with me as a mortal horse. His nickname will be Cele, so no one will know who he truly is.'

"Once Queen Alexis had her emotions in check, she said, 'Your secret is safe. Now come, Daughter, we have a celebration to attend.'"

Chapter IL

"Once inside the courtyard of their home, everyone greeted Queen Alexis and Princess Larentina. There must have been at least five hundred people in the large courtyard. Tables were already set up and overflowing with food and wine. Larentina deeply breathed in the smells of the delicious foods that surrounded the courtyard. The women wore beautiful tunics of many styles and colors, with gold and colorful jewelry. Some of the men wore different colored tunics, and others were dressed in traditional Spartan military garb. Beautiful music played in the background. This was truly a celebration fit for a king.

"After Alexis and Larentina dismounted Celeris, and he was taken to the stables to be pampered and fed, Alexis turned to her daughter and proudly commented, 'We must dress you as a true princess of Sparta. After all, my child, you are my blood as well, and I have not been able to dress you properly because our kings have been too busy teaching you how to be a prince instead of a beautiful princess.' Alexis blushed ever so slightly as she giggled.

"Larentina simply smiled, nodding her head in agreement with her mother. Larentina did not dare displease her because, in Larentina's heart, she was truly her mother. She knew in her deepest thoughts that if it were not for Queen Alexis, she would not be here this day. Besides, Queen Alexis deserved the right to dress Larentina if she chose to do so.

"Androcles and Lycurgus walked up to greet Larentina; Lycurgus teased his sister, with a twinge of pleasure, 'Please, Sister, tell Androcles that you love him, for he gives me no peace with his nagging like an old hag over you.'

"Larentina giggled as she blushed. She put her arms around Androcles's waist, kissed him passionately, and simply reassured him, 'You know I love you. I gave you the greatest gift I could give a man: my heart.'

"Androcles blushed slightly and smiled as he gazed into Larentina's beautiful face.

"Lycurgus became agitated and confused; he asked Larentina, 'What in Hades's name does that mean, anyway? Androcles has been spewing that dribble all day; we even got into an argument over it.'

"Androcles and Larentina smiled at Lycurgus as if they knew a secret that he did not know. Androcles answered, with a bit of sarcasm, 'And that, my friend, is none of your concern.'

"Alexis gently grabbed Larentina by her upper arm and walked toward the palace. Larentina turned to the young men and commented, 'Mother is determined to take me, so I must follow.' She turned away from the princes and headed to the palace with her mother.

"Queen Alexis kept her grip on Larentina's arm as they casually walked toward the main entranceway of the palace; they softly chatted with each other as they walked. They were almost to the wide steps leading into the house when King Alcaeus stopped them. He kissed his wife on the lips and asked, with a smile of delight, 'Now, ladies, what are the two of you up to?'

"He gently kissed his wife again. Larentina and Queen Alexis giggled and blushed slightly as Queen Alexis answered, 'Well, my husband, I thought it only fitting that your daughter dresses this evening as a princess and daughter, instead of a son and warrior.'

"King Alcaeus slyly chuckled and kissed his wife one more time and suggested in a proud, fatherly way, 'Good. She will dance for the entertainment of her father and guests this night, like a daughter should.'

"Queen Alexis smiled at her husband, batted her eyes at him seductively, and replied, 'I'm sure your daughter will not have any problem doing so.'

"Larentina giggled at her parents as she teasingly commented, 'A daughter's duty, always, with the two of you.'

"King Alcaeus asked his daughter, 'Is that not what you are? A goddess of duty?'

"Larentina moved beside her father, opposite of her mother, stood on her tiptoes, kissed him on the cheek, and proudly commented, 'Then I must give a dance like no other. After all, Father, you are a king!'

"Queen Alexis took her daughter's hand, and King Alcaeus watched his wife and daughter disappear inside the palace.

"The festivities continued. Within an hour, Queen Alexis emerged from the large main entrance of the palace. Silence fell upon everyone in the courtyard as they gazed upon their beautiful queen at the top of the stairs. She wore a beautiful lavender chiton that flowed outward to her ankles. She had on beautiful gold jewelry, and her hair was pinned up with a gold crown that was about two inches wide.

"Then everyone gasped as Larentina emerged and stood beside her mother. She wore a pure white two-piece chiton with deep purple waves at the bottom that brushed against the tops of her feet, and the side slits went almost to the tops of her thighs, revealing her beautiful muscular legs. There were deep purple waves along the lower part of her top as well. Both pieces were trimmed in gold. The material was so thin you could almost see through it. Her back was completely bare, and she wore her wolf head gold jewelry.

"A gold double band wrapped across Larentina's head, with a teardrop amethyst stone resting slightly above her eyes in the middle of her forehead. Larentina's skin was a deep golden suntan. Her curly white hair was pulled back with gold combs and draped down the center of her back like a ponytail. Queen Alexis had arranged the curls perfectly around her head. Her hazel brown eyes had more green in them than brown this night.

"Larentina wore a small diamond in her right nostril as well as a large diamond in her belly button. She wore large earrings that almost brushed the tops of her shoulders. The earrings were comprised of many small S shapes that were linked together.

"Androcles let out a soft groan; he could not help himself, for he had never seen Larentina dressed like a woman before. The two-piece chiton showed many bare parts of her perfect body, and he could not believe how she had transformed into an even more beautiful woman.

"Androcles got up from his table, but before he could move from his spot, King Alcaeus appeared at Larentina's side. The king proudly announced, 'My daughter shall dance for us this night.' He then took his wife's hand, and they sat at the head of the table beside King Karpos and his wife.

"Lycurgus sat on one side of the table beside his father, and Androcles sat beside his father on the other side of the table. The musicians started to play, and Larentina started to dance seductively to the music. Androcles loved this woman even more; she still amazed him.

"Aphrodite had been watching; she had to admit even she lusted for Larentina. Aphrodite was pleased; Larentina had been an easy pupil to train. She never gave herself to any man during their travels together, but like Aphrodite, Larentina had the knack to keep them wanting her. The question was, could Larentina keep Androcles, the powerful young future king of Sparta?

"Aphrodite appeared to the crowd, proclaiming, 'I'm Goddess Aphrodite, great-aunt of Larentina.' She started dancing with Larentina, seductively touching her as they danced together. Aphrodite was showing that she approved of her great-niece and considered her an equal, as well as a friend.

"After Aphrodite softly kissed her great-niece on the lips, she leaned toward her and whispered, 'Let the world know, my niece, that you are my friend, and show how much you love me.' Aphrodite never before trusted another woman or had a woman as a friend, and she had never truly cared for such a beauty. But this night, Larentina would break Aphrodite's heart.

"As Queen Alexis looked on, she became jealous of Aphrodite for trying to take the spotlight from her daughter, so she joined in the dance, keeping herself between Aphrodite and Larentina.

"Queen Irene could tell that something was amiss, and she decided to help Queen Alexis by keeping Aphrodite apart from Larentina. Both queens knew exactly what type of goddess Aphrodite was, and they knew she was a bad influence on Larentina. They knew Larentina represented a change in women's rights, and Aphrodite represented the total opposite.

"At all costs, the two queens wanted to protect Larentina. Of course, neither queen knew that Aphrodite had taught Larentina to dance so seductively, but they were very seasoned in seduction and could easily put a damper on Aphrodite's plans.

"Aphrodite knew exactly what these silly mortal women were doing. They were trying to protect Larentina from her, but Aphrodite truly loved Larentina in this moment and time. She could not help it; she saw so much of herself in the young woman, but Larentina had great strength—something Aphrodite had never seen before in any woman, not even the goddesses on Mount Olympus.

"Aphrodite knew Larentina held a place in Zeus's heart like no one before her. Aphrodite had started out trying to use Larentina against Zeus but soon found herself in love with the half goddess. This would be a fleeting moment for Aphrodite, because she was fickle and still enjoyed playing with mortal men's hearts.

"Larentina pleased Aphrodite as no man could, simply with her companionship, respect, and love. After feeling such love from Zeus's own daughter, she did not want to share it with anyone else. It was like an addiction with Aphrodite: once she had Larentina, no one else could fill the space in her heart, but Aphrodite's still felt that she must corrupt Larentina's soul and cage it forever for Aphrodite's true master, Lucifer.

"As Aphrodite danced between the two queens, she watched Larentina dance with Androcles; she grew jealous of the young prince, because he was taking Larentina's attention away from her. Aphrodite became more agitated as her great-niece showed such affection toward Prince Androcles.

"Aphrodite decided she would flirt with King Alcaeus, knowing it would anger Queen Alexis. Of course, it did. Queen Alexis and Aphrodite began fighting, which drew Larentina's attention from Androcles toward Aphrodite.

"After Queen Alexis pulled Aphrodite's hair, the goddess threatened to turn the queen into an ugly old hag, but Larentina grabbed her great-aunt's arm and commanded, 'If you do this, I will kill you here and now, great-aunt or not. Have I made myself clear?'

"Aphrodite cried in a whiney voice, hoping to receive sympathy from her great-niece; she answered, 'I wanted your attention, and besides, only you can entertain me and since you are so busy entertaining others only your father could replace you, because this celebration is becoming boring without your attention.'

"Larentina slyly chuckled at the beautiful goddess and mentioned what Aphrodite had overlooked: 'Why seek my attention when you can have my brother's? Is not Lycurgus just as charming and beautiful as me, in your eyes anyway? Take him. I'm sure he will love your company as much as I do, if not more. After all, he is a man and I am not.'

"Aphrodite devilishly snickered at her great-niece. 'Well, Larentina, are we not the clever one this evening? You are my friend, and I long for a woman's friendship, which I have never had. Granted, women pray to me and ask things of me, but it's not the same. You have made a valid point. Why not have a younger, handsome man to charm instead of an older one on this evening?'

"Larentina drunkenly giggled at her great-aunt and walked toward Lycurgus. She was a bit drunk from the wine she had been drinking. She bent down and whispered in Lycurgus's ear, 'Brother, I may have caused you some trouble this evening, for now Aphrodite has her eyes on you.'

"Lycurgus turned and looked up at Larentina with a devilish smile on his face. 'No man would refuse Aphrodite and her charms. For once, Sister, you have not caused me any trouble at all. I praise the gods, for this time your troublemaking will not cause me pain, but pleasure.'

"The twins devilishly chuckled between themselves, as Androcles watched Larentina's every move.

"Lycurgus rose from the table and approached Aphrodite, who softly laughed as Lycurgus whispered in her ear.

"Larentina walked over to her parents as Queen Alexis sat on King Alcaeus's lap; they were talking with King Karpos and Queen Irene. Larentina kissed her mother on the cheek and whispered in her ear, 'Now that everything has calmed down, and you have everything in control, I'm in need of some rest, for I have drunk too much wine this evening.'

"Queen Alexis reached up, touching Larentina's cheek, and said in a soft tone, 'Rest, Daughter, and sleep the wine off.'

"Larentina quietly walked to a side entrance, and no one was paying much attention to her as she slipped inside the royal home to go to her room for some well-needed sleep. The wine was taking its toll on her.

"Larentina knew Androcles would follow her, because he had been watching her all night. She lit a candle and walked through the darkness to her room at the back of the palace. When she opened her door, she immediately noticed that rose petals had been strewn across her bed. She knew exactly who the perpetrator was, so she called out, 'Cupid! You mischievous rascal, show yourself, for I know you are hiding in the darkness with your potent arrows.'

"Cupid giggled mischievously and asked, 'Pray, tell me, Larentina, how did you know it was me?'

"Larentina shook her head in annoyance and simply answered, 'No one else plays with mortals' hearts so cleverly and mischievously as you do. Now leave before I tell your mistress on you!'

"Cupid became scared, and his voice quivered. 'Okay, okay, but do not tell, because she can be so cruel to me.' He disappeared quickly from Larentina's sight.

"She opened her window and looked up into the sky, which was illuminated by thousands of shining stars and a full moon. She looked at the moon and smiled, for she was truly happy this night, with or without the wine. She undressed and stood completely naked in front of her open window. She heard her door open. As she had predicted, Androcles had followed her. He stood in the doorway holding two goblets and a pitcher of wine.

"Androcles almost dropped the pitcher and goblets when he saw Larentina's beautiful naked body illuminated by the moonlight.

"Larentina asked in a seductive voice, 'Did I invite you?'

"As Androcles closed the door and walked into the room, he answered, 'Yes, you did with your dance.'

"Larentina blushed as she giggled softly and asked, 'Do you plan to seduce me with wine?'

"Androcles answered with a devilish smile on his face, acting as if he was innocent of such a thought. 'My goddess, do I need to stoop that low? I just thought you might be thirsty.' He poured the wine into the two goblets and handed her one of them.

"Androcles actually blushed before making a toast: 'Let the gods bless us, so you have a crown of laurel leaves placed upon your head after a glorious victory in the games.'

"Larentina smiled, took a sip of wine, and cleverly commented, 'Yes, for when that day comes, I will marry you properly and be yours for all times.'

"They both took a sip of wine and then put their goblets down on the dresser beside them. Larentina hugged Androcles, and they kissed passionately for several minutes.

"Androcles picked up Larentina and laid her on her bed, where they continued to kiss passionately, but he refused to take advantage of her, and they fell asleep in each other's arms."

Chapter XLI

"The following morning, Androcles woke to a rooster crowing right under Larentina's bedroom window. As he shook the cobwebs from his mind from drinking too much wine the night before, he wondered if Larentina had left his side again, but when he regained his his senses, Androcles realized she was still beside him. His arm was draped around Larentina's naked waist, and the back of her head was nestled in his neck. As he kissed her bare shoulder, he could still smell the sweet smell of wildflowers on her. She started to stir and turned, so that she was lying on her back; Androcles reached down, kissed her, and softly murmured, 'Soon, my love, you will be mine.'

"He loved this woman more than life itself. He knew he would never be able to live without her; no matter how complicated she was, with or without magic, there could be no other woman for him. Death and war had surrounded them all their lives, and it had become normal somehow; basically, it was part of them, but somehow she had taught him that the love between a man and woman was worth more than glory on a battlefield.

"Larentina softly giggled as she blushed, kissed him gently, and responded, 'Soon, my love.'

"Androcles lay there lazily, but Larentina immediately got out of bed and frantically threw his garments on top of him, whispering, 'Androcles, hurry! You must leave from my window. If my father discovers you here with me, he will be furious.'

"Androcles grudgingly obeyed Larentina. As he slowly dressed, he defended his actions, saying, 'Larentina, you are practically my wife, so why would your father disapprove? We have done no wrong.'

"Larentina irritably answered, 'I had too much wine this past evening, and I'm in no mood for an argument. Now just go. I should not have allowed you to stay.'

"Androcles was totally baffled and asked, 'Must I leave through the window?'

"Larentina pushed him toward the window as she ordered him impatiently, 'Just go, now, before we are discovered. Besides, we may start training for the games today.'

"She quickly kissed Androcles, and as he climbed slowly out the window, Larentina pushed him completely out. He landed on his feet, but because he was unprepared for the landing, he lost his balance and fell to the ground. Larentina covered her mouth with her hands to muffle her giggles at her future husband's clumsy escape.

"Androcles looked up at her and, in a half whisper, protested, 'You will be the death of me yet, Woman.'

They both heard voices on the other side of the palace; Larentina waved her hands at Androcles as if she was shooing away a fly. He shook his head from side to side, bewildered and disappointed, and ran to the stables to retrieve his horse.

"There was a knock on Larentina's bedroom door, and she quickly put on some clothes as the door slowly opened.

"Queen Alexis peeked around the corner of the door and asked, 'Daughter, may I come in? I must speak with you regarding last night's events.'

"Larentina met her mother at the door and opened it completely as she answered, 'Please, Mother, come in. I think I drank too much wine last night.'

"Queen Alexis smiled at her daughter and said in a soft voice, 'I think we all did, but that is not the reason I'm here.'

"Queen Alexis walked to Larentina's bed and sat on the edge of it. She patted one side of the bed for Larentina to sit beside her. Larentina looked at her mother with an inquisitive expression and sat down.

"Queen Alexis took Larentina's hand and voiced her concerns. 'Daughter, I know that you like Aphrodite and you believe she is your great-aunt, but she is not what she appears to be.'

"Larentina looked puzzled and asked, 'What do you mean?'

"Queen Alexis hesitated for a moment before answering, 'She is a goddess that came from the lands of Egypt. Before Egypt, I do not know whence she came. She went by a few names that I know of: Isis, Hesiri, and Hathor. She was the goddess of war. She is truly an evil goddess who preys on mortal men and enjoys the bloodthirsty wars that she creates between them. When she is unable to trick mankind any longer, she flees and changes herself into something else. I have no idea how she has tricked our gods into believing she was born by Zeus's grandfather, but I believe she is up to something very evil, and it will be up to you to stop her. How, I do not know.

"'I also do not know why she has taken an interest in you, because you are a woman not a man, but she is using you, my daughter. I just do not know for what purpose.'

"Larentina solemnly looked upon her mother's face and saw her worried expression, then kissed her on the cheek to reassure her, and spoke her thoughts. 'Do not fear, Mother, for I know her actions were very strange last night, and I have not truly trusted her since I met her. Her deceit, I'm sure, will reveal itself in due time, and I will take action, for I do not want to anger the other gods by destroying her outright.'

"Queen Alexis let out a worried sigh and said solemnly, 'Daughter, I worry that you may be playing a wicked game that is above all of us, for she is a powerful being and can cause great pain and suffering not just for you, but for all of Sparta, well above our discipline. You may not be strong enough to destroy her.'

"Larentina contemplated this and said to her mother, as she looked into her eyes, 'I just can't believe any type of being would try going against their own blood.'

"Alexis responded, 'Daughter, all I know is the Amazon warriors almost destroyed her, and she fled from their land as well. So maybe you can defeat her, if what I'm saying is true.'

"Larentina asked, 'But, Mother, she is a ward of Zeus; how could she trick him?'

"Queen Alexis honestly answered, 'I do not know, Daughter, but I do know our gods on Mount Olympus have been deceived by her somehow. I believe she has been forced into some type of servitude, just like we mortal women are. I fear she is using you simply because you are Zeus's daughter. She could be using you to start the war between the gods that was foretold by the Oracle. I fear this maybe the end, not only the destruction of the gods, but all of mankind as well.'

"Larentina vowed with conviction, 'When the truth shows itself to me, I swear on all of our ancestors' spilled blood that I will destroy her myself.'

"Queen Alexis shook her head as she voiced her fears. 'I fear the gods may not be strong enough to take on such evil. You and your brother are all the blood that I have left from my sister Agape—my family, my blood, my pride, my joy.'

Larentina hugged her mother and kissed her on the cheek, trying to console her.

"Larentina asked, 'No one has ever said where our gods came from and how they came to be. Do you know?'

"Queen Alexis looked at Larentina with a puzzled expression and shrugged her shoulders. 'Daughter, I do not know the answer. I only know the same stories you know. Some of those stories tell how the gods were born.'

"Queen Alexis got up from the bed and walked to the door. She warned Larentina before leaving the room, 'Daughter, you are mortal and she is not. She is a very powerful goddess. Please, promise me you will be very careful. Zeus may not be there to protect you.'

"Larentina nodded and said, 'Yes, Mother,' as Queen Alexis left the room.

"As Larentina washed herself and prepared for the new day, she realized that she would have to be very careful. She did not have powers like Aphrodite, as her mother had just reminded her. Larentina knew she would have to rely on her wits to destroy this goddess, and she would have to time it perfectly.

"Larentina then decided that none of the gods really seemed to be what they said they were. Where did they all come from? No one could answer this question. She shrugged off her thoughts as she said aloud, 'I will not worry about this today, but another day.'"

The Ancient City of Babylon

Chapter XLII

"There was another knock on Larentina's bedroom door. She said, 'Come in.' The door opened and Corinna walked in. She asked, 'Princess, do you wish me to prepare some warm water for your bath?'

"Larentina answered, 'Oh, no, Corinna, for I have already bathed.'

"Corinna turned to leave when Larentina recalled her earlier thoughts and asked, 'Corinna, do you know much about the gods?'

Corinna looked at her mistress with a puzzled expression; she boldly, but respectfully, answered, 'I do not know of your gods, only mine. You know of this.'

"Larentina became curious about the helot's response and asked, 'So what god do you worship? We never discussed it after that day, in fear we would be killed.'

"Corinna hesitated for a minute and just looked at the ground without answering.

"Larentina asked again in a softer tone, 'Corinna, fear not, for you are speaking to me, and this time we are in my father's house. There will be no one listening. Besides, Corinna, you have told me a few tales over the years, but you never told me your God's name, just simply a few stories of your people who worshiped this God. I understand your fear, but have courage, my friend. I would like you to answer me truthfully.'

Corinna became less fearful of her mistress and looked into Larentina's eyes as she answered, 'I worship the one true God.'

"Larentina became confused and asked, 'And what is your God's name?'

"Corinna answered, 'God.'

"Larentina responded, still confused, 'Do you mean your God has no name?'

"Corinna answered, 'His name is God; the God of my people; the one true God of the Israelites, the Hebrews. His name is so powerful we are forbidden to speak it. Your gods are nothing more than fallen angels banished for rebelling against my God.'

"Larentina's eyes widened. She had heard a few tales of the Hebrews from Corinna, but never paid much attention because they were always being conquered; she considered them weak because of some of the stories that had been told to her. So Larentina asked Corinna, 'How can your God be stronger and more powerful than my gods? After all, your people have been conquered over and over again throughout the ages. Why does not your God destroy your enemies and protect you if he is so powerful?'

"Corinna let out a soft sigh and answered patiently, 'My mistress, you do not understand God at all; he created the world in six days—all of life and mankind. On the seventh day, he rested. He gave us free will, but when we ask him for help, he gives it by intervening to protect us; he even punishes us throughout the ages. Of course, you have not heard these stories. Ask the Egyptians how they suffered the wrath of the God of my people. My God is everything and everywhere. Your body is his temple. In fact, we all are a piece of him. He is the creator of all.

"'Lucifer was the first angel to sin. Lucifer was banished from God's kingdom because of his egotism and malice; his sin was pride. Because of the misreading of the Holy Scriptures, many people believe that Lucifer and Satan are one in the same, but I believe that they are two separate fallen angels. Satan had an army of other angels that were cast out after him. Many of these fallen angels fell in love with the mortal women God had created and laid with them. God was very displeased and once again ordered these fallen angels not to interfere with his children, but they still disobeyed him. Your own people worship Lucifer; he changed his name to Eosphorus. Your people even state his mother was Aurora, but this is false because Lucifer has no mother.

"'You yourself are one of God's children. You just do not know it. You are not the daughter of the fallen angel Zeus, but even if you are, you are still my God's child, for you came from the womb of one of his daughters.

"'What you do not know, Princess Larentina, was that I too was there the night of your birth, and I know who your true mother was. So I know who you really are.'

"Larentina ignored this confession; she did not care that Corinna knew who she was. She wanted to know about her gods and Corinna's God; she said, 'Corinna, please sit down beside me. I want to hear more.' As Corinna obeyed her mistress and sat on the bed, Larentina asked, 'Tell me more about your God and his fallen angels, especially about the Goddess Aphrodite; do you know where she came from?'

"Corinna was still fearful as she asked, 'Are you sure, my mistress, you want to hear this tale? I fear you may become angry with me.'

"Larentina answered, seriously and thoughtfully, 'Corinna, you know me. I have never been angry with you, ever, but if it will help you open up to me, I promise I will not become angry. I truly would like to hear the tale because I do not know the true story.'

"Corinna softly smiled, feeling more confident and safe telling her mistress these stories, and began the tale of the Greek deities by asking Larentina, 'Have you heard the tale of the great flood and Noah?'

"Larentina looked at the young helot with a puzzled expression, but she answered, 'I am not sure. Is your great flood the same as the tale of Deucalion?'

"Corinna answered, 'Yes, it is, but the version you know is completely different from the real one. Noah, I believe, is your Deucalion. Did the stories that have been told to you explain why Deucalion had prepared for the flood, when no one else on earth knew it was coming?'

"Larentina answered the helot, 'Um, I do not think so.'

"Corinna looked at her mistress, let out another soft sigh, and told Larentina the entire tale, adding, 'The reason Noah knew of the great flood was because God came to him and told him what he was preparing to do. Noah asked God why, and God told him because there was too much wickedness in mankind, and he wanted to destroy all the creatures that the fallen angels had created, as well as the fallen angels themselves. God wanted to purify earth and cleanse it from all the wickedness. Now that you know the tale of the flood, I will tell you what happened to Noah and his family.

"'After the flood waters receded, Noah and his family left the ark and made their home in the northern foothills of Ararat. All the members of Noah's family traveled into the surrounding lands of northern Iran, Syria, and other areas, creating settlements there. After a few generations, Noah's descendants scattered across the lands because there was dissent between the Japheth, Shem, and Ham families; Noah's descendants migrated into Mesopotamia.

"'The first seven cities to be built after the great flood were in the lands of Mesopotamia. Nimrod, who was the son of Cush, grandson of Ham, great-grandson of Noah, conquered all the new cities and created an empire of these lands, called Babylon.

"'The Goddess Aphrodite, as you know her, had gone by hundreds of names over the ages, but her first name as a mortal woman was Semiramis.

"'During Nimrod's conquests of the region, he met Semiramis in a brothel and fell in love with her, but it would look bad if a king married a harlot, so he started the first myth about her, proclaiming she was a virgin who fell from the heavens in an egg and was reborn from the sea. Of course, no one doubted his story—after all, he was a king and conqueror. Ultimately, this would be his downfall because he had made her into a deity from the beginning.'

"Corinna giggled and said to Larentina, 'I'm sure you know, my mistress, all too well that even the greatest of men do stupid things regarding a very beautiful woman.' Both women girlishly laughed at the statement.

"Larentina, still giggling, commented, 'Shame on you—how would I know of such things? Now continue the story; I want to know more.'

"Corinna cleared her throat and began the story where she left off. 'Semiramis wanted to create a false religion; her reasoning was to strengthen and preserve Nimrod's rule; of course, he accepted this idea and actually encouraged her to set up this religion. Nimrod never took this powerful duty from her, and this would be his second mistake.

"'Semiramis resurrected the same religion that Noah's own ancestors practiced before the great flood. After all the cleansing that God had done, Semiramis resumed all the corruptions once again. Of course, she was being controlled by Lucifer himself, and the religion was basically a twisted truth. They could only worship God through Lucifer, even though the Holy Scriptures did not say that at all, but she tricked the people by claiming she was the queen of the heavens. She even had the people worshiping her and all the fallen angels that had survived the great flood.

"'Semiramis became pregnant with another man's child, and Nimrod threatened to expose her as the harlot that she really was. Semiramis was not about to allow that. Nimrod never took control over the false religion, and Semiramis used this religion against him.

"'Semiramis had created a festivity to honor Nimrod's rule, which was only celebrated by the royal family, the upper society, and the priests and priestesses who were loyal to Semiramis and no one else. Semiramis served them great feasts in which the food and drink were drugged, and they would sacrifice a newborn lamb every year. They would tear the lamb from limb to limb while it was still alive and eat the raw flesh.

"'On this year, Semiramis replaced the lamb with Nimrod himself, and they tore him limb from limb, killing him. She immediately placed her bastard son, Damu, upon the thrown and proclaimed him as a god. She also proclaimed herself as a god, because a god could only be borne by another god.

"'After the horrendous murder of King Nimrod, the military broke into two camps, one supporting Semiramis and one against her. Through most of her reign, there was civil war, and when Damu came of age and wanted to take the throne, she refused him. Of course, Damu was just as evil and vile as his mother, so he planned to have her killed. Semiramis ruled over Babylon for a hundred years. She was old and her beauty was long gone, so she prayed to her god, Lucifer. Lucifer appeared in front of her and made a deal with her. Lucifer gave her a green crystal that gave her eternal life, beauty, and magical powers; what she offered in return to the evil one, no one knows.'

"Larentina looked upon Corinna seriously and confessed, 'Now I know the truth of this harlot, but her story is similar to mine. I do not want to become like her. I want to be good and decent. I would love to see mankind treat each other as equals.'

"Corinna took her mistress's hands in hers and, with tears that began to form in the corners of her eyes, said sadly, 'Your mother and aunt created this falsehood, and Zeus wanted to be God himself by trying to pretend that he gave you free will instead of our true God.

"'You have a choice, Princess Larentina; you always have. I thought my God had forsaken me, because I am the second generation of slaves to your people. I'm very far from my homelands, but I still always pray to my God to free me and reunite me with my people. I now know my purpose is to be here with you to help guide you to God. He has a purpose for you and the way you have lived your life. It was unclear until now. I believe you are the only one who will be able to destroy Aphrodite; even our Holy Scriptures said that she is an abomination.'

"Larentina looked into Corinna's tear-filled eyes as she vowed with conviction, 'I think you are right, and someday I will give you your freedom. From this moment forward, you will be my secret confidante and religious adviser. I know that if I am discovered, both of us shall be killed. I hold no power and probably never will, but I promise that if the opportunity presents itself to me, I will find some way to give you your freedom.'

"Corinna softly laughed because her mistress did not fully understand, so she shared her wisdom. 'I am already free; my body may be chained as a slave, but my spirit will always be free.'

"Larentina looked upon the helot's face with a puzzled expression, for she did not understand this.

"Corinna unexpectedly uttered, 'I feel I must tell you the story of Medusa's fate and what really happened to her. I do not know why, but I just thought of her.'

"Larentina was puzzled by this change in subject but simply requested, 'Then tell me the story.'

"Corinna began, 'Medusa was a beautiful virgin priestess of the Temple of Athena, which you know as part of the Acropolis in Athens. Poseidon, the fallen angel that you know as the god of the sea, lusted over Medusa for a very long time, and he savagely assaulted her, impregnating her in Athena's very own temple. When she came out onto the streets begging someone to help her, they threw rocks at her instead and cursed her.

"'The Goddess Athena was so jealous and angry at Medusa for causing this, instead of protecting her and asking Zeus to punish his brother, she punished Medusa, who had already been violated in such a vile way. Athena turned her into the most disgusting creature you could ever imagine and then gave her eternal life in the form of a hideous gorgon. She was so vile, just one look would turn men into stone. She was banished to the island of Hyperboreans, in what you know as the underworld. The only way you can reach this island is by paying Charon a coin to cross into the underworld. She was, and still is, completely alone, except for the two sister Gorgons, Stheno and Euryale. As I hear it, they were born as gorgons, while Medusa was transformed into one.

"'Through the ages, warriors from all across the lands would hunt her down, just to seek her head as a trophy. Then, they created this myth about her being evil and deserving of her fate, and saying it would be glorious to bring home her head.

"'Perseus felt empathy toward her, and instead of killing her, he killed Stheno and threw her head into the sea, which created the beautiful creature known as Pegasus.

"'I believe God wants you to give these creatures the opportunity to believe in the one true God, so their souls can be made free; if you do this, the curses they are under will be lifted.'

"Larentina covered her mouth as tears streamed down her cheeks. "That poor woman. What a terrible tale. Not even her people would seek justice on her behalf, and she was so faithful to the Goddess Athena. Even Agape told me a different version, because Poseidon still lusts for Medusa in her former beauty.

"'I must admit, I believed she was vile and deserved her fate. I would never have realized that the Goddess Athena was the one who is truly vile. Why did you tell me this version of this tale and ask me such an impossible task?'

"Corinna was confused as to why she had told the tale and said, 'I do not know. For some reason, you must have this knowledge to help free these poor souls. Everyone deserves to know the truth of God, so they can truly make a choice. If we can help bring the truth to at least one of these beings, then maybe, just maybe …' Corinna stopped speaking, for she feared she might have spoken too much."

Chapter XLIII

"There was another knock on the door; before Larentina responded, she whispered to Corinna, 'From this moment forward, I believe in this one true God. I will never put another god before him, but I want to know more about your God. I want to know everything you know. We must talk more when the opportunity presents itself.'

"Corinna nodded her head in agreement as Larentina opened the door. It was her father, King Alcaeus, standing on the other side.

"King Alcaeus could tell that a very serious conversation had been going on between his daughter and the helot, but he simply asked, 'Did I interrupt something?'

"Larentina nervously chuckled as she kissed her father on the cheek and answered, 'Oh, we were just talking about perfumes, Father.'

"Of course, King Alcaeus knew better, because he knew that Larentina was not interested in that, but he just shrugged his shoulders and asked the question he came to ask: 'Do you truly want to compete in the Olympic Games this year?'

"Larentina answered, 'Of course I do, but I understand if I am not allowed.'

"King Alcaeus let out a heavy sigh. 'Well, we need to have a meeting then with the gerousia council to be certain that you can compete. I believe they will intercede on your behalf because, after all, Daughter, you are a Spartan. Nothing would please them more if the first woman allowed to compete was a Spartan.' He nervously chuckled and asked, 'Did you truly vow to marry Androcles if you were crowned after victory at the Olympic Games?'

"Larentina gazed into her father's eyes and asked, as she softly smiled, 'Before I answer, Father, would it displease you if I had?'

"King Alcaeus furrowed his brow, looking at his daughter. Then he let out a hearty laugh and answered, 'Of course not, Daughter, for it would please me greatly to unite the Agiad and Eurypontids houses. It simply is a good match, but the question is, Daughter, do you love him?'

"Larentina blushed as she confidently answered, 'Yes, Father, I do love him. After all, I believe he is the only man in this world that is strong enough to handle me.'

"King Alcaeus guffawed, and after kissing his daughter on the forehead, he commented, 'That was the same reason Karpos gave when he tried to arrange the marriage between you and Androcles. I do not believe he is the only man; after all, Daughter, you have put me through the underworld and back your entire life, and after the encounter with Zeus, I fear you think of me as a coward.'

"Both King Alcaeus and Larentina had solemn expressions on their faces as Larentina voiced her thoughts. 'Father, I do not think of you as a coward, for you spoke up against Zeus, and that is courage in itself. You are the strongest and bravest man I know, you are my father and a mortal god in every sense of the words, and I love you and I am proud that you call me Daughter.'

"After hearing this, King Alcaeus became his old self again as he confidently ordered, 'Laying around and gossiping all day is not going to put that laurel leaf crown upon your head. I want you to get with your brother and Androcles today and start your training. I will speak with the gerousia council.'

"Larentina kissed her father on the cheek and simply nodded her head in agreement.

"After King Alcaeus left Larentina's room, Larentina turned and looked at Corinna as she spoke her plans to her. 'I meant what I said earlier. I want to learn more about your God, Corinna.'

"Corinna simply nodded her head in agreement and then left Larentina's bedroom, closing the door behind her.

"As Larentina braided her own hair, she thought to herself, 'Now I know these gods that I worshipped, as well as my own people, are not truly gods, but are they fallen angels of another God? I must know more and learn their secrets so that I can destroy the ones who are vile—or at least try to. I will destroy them by pitting them against one another and using their own powers against each other.' As she laced up her sandals, she thought of an even better plan: 'All the poor creatures they have turned into beasts and monsters were once mortals like me. If I can somehow convince these creatures to unite with me, I will then have a powerful army to take down these evil gods. Just having one may be enough, but having many of them would be even better. I believe Zeus is a noble and good deity, and there may be several more of these beings as well. The question is, how will I know which beings are bad and which are good?'

"Then Larentina thought of Corinna telling her that she was present during Larentina's birth. Larentina had learned that the helmet the gods gave her only worked on your own past, so she could use it to see if that was true. Larentina put the magical helmet on and saw more of the truth of her birth; she could see that the helot had been telling her the truth.

"As Larentina walked out of her bedroom, she put all her planning and scheming to the side and decided to think about all this another day. She wanted to compete in the Olympics more than anything else at this moment in time.

"The main reason Larentina easily accepted this new idea was because, all of her life, she had felt out of place regarding the idea that she was a demigoddess. If she truly was this, why should she worship her own family, which she considered herself equal to or close to? It was better for her to worship the creator of the gods now that she knew this powerful being had always been there looking over his children. She felt more at ease with this idea and accepted it as truth.

"As one last thought, she decided to pray to the one true God for the first time in her life. 'God of Corinna's people, I believe that you are the one true God. I pledge my allegiance to you and ask that you give me the strength and power to be glorious in these upcoming games. Give me the will to do your bidding by destroying as many of these false gods as I can. Help guide me to find peace and equality among all of your children. Give me the insight to be a noble and honest woman. Do not allow me to fall from grace as Aphrodite and the others have done.'

"Tears fill her eyes because this was a much more powerful God, and even though she did not know much about him, she felt something at that moment that she had never felt before. Her tears were tears of joy because she felt God's presence all around her and within her. She felt tingly from head to toe. She smiled as she closed her bedroom door behind her."

Chapter XLIV

"By midmorning, the day had turned beautiful and warm, and a very happy Larentina walked toward the stables. On her way, she saw her brother and greeted him. Lycurgus was riding bareback on one of his stallions; he stretched out his hand and commanded, 'Come, Sister, join me, for we must talk where there are no other ears around.'

"Larentina grabbed her brother's outstretched forearm, and he pulled her up onto the back of his stallion. Larentina wrapped her arms around Lycurgus's waist. She kissed him on his cheek and rested her face on his shoulder, so that she could share his view as the black stallion took off in a gallop. They were both smiling and enjoying their ride as they often did. It was the closest to freedom they had ever felt in their lives.

"After about a half hour of riding the solid black steed, Lycurgus stopped the strong horse at an isolated spot beside the riverbank. They dismounted and hugged each other.

"Lycurgus picked up some flat rocks and skimmed them across the calm water of the river as Larentina watched, smiling at her brother. She decided to join in the fun and looked for some nice flat rocks so that she could do the same. Lycurgus skimmed another small rock across the water and asked sadly, 'Sister, do you truly forgive me for the wicked things I did to our real mother and father? I know that Zeus himself said I did not do these things, but you were not there.'

"He stopped throwing the rocks that he had collected and looked at his sister with tears in his eyes, for he truly regretted going to Agape's home and providing an opportunity for Hera to kill their parents.

"Larentina let out a heavy sigh, sadly smiled at her brother, and thoughtfully spoke as she walked toward him, after dropping the small rocks in her hands. 'Brother, as I have said before, there is nothing to forgive, for it was not you, but the Goddess Hera. You already know this.

I know you did not do this, but if it makes you feel at ease, you have my forgiveness once again.

"'If you choose to side with me to battle the gods, you can take your vengeance on the battlefield against her and all other beings like her, but I would like to see Zeus, himself, kill her. My stronger feelings are that I would like to see her punished by him for all of eternity. I believe Zeus is good and noble, as many of the deities are. I believe my purpose is to save him somehow, but I do not know from what. In the end, it will be his choice.'

"Lycurgus picked up another handful of rocks and skimmed them across the river one at a time, as he contemplated his very own sanity for a few moments. He solemnly shared his thoughts as he skimmed the rocks. 'Sister, you should know by now I will follow you to the end of the world just so I can be by your side, to share in the glory of battle with you and to kill or be killed in the name of honor and glory.

"'I cannot swear that I will never doubt you, but I will worship the same gods you do. There is no doubt in my mind that anything you believe in will be the truth. I will die to protect you. I will fight for your beliefs, for they will be mine as well as yours. I will spill blood for your country, for that country will be mine as well. I swear it. I love you, Sister. You are my family, my blood, and a part of me. You are everything that I am not. From this moment forward, you are my queen, my commander, my life, and everything in between.'

"Larentina hugged her brother tightly and whispered in his ear, 'Brother, you do not need to swear this to me, for you will not be able to keep this vow. You will be king someday, and it will be me spilling blood for you.'

"Lycurgus stepped back from his sister's hug, looked into her soft brown eyes, and vowed with conviction, 'That may be true, Sister, but even in secret, I will be your soldier to command. Do you understand?'

"Larentina hugged her brother again and answered softly, as she hugged him, 'I understand, and I pray I do not see you killed because of my impulsiveness.'

"Larentina decided to tell him the stories that Corinna had just told her. She added that she now worshiped the one true God of Corinna's people. After listening to the stories, Lycurgus also vowed that this God would be his as well, even though he truly did not believe in him, but he had promised that he would worship the gods she believed in.

"She smiled at her brother as she looked into his eyes with joyful demeanor. 'Come, Brother, for we need to prepare for the games ahead of us. Too much serious talk this day; let us have fun instead.'

"Lycurgus laughed and Larentina joined in with him, because she was acting like a little girl with a new toy.

"Lycurgus, as well as Androcles and their fathers, King Alcaeus and King Karpos, did not have many pleasures in life, but the feeling of joy to spoil a beautiful woman and to give her all of her heart's desires seemed to be the most joyful pleasure in the world—whether it was a sister, a daughter, a wife, or a lover. The Spartan women always had this power over their men, but it was Larentina who had given the men courage to display it.

"The twins started planning for the Olympics, which would take place in a few months. After a few hours of planning, they decided to go and visit with Androcles.

"They mounted Lycurgus's horse and rode to King Karpos's home. They dismounted in the courtyard, where Androcles was already running up toward them. They planned more with Androcles and dined with him that night."

Chapter XLV

"Despite all the planning for the games, which Lycurgus, Androcles, and Larentina thought would be simple, the next couple of months were full of problems for Larentina.

"Although Celeris wanted to participate in the games, he was resistant to having another horse join him. Larentina, exasperated with Celeris, scolded him, 'Celeris, you are as stubborn as a mule! I can't believe that none of the strong horses in my father's stables suit you. I must have three more horses to compete in the chariot races.'

"Celeris was so upset with Larentina that he shook his head and neck up and down, making loud disapproving whinnies and nickers at her. Finally, his wings appeared, and she understood; she leaped on his back and he took off into the sky.

"The next thing Larentina knew, Celeris had landed on the rooftop of a perioikoi's house. After five minutes or so of convincing Celeris to get off the very rare terracotta shingled roof, he did so. Then, he galloped into the field and that was when Larentina saw the three sister mares grazing.

"Larentina dismounted Celeris and walked slowly toward the most beautiful mares she had ever seen. She could see why her stallion liked them; they appeared to be very strong and powerful horses.

"Celeris kept nudging her to move faster, but Larentina did not want to spook the mares. She stopped within a couple of feet of them, and Celeris stood beside her. As Larentina rubbed his neck and fed him a carrot from her leather pouch, she voiced her concerns. 'Celeris! How am I to pay for such magnificent horses?'

"Larentina then heard movement behind her. She turned and saw a perioikoi running toward her with a pitchfork in hand. Larentina immediately realized he must be owner of the three horses. She hoped that this man and his family did not see Celeris on top of his richly tiled roof.

"The perioikoi demanded breathlessly, 'Who are you? And what is your purpose? Are you trying to steal my horses?'

"Larentina remembered that the horses truly belonged to the state, so she answered, in an annoyed tone, 'I'm Princess Larentina of the house of Agiad. How dare you insinuate that I would steal? If I choose to take these horses, I shall do so because they are property of the state. I could have your tongue cut out for such an assumption.'

"The perioikoi immediately dropped to one knee and bowed his head to the ground; he begged her, 'Please forgive me, Princess, for I did not know who you were. Of course, take the horses, they are yours.'

"Larentina patted the man on the shoulder and commanded, 'Rise, Perioikoi, for you do not need to bow down to me. My horse loves your horses and feels very strongly toward them. He would like them to compete in the Olympic chariot races with him. All I ask is to train them and compete with them. After that, we will return them to you, if we can.'

"As the perioikoi rose to his feet, he took Larentina's hands in his and gratefully answered, 'Of course, my princess, you can take whatever this humble perioikoi has to give for the sake of Spartan glory. They are yours; you do not need to return them to me.'

She thanked him and led the three horses back to King Alcaeus's stables.

"Larentina did not have any other problems with Celeris after that, but she did scold him for using his wings. They were very lucky that they were not discovered.

"As predicted by her father, the gerousia council debated with the Delian League for weeks on end. The Spartan gerousia council argued that there was nothing in the Olympic rules stating that a half goddess could not compete, and Larentina was a virgin, unmarried, of royal blood, and the daughter of Zeus himself. The Spartan gerousia council also argued that Hercules, the son of Zeus, had competed in the Olympics, and Larentina was a descendent of Hercules because she was born of the house of Agiad.

"The number one argument among the gerousia council to the Delian League was that the games were created to honor Zeus; how could they keep his daughter from competing in them?

"The Delian League argued that the Heraea Games were set up for girls to compete in, and honor Hera, Zeus's wife, and there was no need for Larentina to compete in the men's games.

"Of course, both kings of Sparta were at these meetings and heard these petty arguments. King Karpos himself defended his future daughter-in-law, passionately yelling at all the men present, 'Come! Come! Why on earth would our Spartan warrior and goddess want to compete against mortal women to honor Hera, who is no relation to Princess Larentina whatsoever?'

"In the heat of anger, King Alcaeus also argued, 'Do you fear that Spartan women can shame your men? That, indeed, would show that our mere women are stronger than your own male warriors; and what would that say about our male warriors? Indeed, that is the question to ask of you, and I will ask it again. Do you fear that our women will shame your men?

"'Zeus himself has shown his presence to us while protecting his daughter, and I have been bestowed the honor of being her ward. Do not forget, free men of Greece, if you deny Zeus's daughter entrance into these games, you will have the wrath of Zeus upon each and every one of you.'

"The Delian League finally gave in but vowed they would change the Olympic rules for the future: 'neither god nor goddess could compete because the games are intended strictly for mortal men to honor Zeus.' But there was nothing they could do for this year's games.

"It was also decided that Larentina would be the only one competing in the chariot races because the Delian League did not want Larentina to have any help from the Spartan princes because they would consider this cheating. The Spartan kings did not want to press their luck any further, so they agreed.

"A week later, a messenger brought the Olympic invitation to Sparta, as well to other city-states, to honor the gods and compete in the Olympic Games.

"Because of the many different types of calendar years, the Olympic Games were also a form of timekeeping. Every four years, all the city-states were calibrated in time with one another. For the coming months, Larentina, Lycurgus, and Androcles trained rigorously to prepare for the upcoming Olympic Games."

Chapter XLVI

"The day arrived when they would be leaving to attend the games. Larentina woke up and excitedly put on her military garb. There was hustle and bustle throughout King Alcaeus's home as everyone completed last-minute packing and loaded the wagons for the journey to Olympia. King Karpos, Androcles, and several of the gerousia council were already waiting on the Agiad household.

"As they traveled, Lycurgus and Androcles rode up on either side of Larentina, who was riding Celeris.

"Lycurgus boasted, 'Our names will be remembered for all of eternity, Sister, for the Spartans will win every game we compete in!'

"Androcles proudly agreed, 'Our deeds will be celebrated throughout the ages!'

"Larentina chuckled at her brother and Androcles because they were acting like typical Spartan warriors, with their attitude of being better than anyone else. Larentina reminded them that there could be athletes who were better than they were; she warned, 'I hope that you are correct, but we will be competing against some of the greatest athletes throughout Greece.'

"Lycurgus arrogantly commented, 'We will see, Sister, we will see.'

"Larentina smiled and shook her head from side to side, as she thought how arrogant her brother and Androcles could be. This thought had crossed her mind many times in the past, even though they had been taught never to underestimate their enemies. Even though these were games, they would treat the other athletes as the enemy because, after all, they were competitors.

"As they traveled slowly through the countryside, Larentina grew bored and became increasingly impatient to arrive at Olympia for the upcoming events.

"They reached a city and slowly rode through the main street; the kings decided they would set up camp on the other side of the city, where they could purchase food and supplies for the rest of the journey.

"Merchants had set up canopies that stretched endlessly down the busy street of the city. The smells of all the Greek delicacies filled the air. They heard the hustling and bustling of thousands of people bargaining with the merchants on the main street as well as along many side streets.

"King Alcaeus was at the head of the convoy and rode past a disturbing sight; he decided to fall back and join his daughter, because he feared her reaction to the sight he had just witnessed. He stopped his horse until Larentina, who was slowly riding through the city looking and observing the people, caught up to him.

"As King Alcaeus watched her, Larentina rode past six tall, dark-skinned women in bondage. All six women were missing their right breast. Although she had heard stories of Amazon warriors removing one of their breasts to improve their aim when they used their bow and arrows she never truly believed this part of the story until now. Larentina had never seen people this dark before, and she was amazed to see such beautiful women; their skin was much darker than her own, and they had black, piercing eyes.

"The first woman was tied by her ankle to a large post. She looked at Larentina with a fierce and deadly stare; Larentina stared back curiously at the beautiful woman, who stood almost six feet tall, as she and Celeris slowly walked passed.

"All the women were connected by a metal chain that went through a metal loop on their shackled ankles. The chain was then connected on both ends to a wooden pole. The six women looked like they were starving. Their bare feet were covered in dried blood, and two of them had severe wounds. Larentina did not think their wounds were life-threatening, but they did need medical care. Despite their condition, Larentina could see in their eyes that all six women still had the spirit to fight. She instinctively knew they were warriors.

"Four Athenian guards were poking the women with sticks and taunting them. The guards all boasted that the Amazon women were not as fierce and strong as the legends had said they were. They claimed how easy it had been for them to take down twenty of the female warriors; these were the only six who survived.

"Larentina saw twenty more soldiers walk toward the guards, and they also poked at the prisoners with sticks until they bled. To Larentina, this was an unfair and dishonorable way to act.

"Before Larentina had a chance to react, King Alcaeus grabbed his daughter's arm and ordered in a stern tone, 'Daughter, do not even think about it. Your aim is just fine without removing one of your breasts. I have tolerated all those piercings on your body, but I will not stand for a daughter of mine to have a part of her body removed to try to emulate an Amazon.'

"King Alcaeus let out a heavy sigh as he continued, 'Daughter, these soldiers are acting dishonorably, but we are guest here and cannot object. I completely understand your feelings, but these soldiers are not Spartan, so for diplomacy sake we cannot interfere. Have I made myself clear?'

"Larentina was not even thinking of this, but she looked at her father as her eyes were still filled with awe regarding these powerful women and answered, 'Yes, my king, I completely understand.'

"King Alcaeus asked one of the Athenian soldiers in a loud, authoritative voice, 'What will be done with these women?'

"The guard approached King Alcaeus as he sat on his horse and answered, 'Our king wants to keep one of them, and the rest will probably be sold as slaves.'

"King Alcaeus nodded his head.

"As they approached the other side of the city, Larentina thought of the stories she had heard about the Amazon warriors. She remembered the story of Hercules, her older brother, and his twelve labors.

"Hercules was the son of her father, Zeus, and Alcmene. Hera was so jealous that she vowed to destroy all of Zeus's offspring that were conceived from his infidelities.

"Larentina knew that Hera had already tried to harm her by killing Agape and her family. If Zeus had not interfered when he did, Larentina knew she could have killed her brother for the murderous act, or King Karpos for that matter, creating a civil war. As Larentina continued thinking of the story of Hercules, she realized just how gullible and naive she truly was.

"Larentina now knew that she would have to always keep her guard up, because it was just a matter of time before Hera tried something else. Larentina knew she could not depend on Zeus. She was just lucky that Zeus had interfered earlier.

"Larentina remembered that Hera had tried to kill Hercules numerous times during his life; the goddess hated Hercules deeply. Only the gods knew how much Hera hated Larentina.

"Larentina remembered more of the story; Hera finally succeeded in driving Hercules mad, and he killed his wife and their three children. With the remorse and horror of killing his family, Hercules decided to kill himself; he could not live with the murderous deed that he had committed, just as Hera had tried to do with Lycurgus, but Larentina was thankful the goddess was unsuccessful in driving her brother mad.

"Hercules had taken his sword and was about to thrust it through his chest when the Oracle of Delphi entered the room, startling him as she said, 'Fear not, nor blame yourself, for it was Hera that drove you mad and made you commit such a heinous crime. You are not the bearer of blame. Zeus appeared to me and had me rush here to prevent you from killing yourself. To purge yourself, you must become a servant of your cousin, King Eurystheus.'

"Hercules went to King Eurystheus. Hera discovered that her unfaithful husband, Zeus, was behind Hercules's survival, and she told King Eurystheus to present Hercules with twelve difficult tasks, which King Eurystheus did. One of the tasks was to retrieve the belt of strength worn by Hippolyte, the queen of the Amazons.

"Hercules sailed to the shore of the Amazon territory; Queen Hippolyte was curious to meet the courageous sailors who dared to anchor in her waters, so she went to the shore to see who these strong men were.

"Hercules introduced himself and told Queen Hippolyte who he was. They talked for two days. Hercules told her about his murderous deed and said he wanted to cleanse himself; he explained that his ninth task was to retrieve her belt of strength. Queen Hippolyte fell in love with Hercules because of his honesty, not to mention his physical perfection, so she agreed to give him her belt. It was rumored that this belt had given her the strength of ten men.

"Hercules also fell in love, and he and Hippolyte stayed on his ship for several weeks, making love. They would walk along the shoreline as Hercules showed off his strength to impress Queen Hippolyte. Hercules even lived with the Amazon queen for over a year. His men even took wives. Hercules had finally found peace and love.

"Larentina thought it was a beautiful love story, until Hera became involved. Hera once again caused trouble by telling the Amazon warriors that Hercules was going to take their queen away with him. Hera convinced the Amazons to take up arms against Hercules.

"The Amazon warriors stormed the shoreline on horseback, carrying their spears. Hercules and his crew were no match against the powerful Amazon army. Hercules thought that Queen Hippolyte had planned to trick him all along, so he killed her on the spot and removed her belt of strength.

"Larentina had also heard that the female Amazons were savages, barbarian warriors who lived in a matriarchal society. Men were of no use to the Amazon women except for mating purposes and to serve as slaves. It was even rumored that male babies were often killed.

"Larentina realized that Sparta was changing the roles of women; the Spartan government was already giving Spartan women so much more freedom than they had before. Now Larentina realized that these stories about the Amazons were not true because Hercules had not killed them all.

"Larentina could not help herself, but she admired these fearless female warriors. She could not ignore her conscience any longer. She had to right the wrong done by her half brother, Hercules, even though she knew Hera had tricked him into killing the Amazon queen.

"She quickly turned Celeris around and galloped back to the six Amazons to rescue them; she considered them her spirit sisters. She also was furious at how those soldiers had poked and taunted the Amazon captives; it reminded her of when the older agoges had poked her with sharp sticks, piercing her flesh. The memory was degrading and she became even more furious.

"Larentina dismounted Celeris before he came to a complete stop; as she wielded her sword, the Amazons watched in fear because they thought she was going to slay them. To their surprise, with one strong blow of her sword, Larentina cut through the metal chain that was binding the women. They were amazed that she had freed them.

"One of the guards ran toward Larentina, brandishing his sword, but the young Athenian soldier was no match against her. As the Amazons removed the chain that had tied them together, Larentina killed the young soldier.

"Larentina prepared herself as several Athenian soldiers came toward her with their swords ready for combat. She was furious and yelled every vulgar name she could think of at them; she taunted them as they had taunted the Amazons. She thought that the angrier they became, the more mistakes they would make. Larentina took on three of them at once, and she killed them all within minutes, but there were many more of them coming.

"Larentina was livid because she considered this behavior totally unbecoming of a warrior; not only were they fighting many against one, but she was a woman and was considered in polite society the weaker of the sexes. She worked herself into frenzy and lost total control of her temper. She said to herself, *I will teach these bastards a lesson they will never forget!*

"Instinctively, Larentina's eyes changed as the wind picked up momentum and the objects around her violently flew into the air. Rocks and pitchforks started attacking the Athenians as the onlookers ran away from the chaos that Larentina had created. Marble and bronze statues came to life and started attacking the soldiers and killing them. It was a scary sight for anyone who witnessed this.

"As Larentina fought the Athenian soldiers, the Amazons picked up the swords of the soldiers Larentina had already killed. The Amazons instinctively fought the soldiers with no fear of the chaos that now surrounded them, because they knew Larentina was there to protect them, not hurt them. They formed a circle around Larentina as they fought the Athenian soldiers, to protect her against any harm.

"By this time, Lycurgus and Androcles had joined the battle as well. The two princes fought their way to Larentina's side. The sword fight continued as lightning bolts struck the ground and killed several of the Athenian soldiers. A large crowd surrounded the area and more watched from farther away in fear of the lightning bolts.

"King Karpos and King Alcaeus rode up to the battle scene. King Alcaeus remained on his white steed and bellowed orders to the three young Spartans: 'Enough! Enough! I command you to disengage. Damn it, Larentina! I command this to stop!'

"King Karpos was just as livid and bellowed, 'Stop, Androcles, now! I command you!'

"The kings and several of their military escorts dismounted and ran toward the battle scene. The head Athenian commander had just left one of the public spas, and when he saw the commotion, he ran to the scene and met up with the two Spartan kings. He demanded in a frantic tone, 'What in the name of Hades is going on? What god has been angered? Did Zeus do this? Where is he?'

"Both Spartan kings ignored him.

"Even though the kings had never witnessed these other types of magical powers that Larentina just displayed, they knew she would never use her powers against them. They tried to hide their amazement; after all, she was a Spartan goddess, not an Olympian goddess. She not only came from them, but she belonged to them—in their eyes anyway. She had gone too far this time, and both kings felt as if they had lost some control over the princes and Larentina.

"The head Athenian commander commanded his soldiers to disengage. They obeyed him as the three Spartan soldiers, along with the Amazons, stopped fighting.

"King Alcaeus was extremely angry. He grabbed his daughter's arm, turned her to face him, and furiously yelled, 'In all the gods! I knew you would do this! This is not our concern! These females are nothing but barbarians and deserve their fate! Let it go, Larentina! I command it!'

"Immediately, the winds calmed down and dispersed as all the objects fell to the ground, and the statues became lifeless once again.

"King Alcaeus was pleased that she still obeyed him and honored him. He felt he had regained control over her once again, but he was still angry with her for disobeying him in the first place.

"Larentina felt some vindication as she wiped the blood from her face. She defiantly and passionately uttered to her father, 'No! These Amazons are kindred spirits of mine! No matter how much I want to obey your commands, my king, I am unable to do so! So you must kill me for disobeying you!'

"King Alcaeus hesitated but slowly drew his sword; as he did, Larentina threw her sword to the ground and fell to her knees, awaiting her father's blade. He truly did not want to do this, but he was the king. She truly was Alexis's daughter—full of fire, stubbornness, passion, and strength—but Larentina's strengths were more than a handful. She lacked the wisdom and grace of her mother, Alexis. He put the point of his blade in the center of Larentina's throat. Larentina closed her eyes and awaited death. Lambda was growling and barking at King Alcaeus, but the wolf did not attack him. The king, with anger written all over his face, just stood there with the point of his blade on Larentina's throat, but he still had not broken the skin. Lambda was snarling and getting closer to King Alcaeus, but still she did not attack him.

"The tallest Amazon, who was Queen Almez, took her sword and knocked King Alcaeus's sword away from Larentina's throat. As King Alcaeus wielded his sword to engage the Amazon, both Lycurgus and

Androcles crossed each other's blades, entrapping King Alcaeus's blade in front of the Amazon because the Amazon protected Larentina from their king, something they should have done. They know their destiny is to protect Larentina, even if that means to go against one of their kings.

"King Karpos walked up behind King Alcaeus and lightly touched his shoulder; he murmured in his friend's ear so no one else could hear, 'You do not need to kill your daughter for disobeying, simply have her lashed a couple of times to show you are not weak, but merciful. Alcaeus, she cannot help who she is.' Karpos knew Alcaeus did not want to kill his ward, and he also feared that Zeus would destroy the Spartans if he did.

"King Alcaeus turned his head to the side but kept his gaze on Larentina as he murmured back to King Karpos, 'Thank you, my friend, for I do not know what I would have done. You are right; I truly did not want to kill my daughter.'

"King Alcaeus stared directly at his daughter, hesitating for a moment as he contemplated what he would say. As she knelt in front of him, King Alcaeus commanded, 'Daughter! This is your fight, not ours. If you must fight for these Amazons' freedom, so be it. You will fight alone without any interference from your brother or Androcles. You will not use magic; you will fight the way Sparta has trained you. If you survive, then I will lash you myself for defying me! Now stand and retrieve your sword, and fight like a true Spartan warrior! Prove to the world this day why you are the first Spartan woman who has earned the right to be called a warrior!'

"King Alcaeus glared at the Athenian commander and bellowed, 'Pick out your strongest champion to settle this matter, and I will pick out mine!' The Athenian commander assumed the king would choose a man to fight against one of his soldiers; no one who witnessed the magical chaos realized the chaos had come from Larentina herself. The Athenian commander nodded his head in agreement and ordered his strongest and bravest soldier to step forward.

"King Alcaeus then commanded Larentina to step forward as well. When he saw this, the Athenian commander barked at King Alcaeus, 'What is this? She is no match against my strongest soldier! He will shred her into pieces. This is an insult!'

"King Alcaeus guffawed loudly and made a wager with the young Athenian commander, saying, 'This is my daughter's fight. She will fight against your strongest for the freedom of these Amazons. If my daughter loses and dies, you may have her horse; if she loses but lives, you may give her and all her belongings to your king. I believe a Spartan warrior is worth more than a hundred Amazons. Do we agree?'

"The Athenian commander, with a puzzled expression, thought this was a foolish wager, because his strongest man would kill this poor helpless woman within seconds. It was a wager that he could not lose. He agreed to King Alcaeus's wager, saying, 'You are a foolish king; this is too easy; so be it, I agree!'

"King Alcaeus arrogantly snickered as he responded, 'We shall see.'

"The Athenian soldier who was to fight Larentina was a giant; he weighed at least 350 pounds and was solid muscle from head to toe. Larentina weighed but 130 pounds, and she was at least a foot shorter, even though she was taller than most women. It did not matter to Larentina, because she was going to take the Athenian down. She had no fear whatsoever, because her mortal father had displayed confidence and even had used an old trick of hers: 'Let your enemy underestimate you.' This tactic worked every time.

"Larentina stooped down and grabbed a handful of dirt as she stared at her opponent. She crumbled the dirt and let it spray to the ground, grabbed her sword, and stood back up. Lycurgus handed Larentina her shield and helmet, but she did not take her deadly gaze from her opponent. Larentina took her shield but refused her helmet.

"The Athenian commander yelled at the crowd, 'Get back! Get back! Allow these soldiers some breathing space! I will not be responsible if you are killed!'

The crowd quickly moved backward, forming a large circle around the Athenian soldier and Larentina. Larentina could hear Lambda barking and growling.

"Larentina waited for the command to engage. There was total silence among the audience that surrounded her and the giant. The Athenian commander yelled, 'Engage!'

"King Karpos, King Alcaeus, Lycurgus, Androcles, the gerousia members, and the Spartan military escorts anxiously waited to see what their female warrior would do.

"The Athenian giant charged toward Larentina, but she did not move. She just stood there, holding her sword loosely in her right hand and resting her shield on her leg; she did not appear ready for the giant's onslaught. In fact, she had an expression of fear upon her face.

"Androcles thought that Larentina was paralyzed by fear; he frantically yelled from the crowd, 'Prepare yourself, Woman! Prepare yourself!'

"King Karpos glared at his son with annoyance and simply whispered, 'Silence.'

"Larentina ignored her future husband and stood still until the giant was just a foot from her; he held his sword high in the air, and his shield swung back and forth as he charged full speed ahead toward her.

"As the Athenian giant charged toward her, he thought she was as easy to kill as a newborn lamb; he also thought it was such a waste of beauty. His last thought before striking her down was that he would rather take her as his woman.

"Larentina still waited like a spider waiting for its prey, giving the illusion of being cowardly and not knowing what to do. She saw the giant's sweat and could feel his breath; he held his sword high in his right hand to strike down and kill her with one blow. He did exactly what she expected him to do: by thinking she was an easy kill, he left his right side open for the taking, because the giant had no way to know that Larentina was left-handed. She quickly transferred her sword to her left hand and grabbed her shield; that did not need to be strapped to her arm because it had a hand clasp instead, and she crouched and raised her shield into an almost Hoplite Phalanx formation position. She stood with one leg slightly bent in front of her, and her other leg was slightly bent preparing to take the attack directly in front of her. She thrust her sword directly into the right side of the giant's midsection with all of her strength. She quickly pulled her sword out as the giant fell to his knees; she thrust her sword into his stomach area, slicing at his abdomen in a horizontal line; his intestines started to spill out.

"By now, the giant was on his knees, and she pulled her sword from his body and pushed him to the ground with her shield. He screamed in agony as he tried to keep his intestines from spilling out any further. Larentina looked down at the giant and passionately yelled, 'This was a good day to die!' Then, she took her sword and decapitated the giant to put him out of his misery quickly. She may have hated the beasts of man, but she could not stand to see another being suffer.

"She turned to face King Alcaeus, and she bowed before him and all the Spartans as the crowd cheered. The entire Spartan party was completely proud of her.

"King Karpos looked at his son and then at Lycurgus as he proudly, in a half chuckle, but a stern voice commanded, 'Take those ridiculous peacock smiles off your faces. You should not act surprised. After all, she is a Spartan goddess, not an Olympian goddess! You have trained her well, son. I'm very proud of you. What an accomplishment: to turn a girl into a Spartan warrior.' With a proud smile, he nodded his head, totally pleased with his son's accomplishment.

"Androcles thought back to his childhood and his first dream of achieving this success. Now, he was receiving the glory. He proudly shared the credit with his friend, saying, 'This task may not have happened without the help of Lycurgus; I must share the glory with him.'

"Androcles and Lycurgus just looked at each other as they tried to suppress their pride.

"King Alcaeus was very proud of his daughter for expending very little energy and using her weakness as her strength in taking down the Athenian giant, but he still had to discipline her for disobeying him to begin with. Nonetheless, he confessed to Lycurgus, 'You were right, my son. Your sister is clever, very clever indeed. She creates the illusion of strength by using her own weaknesses against her enemies. I'm very pleased because she did this without using her magic. I'm very pleased indeed.'

Both kings now understood the ridiculous heated argument of the princes in the assembly hall before Larentina had returned to them.

"As King Alcaeus slowly walked toward Larentina, the tallest Amazon ran to her and dropped to her knees as if she was praying to Larentina. The Amazon spoke in a dialect unintelligible to everyone present except Larentina, who was very rusty in the language but managed to understand her.

"As she was on her knees, she introduced herself to Larentina and explained how she ended up in this situation. 'My name is Almez, queen of the Amazons. We were on a quest to recover the golden belt of strength of our ancestor, Queen Hippolyte, a gift from the God Ares that Hercules removed from her body after he seduced and then killed her. He also kidnapped the daughter that resulted from their union. The descendant of this girl child is the true queen of my people and belongs with us. This is why the Amazon women treat our men as filth; they have been and always will be. They have no use to us except for mating and cleaning our feet.'

"Queen Almez paused in telling her story and looked critically at Larentina.

"'How can a great female warrior such as yourself treat these peacock males as if they are your equal?' she asked. 'Why did you kneel in front of that old man and let him put his sword on you without a fight?'

"Larentina grew angry but answered in the Amazon queen's own tongue, even though she was a bit rusty. 'Rise, for I am not a goddess to be worshiped. I fought for your freedom because I consider your people kindred spirits to me. You do not understand our customs; my father is a king, and I disobeyed him to fight for your freedom. Instead of killing me, which our king had every right to do, he will lash me. He has no other choice in the matter to keep the respect of our people. I hold no ill will toward him.

"'I believe that all men and women were created equal. In some aspects, I'm envious of your culture because your sex rules, but for good or bad, I was born in this culture, and I know nothing else. Now leave, before my father changes my mind for me.'

"As the Amazon women walked away from Larentina, Queen Almez turned to look at the Spartan princess who so valiantly fought for her freedom and watched, bewildered, as King Alcaeus lashed her twice across the back.

"Queen Almez was amazed at the strength this light-skinned woman possessed, for Larentina did not scream, whimper, or shed a tear. Larentina just stood there without even being tied up and took the lashes from King Alcaeus. Queen Almez did not understand this at all; a powerful goddess allowing such abuse from a mortal man? She did not act like an Olympian deity. Could she be a descendant of the Titans? Could she be the Amazons' lost queen?

"Queen Almez and her warriors walked back to Larentina, who bent to pick up her sword. Larentina looked up at Queen Almez with surprise that she returned, and the queen extended her hand and hugged Larentina, whispering in her ear, 'I do not even know your name, but I know you are a princess of great strength. There is a custom among my people: if you save a life, that life is yours until the favor is returned. So therefore we owe you our lives, and we will not leave your side until the debt is paid in full.'

"Larentina let out a sarcastic laugh because she was in pain and was losing her patience with this young queen, who did not understand. Larentina showed her impatience in her tone. 'Well, it will be a long time coming to pay the debt back, for where we are going no women are allowed.'

"Queen Almez was insulted because of Larentina's demeanor, and she voiced her displeasure. 'I am an Amazon queen. I do not need permission. I come and go as I please. These vain men's foolish little rules will not stop us. How dare you mock our customs?'

"Larentina said with a half smile, 'I humbly apologize; it was not my intent to offend you. What if I command it?'

"Queen Almez graciously accepted Larentina's halfhearted apology as she formally answered, 'Your apology is accepted. If you command it, then we will stay away and wait for you.' Queen Almez could not be so easily dismissed; she was now more determined to follow Larentina to seek her help with their quest.

"Larentina ordered, 'Then I command it.'

"Queen Almez replied, 'So be it.'"

Chapter XLVII

"Zeus once again found himself watching Larentina from his throne chamber. He had been observing her more frequently as she displayed more and more of her powers. He became more concerned with her growing powers. To him, it seemed as if her powers were increasing the older she became. She was learning to harness and control these powers that she had inherited from him, or so he thought. Even the archangels were becoming more brazen, but then he thought, *When they become upset with the Olympians, or the dark one, even the mortals, they go after the Olympians first.* It had been that way for as long as he could remember.

"Zeus had always been a bit absentminded; he had a bad habit of not remembering what he considered to be trivial details. For example, when it came to mortal beauties, he often forgot those he had once been with, except for on rare occasions. Nevertheless, Larentina's powers were disrupting the natural order of things, and Hera (and many of the Olympian deities) had started voicing her nagging fears more frequently. Zeus just shrugged his shoulders; he had all the confidence in the world that Larentina would never become that strong.

"Of course, Hera was also sitting on her throne and watching as this supposed She Wolf displayed continually greater powers. Hera was increasingly becoming paranoid of Larentina's strength. She feared that this She Wolf would become so powerful that she could destroy all the deities with just a thought.

"She decided to voice her concerns, and she chose her words carefully. 'My husband, are you going to allow that pompous mortal king to kill your daughter?'

"Zeus rolled his eyes at Hera and let out an irritated sigh. 'Hera, my love, Alcaeus is not going to kill Larentina. What you fail to see is he is not only Larentina's ward, he is also her king. She disobeyed him and he must punish her in some form to show he is not weak, that he still possesses control over her. I have no problem with his actions because he must keep control and power at all times. This is something that you could not understand, but Larentina does. That is just one small difference between her and you. She understands the beast and respects it; you do not.'

"Hera was coy in her comments and chose her words carefully once again. 'Zeus, it seems to me that your daughter is becoming stronger each passing day, now that she is a full-grown woman. I wonder if she will become more powerful than her sister, Athena.'

"Athena had been watching the mortals with her father and Hera. Athena was becoming more jealous of Larentina each passing day, because Zeus was showing this mortal more attention than he had ever shown her. In fact, Athena did not have any problems with Hercules and Perseus when Zeus showed pride and love toward them, because they were men, and she understood that, but she did not like for Zeus to feel this way toward Larentina.

"Athena had assumed it was because Hercules and Perseus were half-mortal men and his sons, but Larentina? Athena did not understand, and she hated Larentina even more. Even though Athena was jealous of her half brothers, she never did anything nasty to them, but she was already planning something nasty for little 'Miss Priss.' Athena would not allow Larentina to succeed in her destiny; she planned to destroy her because she had the audacity to use her powers against Athena. Athena would not allow Larentina to become Zeus's new favorite daughter. She did not think it was fair.

* * *

"Athena recalled the day when she tried to kill Larentina. She had disguised herself as a mermaid when Larentina, as a small child, was swimming in the river.

"Athena pulled Larentina under the water and held onto her legs, hoping to drown her. The next thing Athena knew, a wolf attacked her, forcing Athena to let go of Larentina's legs. Larentina had used her power over the wolves, and the wolf saved her.

* * *

"Athena did not discover until years later that Zeus barely knew Larentina was his child and did not show her any attention until years later in her life. This thought just made Athena angrier.

"Athena could not believe Hera had not killed Larentina outright, because there would be nothing Zeus could do about it. After all, Hera was the queen of the gods and was almost as powerful as the king of the gods was.

"Athena viciously chimed in, 'How dare you? That wild dog will never be as strong, powerful, or even as smart as I. She is nothing but an ugly, mangy dog. She will never replace me in my father's heart. Is that not right, Father?'

"Zeus had become annoyed with Athena and uttered in disdain, 'You are spoiled, Athena. Larentina is not.' That was all he said on the matter.

"Athena's feelings were hurt, and she was very angry as she let out a loud sigh, threw her long hair back, and stormed out of the throne chamber.

"Zeus and Hera completely ignored Athena's temper tantrum, which was something to which they were accustomed.

"Hera became more brazen as she asked, 'Zeus, pray, tell me, since you refuse to take my fears seriously, what if this She Wolf of yours is more powerful than the two of us? How will we be able to destroy her? If you do not want to destroy her, why not command her to stay in this realm so you can keep an eye on her. After all, she is apparently part of us.'

"Zeus let out a heavy sigh and refused to make a decision on anything regarding Larentina. Instead, he simply shared some of his thoughts. 'Hera, I am quite aware of your fears; you have been nagging me for quite some time now, but I have not made any decisions about Larentina yet. As soon as I have an answer, you will be the first to know.'

"Hera politely excused herself from Zeus's presence; once she was in her bedroom chamber, she summoned Athena. Hera was scheming again and decided to use Athena's insecurity and jealousy to her advantage. She also decided to use Aphrodite.

"Of course, Athena had no problem being a part of Hera's plan to destroy Larentina. Aphrodite was jubilant as well to join in Hera's devious plan. Aphrodite told Hera that if she succeeded, she wanted Larentina's flesh. Hera promised that she could have it if Aphrodite was able to destroy Larentina. Hera knew Aphrodite considered herself the most beautiful goddess of all, and so she did not understand why Aphrodite wanted Larentina's body, but she just shrugged it off. She assumed Aphrodite just wanted Larentina's body as a trophy of some sort, even though Hera considered that morbid.

"The problem was that Zeus could never find out that Hera was behind the plan to destroy Larentina. Those three nasty goddesses planned for many hours and reveled in the idea of seeing Larentina dishonorably killed. They could not wait to see Zeus's face after he learned that his precious pet had died."

Chapter XLVIII

"The Amazon women camped with Larentina and her party. Queen Almez told stories regarding her way of life and the great battles that her people had fought throughout the ages. Larentina was intrigued at how different Queen Almez's society was from her own. She was fascinated by the Amazon culture, but she still believed that men and women were created equal, and nothing could change her mind.

"One of Queen Almez's stories caught Larentina's attention. When she told of the love affair between Hercules and Queen Hippolyte, there was a twist to it.

"Larentina moved closer to Almez as she continued the story. 'Hercules was loved by all the Amazons, not just Queen Hippolyte. They loved him because he was strong, but he did not act superior over them. He treated them as equals. Queen Hippolyte presented the Amazons with a girl child from her love affair with Hercules; the baby was named Aristomache, which means "battle." We seek to find this child's descendant and recover the belt of strength that Hercules took; it had been given to Queen Hippolyte by Ares. We are determined to right the wrong that was done to us.'

"Larentina inquired, 'Almez, how can we help you right a wrong if we do not know the entire legend of your ancestral queen? All I know is Hercules killed her, but does your legend say why he killed her?'

"Almez shook her head and continued, 'It was rumored by fellow warriors that Hercules was going to steal our queen from us and take her to his lands along with our future queen in tow because several weeks later Hercules was about to set sail and Queen Hippolyte was aboard his ship with her daughter. The rumor was believed because Hercules and his men lived among us for over a year.

"'Our story tells us that several of our commanders convinced the warriors to take up arms against Hercules and his ship to recover our love-spelled queen, which we did. In the battle, Hercules killed our queen and dumped her body into the sea, and then he set sail with her daughter in his arms. When our ancestors recovered Queen Hippolyte's body, her belt of strength was gone.'

"Larentina, Androcles, and Lycurgus shook their heads in unity because they now understood the entire truth of the legend.

"Other than Larentina, only Lycurgus and Androcles could understand the Amazon language. Queen Almez realized that they understood her story, but she ignored the men as if they were not even present.

"Larentina then spoke after choosing her words carefully. 'Queen Almez, I know that you speak truth as you know it. In fact, there was a huge piece of this story that we did not know, but there is an important part of it that you do not know either. It was Hera that deceived you. She disguised herself as an Amazon warrior and spread the lies about Hercules's intentions. From our stories, he was not going to kidnap Hippolyte; he was going to complete his tasks, which he needed to do to purge his guilt over murdering his wife and sons. His tasks were for the purpose of cleansing his soul. You were deceived just as my brother and I were; Hera tried the same tactics with us.'

"Almez's eyes widened, but instead of getting angry with the young princess, she believed her story. It now started to make total sense to Almez.

"Almez simply said, 'I believe you and I must think about this new truth. We will speak again tomorrow regarding this new insight.'

"Larentina sat by the campfire throughout most of the evening rubbing Lambda's head as she listened to the Amazon's tales. Everyone else ignored them since they could not understand Queen Almez.

"The following morning, when the sun began to rise, they broke camp and continued their journey to Olympia. They arrived at the outskirts of the city before sunset and set up camp before they entered the restricted area. As they sat around the campfire eating, Larentina told Queen Almez with concern in her voice, 'If you truly wish to serve me, then you will have to wait here for several days before my return. I want to make this perfectly clear to you: you owe me nothing; you are free to stay or go. The only reason I am allowed to go further is because I am blessed, for I am allowed to compete in these great games to honor my father, Zeus.'

"Queen Almez put down her plate, looked at Larentina with a puzzled expression, and asked, 'Why must you honor your father, when it should be your mother you honor? This god you speak of, he did not raise you, nor did he train you to fight. I can understand your loyalty to these peacock kings and your country, but what has Zeus done, except to ignore you?'

"As Larentina rubbed Lambda's head, she glared in frustration at Almez's ignorance before answering. 'I do not understand how you can ask that, because Zeus made me. Of course, my allegiance is to my kings and my country, as well as to my family. What other purpose was I created for?'

"Queen Almez simply responded, with wisdom, 'I believe you were created to change your society, to show the world that women are stronger and smarter than men no matter what god you worship. You are a natural-born leader with the strength and intelligence to back it up. I have seen this with my own eyes. You belong with us. You would be treated as a great warrior and queen in my lands. I swear it! I believe you are the descendant of Queen Hippolyte. You are the chosen one; I feel it in my soul.'

"Larentina blushed as she laughed along with her brother and Androcles. 'I am the daughter of Zeus; maybe that is why you think I'm an Amazon.'

"Queen Almez became irritated because they were mocking her. 'How dare you laugh at my beliefs and what I know must be true? How dare you make light of this?' Almez did not believe that Larentina was the daughter of Zeus, she thought she was something else. She just didn't know what.

"Larentina became more sensitive to Almez's feelings. 'Forgive me, my Amazon Queen, but I'm only half the woman you are. There is no reason for you to think this.'

"Queen Almez controlled her anger and simply agreed, 'You may be right, Princess, but we shall discover the true identity of you. We shall see.'

"Larentina decided to take advantage of this and decided to form an alliance with Queen Almez. 'If this is so, then I will make a deal with you. I will help you complete your quest for your ancestor's belt of strength, if you will help me raise an army to take down the gods. I will then personally help you find the true descendant of your ancestral queen.'

"Queen Almez was shocked at what she just heard and prayed that the young princess misspoke; she confessed her confusion. "I do not think I understood you. You may have translated in my tongue incorrectly.'

"Larentina, still smiling, simply responded, in a more serious tone, 'I did not translate into your language incorrectly, my Amazon Queen; you heard me correctly. I believe these false gods may be powerful beings compared to us mortals, but they are not gods, and I will die trying to destroy them.'

"Queen Almez asked, 'Surely you do not mean your father, Zeus?'

"Larentina answered, 'Of course not, I mean the evil ones. I will not even try to pretend I could take him down. Some of them are unbelievably evil and vile, but if I'm to die, then I will die a glorious death in battle, fighting for a noble cause. I pray I am able to see the dark ones through the many colors of gray behind which they hide.

"'I will not even pretend I have the strength or power to take on the more powerful false gods. My God, the one true God, is more powerful than all these others, and he will take them down. We will never see the ending of this battle that I will start, because it will continue in the heavens.'

"Queen Almez thought she finally was going to convince Larentina to help her, but what a price to pay for her help. Nonetheless, she thought the price would be well worth it. 'So be it! I will fight alongside of you, but first you will have to honor my quest. Tell me, do you know where my ancestor's possession is?'

"Larentina studied Almez's facial expression, hoping to find a response beforehand, but she saw none and decided to take a risk as she answered, with reservation, 'You will not like my answer, but I will try. I am the daughter of the house of Agiad; we are the direct descendants of Zeus's son Hercules, the one who stole your ancestor's belt of strength. I am the daughter of Zeus, father of Hercules, which makes me his half sister of blood.'

"After hearing this, Queen Almez became extremely angry and planned to take vengeance; she now believed Larentina. She stood up quickly, grabbing her spear as she stood, but Larentina stayed seated as she watched the queen's expressions and movements. Queen Almez was puzzled, for Larentina did not take a defensive position. She remained seated, so Queen Almez controlled her temper and sat back down, but she continued to hold her spear.

"Larentina continued to tell her tale, as if Queen Almez's hostile movements had never occurred. 'Hercules took the belt because it was one of the labors he had to perform to purge his guilt from killing his family. I have said this to you already. He committed this wicked crime because he was driven mad by Zeus's wife, Hera. Hercules did not know that King Eurystheus was being directed by Hera regarding the twelve labors he would have to accomplish. He was only to serve Eurystheus, but of course, Hera got involved again.

"'I cannot blame Hera for her actions, but she should take it out on Zeus, not the offspring of his infidelities; after all, we are the innocent. Therefore, I consider this goddess evil and vile. She needs to be destroyed.

"'I consider you and your people kindred spirits to the women of Sparta, and I believe we are related somehow, in blood or spirit, for it does not matter to me. I will not be like my brother Hercules. I truly want to right the wrong that has been done to your people as well as my family. This is why I fought for you.'

"Queen Almez's anger and desire for revenge melted like butter after hearing the words spoken by this great, young female warrior. She was so impressed with Larentina's wisdom and understanding that she responded, with strength and conviction, 'So I now know the truth, which makes total sense to me. I truly did not believe you, but you have given me more understanding, so therefore I believe you. I think we both have learned more truth than before. My hatred and vengeance should be taken out not on you or your people, but Hera herself. I totally agree with your logic and understanding between myth, legend, and the truth. Behind every legend is a twinge of truth. It still confuses me why the gods always toy with us. It appears to me that you are partially right regarding all these gods. I know the evil ones must be destroyed, along with the beings that were created into monsters. I and my people will fight and die for the cause of destroying these wicked creatures …'

"Larentina interrupted Queen Almez; she stood and blurted out, 'No! No! The creatures that were mortals before they were turned into monsters will be given a choice to join us or die. I want them to be part of our future army to help us take down the gods. After all, they have been wronged as well.'

"Queen Almez nodded her head in agreement with Larentina. She then vowed, 'This will be the way then. My people and I will follow you to ends of the earth and back if need be. This is a noble cause and worth dying for. Instead of waiting for your victory at these games that you regard so dearly, I will gather my army and meet you in your country in six months' time.'

"Larentina knew the Spartan kings and the gerousia council would not tolerate this. If she was concerned, however, she did not show it as she spoke of her plans: 'We will first retrieve your ancestral belt. I believe it is still in the palace of King Eurystheus of Mycenae. The stories dictate that

Hercules gave it to him. As soon as I have completed the games, I will go directly to these lands and retrieve it. I will meet you in your country.'

"Queen Almez had no problem with the plan at all; she agreed, 'We will leave before first light. May your god of glory grace you with victory; may my god Ares keep you safe and protect you, my queen!'

"The two women warriors grabbed each other's forearms and strongly patted each other on the shoulder, and then Almez retired."

Chapter XLIX

"Androcles and Lycurgus had been sitting by the fire in silence, listening and studying the two women. As soon as Almez was out of sight, they immediately moved to Larentina's sides and sat down.

"Androcles was annoyed and murmured into Larentina's ear, "Are you mad? You know we will not be able to take down the gods. Why would we do this? They will destroy all of us with a blink of an eye. I do not give a damn what the Oracle foretold.'

"Lycurgus was totally disappointed and concerned for Larentina's sanity; he whispered in her other ear, 'Larentina, this is crazy talk. Hera is the queen of the gods; your power will never match hers. You are out of your league. We will not defeat her. I know what she did to me, but there must be another way. I cannot believe you made a promise that you cannot keep. If the kings find out about this madness, we will all pay very dearly, maybe even with our lives.'

"Of course, Androcles had no idea what Lycurgus meant by what Hera did to him, but he did not question the conversation.

"Larentina looked at the men on either side of her with disappointment. She then gazed ahead at the fire as she solemnly expressed her thoughts and concerns. 'You heard the stories of what Hera did to Hercules, my half brother, and your ancestor. He is our blood. We all know what she did to him; she will do the same to me, and she will use those closest to me to destroy me. She will do anything, and I mean anything, to destroy me. If that means destroying Sparta, she will do just that. I put nothing past her. She and all these other Olympian deities, I believe, are just like me. Why do they possess these divine gifts, as I do? Why do I possess these strange powers? I was conceived through betrayal on Zeus's part. She should seek her betrayal at Zeus himself, not his offspring; we have no other choice. Do you want this, Brother?' she asked, as she looked into Lycurgus's eyes.

She then turned her head and looked directly into Androcles's eyes as well. 'Do you, my future husband?'

"Without answering, Androcles and Lycurgus wiped their faces and stared into the fire. There was complete silence for several moments as they contemplated the seriousness of Larentina's question.

"Larentina broke the silence by stating with conviction, 'I do not need you to protect me; I will do this alone. Hera is not the only god I am going to take down. I want Aphrodite's head as well. She has deceived us all. I do not have proof of the whore's deceit, but when I discover the entire truth of what she really is, I will destroy her as well.'

"Lycurgus became angry, but kept his voice low. 'Damn it, Larentina, Aphrodite has done us no wrong. Why would we seek vengeance against her?'

"Androcles added, 'Aphrodite is a noble and good goddess. What you state has no merit. You are just jealous of her because Lycurgus has had her.'

"Larentina let out a factitious laugh. She then put her hand over her mouth to muffle her obnoxiousness in fear she might awaken someone near the fire. She became serious once again and confessed to both men in a low sarcastic tone, 'Please, I journeyed with the silly goddess because she felt she had to teach me how to seduce men. She is no more than a common whore. She would make love to a fly at twenty paces. You know the stories of her.'

"Both men teasingly snickered. Lycurgus picked up a flask of wine that was sitting by the fire and then stood up, suggesting, 'Come, let us walk away from camp so we can talk without fear of being overheard.'

"Both men tried to contain their laughter over Larentina's last statement, and they knew she was becoming angrier as they continued to playfully laugh at her, making her the butt of their joke.

"When they were finally out of hearing range, Larentina could not hold her anger in any longer, and she strongly smacked both men in turn on their upper arms. Androcles was the first to rub the sting away from his arm. As he was laughing, he commented, 'Damn, Woman, that stung.'

"Lycurgus was still trying to stifle his laughter and said, 'I'm honored that my sister thinks I can do better than Aphrodite,' as he continued to teasingly laugh louder at his sister's reaction.

"Larentina angrily snatched the wine flask from Lycurgus's hand and took a swig of the nectar. She wiped her mouth off with her lower arm and impatiently tried to share her knowledge of Aphrodite so that they would understand. 'This is no laughing matter. You two do not know the entire story of Aphrodite. She has gone by many names throughout the ages. She is also the goddess of war. I swear, my gut feeling tells me she will cause Sparta chaos.'

"Lycurgus playfully said to Larentina, 'Now, that I can believe, because who would not fight for her, just to lay with her, to love her? She is so beautiful and knows how to use her charms. I should know, I had her, but I do not know what all the fuss is all about, because I do not love her. I want not only a beautiful seductress, but also a strong, powerful, and intelligent woman to be my queen, someone like you. Now, you are worth fighting and dying for.'

"He bent down slightly and proudly kissed his sister on the forehead.

"Androcles chuckled playfully and turned to Lycurgus. 'Too bad, Brother, for Larentina will be mine. I have already won her heart!' He grabbed Larentina and kissed her passionately.

"Larentina blushed, letting go of her anger toward her brother and Androcles. She began to explain her plans to them both. 'Enough! This is serious! I am going to Mycenae immediately after the games.'

"Lycurgus thought that he and Androcles had talked her out of this madness. In exasperation, he blurted, 'What? You know the kings and the gerousia council will not allow that. In fact, they will not allow you to wage war against the gods. You know they will not even provide you with a soldier, not even one single agoge. Not for this ludicrous cause. Larentina, I thought this matter was closed. You will never get away with it, not even in your wildest dreams. It will take weeks to reach Mycenae, even with the fastest horse in all of Sparta.'

"Larentina replied, with a hint of superiority in her tone, 'Who said I was going to get their permission? I am half goddess; I do not need anyone's permission.'

"Androcles brazenly barked, 'Woman, you must have permission to even leave the state. What is the matter with you? I will not allow you to do this.'

"Larentina retorted, 'You are not my husband, not yet! If you keep this up, you never will be. I will not be ordered by any man: king, prince, or whatever title he may possess. Besides, they will not even know I'm gone because my horse is faster than all the horses in Sparta. I will not be missed until the journey home. The two of you can make up something, but you can tell the kings I will be home before they are.'

"Both Androcles and Lycurgus were totally taken aback, because it was impossible to travel to Mycenae and back in such a short period of time no matter how fast her horse was. They blurted out in unison, 'What?'

"Androcles, still stunned at Larentina's madness, asked, "And pray tell, how on earth are you going to accomplish such a feat? Your horse may be fast, but not that fast.'

"Larentina kept them guessing, as she cryptically answered, 'I have my ways.' She changed the subject, saying, 'I'm tired, and we have a big day tomorrow.' She kissed both men on the cheek, leaving them with bewildered expressions. She walked into the moonlight, knowing they were watching as she walked back toward the campfire and retired for the night.

"Before drifting off to sleep, Larentina's thoughts were, *That will teach them. Let them chew on that for a while, for I have Celeris.* She chuckled softly to herself with delight over her victory as she drifted into a deep sleep.

"Androcles voiced his concerns to Lycurgus. 'How are we going to control her, Brother? She gets all these crazy ideas, and it's deadly not just to her, but to all of Sparta as well.'

"Lycurgus answered his friend with conviction, saying, 'I will follow her into the mounds of Hades's underworld to fight by her side and protect her. Anything she says must be true, I can promise you that, but I have to admit, even I have my doubts sometimes. That is why I question her. Even she makes mistakes in her own crazy quests. Basically, I have given up arguing with her. I seem to be learning the hard way. Zeus is right; she is just as bull-headed as he is. Once she has set her mind to something, no matter how ludicrous, she'll argue with you until Hades has frozen over. There is no need fighting her craziness; I'm just going to join her and be done with it. At least I'll have some peace from time to time.'

"Androcles was astonished by what Lycurgus just confessed to. He bluntly let his friend know his thoughts. 'You are fickle and just as crazy as she is! You can't even make your own mind up. What have I gotten myself into?' He rubbed his face with his hand.

"Lycurgus put his arm around Androcles's shoulders and drunkenly rambled after a hearty swig of wine, 'I'm drunk, and I'm tired of trying to fight against the prophesies; it seems no matter how hard we fight to prevent this war, it comes closer and closer toward us. You know as well as I do that she would not be a Spartan warrior if she did not possess magic; she would have never survived.

"'Brother, there is much you do not know of my sister and our family. If you did, you would not have come this far to be with her. All I can say is you must trust us, for it must be done, no matter the cost.'

"Androcles just nodded his head, agreeing to some of Lycurgus's drunken ramblings. He simply explained his decision, as well as his beliefs in Larentina. 'I'll probably regret this, but I trust you. You will always have my support, both you and my future queen, but you are wrong, Lycurgus. If Larentina did not have the powers of the Olympian deities, she would still have her power over men's hearts. She has inherited this from her own bloodline, Queen Alexis and her twin sister. Even though my father's wife is very beautiful and possesses great strength, she is not as bewitching as the twins. My father still pines over Agape to this very day. Your own father would die for Queen Alexis, and you know it.'

"Androcles and Lycurgus shook hands, sealing their commitment to protect Larentina at all cost and reaffirming their friendship. Only the gods knew what their wild, crazy Spartan She Wolf would do next. It was now clear that, woman or goddess, they both loved her, may Larentina's God have mercy on their souls. They knew it would take both of them to protect Sparta and Larentina from the Olympia deities' wrath once they discovered what Larentina was doing. With these thoughts in mind, they both retired for the night."

Chapter L

"Almez and her small party of warriors left quietly in the early morning hours. Larentina felt relief when they left, knowing that she would not have to worry about Almez creating any more conflicts among Larentina's traveling companions.

"Larentina's group arrived on the edge of Olympia in the midafternoon. Larentina gazed at the sight before her and was amazed by the beautiful marble buildings and temples sprinkled throughout Olympia. In the brilliance of the afternoon sun, the buildings glistened. Even the countryside was spectacular, as it, too, had marble monuments scattered around; the landscape was spectacular.

"As they were nearing the city gates, Larentina spotted one of the larger temples; she pointed to it and asked, 'Father, is this Zeus's temple?'

"King Alcaeus chuckled at his daughter as he answered, 'No, Daughter, that one is Hera's.'

"Larentina became agitated. 'Hera? How can that be? Her temple is bigger than all the others in Olympia. She of all the gods does not deserve such an honor.'

"As they passed the various temples and buildings during their trek through Olympia, King Alcaeus pointed to each one, telling Larentina what they were. He showed her the Heraion and the Temple of Zeus that rested on the top of the mountain. He pointed out the Metroon, the Philippeion, the precinct of Pelops, and the Echo Colonnade. King Alcaeus even pointed out the spas and swimming pools as they casually rode their horses through the great city.

"Larentina was excited to see that Zeus's temple seemed to tower above all the others; it rested atop a very large mountain. She excitedly asked, in a girlish tone, 'Father! Father! Can we ride to the top and explore inside his temple?'

"No sooner had the words left her lips, when all the men in the party, who had heard Larentina, burst into laughter at her question and her level of excitement. King Alcaeus patiently answered, 'Daughter, we shall. We will even pay tribute to Zeus with sacrifices as soon as we are settled; so be calm, Daughter. Remember, you are the first daughter of Sparta to be given the privilege to be here at this time. So conduct yourself as a Spartan princess, warrior, and athlete.'

"Within moments, they dismounted their horses, and King Alcaeus, before Androcles or Lycurgus had a chance, helped his daughter dismount from Celeris, even though he knew she did not need any help. King Alcaeus realized this might be the last time he could actually treat his daughter like a little girl.

"He remembered the joy it gave him, doting over her when she was a child. He truly missed it, because she looked so much like his beloved wife, Queen Alexis. Just as he loved spoiling his wife, he could not resist the pleasure it gave him to spoil Larentina. After all, he did not have many pleasures in life.

"King Alcaeus just could not bring himself to believe Larentina was Zeus's child and not his. At this moment, Larentina was his child because he had raised her. Let Zeus throw his thunderbolts, proclaiming Larentina as his; Alcaeus was the one who had been there when she had a nightmare or was sick. He was the one who was there the night her back started bleeding, not Zeus. He just could not help adoring Larentina and believing that she was his flesh and blood. He was overcome with love for his daughter as he kissed her on her forehead with a smile that reflected his pride for her. 'You have truly proven yourself these past few days, Larentina. I am very proud that you are my daughter, my ward, my joy, and despite my numerous efforts to resist your charms, you have captured my heart. I'm truly sorry I had to discipline you the other day. You do not realize how much it hurt me to have to punish you in that manner. I pray you never put me into that position again.'

"Larentina hugged her mortal father as tears of joy rolled down her cheeks. She whispered in his ear so that no other could hear, 'I'm truly sorry, Father, for causing such hurt and putting you in a very precarious position. I am truly sorry. I cannot promise that my wildness and lack of discipline will not put you in that position again, but always remember this: you are my king, and I will always try my best to obey you. In my heart, you will always be my father, my king, and my mortal god who I look up to and respect, as I do my brother and Prince Androcles. I love you and always will, Father, for you have always been my true champion.'

"As Androcles and Lycurgus stood on either side of the king, they also smiled with pride to hear the king proclaim what they had always felt.

"At that moment, Lycurgus felt inspired as he realized there was no real shame in showing his affection, pride, and joy to his only sister. He was confident that he would never have to hide his true feelings again. He would not have to fear that someone else would consider him weak for displaying his abounding love for his twin.

"Androcles, who like the rest of the Spartan party was privy to the intimate exchange between father and daughter, shared Lycurgus's thoughts. They were proud of their king for daring to break the bonds of tradition by showing his love and affection toward his daughter. They all considered that act more courageous than the bravest act ever shown on the battlefield.

"When they reached the palace gates, the Spartan travelers were greeted by King Archimedes, a longtime friend of King Alcaeus, and several members of his court. They were then escorted to the gardens, where they were served wine, fruit, and cheese. Once the wine had loosened his tongue, King Archimedes, with a sly grin, boldly asked, 'Please tell me, Alcaeus, how you were able to convince the Delian League to allow your daughter entrance into the games? How did you convince them that she was a goddess as well? You know as well as I do that almost every great state has tried to proclaim one of their children a child of Zeus. If I were present at that meeting, she would never have been accepted.'

"After taking a sip of wine from his goblet, trying to conceal his anger over the implied accusation from King Archimedes, King Alcaeus let out a facetious laugh and answered his friend, without revealing his true emotions, 'Larentina is the daughter of Zeus—*that,* my friend, is a fact known throughout all of Sparta. Raising a daughter of Zeus is the greatest challenge a mortal man could face. She has the temperament of her father and the charms of her mother, and it was to the point that her mother and I were unable to control her until Zeus himself showed up and told her to behave. We have been graced by his presence on several occasions. I would never presume to offend the great Zeus by proclaiming my flesh and blood to be his. It was Larentina's greatest desire to participate in the games to honor her father Zeus, and since that was what she truly wanted, I had no problem helping her achieve her dream. After all, I am her guardian and her mortal father in every sense of the word.'

"King Karpos guffawed at King Alcaeus as he teasingly added his own thoughts to the conversation, 'That, Alcaeus, is totally an underexaggeration of what truly happened. Larentina is truly a handful. I have seen this with my own eyes on multiple occasions.

"'In all honesty, she ended one battle completely by herself, but that is just my personal thoughts of one event on the battlefield. In this particular instance, my son as well as Alcaeus's son vowed to take the glory for Larentina's actions because that is what she requested of them. She used her divine powers and considered that dishonorable but necessary; nonetheless, I managed to extract the truth from one of the soldiers who had participated in this secret battle. Larentina should have been given the glory for that victory instead of the princes of Sparta, but because of her intense desire to remain in the shadows, I stayed silent.'

"King Alcaeus was shocked that King Karpos had kept this secret from him and asked, 'What do you speak of? Why did you not tell me?'

"King Karpos just shrugged his shoulders with indifference as he spoke. 'Alcaeus, I thought it not important, and I truly didn't think of it until now, but I will tell you the secret in private, since this is a matter of the state, and no matter how trivial it may appear to us, we cannot risk the secret leaking out.'

"King Alcaeus nodded his head in agreement. 'Yes, I too agree. It must not have been a glorious event for it to slip your mind until now. I only knew of Zeus's presence that day, and I am grateful he healed Larentina.'

"King Archimedes became bewildered by the conversation of the Spartan kings and asked with confusion, 'What are the two of you speaking of? No one outside of Sparta has ever spoken of anything of great importance that Larentina has ever done. I have only heard tales of her greatness from common Spartan warriors, but if you believe all this is true, then I will respect your beliefs.

"'I have just one more question on the matter for you, Alcaeus. Please tell me, why would you proclaim your daughter as Zeus's child, and not your son?'

"King Alcaeus became indifferent to King Archimedes and simply answered, 'To be perfectly clear on the matter, I did not choose my daughter, it was Zeus who did. I had asked the very same question when it became known that Larentina was the seed of Zeus and not Lycurgus.

"'I do not care if you believe us or not, for Larentina, herself, will show you in the games who and what she truly is. You will believe, that I promise you, my friend; it's just a matter of time until you will see, as we see.'

"King Karpos just nodded his head in agreement with King Alcaeus."

Chapter LI

"Larentina helped the helots groom the horses and settle them in the stables. She made sure each horse had plenty of fresh, clean straw, food, and water. As she was brushing Celeris, she started thinking of the events ahead of her. Larentina knew the festivities would start the next day and could not wait to explore what she considered the greatest of the numerous temples—the Heraion, which was built to honor and worship Zeus. She could not wait to explore it, speak with the priests, and learn more information about her true father. She wondered if Zeus himself would make an effort to visit his temple while she was in it. Maybe he would even show himself during the games that would take place in the next few days. The excitement she was feeling was almost uncontainable, but because of her Spartan discipline, she was able to control her emotions. She certainly did not want to act like a silly girl and cause any embarrassment to the kings, her brother, her future husband, other Spartan soldiers, and especially, the gerousia council members who had accompanied them.

"Lycurgus was looking for Larentina and found her in the stables. He casually strolled into the stable, where Larentina was brushing her horses that would compete in the chariot races, and immediately started to lecture her. 'Larentina! By the gods, what are you doing? This is a helot's work. You are a princess, so start conducting yourself like one. Father will be very displeased if he catches you in here. Come, Androcles is waiting for us. Androcles and I want to go to the swimming pool and spa. This is a once-in-a-lifetime chance, and we want to indulge and relax before the games begin. You know we never had this type of luxury before; hurry up, put down that brush and come.'

"Larentina gave Celeris a loving pat and a kiss on the side of his face; she followed her brother out of the stables and agreed, 'You are right, Brother. I do not want to cause any embarrassment. Are you sure I'm allowed to go with you?'

"Lycurgus shrugged his shoulders with a puzzled expression on his face. 'I do not see why not. After all, you are an athlete and are competing in the games, as well. If there is any trouble, Androcles and I will take care of it. I do not see why anyone would dare cause trouble; after all, you are considered a goddess, and the rules have changed for you. Besides, they have not requested the women to leave this great city yet or stay inside their homes. I believe the women are still allowed to roam up until the day the games start.'

"As Larentina was walking beside her brother, Androcles met up with them. Androcles kissed Larentina on the cheek as two older men walked by them. The Spartans watched as the two Olympian men gave them disapproving looks.

"Androcles became curious and asked, 'What was that all about?'

"Lycurgus shrugged his shoulders indifferently. 'Who knows?'

"Of course, Androcles, Lycurgus, and Larentina had spent their entire lives in a military camp and apparently did not fully understand that women were considered lower than men. For the majority of their lives, Larentina had been treated as an equal. Granted, Androcles and Lycurgus knew this was largely because of their own behavior toward Larentina, but they thought the idea of women being property was falling out of fashion, especially after the increasing amounts of affection and protection that the kings and the gerousia council had shown of late, toward not only Larentina but all of the Spartan women. In fact, women throughout Sparta had experienced an increase in freedom and affection from the men in their lives. They were being seen as good for more than just giving birth to strong male children. Women were becoming valued for their intellect and strength, so they naturally believed this new idea was taking place throughout all of Greece, even though the Spartan kings only recently made this law.

"As they casually meandered down the dusty streets, Larentina walked between the two men. As they walked, Larentina noticed the frequent disapproving glares from the men, and she became angry as she had when she was younger when the women always trailed a few steps behind the men. She did not say anything about her observations to her companions. Instead, her eyes transformed as she noticed a pile of firewood beside a blacksmith's forge. With her mind, she grabbed a piece of firewood and carved it into a paddle. She used her index finger, and with a snap of her wrist, the paddle found its target and started spanking a passing Olympian man. The paddle beat him unmercifully as he attempted to flee, and the man found himself upside down in the air as the paddle continued spanking his backside.

"Larentina noticed another man with a woman trailing behind him. Her paddle swiftly moved through the air and started spanking him. She paddled at least six Olympian men before Lycurgus realized what was happening behind him. He grabbed Larentina by the arm and scolded her, as Androcles also turned around and saw what Larentina was doing. Androcles chuckled to himself. He loved it when Larentina used her divine powers for pleasure instead of chaos.

"Lycurgus commanded, 'Larentina, stop this at once. You were given a direct command by our father not to spank anyone else again.'

"He added, 'Androcles, this is not funny. The Delian League could change the rules again and prohibit goddesses from taking part in the games at any moment they choose. Stop encouraging her.'

"Androcles nonchalantly shrugged his shoulders and asked, 'Can we not have a little fun from time to time? I thought what Larentina did was amusing. Besides, Lycurgus, your father prohibited Larentina from spanking Spartan men. He said nothing about men outside of Sparta.'

"Lycurgus was agitated as he responded, 'Androcles, I have warned you time and time again, Larentina needs to be very careful using her divine powers, because mortal men will fear her and hate her. The Spartan kings cannot protect her from the laws of other Greek city-states. You know this. Larentina, you know this as well. This is a very dangerous matter. We must be careful. But I must admit, it was amusing.'

"Larentina chimed in, 'Androcles, my brother is right. I should not have done this. I do not know why I do such foolish things.'

"Little did they know what was about to happen to the three of them simply because Larentina was walking as if she were equal to a man; they also were about to enter a world that was strictly for men only. This concept was foreign to these young soldiers. It had never occurred to their fathers that they needed to be educated about how other cultures viewed women and treated them as property instead of equals—a practice that the three young Spartans never really saw or thought about, even though it was still practiced in small parts of their own society. They knew there were different laws throughout the Greek city-states, but they never thought that men would show their contempt directly to them for treating Larentina as an equal. They were unprepared for the reactions from the rest of the world because they simply treated Larentina as an equal in front of everyone.

"Androcles and Lycurgus were used to swimming and doing almost every recreational activity with Larentina, so when they arrived at the swimming pool, all three of them jumped into the cool water without any hesitation. They were all excellent swimmers and competed against each other, splashed each other, dunked each other, and pretty much played in the water like children. They were having fun and were completely oblivious to all the older men's disapproving eyes upon them.

"Other young athletes in town for the games were at the pool. They watched the friends in amazement because they had never witnessed such a sight; not only were free men treating this woman as an equal, but they were also amazed at Larentina's physical appearance. Never before had they seen a woman as beautiful as the suntanned princess before them. They had also never before seen a woman with white hair. They were amazed that she did not have hair on her legs or under her arms. When they were able to tear their gaze away from Larentina, they noticed that one of her companions also had thick, snow-white hair on his head, and the other Spartan male had sandy blond hair and deep blue eyes. The athletes stared in awe at the examples of perfection that were playing in the water without a care, oblivious to their audience.

"The other athletes had heard stories of the perfect bodies of the Spartan people, but they also had heard that they were a race of warriors, and if you saw one coming toward you, that could be the last thing you would see before they killed you. Several of the young Greek athletes started whispering among themselves in the water as they watched; they thought these people might not be Spartans, but something else because they did not appear to be noticing the other athletes.

"One of the young athletes could barely contain his curiosity as he watched the blond male cup his hands together to hold the white-haired beauty's heel. They watched him as he pushed the beauty up, out of the water, and she dove back into the pool. She did the same with the other white-haired male; they did this many times, back and forth with each other.

"They stared in amazement as one of the men wrapped his arms around the young woman's waist and kissed her passionately. Then they heard the white-haired male laughing hard at his friend as he dunked him into the water, saying, 'Androcles, how dare you take advantage of my sister in front of me?'

"They watched as Androcles did not come back out of the water, but instead he propelled the white-haired male directly out of the water. The three Spartans were having so much fun with each other, the observer could not restrain himself any longer; with a smile on his face, he asked, 'You all are having so much fun; may I join in?'

"After the boldness of the question, several other athletes also found their courage and asked if they could join in as well.

"Then the first athlete swam very close to Larentina and stood in front of her. He addressed all three friends, but looked only at Larentina as he introduced himself, saying in a very seductive voice, 'I'm Lucius, the future king of the Roman Kingdom.' Lucius also introduced his fellow competitors. They had all traveled from Rome. Androcles glared at the brazen young man with jealousy, and Lycurgus wanted to jump in and shield his sister from the unabashed longing he saw in the Roman's eyes.

"Lucius was a very handsome young man. He had long, wavy, thick black hair; hazel eyes; and a strong Roman nose. He was shorter than the young Spartan princes by at least five inches, but he had darker skin tone than they did and was just as muscular as they were. His voice, while not as deep as theirs, boasted a heavy Roman accent.

"Lucius continued to gaze at Larentina's face, specifically the beauty's lips, which was within inches of him. He engaged in small talk with all three Spartans, saying, 'This is the fifth time that the Greeks allowed outside competitors to join in these games, which are known throughout the world. Are you Spartans? I have never seen a woman who looks like you before, not even in the far reaches of the Roman Kingdom. Please enlighten me as to why, as free Greek men, you give so much freedom to your women? After all, they are nothing but women, no matter how beautiful. Don't you know you should keep your women locked up to protect them from predators like me?' Lucius was just full of himself, as he goaded the two young men.

"Lycurgus and Androcles moved through the water as one and forced their way into the small space between Larentina and Lucius. Lycurgus proudly answered the young Roman, who took a step back in the water, 'Yes, we are Spartans. I am Lycurgus, prince of the Agiad household.'

"Androcles also introduced himself, saying with pride, 'I am Androcles, prince of the Eurypontids household.'

"Larentina moved closer to her brother and Androcles. She peeked between their shoulders and proudly chimed in, 'I am Larentina, princess of the Agiad household, and sister to Lycurgus. You may well indeed be a predator of mortal women, but I am a wolf.'

"Lycurgus and Androcles turned their heads in unison and glared with annoyance at Larentina, who was now standing between them. Lycurgus bluntly remarked, 'We cannot help it if you keep your women locked up. I think all women outside of Sparta are flabby, pale, homely, and weak.'

"Androcles jumped into the conversation and was just as blunt. 'That is correct. Strong women produce strong warriors. Weak, pale, flabby women produce weak warriors. That is a known fact. You suppress a woman, and they will give you nothing but girls and weak sons. It is more challenging to be able to fight a strong woman and to capture her heart than to just lay with a pale, weak one.'

"Lycurgus spoke candidly. 'My brother speaks the truth; it would be like lying with a corpse. You must keep your woman strong and smart, because who else can you trust to protect your lands when you are off at war? My sister has proven this, and that is why our kings and the gerousia council have given so much more freedom to our women, as well as encouraging them to become educated and trained in the art of warfare. You introduce yourself as the future king; are you not of royal blood?'

"Lucius had a curious expression on his face and was about to speak when an older athlete rudely interrupted, 'That may have some merit to it, but as the old saying goes, if you give a woman an inch, she will take a mile.'

"Before Lycurgus had a chance to respond, Androcles, who was becoming increasingly irritated with this narrow-minded idiot before him, responded, with animosity, 'Why not give her ten miles? The question is, will she return to you? I will follow my future queen through the mounds of Hades's underworld even though I know beyond any doubt that she is extremely capable of not only protecting herself but also all that I own when I am off in battle. Lucius, you have not answered Lycurgus's question; are you not a prince now?'

"Lucius had an arrogant smile on his face as he answered, 'No, I am not a prince, but I plan to marry into the royal family, and I will be the next king.'

"Larentina was becoming more agitated with her brother and Androcles; she forcefully pushed both of them to the side. She was completely annoyed with the entire conversation, and her voice showed it when she chimed in, 'I need no man to cage me, order me, or protect me, for I can take care of myself. If any man tries to control me or take away my freedom to come and go as I please, I will cut his manhood from his body, shove it down his throat, and laugh as he chokes to death on it! And as for you, Lucius, taking a king's daughter to your bed does not make you a king! You must earn the title on the battlefield.'

"The older athlete's face grew red with anger, and veins were popping out of his neck and forehead. 'You are nothing but a silly girl whose purpose in life is to produce male babies for men. You will never be like a man. How in Hades did you come to be here to begin with? Women are not allowed to step foot in Olympia during the games. This is strictly for men.'

"Androcles and Lycurgus instinctively knew what Larentina was going to do next as her eyes started turning, but before she had a chance to break the cretin's neck, Androcles grabbed her by the waist and Lycurgus stepped in front of her so she could not attack the older athlete.

"Lycurgus looked down at his sister's angry face and softly murmured, 'Larentina, this fight is not worthy of us, for if you kill this idiot, our kings are going to be very displeased.'

"Larentina looked at Androcles, who wisely agreed, 'He is right, we will have our chance to regain our honor in the games. We can always kill him later.'

"Of course, the older athlete heard every word and uttered his disbelief, 'Come, come. She is too beautiful to hurt a fly. Besides, she is no match for me.'

"Lycurgus, who had been facing his sister, turned to face the older athlete and angrily said, 'You are an ignorant man! You are too stupid to realize that we have just saved your life this day, you donkey's ass, because my sister can very easily break your neck as you stand there. You should never underestimate a Spartan woman!'

"All three young Spartans got out of the water and casually dried themselves off. As they left, Lucius yelled over at them, 'It was an honor and privilege to have met you! I wish you luck in the upcoming games, for I doubt you will beat me and my comrades!' He ended his statement with a conceited chuckle. The Spartans just looked at him and gave him an artificial smile as they walked away from the swimming pool.

"That is when Lucius noticed the fresh lash marks on Larentina's back. He thought the wounds looked like they were only a few months old. If he had known they were only a couple of days old, he may have believed what the two princes were implying. If she was given so much freedom, why was she beaten? But at the same time, he saw old lash scars on her companions as well. He brushed the thoughts away and hoped he would see Larentina again. She was so beautiful, and he wanted her. What a trophy she would make: 'a Spartan warrior princess'!

"Since the three young Spartans had worn out their welcome at the Olympia swimming pool, they decided to go to a nearby spa."

Chapter LII

"As they entered the spa, Larentina, Lycurgus, and Androcles stared in amazement at the intricate mosaic tiles that covered the floors and the paintings that covered the walls of the beautiful white marble building. Once again, all eyes were upon them when they climbed into the warm water.

"No sooner had Larentina stepped into the water than an older male sharply ordered, 'Remove that woman immediately! In fact, you need to remove her not only from this building but from Olympia entirely. Do you fools not know the laws? There will be no tolerance for bringing a worthless woman among greatness and perfection of the male body.'

"To Lycurgus, this was insult added to injury. 'Shut your stupid mouth, old man! You do not know what you speak of!' Lycurgus had no idea who he was speaking to, nor did he care.

"The man immediately stood up from where he had been resting in the water; a slave passed him a towel, which he wrapped around his waist like a skirt before he spoke. In a calm, threatening voice, the older man responded, 'Do you have any idea whom you speak to, in such a disrespectable manner?'

"Lycurgus stepped out of the warm water, followed by Androcles. They also accepted the towels offered by the slave. Lycurgus glowered at the older man and retorted, 'I really do not care who you are; you have no idea who you are talking to!'

"The older male scratched his bearded chin and nonchalantly remarked his observations with an arrogant smile upon his face. 'You are too young to be a king or anyone else of any importance. You and your companion look like pretty athletes, nothing more.'

"This brazen statement infuriated not only Lycurgus, but Androcles and Larentina as well. Larentina quickly got out of the water and waved the slave away like a little fly. Several other men had climbed out of the spa waters also, eagerly anticipating the fight that was sure to ensue.

"Lycurgus was about to physically respond to the verbal assault, but Androcles stopped him by putting his hand up. Lycurgus continued to scowl at the boorish old man, but he restrained himself out of respect for his friend.

"Androcles diplomatically introduced both of them. 'I am Prince Androcles, my hot-headed friend here is Prince Lycurgus, and the woman of whom you speak is a Spartan goddess, Princess Larentina, the daughter of Zeus himself, and the sister of Lycurgus. You have made a grave mistake by disrespecting us and our customs this day, for we are not just pretty athletes.'

"Lycurgus could not hold his tongue any longer and scornfully uttered his threats. 'I promise you this day that I will remove your arrogant tongue from your mouth before these games are completed for acting as if my sister, who is the same as myself, is less than you because of her gender.'

"Once again, the older man condescendingly scratched his chin with that same smirk upon his face, and glibly introduced himself. 'I am King Draco, ruler of Mycenae. To prevent you from cutting out my tongue, I truly apologize to you and your sister. In fact, I apologize to all the Spartan people for disrespecting you. I have already heard that your sister will be competing, and I would rather have Zeus's daughter as my ally than my enemy, for I may not fear you or your companions, but I do indeed fear Zeus.' He then extended his hand in friendship, leaving Lycurgus no other choice but to accept it for diplomacy's sake.

"Larentina realized at this moment that she was standing in the presence of the direct descendant of King Eurystheus, the king that Hercules gave the Amazon belt of strength to, so she abruptly asked the king, 'Are you the direct descendant of King Eurystheus?'

"King Draco proudly answered, 'Yes, I am.'

"Larentina asked, 'The same King Eurystheus who legend states gave the twelve labors to my brother, Hercules?'

"King Draco answered, with an even broader smile, 'Yes.'

"Larentina then asked the king, 'Does your family still possess the Amazon belt of strength?'

"King Draco proudly answered, 'Yes. In fact, ever since King Eurystheus gave the belt to his oldest daughter, it has become our family tradition for the firstborn daughter of each generation to receive the belt of strength.

She is then trained from an early age in the ancient fighting skills of royal Egyptian women, as well as most other great battle techniques.'

"As King Draco looked at Larentina with a serious expression on his face, he asked her, 'Are you familiar with these fighting skills? My daughter Poulxeria has not had any real competition in quite some time now. In fact, she has never fought a woman who could equal her strength, so I have never had the pleasure of witnessing her talents against another woman in combat. I allow her to fight against any suitor who desires her hand in marriage; this is merely amusement and entertainment for my guests and me. Unfortunately, none of them had the training or even the cleverness to survive; therefore, she rapidly disposed of each one.' With those words, he broke into a malicious snicker.

"His tone, as well as the words he spoke, infuriated Larentina, but unlike her brother, she was able to contain her emotions as she answered him calmly, 'Yes, I'm very familiar with these fighting techniques.'

"King Draco removed his attention from Larentina and looked directly at Lycurgus and Androcles with a smile upon his face. As if Larentina were not standing right in front of him, he confidently made a wager to the two young princes. 'I will make a wager with you: if your young princess wins in the games, I will bestow upon you and your kings the honor of having her fight against my daughter using the ancient techniques of the Egyptian pharaoh's daughters. Come to think of it, I believe they still currently practice these techniques as a form of entertainment.'

"Androcles let out a factitious laugh as he responded, 'That is a fool's wager, for your daughter possesses the Amazon's belt. Larentina would not have a fighting chance as long as your daughter wears the magic belt that gives her the strength of ten men …'

"Lycurgus cut his friend off before he could complete his thoughts. 'Androcles is correct; what do you take us for, fools?'

"King Draco answered, 'You boast of how strong this princess of Sparta is; why not prove it? This is an honor that I grant you.'

"Androcles agitatedly asked, 'What kind of honor is that? What would we get out of it?'

"Lycurgus chimed in, 'If we even considered it, the victor would be given the belt as her prize, and to make the fight fair, your daughter could not wear the belt when fighting my sister.'

"Androcles added his two cents. 'Just so you know we are not as gullible as our ancestor Hercules was.'

"King Draco glibly answered, 'I agree the victor would get the belt, but it would not be a fair fight unless my daughter wears the belt because of the strength you claim your princess possesses, so I will not agree to that part of the wager. My daughter will wear the belt to fight against the Spartan princess.'

"Larentina broke into the conversation and made her presence known once more as she accepted the wager's terms in a loud and serious voice. 'I accept your wager that the victor is given the Amazon's belt as the prize.'

"Lycurgus grabbed his sister's upper arm, bent his head down to where his lips were almost touching hers, and he solemnly stared directly into her eyes as he whispered his dismay, so that no one else could make out his words, 'You are an arrogant woman; do not be so foolish. If Princess Poulxeria wears that magic belt, she will cut you into shreds. You may be strong, Sister, but you are not that strong. Granted you are a clever warrior, and you can fool many men, but the truth is you are not as strong as a man. We will not be able to protect you if you allow yourself to be put into this type of combat. Our father will kill us if I let you die because of a foolish wager.'

"Before Androcles had a chance to let Larentina know his thoughts on her proposed wager, which incidentally echoed those of her brother, Lycurgus turned around to face King Draco and cleverly voiced what both princes were thinking: 'Neither my sister, nor my friend, nor I can accept this wager, for we do not possess the authority to do so. This wager must be presented to our fathers, the kings of Sparta. The decision is theirs to make, and theirs alone.'

"Lycurgus was positive this would end the matter once and for all and would keep his sister in check, but to the young Spartans' surprise, King Draco agreed, 'That is acceptable. I will speak directly with your kings regarding this matter. It has been a total waste of my time speaking with you, for as I announced earlier, you are too young to be of any importance.'

"Lycurgus just ignored King Draco's pompous attitude and simply replied, 'Then it is settled.'"

Chapter LIII

"As Larentina, Androcles, and Lycurgus walked back to King Archimedes's Olympian palace, Larentina could no longer hold her tongue and uttered her disappointment, 'How could you do that, Brother? You made a vow to me! How easy it is for you to forget a promise.'

"Lycurgus's face flushed with anger, but before he could respond, Androcles jumped in and furiously whispered, 'Larentina, you are foolish. There is no way you could best the daughter of King Draco as long as she wears that belt. I thought what Lycurgus said to King Draco would prevent us all from getting into trouble, not only with our fathers, but also with the gerousia council. You know perfectly well that our fathers will not accept this foolish wager, because you are putting not only yourself in harm's way but also Sparta.'

"Lycurgus voiced his concerns as well. 'Sister, I have already told you how I feel about this idiotic plan of yours. Your first plan was mad, but this is even worse than the first one. Get it out of your head, because you are never going to retrieve that belt. Your rash promises may result in war with the Amazons because you are not going to be able to keep your promise to them. You have not thought this through; there must be a better way.'

"Larentina was livid as she yelled at her two companions, 'You foolish, stupid, idiotic men! You have forgotten one little detail, or it has not been revealed to you; the belt of strength only works on men, not women! I will be fighting against a woman of mortal strength! How clever she is, I do not know, but I will be fighting with my strength and wit against a mortal! The magic will not work with me! Remember, the magic was created from a male god; it works against mortal men, not women!'

"Larentina shook her head from side to side in disappointment at the stupidity of Androcles and Lycurgus. She simply took off running toward the palace where they were staying. Once again, her brother and Androcles doubted her.

"Both young men stopped dead in their tracks as they watched Larentina run off in anger. Androcles asked Lycurgus, 'Did you know that?'

"Lycurgus shook his head and answered, 'I did not know that, but she is probably right. Now I feel like the foolish one. I should not have thought so little of my sister's insight. I should have known that she is not impulsive and always has a good reason for every word and action.'

"Androcles simply suggested, 'We will talk with our fathers this very night.'

"Both men agreed as they casually meandered toward the palace enjoying the sights, sounds, and aromas of the city.

"When Androcles and Lycurgus reached the palace, they immediately asked the first slave they saw to direct them to their fathers. They followed the slave to a large meeting room where their fathers were sitting at a table near an indoor fountain with several other men of importance, conversing and drinking.

"Androcles approached his father and the group of men and requested an audience with him and King Alcaeus. Lycurgus did the same with his father.

"All four men left the crowded room and walked outside the palace. Once outside, they were surrounded by the palace's beautiful lawns and gardens.

"Androcles and Lycurgus told their fathers the story of King Draco's wager of the Amazon belt of strength. They also told them of Larentina's foresight regarding how the belt's magic only worked against men and not women. They did not mention why Larentina wanted the belt, or about her wanting to settle a score with the deities. Even though the Oracle foretold this, they knew their fathers would not go along with her madness.

"After hearing this, King Alcaeus voiced the obvious. 'Larentina will shred that poor girl to pieces, but if the fool wants to wager the belt at the expense of his daughter because he does not know the weaknesses of it, that is his own damn fault.

"'When Larentina was young, Alexis told me about the ancient dja fighting skills. She had heard that they were only taught to the pharaohs, and in many cases, the pharaoh would have his daughters taught to use these weapons for their amusement. These dja three-pronged spears sounded like they were primarily used for entertainment of some sort. The description sounds more like a dance than a fight. She pestered me to allow Larentina to be trained by one of the pharaoh's older daughters;

I saw no harm and thought it to be a good idea. Larentina became good friends with the pharaoh's daughter. She was just a child then; does she even remember how to use these ancient weapons?'

"Lycurgus and Androcles slyly chuckled at King Alcaeus's question, because they knew she did. In unison they answered, 'Yes.'

"Lycurgus completed the answer by stating, 'I remember Larentina would always be playing with these when we were children. I thought they were just toys; she would throw them into trees testing her strength, as well as sharpening them like swords, but I have not seen her play with them for many years. I assumed she had outgrown them. I even asked her why she was not playing with them anymore, and she answered that she grew tired of them because they gave her no challenge, but she still carries the metal tips of them wherever she goes.'

"King Karpos simply commented, 'Then she is rusty.'

"Androcles chimed in, 'Possibly, but even if she is, she still can shred the girl because of her Spartan training.'

"Lycurgus simply agreed, 'That is true,' as both kings nodded their heads in agreement with their sons.

"King Alcaeus voiced his observations. 'The two of you are leaving out part of the story. Why would Larentina want or need the Amazon belt of strength to begin with? After all, she is protected by our own legions. Not to mention just our two households should be enough. Do you take us for fools? We know she was talking with that Amazon the other night. There is more to this, so tell us, my son.'

"King Karpos nodded his head again in agreement with King Alcaeus.

"Lycurgus once again let out a sigh, because he truly did not know how to answer his father. Instead, he blurted the truth, 'Yes, Father, there is more. She has it in her head that she must right a wrong that our ancestor, Hercules, committed against the Amazon's queen, Hippolyte. I hate to admit it, but it is a noble and just cause because Hera tricked everyone involved because she wanted Hercules dead.'

"The three men shook their heads in agreement with Lycurgus.

"King Karpos solemnly looked at King Alcaeus as he spoke. 'It seems Larentina has stumbled onto something that could benefit Sparta in the future. You know no one has been able to conquer the Amazons and take over their lands. They are barbarians, but we could use them as allies for the future of Sparta. If Larentina is able to pull this off and retrieve the belt to return it to the Amazons, they would be forever beholden to her;

not to mention we could add to the wager that if Larentina is the victor, King Draco must pledge his allegiance to Sparta, and then we would also have control of his armies.'

"King Alcaeus rubbed his chin, contemplating the situation, before speaking. 'That is a very valid point, Karpos, but was it not Hercules that betrayed the Amazons to begin with?'

"Androcles chimed in, 'My king, Lycurgus and I were present during this conversation with Larentina and the Amazon. Larentina explained to the Amazon queen that it was Hera who tricked the Amazons into attacking Hercules, and Hercules thought their queen had betrayed him. I heard with my own ears the Amazon queen vowed her and her people would follow Larentina to the ends of the world, but she would first have to return the belt to her.'

"Again, Lycurgus and Androcles did not mention the rest of Larentina's plans.

"Both kings were pleased with this information and in unison said, 'Good.'

"King Karpos inquisitively asked his son, 'How and when did you learn the Amazon's tongue?'

"Androcles shrugged his shoulders with indifference. 'I never really thought about it. It was Larentina who taught me the tongue, as well as many other languages. Remember, I was her eirena and it was decreed by King Alcaeus that I had to train her in controlling her powers. Larentina discovered she could read men's minds like the Olympian deities could, but she never quite mastered it. We played a game in which she would put the languages somehow into Lycurgus's mind and my mind, but it only worked to some degree. It was enough that we could speak it, and understand it, but we had to practice at it verbally.'

"King Alcaeus asked his son, 'Lycurgus, why did you not tell us of this power that Larentina possesses?'

"Lycurgus shared Androcles's attitude in his answer. 'Larentina never really mastered it, and we never really thought about it since we were children. I guess we never considered it important.'

"King Alcaeus and King Karpos both shrugged their shoulders as they realized it was not all that important.

"King Karpos ordered, 'Lycurgus, fetch your sister; Androcles, gather the members of the gerousia council and bring them all here so that we can all talk.'

"Both young princes obeyed King Karpos's commands and went in search of the requested parties.

"Once everyone had assembled in front of the two kings, King Alcaeus simply asked Larentina, 'Can you truly be victorious in the upcoming games for your people?'

"Larentina answered, 'I can only give you my best, and pray to my God that I triumph.'

"King Alcaeus asked her, 'If the gods do grant this favor to you, can you defeat this young princess in the ancient Egyptian ways?'

"Larentina confidently answered, 'Yes, that will be no challenge to me; she is incredibly vain because she wears the Amazon's belt.'

"King Karpos commanded, 'Then our decision is made. Off with the three of you, so we may speak to the gerousia members in private. May the gods grant you and the Spartan people glory in the upcoming games.'

"All three young Spartans did as they were commanded, and the gerousia members watched them leave.

"Once the three young Spartans were out of hearing range, Lycurgus grabbed his sister by the upper arm and scornfully whispered in her ear, 'You need to be careful of the God you speak of to others. Do you understand, Sister?'

"Larentina jerked her arm from her brother's tight grip as she gave him a hurtful stare and simply nodded her head in agreement. She could not argue with him because she saw the fear in his eyes, even though he was angrily preaching at her. People do not accept new gods so easily, and they both could be killed.

"Both kings were completely surprised that the gerousia members who were present to watch the games did not argue with them, but they agreed with the kings regarding the entire idea."

Chapter LIV

"Larentina awoke, jumped out of the bed, and dressed as quickly as she could. She was so excited because the day had finally come! She and all of the Spartan party had participated in many festivities over the past few days, and they were given a royal tour of the great city by King Archimedes himself. King Alcaeus fulfilled every promise he had made to Larentina by taking her to the temple of Zeus, sacrificing a lamb, allowing her to speak with the priests of Zeus, and so much more. She finally felt she had the respect and love she craved for from her mortal father, and she vowed at this very moment she would do everything in her power not to let the Spartans down.

"At this point in history, the athletes did not compete in the nude. This tradition started later because another great Spartan princess, with the help of her father, disguised herself as a man to compete in the chariot races, and that's when they changed the rules to keep that from happening again.

"The morning flew by, and before Larentina knew it, they were in the large coliseum's center ground. The first competition was the disc, which Lycurgus won. Next was the javelin competition, which Androcles won. Many other athletes in addition to the two princes and Larentina competed for Sparta. Spartans also competed in wrestling, the long jump, foot races, and so many other games. They were victors in each event they entered.

"Larentina competed against the best archers in the world. She never missed a shot. In fact, she spliced down the middle of numerous arrows during the heated competition, hitting the bull's eye every time. It seemed to Larentina that the competition was very short, and the next thing she knew, she was being crowned as the victor.

"The games continued for several days, and then it was the day for all three royal Spartans to compete in the relay races. Lycurgus started the race; he had a very large lead over the other teams as he passed the baton to another Spartan athlete. When the baton was passed to Androcles, the Spartans had kept their lead. Androcles had made even more headway when he in turn passed the baton to Larentina, but she did not take this large lead for granted. She ran as fast as her strong legs would allow, increasing the distance between her and the other runners. She crossed the finish line well before any of the other runners.

"Once again, the crowds cheered the young Spartan victors. The entire team ran together to the center of the great arena for the crowning. Larentina was the last to be crowned, and after King Archimedes placed the crown on her head, he yelled to the spectators, 'This is the greatest tribute to Zeus, for his own daughter has competed in the games and has proven herself to him! The Spartan people are truly above all others for showing the Olympian deities that the children of Sparta are the greatest athletes of the world!' King Archimedes did not actually believe Larentina was the daughter of Zeus—most people did not—but it sounded good and that is why he said it.

"Larentina was smiling with pride as she watched King Alcaeus, King Karpos, and the rest of the Spartan party cheering and clapping as loud as they possibly could for their new generation.

"On the final day of the games, the competition that was the most important to Larentina, the chariot races, were held. As Larentina, her horses, and chariot were receiving last-minute inspections by King Alcaeus, King Karpos, Lycurgus, and Androcles, as well as their helots, King Alcaeus asked with fatherly concern, 'Daughter, are you sure you are up to this? No woman has ever competed in this dangerous race before. Are you sure you are strong enough to handle these powerful beasts?'

"Larentina just nodded her head in affirmation. All the men kept trying to get her to wear body armor, but she refused, stating, 'Why do I need protection? After all, this is just a game. I'm not going into battle.' Finally, she partially gave in and put on her shin guards, and she agreed to wear her helmet for protection. Androcles even made her take her dagger, which she concealed in her shin guard.

"They continued fussing and fussing over her, tugging and adjusting her militaristic tunic, urging her to put her helmet on so they could ensure it was secure, making sure her shin guards and sandals were properly fitted, and double checking the harnesses on the horses as well as the chariot's wheels. They fussed over her like a bunch of old women. Each man gave last-minute advice and commands as they were all huddled around her. They kept it up until her head hurt.

"Of course, all the other kings and wealthy free men from other Greek city-states watched this spectacle in total disgust. They all whispered to one another, 'The Spartan kings have no shame.' Everyone completely understood that the Spartans were putting their entire reputation on the line, allowing a mere girl to compete despite what King Archimedes said when he crowned her after the relay victory. The other spectators thought that the Spartan kings were doing everything in their power to get the rest of the world to believe that this girl was the daughter of Zeus, which no one really believed.

"As she prepared to climb up into the chariot, all the Spartan men clamored to help her; she finally commanded to all of them, 'Enough! I'm not a rag doll that needs to be pampered! I completely understand your concern; I promise I'll come back either with a crown on my head or dead on my shield!'

"Lucius watched this entire spectacle of the Spartan warriors fussing over just a young girl, but he wanted these people as future allies, even if the Romans had lost most of the games to them, and he felt he needed to warn her about his king, who was competing in the race with her. As he watched the Spartan kings and their entourage leaving to take their seats in the stadium, he seized the opportunity to approach her.

"Larentina stood in her chariot and heard someone call her name; as she looked down, she saw Lucius. She leaned down to the side of her chariot where Lucius was standing and asked him, annoyed, 'Lucius, what trickery is this? I'm competing against your king in addition to the others. You should not be here.'

"Lucius just smiled as he looked up at the Spartan beauty, and sincere concern filled his voice. 'I'm here to warn you about my king. He is a beastly man. King Servius will do anything to win in this race; he will kill everyone that gets in his way. Look!' he said, as he pointed to the Roman king's chariot. 'See those jagged sharp spears in the center of his wheels? I have watched him shred the wheels of other chariots with those spears in battle. Be careful, my Spartan princess, for if you get to close to him, he will kill you and your beasts.'

"Larentina scowled and said, 'You think you can scare me into losing to your king? I do not think so. It will take much, much more than that; and besides, these are games, not a battlefield. What you say is cheating, and I do not believe your king would do such a thing.'

"Lucius, still with concern in his voice, pleaded with her, 'My princess, I have watched him murder his own sons because he feared they would kill him and take his throne. He is mad.' He let out a heavy sigh, hesitating before telling his secrets. He truly was smitten with the Spartan beauty and did not want to see her slain. "I warn you because I believe Rome may need Sparta as her ally. I warn you because your father may grace me by allowing me to train with your armies as a favor for helping Sparta win this day. I believe Sparta may be the key to my future and to Rome's.'

"Larentina inquisitively looked down at him, and with a change of heart, she decided to believe he was sincere. 'Lucius, if what you speak is true, I am grateful, but it is much harder to get into our agoge training than you think. For one thing, you are too old. We start training at the age of seven, but we will see what my kings have to say.' Larentina bent down further and kissed Lucius fully on the mouth; Lucius reached up and gently kissed her back. Larentina blushed as she said, 'Thank you; I will do my best to stay away from your king, but my kiss of gratitude was not meant to linger; you have turned it into something else.'

"Lucius softly smiled as he said, 'I cannot help it that you have the ability to bewitch the strongest of men.'

"Larentina girlishly chuckled; she blushed and turned her attention back to the races, without giving a response to Lucius.

"Naturally, Larentina did not think about what her kiss to Lucius would look like to others watching. Androcles was the first to stand up from his seat; King Karpos grabbed him by the arm and commanded, 'Sit. Who was that stranger?'

"Lycurgus casually answered, as he was still sitting in his seat, 'Lucius, supposedly the future king of the Roman Kingdom.'

"King Alcaeus, acting like any concerned father would, asked, 'Who? How did she meet that peacock? How and when has she had time to meet him? What are you not telling me, son?'

"Androcles was growing even more jealous and angrily chimed in, 'We met that ass at the swimming pool before the games, and he was trying to court her the very first minute he laid eyes upon her. Lycurgus and I stopped his advances immediately. He is nothing but a fool. He confessed he would become king by marrying the king's daughter.'

"Androcles and Lycurgus both guffawed at the thought, and the kings joined in.

"King Karpos teased his son, as he continued to laugh, 'Apparently, son, you did not do a very good job at keeping him at bay. Once you are married, heed my advice, and keep a leash on her.'

"Lycurgus became angry because Larentina did not deserve to be the brunt of this mean-spirited joke. 'I'm sure there is an explanation of her behavior this day, and I do not believe the kiss was romantic, but something else.'

"King Alcaeus also became angry regarding what he considered to be disrespect to him, saying, 'I will speak with her promptly after this race! This behavior will not be tolerated! She was raised better than this.'

"Androcles stated his observations from the other day, and his voice was still laced with anger, 'This does not make sense to me at all. She acted as if he was inferior to us the other day.'

"King Karpos commented reassuringly, 'We shall see, my son, we shall see her motives. Right now she must be victorious, and I do not believe she has her mind on anything else, because she knows the consequences of failure.'

"King Alcaeus nodded his head in agreement, and Lycurgus did as well."

Chapter LV

"The chariot races began, and the racetrack was packed with chariots and horses. As Lucius predicted, it was a bloody race. Larentina watched as King Servius, the Roman king, stayed slightly in front of the pack by ramming his chariot into the sides of the other chariots as they came alongside him. His wheels, which were armored with jagged spears protruding from the center, shredded the other chariots' wheels, causing massive wreckage. It happened so quickly that the chariots immediately behind could not maneuver away from the wreckage, causing them to crash as well.

"The slaves and others moved the wreckage off the racetrack as fast as they could, but there was so much. The race was down to four chariots, and Larentina found herself side by side with the cheating tyrant. Celeris was on the inner side of the four horses; he moved further into the inner edge of the track, to try to pass King Servius before he shredded her wheels as well. But it did her no good because the king maneuvered his horses closer to the center edge of the track to get close to her. She would move her horses to slow down and speed up, but she was also concerned that her horses' legs might meet his wheels of destruction as well.

"She became more fearful with every passing moment. If she lost this race, Sparta's reputation of being the strongest and most ruthless city-state in the known world would be lost forever. They would be attacked and conquered over and over again. They would become a joke because of her failure. She became even more determined to win this race at all costs.

"King Lucius matched her as she maneuvered several times, and then suddenly, out of nowhere, Larentina felt the most excruciating pain of her life as his horsewhip made contact with her back. When he saw this, Lycurgus jumped up from his sitting position, gritting his teeth in pain. Both kings and Androcles looked at Lycurgus in shock as they saw the blood dripping down his back.

"King Alcaeus immediately pulled his son back down beside him. He did not want anyone to see for fear that Larentina would be disqualified for using magic, and Sparta would be shamed. Both kings looked at each other in disappointment. They now worried about what would happen to their city-state's reputation if Larentina were to lose this race. Sparta as a whole would become the butt of a nasty joke. The kings began to regret having allowed Larentina to do this. In fact, all the Spartan men knew Larentina would die before allowing this to happen, but they all feared that her best would not be good enough. Goddess or not, she was still a woman, and maybe they should not have expected so much from her. The mood of all became surreal and disheartening.

"Of course, Bion was compelled to vocalize his disappointment and rub it in the kings' noses. 'What did you expect? You and your sons have spoiled her. She has destroyed Sparta. She should have been shipped off to Zeus, so that he could deal with the abomination that he created.'

"Bion was sitting beside Lycurgus. Lycurgus's disappointment in Larentina turned into anger toward Bion. Lycurgus, still wincing in pain, grabbed Bion by his shoulders and shook him fiercely. He gritted his teeth as he glowered at Bion and threatened, 'Shut your insolent mouth. You have no clue of Larentina's capabilities. The race is not over yet. Keep spewing this filth, and I will cut your tongue out myself.'

Bion just sarcastically smiled and glared at the young prince.

"Androcles leaned forward, saying nothing, but he too gave Bion a deadly glower.

"King Karpos jumped into the argument, saying calmly, 'Lycurgus is right, the race is not over. There is still hope that our She Wolf will be victorious.'

"Everyone turned their attention back to the race, anxiously awaiting the outcome.

"Larentina jerked forward after the first lashing, gritting her teeth to keep from screaming. She thought for one second that maybe she had been pampered when she was lashed during agoge training, because it was never as painful as this. Those lashings had been painful, but not like this. She now wished she had worn her body armor. She grew humble for she was arrogant and did not heed her father's warnings, as well as Lucius's warnings. She felt foolish and vain.

"She glowered over at the tyrant, and when he tried to lash her again, she grabbed the whip in midair. The Roman king was astonished that this mere girl had the audacity to fight back. Nevertheless, he thought he would have no problem killing her, the same as he would any man in his way.

"As he tried to pull the whip away, her hand started to bleed, and she noticed that he had tied jagged shards of pottery into his whip. She now understood why it had been more painful than any other lashing she had received in her life. He was not only beating her with it, but his horses as well. To Larentina, that was unforgivable! Larentina glanced down at her hand and pushed the pain to the back of her mind, not realizing she had transferred her painful wounds to her brother.

"Adrenaline coursed through her veins as she continued to grit her teeth, and her eyes started to change. She would not allow this cheater to deprive her of victory. After all, this was her dream, and Sparta had allowed her to compete; she could not lose, not like this anyway. She turned her head, glowered at King Servius, and bellowed, 'I'm going to kill you, you sorry son of a bitch!'

"Unknown to Larentina and the bloodthirsty audience, most of the Olympian deities were watching as the race unfolded. Hera was sitting beside Zeus, and for one split second, she felt empathy toward the She Wolf, but it did not last, because she was rooting for the Roman king to kill her. Zeus, on the other hand, was afraid that his daughter might be killed. If worse came to worse, he would interfere to prevent that from happening; he watched excitedly, quietly rooting for his daughter.

"As the Roman king wickedly guffawed at Larentina, she climbed up on the side of her chariot and frantically yelled at her horse, 'Celeris, take me closer!' The horse led the other horses until they were side by side with the Roman king's horses, matching the pace of King Servius's chariot. King Servius then started whipping her horses. Larentina lost all control over her temper as she heard the chopping sound of her wooden spokes being cut to shreds, but at this moment, she did not care.

"Because of the gymnastic training she had throughout her life, she was able to balance herself on the edge of the moving chariot with ease, but she took no chances as she used her gifts to ensure she landed where she needed to. After balancing there for a few seconds, she leapt onto the edge of his chariot without faltering.

"Hera decided to take advantage of the moment. Hera moved her fingers without Zeus seeing, and Larentina felt an unknown force pushing her off the edge of the Roman king's chariot. Everyone in the audience gasped and rose to their feet, but she rose back into the air and returned to the edge of the king's chariot.

"Larentina knew it must have been Hera who did this. She feared she would have to use her powers in the open to prevent Hera from killing her.

"When Zeus saw this, he glared at Hera and angrily commanded, 'You will not interfere. If you do it again, you will pay a high price for disobeying me.'

"Hera averted her gaze from Zeus's; she looked at the ground trying to act innocent, but she knew she had been caught as she humbly murmured, 'Yes, my husband.'

"Before the Roman king could react, Larentina leapt onto his back. She wrapped her legs tightly around his waist and squeezed her right arm around his neck, cutting off his air supply.

"At this point, Larentina did not care as lightning bolts appeared everywhere around the chariot, striking it at least three times as flames started engulfing it. Winds were swirling around the chariot and lifting it several times from the ground.

"Lucius sat in the stadium and watched the young Spartan beauty's battle against his king. Could it actually happen? Could this Spartan girl rid the world of this tyrant, who was preventing him from becoming the next king of Rome? He stood up with his bloodthirsty eyes taking in every move, and he licked his lips in pure delight as he watched Larentina. He now believed all the stories about the She Wolf of the Spartans.

"Larentina knew this cretin of a king had no idea how strong her legs were, because he grabbed at them, trying to untangle them from his body with his free hand, instead of going for her arm. She reached down as he was pulling at her legs, grabbed her dagger that was tightly secured in her shin guard, and sliced the dagger across his windpipe.

"As he let go of the horses' reins, Larentina released her leg hold, so she was now standing directly behind him. Full of rage, she repeatedly stabbed him in his back. He turned to face her in shock and horror, falling into her as she slit his throat from left to right. Her voice was filled with contempt and hatred as she bellowed, 'Nobody lashes my horses!'

"The bloodthirsty crowd applauded her heroic act. Nothing was more exciting than seeing the underdog win a fight, even if she were a woman. The crowd loved it! Excitement and passion coursed through the audience.

"As the king dropped to his knees, Larentina looked over at the spectators, who were now frantically yelling at her; she looked back at the racetrack and saw the wreckage of one of the crashed chariots directly ahead of her. She leapt back into her chariot seconds before King Servius's horses jumped over the wreckage. The horses cleared the wreck, but his chariot, still in flames, was torn to pieces.

"While Larentina had been fighting King Servius on his chariot, Celeris deftly moved the horses and her chariot away from the Roman king's wheels of destruction. She only lost two of her spokes.

"Before Larentina could react by maneuvering her horses out of the way, she came upon another chariot's wreckage. Her horses were about to jump it, and Larentina instinctively climbed onto the front edge of her chariot and then leapt onto the back of one of the mares. When she looked behind her, the chariot crashed into the wreckage as her horses ran clear. All that remained of her chariot were the wheels and the axle that had held them together. At that moment, as the pieces of her chariot were flying in midair, she used her powers to put the chariot back together again so she could cross the finish line and win the race. She then jumped back onto the few planks of wood that she was able to put together with her mind and completed the last stretch of the race. The audience once again erupted in cheers because they had never seen an Olympian deity use their power like this before. In fact, most had never seen one of their Olympian gods at all. It was not until she crossed the finish line that she realized that she had just won the race.

"She had a headache and was completely exhausted, because she had never used so much energy before; she was relieved it was over because she thought for sure that Hera would have killed her by now. She realized that Zeus must have also been in the audience and stopped Hera from using her powers against Larentina.

"All the spectators were on their feet, and Larentina was overwhelmed by their deafening cheers. With a proud smile on her face, she remained standing on what was left of her chariot; her horses slowly walked around the racetrack once more, as she waved her one hand in the air to the jubilant crowd.

"Zeus, Hera, Apollo, and many other deities disguised as mortals had watched the bloody spectacle from the crowd of spectators. Zeus's face beamed with pride in his mortal daughter while Hera scowled with disgust.

"The entire Spartan party, with the kings in the lead, leapt over the wall onto the racetrack as Larentina passed by. King Alcaeus ran up to what was left of his chariot, grabbed his daughter by the waist, and lifted her into the air as he laughed triumphantly with her.

"Larentina leaned on her father's shoulders to ease the burden of her weight. She blushed as she gazed deeply into her father's eyes, which reflected the pride he felt in his heart. He let her down gently and kissed her on each cheek as he proudly announced, 'This is a glorious day for Sparta! I would not have believed it if I had not seen it with my own eyes. I am so pleased with your victory that I cannot contain it. Your mother is going to burst with pride when she hears this tale!' He then playfully teased Larentina, 'I should have known you would destroy my prized chariot, Daughter!' He kissed her twice more on both her cheeks and lifted her into the air again, gleaming with pride and joy. Once again, he let her down gently, still gazing into her eyes with pride.

"King Karpos grabbed her by the arm and, in a proud and victorious voice, confessed to King Alcaeus, 'You are not the only one who is proud of our champion. You must share the princess!' He then embraced Larentina in his arms and kissed her on each cheek.

"He didn't care whether anyone saw, for she had proven that she was truly a warrior and the She Wolf of Sparta. As he held her beautiful face in his hands and again kissed her cheeks, he realized that she looked uncannily similar to his first true love, Agape. He shook this thought from his mind as he reminded himself that she would soon be his daughter once she was joined to his son. He now had a completely different outlook of women, and Larentina had proven this once again to him.

"King Karpos proudly confessed to Larentina, 'I too am very proud of you this day, Daughter. You had us worried for a moment, but it was just a moment that we doubted your strength and courage.'

"King Alcaeus angrily commented to King Karpos, 'She is not your daughter; not yet.'

Both kings and the surrounding Spartan entourage laughed heartily at that statement. King Alcaeus became embarrassed because he had acted like a jealous father.

"King Alcaeus put his hand on top of Lycurgus's shoulder and solemnly asked, 'Daughter, are you forgetting something?'

"Larentina then realized that she had transferred her pain to her brother; she looked down at Lycurgus's bloody hand and then looked at her own hand, which was miraculously healed as well as her backside from the whipping she had just received. She immediately became embarrassed and felt like a coward.

"She gently took Lycurgus's hand in both her hands and turned his palm upward so everyone huddled about her could see as well as protect what she was about to do from outsiders' eyes. She touched his bloody wounds, closed her eyes, and healed Lycurgus's hand as well as his back. They watched as Larentina let out a soft painful moan and flinched as the pain and fresh wounds reappeared on her flesh.

"After she healed her brother, King Alcaeus whispered, 'You cheated this day, Daughter, but I understand you had to.'

"King Karpos retorted, 'She did not cheat, the Roman bastard cheated first; she did what she had to do to be victorious for the Spartan people.' The large huddle of Spartan men either verbally acknowledged this as fact or nodded their heads in agreement with King Karpos.

"Lycurgus simply confessed, 'I would have done the same, Father, for we are as one. You know we cannot survive without the other. You yourself have instilled this in us, but this was truly the first time Larentina did it. So therefore this was not cheating; it is not the same thing as the pain from discipline. Larentina played this game by the rules of engagement King Servius dictated.'

"King Alcaeus nodded and commanded, 'This will never be mentioned again; not among ourselves or outsiders.' Everyone in the party nodded their heads in agreement.

"By this time, King Archimedes and many other kings of Greece's city-states had surrounded the large Spartan party, which in turn had surrounded Larentina. Many spectators had congregated in the seats in the stadium so they might be able to see what was about to unfold.

"King Archimedes pushed many of the Spartan party out of his way as he walked toward the center of the huddle until he reached Larentina, King Alcaeus, and King Karpos.

"Once all the people started backing away from the three kings and Larentina there was a large circle of open space between them and the growing crowd.

"King Archimedes and many of the Delian League were not happy about what had just transpired in what was supposed to be a peaceful race, and King Archimedes verbalized his disdain. 'Alcaeus, Karpos, Larentina! How dare you act as the victors in these games! You have cheated; these are games, not a bloody battlefield! You Spartans always seem to take something that is supposed to be peaceful and turn it into a bloodbath. It is apparent that even your women are bloodthirsty barbarians! You will not be crowned because of your wicked behavior. Woman or not, you shall be crucified for disobeying our laws.'

"This statement infuriated King Alcaeus; in an angry, thunderous voice, he proclaimed his disapproval of Archimedes's sharp, wicked tongue, not to mention his threats: 'It was your rules that got her into this mess to begin with. It was apparent for all to see: King Servius was at war and murdering all his competitors. Are you blind, Archimedes? Larentina not only conducted herself by this Roman king's rules of engagement, "Kill or be killed," she also righted a wrong for the other competitors who were slain by him. Sparta stands behind her She Wolf. If you truly want to go to war, I have no problem defending the honor of Sparta's She Wolf!'

"Many Delian League members had pushed their way to the inner circle, and most of them acknowledged that what Larentina had done was part of the pact that all the members of the Delian League had pledged their allegiance to. As far as most of them concerned, the Spartan princess had righted a wrong, even though it was not on the battlefield. They had pledged no allegiance to this King Servius. In fact, they had just lost many great kings who were members of the Delian League, not to mention many of their wealthy colleagues who were wounded by the destruction created by this Roman king.

"Before King Archimedes could respond to all the other kings' statements, he heard loud shouting from the spectators standing above them in the stadium; the large circle started splitting down the middle as people moved out of the way, yelling, 'Zeus! Hera! Apollo!' The names of the other Olympian deities were also shouted from the crowds.

"The gods seemed to be walking directly toward them, as if they were ghosts appearing from thin air. Each one wore a hooded cloak of many colors over their clothing.

"As each one of the deities appeared, they removed their hoods so that everyone could see their faces. Shocked by this once-in-a-lifetime sight—seeing the Olympian deities in the flesh—King Archimedes and the entire crowd immediately kneeled down in supplication. Everyone was on their knees except for Larentina.

"King Archimedes peeked up to see this brazen young woman just standing there watching the Olympian deities approach her.

"Larentina became livid the moment she saw Hera; she ran toward the queen of the gods with no fear of the consequences, bellowing fearlessly, 'You wicked, murderous bitch! Stay out of my life!'

"Zeus nervously chuckled as he grabbed Larentina by her waist. No one knew what exactly Larentina was yelling about, and no one really knew what she would have done if she had gotten her hands on Hera. Hera could have easily killed her or put some kind of wicked curse upon her.

"Zeus felt even more pride that his daughter had fearlessly gone after his wife without thinking about the consequences. Not even Hercules was that brazen. Zeus hated to admit it, but Larentina was very unpredictable, and he enjoyed it.

"Zeus kissed her forehead and whispered in her ear, diverting Larentina's attention away from Hera, 'Daughter, be calm. What has been done is done; now I command you to let it go. You are no match against my wife.'

"As Zeus hugged Larentina, she continued to glare at Hera. Hera, on the other hand, stood wickedly laughing at Larentina.

"Larentina finally regained her senses and realized that Hera was a powerful goddess, and she was no match against her; she obeyed Zeus's command.

"Zeus released his paternal hug, and Larentina with frustration in her voice said, 'Father, I have done no wrong this time. Hera interfered again, and I request justice for the crimes she has committed against me.'

"Zeus let out a loud laugh at his daughter's statement, because he did not know what else to do. He calmly ordered, 'Larentina, I will command you only once more: let it go.' After seeing Larentina's facial expression soften, he continued, 'Daughter, I know you did nothing wrong; in fact, you played these mortal men's games according to their rules. You did try to conduct yourself as a mortal, but you had no other choice but to use your divine gifts. That is why I am here; you have proven this past year that you do possess some of the qualities of the Olympian deities, and I believe you belong with us, your true family. This way I can keep a close eye on you. Your power and wit, once again, have caught my eye.'

"The real reason Zeus had appeared was because he knew Larentina was the key to something amiss in the heavens; the archangels of God were becoming increasingly brazen as they were picking off more fallen angels one at a time and casting them into the abyss. Only a couple of the Olympian deities recognized that another thousand-year battle was about to begin, and Zeus knew that his offspring would bring about the beginning of whatever was about to unfold in the heavens. He just didn't know how. He figured if he had her with him that this plot would dissolve, and the true God and his legions of archangels would have to wait for another to choose their side. Larentina was a creature designed of free will, and he had to convince her to join sides with him freely, because he knew the true creator was keeping a close eye on her. He could not even tell what she was thinking, unlike all other mortals. Something (or someone) was protecting her, not only against these silly mortals, but also against himself, her own father. But then, she didn't appear to be able to read his thoughts either.

"Zeus knew he had made a mistake in stopping Larentina from committing the sin of vengeance against an innocent, her brother or Karpos, but his pride had gotten in the way again. He felt very foolish now because he fell into the trap that the creator of all had created for him.

"Larentina protested, 'But Father, I am with my true family, my mother's family, and this is where I belong.'

"Zeus was a charmer as he got down on one knee and kissed Larentina's hand. He looked up at her as he replied with a bit of confusion, 'Daughter, I thought this is what you wanted.'

"Larentina gazed at him as she contemplated her decision before responding to Zeus's request. 'I thought I wanted to be with you, but I belong here. I am neither an Olympian deity nor a common woman. All I know is my choice is here, with my mortal father, mother, and brother. I am still half mortal, and that will never change.'

"Zeus was confused regarding his offspring's decision, but he knew he could not force her or the one true God's wrath would be upon him. Zeus decided to make her fear him, so he said angrily as he stood up and thunder boomed above them and black clouds started to form, 'I must admit you have kept me entertained, but you know as well as I do that you possess the skills of a warrior and healing abilities beyond those of mortal men. I am angry because you do belong with me! What if I command you to join me?

"'This is for your own good; your meddling in man's design is starting to become intolerable. I am tired of interfering with the destiny that you chose, not me, to clean up your foolish messes! You are a goddess, and you must come to terms with this. After all, you are made from my seed, and no other. How could you even choose a mortal over me?

"'I take great offense in this idiotic decision that you have made; you are naive about men; do you truly want to continue down this path leading to the demise of your precious Spartan people?'

"Larentina tried to convince Zeus that she did not belong in his realm. 'Father, look; the wounds that I have encountered are still upon my flesh, and I bleed; does not this prove to you that I am not a deity?'

"Zeus became angry again as he looked at the deep wounds on his daughter's back, and then he took her hand in his and, with one glance, healed Larentina's wounds.

"With his magic, he created from thin air a laurel leaf crown made of gold. Larentina's eyes began to swell with tears. As the tears streamed down her cheeks, Zeus put this crown upon her head and proclaimed, 'This crown represents the greatest gift a daughter could give to her father, courage, and the willingness to sacrifice all for the idea of greatness. Now will you come with me?'

"As the tears fell down Larentina's cheeks, she sadly answered, 'I'm sorry, Father, because for unknown reasons, my destiny is here among mortals, because I am nothing more than a mortal. I have used illusion and deception as my weapons of choice. I will admit I do possess gifts, but I do not believe I have inherited these gifts from you.'

"Zeus tried another tactic to change Larentina's mind. 'These gifts that you speak of came from me, no other. I do not understand why you deny me. You are keeping something from me. Your mind is so strong I cannot hear your thoughts, as I can with all other mortals. This speaks volumes alone. I cannot protect you all the time in this realm, for I will grow weary of trying to keep an eye on you.'

"All who kneeled before Zeus heard this shocking confession, as well as Larentina deliberately denying Zeus. Some, subconsciously, shook their heads with displeasure at Larentina's disrespectful behavior toward Zeus, yet Zeus continued pleading with her.

"Zeus continued, 'I refuse to force you, as I have others. Because of your choice, I will never be able to interfere in your life's journey ever again. You will live and die like all mortals. This crown will be my last gift to you; I crown you as a victor, and if any harm comes upon you from this act, I will not only destroy the king that commits this act against you, I will destroy his family, as well as all his people.' Zeus glared upon all the kings present and asked them all in an angry voice, 'Have I made my command understood?' No one dared reply verbally, but all nodded their heads in affirmation as they continued kneeling before Zeus.

"Zeus said in a pleading tone, 'These mortal men do not care about you. They only care about what you can give them through me. I know what you seek: equality and liberty. Daughter, I will only ask you once more: please, will you come with me?'

"Larentina knew she could never answer yes, because her entire existence was and continued to be a lie, so she answered once more, with tears streaming down her cheeks, 'I cannot, Father. I wish I could say yes and live in your magic kingdom, but my true destiny is here, with my mother's family.'

"Apollo kept his thoughts to himself, but he was very angry that Zeus allowed this mortal beauty to have a choice in the matter, and to make things even worse, he was pleading with this silly girl. Apollo never witnessed such a sight—not to mention, Zeus had rescinded his pledge to give Larentina to him when she came of age. He knew he would get his vengeance against Zeus soon, because this was not the first time Zeus had not kept his word to him, and it was time to dethrone this deity—father or not. He wickedly snickered to himself about how sweet it would be to see Zeus himself begging for his very life. He then would take Larentina just to spite him, take her repeatedly throughout eternity. He smiled after these vile thoughts.

"As Larentina stood there, she watched each Olympian deity fade slowly into thin air. Zeus gave Larentina one last hug and kiss. As he slowly faded away, he warned Larentina, 'Remember my words, Daughter.'

"King Archimedes was the first to stand back up, and he fearfully requested, 'I truly hope you forgive me, She Wolf of the Spartans, for ever doubting you are the daughter of Zeus.'

"Larentina shrugged her shoulders indifferently as she responded, 'I could not care less about your fears of Zeus. You have not only insulted Zeus, but the Spartan kings as well. You and your people are very lucky this day. Your apology should be presented to my kings, not I. There have been wars started over much less.'

"King Archimedes humbly looked toward the Spartan kings; before he could speak, King Alcaeus simply replied, 'Archimedes, the Spartan people and I forgive you. Karpos and I did warn that you would be a believer before these games were completed. Nothing more needs to be said.'

"King Karpos added, 'If it were up to me, this would not have been a peaceful outcome.'

"King Archimedes just laughed as he replied, 'After all, I am just a mortal man as you are, and I am humbly grateful that you have accepted my apology for being so foolish with my wicked tongue. Now enough serious talk, for there is still much festivity before us.

"'I will give you and your Spartans a victorious celebration before you part my great lands. I am proud to call Sparta my ally.'

"Larentina watched as all three kings started talking as if they were best of friends once again, and the crowds around them all cheered once more. Larentina just shook her head from side to side, thinking about how fickle men could be."

Chapter LVI

"The games were over and the last celebration began in the great city of Olympia. King Archimedes went all out for his guests, as promised. It was a beautiful evening, and he had large tables filled with food and flasks of wine spread across his great palace's lawns, showcasing his wealth.

"Everyone talked about Larentina's victory in the chariot race. As with all stories, it was embellished over and over again throughout the evening; with each telling, the tale grew more supernatural.

"Larentina promised her mortal father that she would sing and dance for him and everyone present this evening, to entertain them.

"King Alcaeus and King Karpos had dispatched a messenger to retrieve Queen Alexis and Queen Irene to join them now that the great city of Olympia was reopened to women. Larentina requested her mother to join them, and the gerousia members saw no harm in it. After all, they felt that Larentina could have pretty much whatever she wanted at this point because of the glorious victory she gave Sparta.

"Larentina danced as King Archimedes, King Draco, King Karpos, King Alcaeus, Androcles, and Lycurgus sat at one of the large oval tables.

"King Draco introduced himself and repeated his wager to the two Spartan kings. He explained that they would be privileged if he allowed Larentina to fight against his daughter, Princess Poulxeria.

"Bion became infuriated with the arrogance of King Draco. Naturally, he knew the secret of the belt, that it held no magic over Larentina, but he kept the secret to himself as he spoke before either Spartan king could. 'How dare you insinuate that this is a privilege to us, when it will be a privilege to you. If my two kings happen to agree with this foolish wager, you will have to pledge your army's allegiance to the Spartan kings, at least for the rest of your reign, if our She Wolf is the victor.'

"King Draco was more boastful in his mannerisms than most kings. He wickedly chuckled and vocalized his pleasure. 'Your Spartan She Wolf is no match against my daughter and Ares's belt. I have already pledged my kingdom's allegiance to the Delian League, but if it will get your kings to agree, I will not only give the belt to her if she happens to be the victor, I will also pledge my kingdom's allegiance to you as long as I sit upon the throne.'

"He arrogantly laughed once more, believing the She Wolf of Sparta was no match against his daughter. Then he said to all present, 'But if my daughter is the victor, then you will not only pledge the allegiance of your armies to me, you will give me your She Wolf's armor and sword, since I know they are not earthly.'

"King Alcaeus wickedly snickered at this fool and confidently agreed, 'So be it!'

"Both Spartan kings reached across the table and shook hands with King Draco, symbolically agreeing to this wager.

"King Draco stood to make a toast for all present at the table, and as he did so, he agreed with confidence, 'Then it's settled; you will come to Mycenae as my guests to watch this match!'

"General Nikephoros had sat silently at the table throughout this conversation, but this was not going to happen, not on his watch. After King Draco sat back down, General Nikephoros stood up and angrily said, 'What? You must take us for fools, because once our Spartan She Wolf tears your poor helpless daughter to shreds, we will be sitting ducks for your vengeance. I do not think so; this fight will take place on our soil, Spartan soil!'

"King Archimedes now realized a fight was about to start and immediately stood up and calmly suggested, 'Please, gentlemen, there is no need to fight over where this challenge will take place, for Olympia would be a perfect neutral setting to hold this challenge. Do we all agree? You all will be my guests; this would be a perfect location. Besides, I would love to see this challenge first hand. The Spartan's She Wolf would definitely be entertaining.'

"Everyone around the table agreed.

"King Draco voiced the obvious: 'It will take a couple of weeks for my daughter to join me here.'

Everyone acknowledged this fact and agreed to set the date for the challenge in two weeks.

"Bion rose to leave the table, and a few moments later, General Nikephoros excused himself as well.

"The two men met by the stables. Bion whispered to Nikephoros in anger, 'You are an idiot, you pledged your allegiance to me. Larentina is still alive, and we had an opportunity to have both kings killed and Larentina at the same time.'

"Nikephoros murmured his retort, 'I made no allegiance to you, but to Sparta and to my kings. Larentina has not been killed by my doing because she does not deserve to die, I just do not want her in my army.' Nikephoros said nothing more and simply walked away for Bion.

"No more than a ten minutes later, they both, at different times, returned to the table.

"Larentina knew her mortal father, King Alcaeus, would be speaking with King Draco. It saddened Larentina because she would have to fight another battle, this time against another woman. The night before, Larentina had prayed to God, asking him to keep her faith strong so she could defeat all her enemies and give her the insight when to kill and when not to do so.

"After Larentina finished dancing, she approached the table where the two Spartan kings were sitting. She kissed her father on the cheek as well as all the other Spartans at the table. At this time, the table was almost empty because most of the guests had retired early this evening.

"Larentina was starving after putting almost all of her energy into dancing and singing for everyone. She had watched the heated conversation at her mortal father's table, which transpired through a fraction of her entertainment, but food was more important to her at this moment, for she had not eaten all day.

"Everyone seemed to watch in silence as Larentina ate what scraps were left from the large feast that King Archimedes had provided. King Alcaeus could see the wolf spirit in his daughter as she literally wolfed the food down.

"As one of King Archimedes's slaves poured more wine into Larentina's goblet, she noticed everyone was watching her eat. After swallowing her wine to wash down the mouth full of bread she had finished off with the lamb, she explained why she was famished. 'I'm sorry that I'm being a glutton, but it takes a lot of my strength to entertain you mortal men. And besides, I hate starving and I have not eaten all day.'

"King Alcaeus and the other Spartans who remained at the table guffawed at Larentina's excuse. Androcles was the first to speak, doing his best to contain his chuckles as he playfully teased her, 'Well, my future queen, tell me how that is so, for it appears to me it takes more energy to kill a Roman king than to dance.'

"Everyone burst into laughter once again because of Androcles's teasing, and Larentina started blushing. She understood the teasing because she assumed it was an amusing sight to see. She did not mind it; there was never enough laughter in her world, so if she had to bear the brunt of some innocent amusement in her world, it was fine. She had no problem laughing at herself as well as others. King Alcaeus, as he was still trying to contain his chuckling as he continued teasing Larentina and Androcles, 'Now, come, come, if our She Wolf states it takes more strength to dance for us than killing a tyrant of a king, then it must be true.'

"Everyone laughed even harder, as Larentina blushed even more. She innocently said to her father as she tried to wiggle out of her gluttony, 'But Father, it is true. Have you ever danced and sang for three hours straight, just to entertain your father?'

"Everyone chuckled as King Alcaeus tried to contain his laughter; he playfully teased, 'Daughter, I would not know of such things, since it is a daughter's duty to amuse and entertain her father, but I must admit, it gives me great pleasure for you to choose me as your father over Zeus.'

"King Alcaeus grew serious as he changed the subject, saying, 'I do not understand this, Daughter. How could you give up the Olympian god's kingdom for Sparta? You were very foolish. Now Zeus will not protect you when you need him, because you chose me over him. I would be insulted if I were him. I still do not understand why Zeus gave you a choice in the matter to begin with. I fear he may kill us all and take you from us anyway.'

"Larentina gazed in her mortal father's eyes for just a moment as she too became solemn. She could not help the tears of pride, which formed in her eyes for her mortal father. He had broken all traditions as of late, and in her thoughts, she wished he was her father and no other. 'You are my father in every sense of the word. You may not possess magical powers like Zeus, but you have always been an important part of my life.'

"Lucius had joined the group after several other kings had left their table. He had been waiting impatiently, hoping he would be summoned. When the moment finally arrived, he was very grateful and hoped that things would work out according to his plans.

"Larentina had already told the kings and the gerousia council how Lucius had warned her about King Servius and why she had kissed him fully on the mouth. She had explained that the kiss was for her gratitude to him, his family, and the kingdom he would eventually lead. The Spartan kings and the gerousia council agreed to reward him heartily. King Karpos agreed to adopt him as his son, so that he may have a few months of agoge training and be taught the basics of Spartan warfare.

"So Lucius had become a prince. Not only did this increase his status, but it would also enable him to become the consort of the only surviving daughter of King Servius. He had already sent one of the athletes back to the Roman Kingdom to announce his new title as prince of the Spartan Kingdom and request the hand of Princess Tullia.

"He praised the gods for bringing this Spartan She Wolf into his life's journey. Without her actions, none of this would have happened. He owed his entire future to this She Wolf goddess, and she did not even know how much she had done for him. He would do anything for her, anything.

"He stood up from the table and, with wine goblet in hand, attempted to lighten the mood at the table. 'Princess Larentina, She Wolf goddess of the Spartans, I will love you and worship you until my dying breath. I pledge my allegiance as well as the allegiance of the Roman Kingdom not only to you, but also to your Spartan people. In front of all these witnesses, I vow that the Roman Kingdom will be at your disposal whenever you need us. I swear this on my unborn child's life.

"'Whatever your reasons are for denouncing the great god Zeus, so shall I honor your choice that he has so mercifully given you. You have unknowingly given the Roman people back their freedom from this tyrant of a king. Thank you for the kiss of gratitude that has forever stained my lips and my heart with love toward you. I surrender my very soul to your command. You will always be my true queen now and forever.'

"As Lucius sat back down with pride in his eyes toward this Spartan beauty for giving him everything he desired, a half-drunken Androcles became very angry and punched him squarely in the nose, causing Lucius to tumble to the ground. As blood spurted out of Lucius's nose, Androcles stood above him, yelling angrily, 'How dare you pronounce your love to my future wife, my queen, and my goddess? How dare you?'

"As Androcles wielded his sword to kill Lucius, who was trying to scramble to his feet, Lycurgus grabbed Androcles's right arm before he could strike a deadly blow. Lycurgus gripped Androcles's arm firmly and commanded, 'Stop, Androcles! He has pledged his allegiance not only to my sister, but also to our Spartan people! Stop!'

"King Karpos tried to reassure Androcles, saying, 'He is your brother now, son! There is no rivalry for Larentina's hand; she is yours!'

"Larentina joined in the argument and angrily yelled at Androcles, 'How dare you? I have had enough! I'm going to bed!'

"Larentina started to walk away from the table when Bion commanded her, 'Princess Larentina, do not leave this table, for we have not finished speaking with you.'

"Lycurgus helped his drunken friend walk back to the palace so he could sleep off his anger. Both Spartan kings apologized to Lucius for Androcles's actions, and they they commanded him to leave their presence. Larentina poured more wine into her goblet, and then she refilled the rest of the men's goblets as well.

"Bion was the first to speak. 'Sit, Larentina, for you are not a slave, but something much, much more.'

"Larentina obediently sat in her chair and reached for her goblet full of wine. As Larentina took a deep drink, Bion wondered whether she could beat Princess Poulxeria. He did not want a repeat of the races. He disliked Larentina more and more as her powers grew each passing day, but he did not show it as he asked, 'Are you absolutely positive that Ares's belt does not pose a threat to you? And this fight will be between mortal strength of two women only?'

"Larentina finished off the goblet of wine before speaking. 'Nothing is an absolute in life, but I am positive simply because I do not believe in the belts's magic. I believe in something much, much more powerful than that.'

"Everyone at the table, including Bion, looked puzzled because they did not understand Larentina's meaning.

"King Alcaeus asked with concern in his voice, 'Larentina, what you have just said does not make sense. Can you defeat Princess Poulxeria? Just answer yes or no, Daughter. You were positive the other day.'

"Larentina answered, 'Father, I cannot just answer you with a yes or no, for I do not know how clever this female warrior is. I am certain that the belt does not possess any magic toward me for I do not believe in it, so that makes me more powerful than the belt.'

"Bion was now angry with Larentina; he lost all his patience and let his feelings known to all who were present, saying, 'Larentina, if you do not defeat Princess Poulxeria, Spartans will become slaves to King Draco. Do you not understand this? No more games. You must defeat her or you will be the death of Sparta.'

"Larentina answered, in an agitated tone, 'Why is it that every man in my life must always say I will be the death of them, and now my country. I am a Spartan first; I believe the belt does not pose any threat to me because I am Spartan!

"'Of course I know this, and again I vow I will die if need be to prevent this. I swear it! I will defeat her or die trying. Again, you put very little faith in me. Do I dare say this—that it is only because I'm a woman? I know you would not question my brother or any other man of Sparta if this challenge were presented to them. Is this answer now satisfactory to you?'

"King Alcaeus interrupted the now heated conversation as he simply remarked, 'Bion, she is right. If she were a man, we would not doubt him, as we doubt her. I believe she has earned our faith in her abilities.'

"King Karpos acknowledged this by agreeing, 'I too thought women were merely our property and we as free men could do as we pleased with them, not to mention the only thing women are good for is giving birth, but Larentina has changed my mind and heart toward our Spartan women. She has proven herself time and time again.

"'I can no longer deny her, as well as all our Spartan women, the right to be an equal to all men. I believe she has captured Zeus's heart as well. He may say he will not be there, but I believe he is now very closely watching her and all who surround her. He will be back in her life, and because of this, he will be there for her people. We will leave her fate, as well as the fate of our kingdom, in the hands of the gods.'

"Everyone agreed, and nothing more was spoken regarding the upcoming fight. Larentina was dismissed and retired to her room, still angry and disappointed in her Spartan leaders. Once she was out of sight, the Spartan men continued to discuss Larentina's future in the Spartan army. After the lingering conversation ended, they all retired for the night."

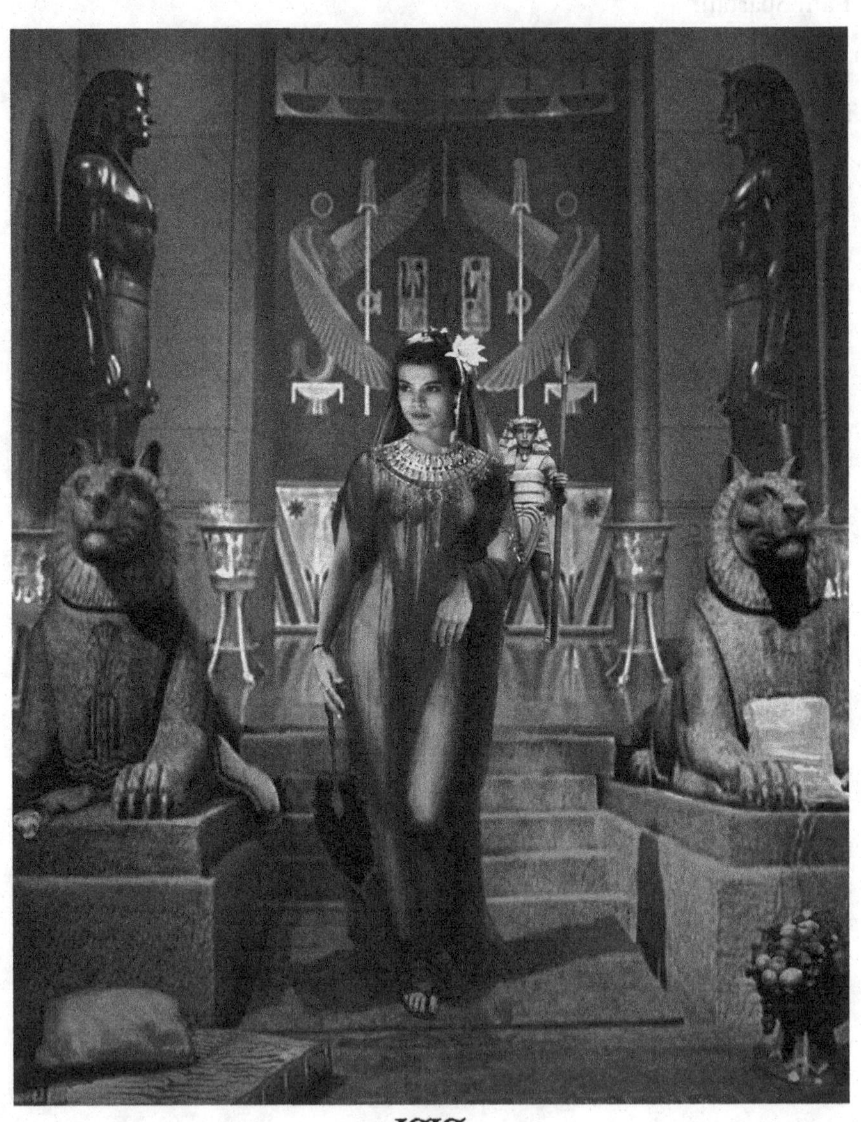

ISIS

Chapter LVII

"Queen Alexis and Queen Irene arrived with their traveling entourage a few days later. Larentina was so excited to see her mother that she ran out of the palace and straight into Queen Alexis's arms, hugging her dearly.

"Queen Alexis was puzzled at her daughter's affection and asked Larentina, with a soft smile upon her face, 'Child, what is this? I heard you were victorious. Let me get settled and meet with your father, and we will talk after supper this evening.'

"Queen Irene giggled because of the daughterly affection Larentina displayed; she voiced her feelings to Larentina. 'I've never seen such longing for a mother. I must admit it is refreshing. We all shall talk after the kings have finished speaking with us.'

"Larentina had truly missed her mother, which is why she behaved the way she did, but there was another reason as well. As Larentina still clung to her mother, they walked toward the palace entrance and met both kings at the threshold. Then, both kings and their wives disappeared into the palace, leaving Larentina standing there alone. She knew she would have to wait until she was summoned so she could speak with her mother, so she casually walked to her room to wait.

"Someone knocked on Larentina's bedroom door. Excitedly, she opened it, thinking it was Queen Alexis, but to her pleasant surprise, it was Corinna. Larentina hugged the helot and invited her into her room, and then she closed the door.

"Larentina asked Corinna to tell her more stories of God and his people to help pass the time away. Corinna told her several biblical stories and prophesies until there was another knock on the door.

"This time it was Queen Alexis, who entered her daughter's room with a serious expression on her face. She commanded the helot, 'Corinna, leave us now.' As Corinna closed the door behind her, Queen Alexis sat in a large chair across the room from Larentina's bed. Larentina sat on the floor beside the chair and looked inquisitively at Queen Alexis in silence.

"Queen Alexis rubbed Larentina's head softly, and then she began to speak, but it was obvious she was not happy with Larentina. 'I told Queen Irene that I thought it best that I speak with you alone. I should have taught you your station in life a long time ago, but I am doing it now. Daughter, you must learn to hold your sharp tongue when you speak to any man. You should not overstep your place when one of the gerousia council members is speaking with you. When they ask you a question, simply answer yes or no. Do not speak unless you are spoken to. This applies to any man you speak to. Sometimes it is better to appear to be humble and stupid while you observe and plan your strategy. Do you understand my meaning? Larentina, you have changed much for the women of Sparta; there is no denying this, but we have much more to accomplish. We must be careful about many things while we change our customs. In this unspoken battle, we must begin to slow down our attacks and be wise about which battle we choose to fight.'

"Larentina just nodded her head, acknowledging that she understood her mother, but her eyes were filled with disappointment over Queen Alexis's commands.

"Queen Alexis let out a soft sigh as she continued lecturing Larentina. 'You have been very lucky. I do not understand why Zeus allowed you to speak to him in such a manner. I do not know why he gave you a choice instead of commanding you to go with him, but what I do know is you have put Sparta in a very precarious position by choosing a mortal king over him. He is a god who does not always keep his word.

"'Because of you, and because we pushed and encouraged you into your life's journey, our gender has been given more liberties than ever before, but it only takes one mistake from you to lose all that we have fought for.

"'I must warn you now. Apollo has spoken to me in dreams and omens, telling me that you were promised to him; Zeus broke his promise to him by giving you a choice in the matter. Apollo is very displeased, and he cannot take back the wolf spirit from you because it has become a part of you. He has made threats through my dreams of harming the Spartan people if you follow through and marry Androcles. If Apollo can't have you, then he vows that no man shall. I promise you, Daughter, Apollo will kill Androcles. You will be blamed for his death, which could lead to a civil war among the Spartan people, breaking the alliance between the Agiad and Eurypontids houses.'

"Larentina became annoyed and asked, 'Mother, how can that be so? Would not Zeus have told me himself? Apollo can have any woman, deity or not; why would he even want me?'

"Queen Alexis patiently answered, 'Because Zeus vowed not to interfere in your life ever again, so now you are easy pickings for any vengeful deity. I tried to warn you many times in the past.'

"Larentina looked up at Queen Alexis with a grim look as she asked, 'How can I undo this without giving up my freedom?'

"Queen Alexis let out a sigh as she calmly answered, 'You cannot; this freedom has all been an illusion. We almost have it, but not quite. Larentina, you are not that naive.'

"Larentina retorted, 'I guess I am that naive, for I thought my destiny was to change Spartan society, giving women complete freedom and enabling us to be treated as equals. I will not lower myself, because I have already been accepted as an equal, and I will not bow down to any man; I know nothing else but the way I have always lived. I am what I am because of you and my birth mother. This is what the two of you designed me to be. Now you want me to be different?'

"Larentina irritably sighed again as she looked up at her mother. Queen Alexis continued scolding her. 'You will do your duty, Daughter. Agape and I also designed you to do your duty to us first, before anything else. You will do as I command. You also put us in a very bad situation regarding the Amazons and King Draco.'

"Larentina impatiently asked, 'How so?'

"Queen Alexis started lecturing her daughter again. 'You first have made a pact with the Amazons. I do not know the deal completely. Then you convinced our kings and the gerousia council to make a wager with King Draco for the belt of Ares to return to the Amazons, but what you do not know, Daughter, is Princess Poulxeria's mother is a direct descendant of Aristomache, the daughter of Queen Hippolyte. So if you kill her and the Amazons discover this, they will come after not only you, but the Spartan people as well. If you do not defeat her, then the Spartans will be enslaved; we must go to war whenever King Draco commands it. Do you understand the magnitude of this dilemma?'

"Larentina contemplated the question and then answered, 'Then I will go and tell the truth to Queen Almez.'

"Queen Alexis wisely responded, 'What good will that do? You cannot tell her the truth, for you must defeat Poulxeria for the Spartan people's honor. That is your duty. I could care less about the Amazons. They are a much easier problem to solve, because you did not have the authority to make the pact with them to begin with. I still do not understand how you used the princes to get us all into this; what power do you possess to manipulate the kings and the gerousia council to go along with this madness?'

"Larentina passionately defended herself. 'I gave my word to Amazons, and I must honor it no matter the cost. Who sent you here to speak with me? It could not be the kings; was it Bion? What you do not know is I have already changed the kings' minds regarding Spartan women, and King Alcaeus has pledged his allegiance to me simply because I have proven myself. I did not manipulate anyone, only you have. You lied, and because of that lie, everything about me is a lie.'

"Alexis became angry at Larentina's accusations. 'If I had not, you would be nothing but a perioikoi like your mother was. The only great thing Agape did was give birth to you and helping me groom you into a woman warrior to prove our gender is equal to men.'

"Larentina quickly changed the subject. 'Mother, what about my destiny the Oracle foretold?'

"Queen Alexis let out a heavy sigh once again as she decided to tell Larentina the complete truth of her bloodline. "Larentina, you have never questioned my wisdom in such matters, but it is time for me to tell you where our mother's mother came from and why I hate Aphrodite. I blame myself for passing this hatred of her to you and not telling the entire truth about this witch.

"'Our family came from the lands of Egypt ages ago. We are the direct descendants of one of the first pharaohs. The names of our ancestors have long been forgotten, but the story of their lives has been passed down from generation to generation of the women in our bloodline. I will tell you this story as it was told to me by my mother.

"'Aphrodite, as we know her today, came to the lands of Egypt proclaiming herself as the goddess, Hathor. No one knew what lands she came from before Egypt. Hathor tried to seduce the pharaoh's daughter, our ancestor, by promising her eternal life and beauty, but our ancestor refused her. Hathor became angry and vowed she would torture our ancestor for all eternity. She tried to warn the pharaoh that Hathor was not what she appeared to be; she pleaded with her father to destroy Hathor, but her pleas fell upon deaf ears.

"'So Hathor seduced our ancestor's twin sister, as I believe Aphrodite is trying to do to you. Hathor, with some type of bloody ritual, took over the sister's body like some kind of spiritual parasite. Hathor then proclaimed herself to be Isis and seduced the pharaoh, giving birth to several children.

"'As long as the pharaoh lived, our ancestor was protected by Isis. Isis performed another bloody ritual by sacrificing the pharaoh himself to the god she worshiped. Isis and her priests and priestesses ate the pharaoh alive during this ritual.

"'Our ancestor vowed that her bloodline would seek vengeance against Isis for this heinous crime.

"'Since our ancestor had no protection after the brutal murder of her father, an Egyptian general who loved our ancestor helped her flee to saftey. After several generations of running from Isis, we became Spartans. There are no other people as strong and brave as the Spartans, and our bloodline truly believed we could not be more protected from the wrath of Isis. We still hope that one day, we will destroy Isis.

"'Our ancestor believed Isis's magic was evil and vile. She also believed her powers came from a green crystal Isis wore around her neck. Isis never removed this crystal pendant, not even when she bathed.

"'I never had seen Aphrodite before that night when she was trying to seduce my husband, but when I saw the green crystal around her neck, I knew she was Isis, and I fear that she knows who we are. I know now she wants your body.'

"Larentina's eyes grew wide because this was almost the same story as Corinna and her people. Larentina now knew it was true without any doubt.

"Queen Alexis looked puzzled and asked, 'What is it, my child? Fear is written all over your face. You now know you cannot fight this evil, vile creature, don't you?'

"Larentina became irritated, but she could not tell Queen Alexis what she knew. So, she simply said, 'Oh, this is not an expression of fear, but of a newfound truth; I will destroy this evil witch. I do not know how, but it will come to me. I will have to talk with the Amazons.'

"Queen Alexis lost all patience with Larentina and said, 'I grow tired of this argument. You will stay away from Aphrodite! She will kill you and everyone around you! Did you not learn anything from this story? You will do what you are told, and you will kill Poulxeria; this is my command. If you do not, Sparta could be destroyed! Now go to sleep, Daughter, and you will be given to Apollo to keep the Spartan people safe. The Spartans have kept us safe for many generations, and we owe them this. Have I made myself clear?'

"Larentina answered with disappointment laced in her voice, 'Yes, my queen.'

"As soon as Queen Alexis left her daughter's room, Larentina put on a hooded cloak and prepared to leave, completely disobeying her mother's commands. She looked around her room and grabbed her sword and her bow and arrows. She slipped out of her room and ran barefooted across the lawns toward the stables where Celeris was. Out of breath, she rubbed her beautiful horse's neck and whispered in his ear, 'Celeris, I need you to spread your wings this night and take me to Queen Almez.'

"Celeris shook his neck up and down, gesturing a yes to Larentina. She led him out of the stables and mounted the stallion bareback. Celeris leapt into the air as his wings flew them quickly to Queen Almez.

"As Celeris approached the Amazon village, Queen Almez was awakened by frantic shouts from her tower guards. She quickly got out of her bed and ran onto the porch. She yelled at one of the guards in the closest tower, 'What is it? Are we being attacked?'

"The young guard solemnly yelled down to her, 'No, my queen. I see the shadows of a winged horse with a human upon its back crossing the full moon's light.' She pointed her index finger at the moving figure coming closer toward them.

"Queen Almez looked up at the shadow in shock; she had never seen such a sight. She thought, *What could this be?* She thought it must be a messenger from the gods. She didn't know what to do at this point, so she decided it would be best to keep her arrow pointed at it and wait to see what it wanted; she did not want to anger the gods unless she had to do so. As the shadow flew closer and closer, she heard her name being called from the figure on the horse: 'Queen Almez! Queen Almez! It is I, Larentina!'

"Queen Almez lowered her bow and arrow and barked orders to the others: 'Hold your fire! It is a friend of the Amazon nation!' All the archers lowered their bows but kept their arrows to the string, ready to shoot.

"Within a few minutes, she could see the large horse and Larentina's face illuminated by the fires at the meeting place of her village. Queen Almez, in a puzzled and angry voice, asked, 'Larentina, what is the meaning of this? I could have killed you. You gave me no warning! This was not what we agreed to!'

"Larentina dismounted Celeris and ran toward Queen Almez. She commanded, 'We must talk, now! I have troubling news.'

"Queen Almez, still confused, simply said, 'Follow me so that we may talk in private.'

"Larentina obeyed Almez and followed her into the queen's home.

"After a male slave served them wine and cheese, he left the room, and Queen Almez then asked, 'So tell me, Spartan Princess, what is the meaning of this intrusion in the middle of the night?'

"Larentina told her what was about to happen. She relayed how she planned to recover the belt, and she explained who the descendant of Aristomache was. She told her the troubling position that she had gotten the Spartans into, and she sought her wisdom on what to do. She did not have much time because she had to get back before she was missed.

"After listening to the entire tale, Queen Almez chuckled and asked, "Well then, my young princess, what is the solution? It is an easy problem to solve, for me anyway.'

"Larentina was irritated that Almez mocked her. 'This is no laughing matter, Almez. I must fight Poulxeria; you know this. Does she even know her true origins? Does she even know the belt does not possess strength against another woman? I know how I can avoid killing her and taking her from the grip of Draco, but it will be at the cost of Sparta.'

"Almez became serious as she answered, 'As I stated, young princess, the solution is right in front of your nose. If what you say about this arrogant fool of a king is true, you can have it all: just take our Amazon queen instead of killing her. Naturally, Poulxeria would rather die than be beholden to you, but we must find a way so I can speak with her. I believe that if the truth presents itself to her, she will follow you as I have.

"'Stop thinking small, young Spartan. If you think large, then you will figure out a solution so that all can win. I trust you, simply because you have risked all just to speak the truth to me. All of the Amazons and I will be forever beholden, and unlike many, I stand by my word. I will leave at first light for Olympia. I will camp outside the city and stay hidden until you are able to speak with me again. At that time, we will decide how to get me into the city so that I may speak with my queen, Poulxeria. Do you agree?'

"Larentina simply answered, 'Yes, Queen Almez, I agree.'

"Almez commanded Larentina, 'Now go before your parents discover you are missing.'

"Larentina hugged Queen Almez and quickly left without saying another word."

PRINCESS POULXERIA OF MYCENAE

Chapter LVIII

"Several weeks passed before Princess Poulxeria, along with the rest of King Draco's family, finally arrived with a military escort. The Spartan royals and other dignitaries gathered to greet the arriving party. Larentina inquisitively peeked between the shoulders of her brother and Androcles.

"The young princess stepped out of the richly embellished carriage behind King Draco's wife. Poulxeria was not dark like Almez, but her skin was browner than Larentina's suntanned skin. Poulxeria had long, straight black hair and green eyes. Larentina thought she was a very beautiful woman indeed, a bit older than herself and possessing great strength.

"Lycurgus whispered to Androcles and Larentina with a devilish smile, 'I think I'm in love. She is as beautiful as you are, Larentina. I think I have found my match. Try not to kill her, Sister, for I want her.'

"Androcles slyly chuckled as he looked at Larentina, but Larentina said nothing; now she had a reason not to kill Poulxeria even though she knew Lycurgus was joking, and she prayed she didn't get herself killed in the process.

"Throughout the evening, Larentina silently studied Poulxeria. Larentina listened and laughed accordingly throughout the evening's feast but never took her eyes off Poulxeria. She listened to the story of how Poulxeria's mother had died in childbirth. King Draco explained he did not know much of her mother's family history, only that she had been the ward of one of his generals.

"As King Draco told this story, Larentina watched as Poulxeria sat with her head down; she never looked anyone directly in the eyes and only spoke when spoken to, and she only answered with very brief responses. She looked like a caged animal, and Larentina did not like this. She did not like this at all. But then, Larentina knew she was one of the few women who had not only been raised with a militaristic background, but had also been treated like an equal when it came to warfare. Larentina had guessed the black-haired beauty would be like her, but it seemed this night her spirit was broken somehow. Larentina was unprepared for this because she expected courage and strength, but she was not about to underestimate Poulxeria because of her weak appearance.

"Larentina watched as King Draco's queen got up from the banquet table and excused herself so that she could retire. Poulxeria followed suit. Larentina waited a few moments and did the same.

"Within a few moments, she caught up with the two women inside the palace walls. Larentina followed them from far enough away so that neither woman noticed her.

"Moments after Poulxeria went into her room, Larentina softly knocked on the door. Poulxeria opened the door and was shocked to see the woman she would be fighting the next evening.

"Poulxeria started to close her door without saying a word. But Larentina put her sandaled foot between the threshold and the door and whispered, 'Wait, Princess Poulxeria, I must speak with you.'

"Princess Poulxeria replied, 'I have nothing to say to you. What? Are you scared that your life will end tomorrow?'

"Larentina just softly chuckled and shrugged her shoulders indifferently, saying, 'No, but are you? I'm not afraid to die; just the part of dying.'

"Princess Poulxeria smiled as she furrowed her brow and let out a soft, sarcastic snicker. Her voice was frank, nonetheless, as she spoke. 'You are puzzling to me. I still do not understand why you must have my belt, when you have the greatest people in all the lands to give you strength, the Spartans. As if that were not enough, you also have Zeus as your father and his protection as well. You will die tomorrow, and that is a shame; I feel we could have been friends.'

"Larentina was sincerely inquisitive of Poulxeria's behavior this evening. 'Poulxeria, my brother fell madly in love with you from the first moment he saw you this day. You do not know much about who you really are. Please tell me, why do you act as a caged animal when I can sense you are a great warrior, longing to be free?' Larentina knew Lycurgus was only kidding, but she thought flattering Poulxeria by using her brother might prompt Poulxeria into speaking with her.

"Princess Poulxeria was now unsure of Larentina's intentions and gazed at her face for a few minutes, studying her before answering. She decided to take a chance and opened the door wider, looked out into the hallway both ways, and whispered, 'Larentina, come in before we are caught and you get us both into trouble for trying to fix the fight.'

"Larentina could not stop giggling as she entered Poulxeria's room.

"Poulxeria continued whispering, 'What is the matter with you? What you are doing is not funny. You will be the death of both of us if we are caught together before our match tomorrow.'

"Larentina became agitated with this woman. 'Damn it! Why must everyone in my life say I'm going to be the death of them?'

"Poulxeria could not help herself and started laughing, covering her mouth so that she was not too loud. Once she controlled herself, she flippantly answered, 'Because you are!'

"Poulxeria continued laughing, and Larentina could not help herself but to join in before she spoke. 'That was funny. I guess you are right, but this time it may be my death.' Both women stopped giggling.

"Poulxeria didn't understand her feelings toward this young Spartan princess, but she felt comfortable and trusted her; she felt sad because she believed she was going to kill this young woman tomorrow. A curse that her father had put upon her; it would figure the first woman she ever fought, she would like. Nevertheless, Poulxeria was still leery of Larentina. 'Are you trying to befriend me so I will not kill you tomorrow?'

"Larentina became serious again as she spoke, still with a soft smile upon her face. 'Poulxeria, killing me will not be that simple. I will not go down without a fight first, but you have not answered my question; I must know, why did you behave like a scared caged animal?

"'Before our fight, I would like to know the history of the belt of strength; did your ancestors have added strength when they wore it or not?'

"Poulxeria answered, with a soft smile upon her face as well, "Fair enough. I am the first daughter that the belt has given strength to, ever since Hercules gave it to my father's ancestor, King Eurystheus, ages ago.

"'As you can see, my father keeps it safe with him and does not allow me to wear it until a few moments before each fight. I had many suitors long ago, but the only way they could win my hand in marriage was to fight me. After I killed every man who loved me, my father picked out opponents to fight against me just to entertain him. Of course, I must kill anyone who tries, or I will be punished severely, even killed. My father has put upon me this curse. I will never be able to love anyone because I have to kill them.

"'The answer to your first question is not so easy, for no one else knows; you will be the first and only person I have told the truth to, so my secret will die with you tomorrow. Telling you this sad story will not spare your life, for I still will kill you tomorrow, because it is my duty.

"'My father did not tell the truth this night about my mother's death. She was fleeing from the lands of Mycenae when I was only thirteen. I had just turned into a woman just eight months prior. My father would come to me in the dead of the night and take me like he would my mother. When he was unable to perform, he would beat me like he beat my mother. He hunted us down and decapitated my mother before my very eyes. He brought me back to Mycenae and has been taking me ever since. I gave birth once, but he killed my son, saying it was an abomination. Now I have answered your questions; you must go.'

"Larentina had tears in her eyes for this woman, and the tears crept down her cheeks. 'Poulxeria, can you love a man after that?'

"Poulxeria shrugged her shoulders, not caring one way or another. 'I guess anything is possible.'

"Larentina decided to tell Poulxeria her plans. 'Before I go, I will explain what will happen tomorrow; and it will be up to you to make the right choice. If by a heavenly miracle I defeat you, I will hurt you very badly, but I am not going to kill you. I know that you will do everything in your power to kill me, but I will only hurt you, and then I will heal you. But before you pass out, you must surrender to me, so that I may proclaim myself as my brother's champion for your hand in marriage.

"'I am not fighting against you for the wager that my Spartan kings made with your father, but for your freedom. My reasoning will become clear to you after tomorrow.

"'If by chance you defeat me and kill me, I want you to promise that my death will not be in vain. I want you to become the She Wolf I know you to be; you must kill Draco, to prove it to yourself.'

"Poulxeria snickered. 'You are an arrogant Spartan, and that will be your downfall tomorrow, but I will promise that, for I know you are truly a Spartan She Wolf to even dare challenge me.'

"Larentina sadly smiled and shrugged her shoulders indifferently. 'That could be true, but we will see. Good night, Princess Poulxeria. May my God look after you this night, for we shall see who the strongest is tomorrow.'

"Larentina hugged Poulxeria and gave her a kiss on the cheek. Instinctively, Poulxeria returned the hug and kiss. As the two women let go of their friendly hug, Poulxeria simply said, 'You are very puzzling, Princess.'

"Larentina didn't respond. She just sadly smiled and shrugged her shoulders again as she left Princess Poulxeria's room."

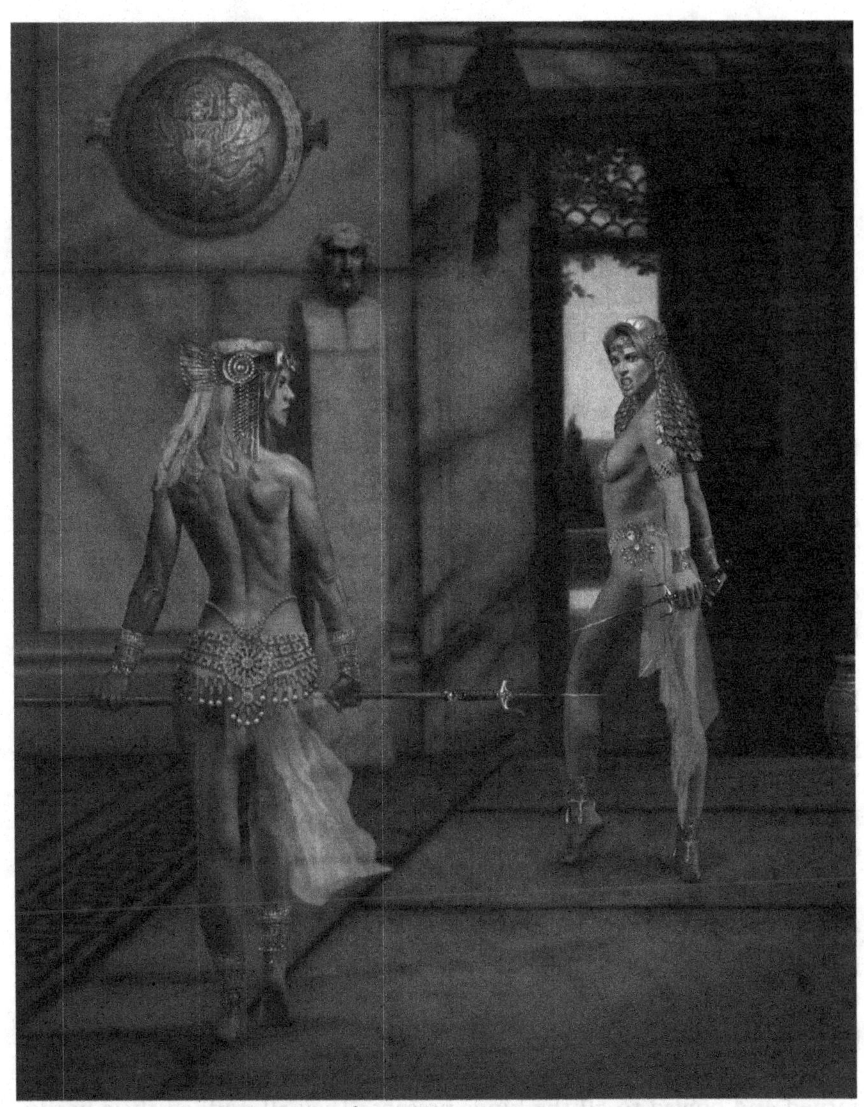

PRINCESS LARENTINA'S FIGHT WITH PRINCESS POULXERIA

Chapter LIX

"Larentina found herself in King Archimedes's throne room. The room was so large that five hundred people could easily fill it, with extra room to spare. Larentina had never seen a throne room so large and so grand in her entire life.

"King Archimedes was sitting upon his throne with his queen seated next to him. King Karpos and King Alcaeus and their queens, as well as their sons, sat beside King Archimedes and his queen. King Draco and his queen sat beside Prince Androcles, and Lucius sat next to Prince Lycurgus. There were three senior gerousia members present, and about sixty soldiers of high rank, as well as another forty to fifty guests. Larentina guessed there were a number of other kings in the crowd as well.

"Larentina was barefooted, and the mosaic floor tiles were cool beneath her feet. She was dressed like an Egyptian with black kohl liner under her eyes and wide bands around her ankles and wrists that were embedded with gemstones. Corinna had braided her hair into four braids that were tight against her head, and at the back of her head, they were braided into one. She wore her wide gold wolf head necklace and armbands as well. She also wore her diamond belly button ring, diamonds in her earlobes, and a small diamond in her nostril. She carried only the tips of her three-pronged djas, one in each hand. She figured if she were going to fight in the ancient Egyptian ways, then she would die dressed like an Egyptian princess as well.

"All eyes were upon her as she walked to the far center of the room. She turned and bowed to all the kings present. They all nodded their heads, acknowledging her.

"Within moments, Princess Poulxeria walked into the large throne room. She too was barefooted and dressed like an Egyptian. She wore wide gold bands on her wrists and ankles, as well as a wide necklace shaped like a lion's head, but she had no piercings. Her long beautiful black hair was pulled tightly back into a ponytail. She walked across the large room to face Larentina. She turned and bowed to all the kings present. They nodded their heads, acknowledging her.

"As the two women stood next to one another, King Alcaeus and everyone else realized that Princess Poulxeria was almost a half-foot taller and at least thirty pounds heavier than Larentina. At that moment, everyone became as fearful as they had been during the chariot races.

"When Larentina saw that Poulxeria held two complete djas, she immediately called Poulxeria on it. Larentina made a tsk tsk noise using her tongue as she sarcastically uttered, without raising her voice, 'Poulxeria, shame, shame on you. You know better. Only pharaohs and kings are allowed to fight with the entire spear. As women, we are only allowed to fight with the tips. You know the ancient ways. This fight is close and personal to me, as it should be to you.'

"No one could tell whether Larentina truly wanted to kill Poulxeria or not. Not even Poulxeria could tell for sure what Larentina was doing. All Poulxeria—as well as everyone in the audience—knew was that Larentina already had started goading her and acting like an arrogant, pompous ass. Poulxeria realized this ruthless woman standing before her was not the same woman she had spoken with the night before.

"Poulxeria looked over at her father for guidance. King Draco nodded up and down once, gesturing that he agreed with Larentina. Poulxeria looked directly at Larentina with a deadly stare; because she wore the belt of strength, Poulxeria had all the confidence in the world. She easily pulled the wooden shaft from each spear and threw them to the floor. She then looked up at the ceiling and snickered loudly and wickedly as she glared into Larentina's eyes.

"The women exchanged deadly stares and stood with their legs spread apart, waiting for the command to attack. King Archimedes commanded in a loud, authoritative voice, 'Let the match begin!'

"Both women moved in a circle, facing each other with dja tips in each hand. Larentina wickedly giggled, as she confidently twirled the dja tips between her fingers, and asked Poulxeria through gritted teeth, 'Are you going to dance or are you going to fight?'

"Naturally, Larentina's goal was to win. She knew no other way to compete when she was fighting to the death for her country.

"Poulxeria lunged angrily toward Larentina with her dja tips, but Larentina easily blocked the blow. Of course, this was why Larentina had started goading Poulxeria. The angrier an opponent became, the more mistakes he or she would make.

"They clashed and jabbed at each other as if they had daggers. For a while, they appeared equally matched, and the crowd grew bored.

"Larentina sensed the boredom of the crowd and decided to stop playing. She side-kicked Poulxeria in her midsection, and Poulxeria flew back. This was just one of the Chinese master's martial art techniques that Larentina had learned as a child, and she had practiced it almost every day of her life since then.

"Poulxeria bent over in pain after she landed several feet from where she had been standing. As Larentina crept slowly forward, Poulxeria ran and did an aerial somersault over Larentina's head, preventing the Spartan from kicking her again. As Poulxeria flew past, Larentina stabbed her in her upper back with one of her djas. Poulxeria fell to the ground but quickly clambered back onto her feet as Larentina turned around. Poulxeria lunged at Larentina with both her djas held waist-high, trying to strike her in the heart. Larentina did a hands-free cartwheel past Poulxeria, and as she went by, she stabbed Poulxeria again—this time in her upper thigh. Larentina knew she had not hit a major artery; she just wanted to put her opponent out of action, perhaps make her hurt, as well as make her bleed. It seemed more like a gymnastics competition, but there was bloodshed as well.

"After Larentina stabbed Poulxeria several times, King Alcaeus realized that she was just playing with her, and he became angry because Sparta depended on her to win this battle. He commanded her, 'Larentina! Stop playing with your food, and kill her!'

"All the spectators could see that while Larentina was smaller, she was much stronger and more skilled than Poulxeria.

"After hearing King Alcaeus's command, King Draco yelled at his daughter, 'Poulxeria! Stop toying with the girl, and kill her! You have the strength of ten men! Stop playing and finish it!'

"King Alcaeus glowered over at King Draco, and King Draco glared back at King Alcaeus. King Draco chuckled sinisterly as he leaned back in his richly cushioned armchair.

"Lycurgus whispered across his mother to his father, 'Father, my king, I told Larentina that I wanted her to spare Poulxeria's life, but I was only joking. She is trying to defeat her without killing her.'

"King Alcaeus was absolutely furious with his son and whispered angrily, 'You are not king, not yet! Joking or not, you did not have the right to command this of your sister. I swear, Lycurgus, if Larentina loses this fight because of your lust for that girl, I will kill you myself. I will deal with you later, and you better pray to the gods that Larentina is victorious, because your life will depend on it.' King Alcaeus leaned back in his chair, filled with anger toward his foolish son. Lycurgus knew that his sister worshipped the ground he walked on. Joking or not, he should not have put that idea in Larentina's head.

"The fight between the women became more intense, and Poulxeria finally caught the young Spartan slightly off-guard and managed to cut a long flesh wound across the right side of Larentina's waist. Larentina facetiously made that annoying tsk tsk sound again at Poulxeria, as she devilishly smiled and said with a low, deadly tone, 'Nasty, nasty!'

"Even though Larentina did not want to kill Poulxeria, she had to give a good show. She had hoped that Poulxeria would work with her, but it was apparent that Poulxeria was fighting for real. If push came to shove, Sparta came first, and if Poulxeria was not going to yield to her, Larentina would not have a problem killing her. Although that saddened her, Larentina decided to turn up the heat, because she really had no other choice.

"Before Poulxeria realized what happened, Larentina stripped her of first one and then the other dja tip; Poulxeria had no weapons to defend herself against this ruthless Spartan She Wolf. Poulxeria realized that the Amazon belt's magic did not work with this Spartan devil, and she became afraid. She did not understand why Larentina was playing with her, instead of just killing her, even though Larentina had tried to warn her last night. Larentina still fought hard, however, as if she was really trying to kill her.

"Poulxeria noticed several swords hanging on the wall behind her. She tried to run toward them, but she could only limp painfully, because of the deep wound that Larentina had inflicted in her thigh earlier.

"When Larentina saw what Poulxeria was up to, she dropped her djas on the floor and ran to the wall.

"Both women ran up the side of the walls after the new weapons. Larentina picked up two battle-axes. Poulxeria grabbed at the swords, but it did her no good, as she could not remove them from their resting place on the wall. Now she had her back against the wall, and she fearfully watched as Larentina ran at her at full speed with not just one, but two battle-axes, tightly gripped in her hands.

"To Poulxeria's surprise, Larentina stopped dead in her tracks and once again made that annoying tsk tsk sound; then, she mocked Poulxeria in a facetious tone, saying, 'Poor little Princess, trapped in a corner like a scared little cat. What should we do now? If I kill you without a weapon, your vile pompous father would scream I cheated; so now I ask: do you yield to me?'

"Poulxeria bellowed at Larentina, as her temper now had the best of her, 'Never!'

"Larentina once again made that annoying tsk tsk sound and said in a high-pitched, annoying voice, 'That is not the right choice. You would rather die as the helpless prey between the fangs of a Spartan She Wolf, instead of having your name live forever and joining me as another She Wolf by my side!' Larentina then threw one of the battle-axes to Poulxeria, who caught it as she stared in complete confusion at Larentina. At this point, Poulxeria understood what Larentina was up to because of their discussion the previous night, but she could not take that chance. This entire fight had been bizarre; Poulxeria had never lost a fight before, but then she had never fought against a woman either.

"Both women ran directly at each other. Poulxeria held her ax high in the air with both hands so she could strike Larentina down with one great deadly blow. However, Larentina held her ax at either end of the shaft at midsection level.

"Larentina leapt onto the upper part of Poulxeria's legs, right above her knees. She leaned forward and pushed her weight into Poulxeria's neck and upper chest, causing Poulxeria to fall onto her back. Poulxeria was dazed because of the hard fall, and she lost her breath. She saw white dots before her eyes. Poulxeria dropped her battle-ax and frantically reached for it.

"Larentina now rested on her knees with Poulxeria lying between them. Larentina reached forward and retrieved one of her dja tips. She slowly pressed her dja into the flesh between Poulxeria's collarbone and shoulder, but only barely piercing her skin. Larentina leaned forward and pleadingly whispered, 'Please, Poulxeria, I do not want to kill you. Please, please, play my game and yield so that we both can be victors, please.'

"Poulxeria stubbornly gritted her teeth in pain and murmured, 'Never.'

"Tears formed in Larentina's eyes and dripped onto Poulxeria's face; Larentina begged in a soft whisper that no one else could hear, 'Please, please, do not make me do this.'

"At that moment, Poulxeria knew Larentina was sincere, and she nodded her head in agreement.

"It appeared to the audience that Larentina had stabbed Poulxeria in the chest. Larentina held the dja against Poulxeria's flesh and asked loudly, so everyone could hear, 'Do you yield to me?'

"Poulxeria remembered Larentina's words from the night before and painfully yelled, 'I yield! I yield!'

"The audience murmured as Larentina pulled the dja tip from Poulxeria's flesh. Right before Poulxeria passed out from the pain, she heard Larentina whisper in her ear, 'Today is a good day to die. Now be reborn as the She Wolf that you are, my sister.'

"Larentina quickly and cleverly smeared Poulxeria's blood all over her opponent's chest to make her condition look much worse than it actually was; it appeared that she had been stabbed several times. No one saw what Larentina did because the wound was inflected on the side of Poulxeria were they could not see because Larentina was on top of her.

"Larentina unbuckled the belt from Poulxeria's waist and stood up as she held it in the air for all to see, and loudly proclaimed, 'Poulxeria has yielded to me, and now by your own customs, proclaimed by your own lips, King Draco, she belongs to me.'

"King Draco immediately stood up and yelled angrily at Larentina, 'That was not the wager!'

"Larentina snickered loudly, 'The wager you refer to was between my two kings of Sparta and yourself. That had nothing to do with me. I fought for Poulxeria as many men have done before me; she is mine if she lives. You have boasted to everyone your pledge, to whomever you chose to fight her: if they won, she belonged to them. You chose me to fight her, did you not?'

"King Draco stumbled for words and yelled defiantly, 'They were suitors! They were men!'

"Larentina chuckled once again as she retorted, 'But you chose me; you did not say that I had to be a man for this honor. In fact, you said it would be an honor and privilege for me, not your daughter.'

"Lycurgus and Androcles spoke loud and clear, saying, 'That is true!'

"King Draco yelled his retort, 'You play with words! You have cheated somehow! Are you mad? Why would you want my daughter? If she is not dead already, she will be in just a few hours. Would you take her away from me?'

"Larentina shook her head from side to side; she looked over at Poulxeria, who had passed out. 'She is not dead, not yet. If she does die, you may have her body, but if she lives, she belongs to me. You may not touch her or see her until she is dead!'

"King Karpos angrily responded to the accusations that King Draco made. 'The question is to you, Draco: are you mad? We all saw it with our own eyes; Larentina beat your daughter fairly, and even gave her several chances to defeat her. You have forgotten that not only is Larentina from the house of Agiad, making her a direct descendant of Hercules himself; she is also the daughter of Zeus himself, making her the sister of Hercules. Do not forget, stupid ass, she has Spartan blood coursing through her veins. If you had thought about that, just maybe you'd see that our She Wolf has the strength of ten and half men. Just imagine if your daughter had to fight against one of our Spartan men, she would have been shredded to pieces, with or without the belt.'

"Everyone in the entire room nodded their heads in agreement and shouted out that King Karpos was correct.

"King Alcaeus grabbed Lycurgus's arm as his son stood to go to Larentina's side with a large leather satchel in his hand. The king murmured, 'You are damn lucky this day, Son. You and your sister once again have gotten yourselves out of a mess that you both created. I hope this girl was worth it.

"'One of these days, your cleverness is not going to work, and I fear all of Sparta will pay a high price for it.'

"Lycurgus responded, 'I'm sorry, Father, but I got Larentina and myself into this one. I truly didn't think she would take my words so seriously.'

"King Alcaeus sadly shook his head from side to side as he commented, with a half smile, 'I have said it numerous times, and I will say it again, the two of you are going to be the death of me yet.'

"Both men chuckled and Lycurgus teased, 'Now I know how Larentina feels.' King Alcaeus let out a boisterous laugh.

"Lycurgus simply said, 'Father, I must get this satchel to Larentina quickly. It is filled with her herbs and healing potions.'

"King Alcaeus asked, 'The two of you had this extra surprise planned, didn't you?'

"Lycurgus reminded his father, 'Was it not you who lectured me on numerous occasions that a great leader always has everything planned down to the smallest detail?'

"Alcaeus proudly answered, 'Very well said, Son. Now go and help your sister.'"

Chapter LX

"Poulxeria awoke after feeling Lambda licking her face. She screamed and pushed the wolf away, bolting straight up in the bed. She looked to her right and saw Larentina sitting on the bed beside her. Larentina gently pushed Poulxeria's shoulders back onto the bed and patiently commented, 'Be still. I cut you a little too deeply, and I am sorry for that.'

"Poulxeria was incredibly angry with Larentina and with the little bit of strength she had left, she raised herself back up and with her right hand, slapped Larentina across the face. Then, she fell backward into the bed, exhausted.

"Lambda immediately resumed licking Poulxeria, who pushed the wolf away and said, annoyed, 'Get this beast off of me!'

"Larentina teasingly giggled at her new friend, as she confessed, 'I guess I deserved that, but you have definitely been reborn as an Amazon and possibly a She Wolf. Lambda likes you.'

"Poulxeria was extremely confused by Larentina's statements, so she asked, 'What are you talking about, you Spartan devil? Where is my father? What happened? Why are you here nursing me?'

"Larentina smiled as she made that annoying tsk tsk noise again. Before Larentina could speak, Poulxeria angrily commanded, 'Stop that! Just stop that annoying noise.'

"Larentina teasingly giggled again and then answered Poulxeria's questions. 'I told you what would happen. Have you forgotten already? Your life now belongs to me. It is time for me to enlighten you as to who you really are.'

"Poulxeria sarcastically asked, 'I already know who I am. So am I now your slave?'

"Larentina said, 'No, you are not my slave. Are you sure you know who you are? Please tell me about your mother's ancestry.'

"Poulxeria impatiently answered, 'I do not know; she was killed before I ever learned her history. I only know what my father has told me.'

"After taking a deep breath, Larentina blurted out, 'You are the direct descendant of Aristomache, the daughter of Hercules and the Amazon Queen Hippolyte. That is why Ares's belt's magic only worked with you and no one else in your father's lineage. I guess you have figured out that the belt does not work on another woman.

"'I did not fight for the wager that was between your father and mine, but rather for you and the belt, because I need to return it to the Amazon people. That is the agreement I made with them, and that is why you live. Once you have healed enough, I will take you to meet Almez, the current ruler. It is time to take your rightful place with the Amazons as their queen, should you choose to do so. Your people have made a pledge to me for this.'

"Poulxeria asked, 'What if I choose to be with your brother instead? I do not want to be with those barbarians. I want something more.'

"Larentina patiently responded, 'So you are interested in my brother? I must confess to you that he was joking, and I used it to try to entice you. My brother does lust for you, and he is a very handsome man, but love you? I do not know about that. You will have to earn his love. That will be up to Lycurgus, not me. I'm sorry that I misled you.

"'I know your history because my mother, Queen Alexis, told me. It made sense because the belt has never worked with anyone else but you. You also confessed this to me. If you want my brother and he wants you; it will be between the two of you, but would you really rather live in my world than your own; as the ruler of your own people?'

"Poulxeria voiced her thoughts on the matter. 'Your brother is very handsome and very charming. I long for a man who really loves me and will cherish me for my entire life. You know this. I do owe you for my freedom. Before I make any decision, I will meet these Amazons. I want you to tell me why you made this agreement. What do the Amazons owe you in return?'

"Larentina told Poulxeria everything she knew and everything that she was planning. After listening, Poulxeria decided that she would follow Larentina to Hades's underworld and back if need be. She owed this Spartan She Wolf her life, her freedom, and her future. Poulxeria pledged her allegiance to Larentina and vowed she would die to protect her so Larentina could accomplish her destiny, because Poulxeria now realized Larentina's destiny was her destiny."

Chapter LXI

"After Poulxeria fell into an exhausted sleep, Larentina told her parents that a small party of Amazons were waiting for her and Poulxeria outside the great city of Olympia.

"Larentina also told King Alcaeus that Poulxeria was the queen for whom the Amazons had been searching in addition to the belt; she revealed who had told her the secret of truth. King Alcaeus looked at his wife and irritably asked, 'Why did you keep this information from me, Alexis?'

"Queen Alexis answered her husband, with conviction, 'Because I didn't see the relevance, and I did not want Larentina to be defeated by this barbarian.'

"King Alcaeus was disappointed in his wife; he asked, 'What else have you kept from me?'

"Since Alexis was already angry with Larentina for disclosing her secret, she told King Alcaeus about how Apollo had come to her in dreams and omens. She explained that Larentina belonged to Apollo because Zeus had pledged her to him, and how Zeus then broke his promise.

"Alexis relayed Apollo's commands: 'There will be no marriage between Androcles and Larentina; she will be given to Apollo; and she may not be touched by man. If the Spartans do not give her to him, then he shall punish all of Sparta. These are his commands.'

"Larentina was now furious with Queen Alexis, but she didn't show it, as she calmly vocalized her thoughts on the matter to her royal mother. 'Zeus has said nothing regarding this to me. I believe Apollo is disobeying his command for giving me the choice and I have chosen Androcles, as he has chosen me, but if what you say is true, then I feel something is amiss among the Olympian deities. I must warn my father, Zeus, somehow, for why else would Apollo be so brazen to disobey him?'

"Before Queen Alexis could give Larentina a tongue-lashing, Bion spoke. 'I believe what Larentina says may be true. This is part of the

Oracle's prophesies, is it not?' Bion solemnly looked at the kings, who nodded their heads in agreement.

"Androcles and Lycurgus could not believe what they were hearing. In fact, both young men were very angry because now the madness that Larentina had mentioned was becoming a reality. Androcles held his tongue, but his thoughts were to fight for Larentina no matter the cost. He would fight Apollo himself to keep Larentina.

"After many hours of discussion, they decided to start their journey back to Sparta at first light. Before they parted from Olympia, they would meet with the Amazons and give them the belt, as well as Poulxeria.

"Bion had suggested during the conversation that they should deal with Apollo after they returned to Sparta by giving Larentina to the god, for fear he would keep his threats regarding Sparta. They had no other choice in the matter.

"Bion was pleased that Apollo had interfered. Now, Larentina would be out of Sparta forever. His next task would be to rid Sparta of Alexis and, if need be, these weak foolish kings as well.

"Larentina went to Poulxeria's room, where she was regaining her strength from her wounds. The two women talked behind closed doors for the better part of the evening. In fact, Larentina left Poulxeria's room at the bewitching hour of midnight. Both women were unaware that Androcles and Lycurgus were planning something as well.

"Lycurgus watched as his sister left Poulxeria's room, and as soon as she was out of sight, he entered Poulxeria's room quietly, as he had done for the past several nights visiting with her. It would help pass the time, so Androcles could speak with Larentina.

"Androcles knocked on Larentina's bedroom door quietly, and Larentina instinctively knew who it was. She opened her door, and stood in the moonlight, the nightgown she was wearing made her body even more enticing. The young couple did not say anything as they greeted each other with a passionate long kiss.

"As Larentina looked up into Androcles's blue eyes, she made her vows to him, 'I vow to love no other as long as you shall live. I will love you and cherish you as my king, my consort, my lover, and friend.'

"In turn, Androcles made his vows to Larentina, 'I too vow to love no other as long as you shall live. I will love you and cherish you as my queen, my consort, my lover, and friend. I swear I will protect you, provide for you, and always treat you as my equal, as long as we both live. Death will not keep us apart.' They kissed passionately for they were now man and wife by their own design.

"Androcles picked up Larentina and carried her to the large bed as he was still kissing her. Then, Larentina gave Androcles the greatest gift a woman can give to a man—her virginity. They made passionate love for several hours. Androcles whispered in Larentina's ear, 'I love you, I have always loved you, and now that I have you, no man or deity will take you from me. I will fight for you and to keep you strong I will give you my last dying breath.'

"Larentina looked deep into Androcles eyes as she smiles softly and whispered to him, 'I love you, and I have always loved you, and I will bear you many great sons, my husband, my king.' They kissed passionately and made love once more.

They both then quietly bathed each other seductively with cloths and water that was provided in Larentina's room. They kissed once more after telling each other their plans and how they would be free. As Androcles was walking toward the door, Larentina whispered in an almost panicked voice, "Wait, my love." She kissed him passionately once more.

"Larentina kneeled down, hugged Lambda, and commanded, in a loving voice, 'Go with my husband, Lambda, and protect him as you would me.'

"Larentina finished dressing in her military armor; she secured her belt with her sword at her side. She quickly looked around the room and walked out of the palace, as she had done numerous times while they had stayed in Olympia. She knew there was no turning back, and she probably would never see Sparta again. She had done all that she could do in her fight for Spartan women's freedoms. Now, she had set her sights on fighting for her God and true freedom and liberty that her God had given to her and all of mankind.

"Poulxeria waited for her in the shadows of the surrounding trees; when she saw her, she whispered, 'Larentina, I'm here.' Larentina ran toward the whispered voice and immediately grabbed Poulxeria's hand, and they both ran to the stables.

"As Larentina quickly saddled Celeris, she whispered to him, 'Celeris, you must fly us to Almez's camp.'

"As Celeris revealed his wings, Poulxeria gasped.

"Poulxeria deliciously giggled as she voiced her delight. 'I should have known that Zeus would provide you with everything. You truly are from Mount Olympus. Magic surrounds you, but you are not like any other goddess. You fight for another's freedom, something I have never seen or heard about.'

"Larentina whispered to Poulxeria, 'Because I am no goddess; I am woman. What good is freedom if you do not have others of your gender to share it with? Now come, we do not have much time.'

"Before the two princesses were able to mount Celeris for their quick getaway, Athena appeared in front of them, giggling wickedly. It was obvious to Larentina that she was a goddess, but she did not know which one. Larentina scowled as she demanded, 'And who in Hades are you?'

"Athena threw her head back and guffawed toward the heavens as she wickedly announced, 'I am your worst nightmare—your sister, Athena.'

"Larentina slowly clutched the handle of her sword as she angrily asked, 'And what do you want of me, Sister?'

"Athena became deadly serious as she threatened, 'I want your head on a platter to present to our father, Zeus, and I will have it.' She giggled at the thought.

"Larentina knew that she was no match against Athena, but on the other hand, Athena believed her to be some kind of demigoddess. Larentina decided to take a chance that these beings were not as strong in her realm.

"Larentina's irises changed from hazel brown to a deep dark maroon as the lightning bolts lit them up, and in the darkness, they glowed like a burning fire. Larentina did not touch Athena as she raised her hands and pushed them about three inches in front of her. The air did not move, but Poulxeria saw some kind of energy move toward Athena at lightning speed, throwing the goddess upward and backward, and then she landed on the ground.

"Poulxeria could see by Athena's widening eyes how shocked the goddess was. Of course, this display scared the living daylights out of Athena, and she disappeared again.

"Poulxeria, still somewhat shaken, was amazed at what she had seen Larentina do. She asked, 'How can you say you did not come from the gods? I've just seen your powers with my own eyes.'

"Larentina was also shaken but wanted to bring Poulxeria to the Amazons to fulfill her bargain. 'Poulxeria, I do not have time to discuss your superstitions; let it go. I am no god, I'm just like you. I just use my mind differently than you do. I cannot explain it because I have no idea what I am, but I am no god. Now let us get out of here before Athena comes back. I do not know if my powers will scare her off next time.'

"Poulxeria remained confused as Larentina gently pushed her toward Celeris. 'But—'

"Larentina's impatience grew. Even though Larentina had showed courage, she was still scared of the Olympian deities and what they could do to her and to her people. 'Please, Poulxeria! I must take you safely to your people. Let it go and let us instead enjoy the magical ride that my horse will provide for us.'

"Once again, they were interrupted when General Nikephoros stepped out from the dark shadows of the night. He walked toward them and began petting Celeris on the nose as he calmly spoke. 'Easy, boy, easy.'

"He looked up at Larentina as he rubbed Celeris's face. 'Larentina, I must admit I am very disappointed in you this night. You are a goddess of duty, yet here I find you shamefully running away from your duty. It is obvious you have angered many Olympian goddesses as well. I do not know what you are, and over the years, I have found myself with mixed feelings about you. I have disobeyed many repeated orders to have you killed.'

"Larentina was shocked by this confession, and Poulxeria was completely confused, but she stayed silent and stepped away from the two Spartans.

"Bewildered, Larentina asked, 'Why do you confess to me now, knowing my king will kill you?'

"Nikephoros looked to the ground and let out a heavy sigh, and then he gazed into Larentina's eyes. 'I find myself filled with pride and joy over your brother's accomplishments, and somehow, I see myself in his eyes. With you, I both hate you and love you for some unknown reason. You may lie to the gods and to our kings, and it is true Queen Alexis and Agape are identical twins, but I see part of the fire of Agape's soul in your eyes. You and your brother have Agape's fire, not Alexis's. I know this deep in my soul. Why Queen Alexis and Agape lied to the world about you and your brother, I do not know, but when I discover the reason, I know I will have peace once more.'

"Nikephoros moved away from the horse and commanded, 'Now go, before I change my mind.'

"Larentina did not understand how General Nikephoros knew the truth or why he was setting her free. She shrugged these thoughts from her mind and was grateful he had allowed them to leave. She commanded Poulxeria, 'Come, we must leave now.'

"Poulxeria returned her attention to Celeris, and she smiled as she mounted the horse behind Larentina. Poulxeria wrapped her arms around Larentina's waist, kissed her new friend on the cheek to lighten the mood, and whispered in her ear, 'You may say you are woman, but you are much, much more than that. Thank you, Larentina, for showing me the way and bringing me into your destiny.'

"With those words, Celeris took a running leap and flew them toward Almez's camp. Poulxeria silently enjoyed the view of mother earth as the gods see her. She relaxed and relished the wind flowing through her hair. She kissed Larentina once again on the cheek and whispered, 'I cannot say it enough, Larentina, thank you. This is the most powerful feeling I have ever felt; I feel so free!'

"Larentina said nothing; she just smiled."

* * *

"A few minutes after Larentina and Poulxeria left Olympia, Corinna was awakened by someone's hand over her mouth. She turned over to discover it was Androcles. Her eyes grew wider as she became scared. Lycurgus also stood next to her straw bed that covered the ground. Lycurgus put his index finger over his lips, indicating for her to be silent.

"Androcles whispered in her ear, 'Corinna, you must come with us now. Larentina is paying a high price for your freedom. Now quickly get dressed and follow us. We do not have much time.' He then removed his hand from her mouth.

"Corinna quickly stumbled to her feet; she watched Lycurgus's face in the moonlight that seeped into the small open windows of the slave quarters. He nodded his head up and down as if gesturing in agreement. Then, he whispered, 'Hurry now, hurry.'

"Androcles and Lycurgus waited impatiently for Corinna as she gathered her clothing in the darkness, but it only took her a few moments.

"When they went outside, five horses were waiting for them. Two of the horses were loaded with supplies. Corinna thought she was dreaming; this day had finally come. Larentina was somehow keeping her word to her.

"Androcles mounted his horse first and waited as Lycurgus helped Corinna mount one of the three mares that Larentina had been given to compete in the chariot races."

Chapter LXII

"Larentina and Poulxeria arrived at the Amazon camp in less than an hour. As soon as they dismounted Celeris, Almez and her warriors, who totaled about one hundred, all ran toward them from many directions of the camp, where they had been sleeping.

"As Almez hugged her lost queen, Larentina lovingly rubbed her horse's neck and softly whispered to him, 'Now go to Androcles and Lycurgus to show them the way.'

"Everyone moved out of the way to give the horse room to pick up enough speed to fly into the night.

"Celeris landed on the roadway within a few feet of Androcles, Lycurgus, and Corinna. Celeris had startled the horses that were moving at a slow gallop. Lycurgus and Androcles recognized Larentina's horse. Corinna was surprised and asked, 'What magic is this, for he is not white?'

"Lycurgus voiced the obvious to Androcles. 'This must be the offspring of Pegasus. Now it makes sense why Larentina could disappear and travel a great distance, and return before anyone missed her.'

"Androcles asked, 'How many more secrets has she kept from us?'

"Lycurgus replied, 'I do not know. I think it would be wise to have Corinna mount him and fly to Larentina, because if we are seen, there will be questions why we have a slave girl traveling with us.'

"Androcles acknowledged Lycurgus, saying, 'This is wise.'

"Androcles dismounted his horse and helped Corinna down. Lycurgus was now rubbing Celeris's neck and saying in a soft tone, 'Easy, boy, easy.'

"Lycurgus helped Corinna mount Celeris. Androcles commanded Lambda to go with Corinna, and Lambda obediently obeyed him, jumping on the back of Celeris and sitting between Corinna's legs. Lycurgus smacked Celeris on his rump as he commanded, 'Now fly her to your mistress!' Celeris took off.

"Both young men mounted their horses once again and galloped into the night. They followed the direction that Celeris had flown, toward the sea.

"Lycurgus spoke his thoughts aloud. 'I am assuming all went according to plan that we spoke of last evening regarding my sister. You already had my permission, but did she agree and did you make the proper vows to her?'

"Androcles simply responded, 'Yes. I hope that you still accept this, for we are brothers now.'

"Lycurgus proudly replied, 'Yes, I do accept this, and I welcome you as my brother. I always have. It is time for you to know all our family secrets, and I pray to the God that Larentina now worships that you still want to be part of our family.'

"Lycurgus told the entire truth to Androcles as they rode toward the Amazon camp."

Chapter LXIII

"All the Amazons touched Poulxeria's hair and examined her skin, which were vastly different from theirs. Almez became irritated with her warriors and commanded, 'Come, come. Give our lost queen some breathing room. I must talk with her, and you all may listen.'

"Almez then asked Poulxeria, 'Are you thirsty, my queen? May I get you something to eat?'

"Poulxeria still did not know what to make of all this. Larentina had changed Poulxeria's world so quickly, and she was having a hard time keeping up with all the changes. Poulxeria looked at Larentina for guidance. Larentina noticed her discomfort and answered Almez, 'Yes, we are both thirsty. Queen Poulxeria is still healing from her wounds, and everything has changed so much for the two of us. I will leave you so that you, your people, and Queen Poulxeria may become familiar with one another.'

"Almez nodded her head in agreement.

"The sun was still rising from beneath the landscape; Larentina watched the orange-yellow ball peek slightly above the distant mountain peaks. Almez had camped on the shoreline about one hundred miles from Olympia, but that was okay for Larentina; the farther she was away from Olympia, the better their chances were of not being tracked down.

"Larentina was walking around the shoreline when she heard Celeris approaching her from the sky. Lambda jumped to the ground and ran to her mistress. Corinna also jumped down from Celeris's backside and ran into Larentina's arms. Almost out of breath from the experience of flying, she exuberantly said, 'My princess, may my God bless you for giving me my freedom and the chance to see the world as he does.'

"Larentina sadly smiled. She remained silent, and a solemn expression spread over her face as she heard her brother's thoughts in her mind, as she had been able to do all her life.

"She said aloud, 'Brother, you had no right to tell Androcles who we really are. That was my place, not yours.'

"She heard her brother's voice in her mind, saying, 'He has a right to know. He should have a choice to follow our destiny knowing the whole truth.'

"Corinna, with a puzzled expression on her face, asked Larentina, 'My princess, who are you talking to? What madness is this?'

"Larentina looked at Corinna with an angry gaze. 'Be silent, Israelite, for you would not understand. Your God has given me great gifts, and that is all you need to know.'

"Corinna silently accepted this, nodding her head. Corinna watched as Larentina spoke aloud, describing their location to someone.

"Larentina felt remorse for speaking so rudely to Corinna, and she asked her to forgive her. Naturally, Corinna forgave her closest and dearest friend. Larentina confessed her battle within herself to Corinna. 'I know that I am a daughter of energy from the light, but I feel I am also the energy of darkness. There is a battle raging within my soul that I have been fighting all my life. I know that I will succumb to darkness, because I have lost this war many times throughout my life, and I have no remorse. My friend, my sister, my confidante, always remember no matter what I do or say, I love you, and I always have. Please forgive me for all the wickedness I have done to you, and please forgive what I may do in the future.'

"With tears welling in her eyes, Corinna ran into Larentina's arms as she too confessed her feelings. 'Since the moment you were born, Larentina, you amazed me with your gifts, but today you fill my heart with love and admiration toward you. There is nothing to forgive, because I have always known you loved me from the day you sacrificed yourself to protect me for telling you about my God.'

"Larentina changed the subject by asking Corinna to tell her more tales of the one true God. Corinna told her more stories from the Bible, and then Larentina abruptly announced, 'Please come, Corinna, I must speak with Almez and Poulxeria now.'

"Larentina rudely interrupted the conversation between Almez and Poulxeria by commanding, 'It is time. We must prepare your ship for our journey. My brother and husband will be here in a few hours.'

"Almez and Poulxeria obeyed Larentina's commands without question. Everyone started breaking down the camp and preparing to leave by sea."

ATHENA

Chapter LXIV

"Androcles and Lycurgus slowed down and were casually riding their horses down the trail when they heard someone following them. Neither of the men said a word as they instinctively dismounted and led their horses off the trail to conceal them in the surrounding foliage.

"As they waited, one on either side of the trail, they silently drew their swords to ambush whoever was following them. When they saw the travelers who were following them, Androcles and Lycurgus ran yelling toward the trail, causing the travelers' horses to bolt; several of the men were thrown from their horses.

"One of the travelers was Lucius; once he had control of his horse, he yelled in his heavy Roman accent, 'Androcles, Lycurgus! It is I, Lucius.' He was accompanied by several Roman soldiers.

"Androcles became so angry that he pulled Lucius from his horse and bellowed, 'I have had enough of you and your interference! If death is what you want, then so be it!'

"Once again, before Androcles could kill Lucius, Lycurgus stopped him as he commanded, 'Androcles, stop; remember, he is your brother now!'

"Androcles retorted angrily, 'He is no brother of mine!'

"Lucius took advantage of the diversion and kicked Androcles between the legs. He got up from the ground quickly and drew his sword. Before Androcles could react, he found the tip of Lucius's sword resting on his neck.

"Lycurgus used his sword to knock away Lucius's sword; he commanded, 'Enough! Why are you following us?'

"Lucius casually picked up his sword as Androcles stood and retrieved his as well.

"Lucius calmly answered, 'Wherever your She Wolf goes, glory seems to follow her, and I would like to be part of it.'

"Androcles angrily retorted, 'Glory? You have it all wrong, Roman! Wherever our She Wolf goes, destruction and chaos follow closely!'

"Lycurgus laughed at the flippant conversation; this young man had no clue. Lycurgus commented, "Androcles speaks the truth.'

"Lucius laughed as well and said, 'You may call it chaos, but I call it glory.'

"All the men chuckled at the joke regarding Larentina.

"Androcles, Lycurgus, Lucius, and the soldiers talked among themselves before continuing their journey; suddenly, the ground started to tremble as if small earthquakes were occurring. They could hear and feel the earth move: 'Thump, thump, thump!' It was coming closer and closer to them. They heard the sound of trees breaking and crashing to the ground as it approached them.

"Athena appeared in front of them in all her glory, wickedly laughing as she spoke. 'You foolish little mortals, did you actually think we would allow you to take our She Wolf from us? She will die, as will our father. I am tired of all you mighty Spartans interfering and protecting that dog. I should have turned her into a gorgon long ago. But we have plans for her, and they do not include you.'

"Athena stood a little over five feet tall. She had beautiful gray eyes and a pert nose. Her face was round and full. Her skin was fair, and she was lean from head to toe. She wore military garb, and the plume of her helmet was purple and gold. She stood straight with her legs spread apart; she held a spear in one hand with the tip pointing toward the heavens. Even though she was shorter than most Spartan women, her posture demanded respect. Athena was one very angry goddess, and she wanted to destroy everything Larentina loved, along with Larentina herself.

"Androcles charged toward Athena with his sword in hand. Athena simply waved her hand, and Androcles found himself tied up to a tree. Lycurgus ran to the tree and scrambled to untie him, as Lucius and the Roman soldiers guarded them.

"The mortal men feared for their very lives as a giant appeared between two large trees and looked down at the men with his one eye. The giant had the body, legs, and arms of a man, but his head and teeth were like a dinosaur with one large eye in the center. The giant had the skin of a reptile and the color of charcoal.

"As Lucius looked up at the creature, he said, 'Androcles, I believe you were right; your She Wolf seems to bring the worst out in the Olympian deities. I have only heard of these creatures from fairy tales. Pray tell, how are we going to kill it?'

"Athena viciously laughed as she chimed in, 'This is my version of a Cyclops. You cannot kill him, but he will eat you for a snack!' Athena looked up at the Cyclops and commanded, 'Eat them, for I know you have not had mortal men in a long time!'

"Still laughing, Athena disappeared; she sat, invisible, on a tree branch to watch.

"Lucius was no longer arrogant; he started running, as he remarked, 'I do not know about you, but I think we have bitten off more than we can chew.'

"Androcles laughed and said, 'I did warn you. Are you still seeking glory?'

"Lycurgus slyly snickered at Lucius and then asked, 'Androcles, do you have any idea how we are going to kill this thing? This is not a Titan, but something Athena had just conjured.'

"Androcles shrugged his shoulders as he answered, 'If Larentina were here, she would know, because she listened to the fairy tales. I never paid much attention to them. Besides, this is different from the Cyclops in the tales.'

"Lycurgus reached out to Larentina's mind and yelled aloud, 'Larentina! Larentina! We need your help!'

"Lucius was completely confused as he voiced his thoughts. 'Are you ill in the head? Larentina cannot hear you.'

"After they used all their spears trying to hit the creature in its eye, they ran through the woods to keep out of its reach. The Cyclops was gaining on them as it tore down trees chasing them. Their arrows did not even make it flinch. The Cyclops finally caught one of the Roman soldiers. The soldier screamed as the Cyclops's clawlike hand grabbed one of his legs; the monster dropped the Roman soldier into its mouth, head first, and started chewing. He swallowed the soldier and then burped!

"Lucius watched, horrified, and said, 'I think I am going to be sick!'

"Androcles and Lycurgus blurted in unison, 'So are we!'

"Lucius frantically yelled, 'I think we had better start running again, it is getting closer now!'

"As the men ran, they heard Larentina's voice from the sky above. She was being dismissive about everything as usual, saying, 'You are an ugly, nasty, rude Cyclops! Did your mother not teach you better table manners?'

"Celeris dropped to the side of the Cyclops's head as Larentina thrust her spear into the Cyclops's face. Celeris and Larentina looked like a mosquito trying to land on its prey; the horse dodged the swings and snaps from the Cyclops's mouth and clawlike hands.

"Larentina frantically yelled down to the men, 'The eye! The eye! You must blind it!'

"Lycurgus sarcastically yelled up to his sister, 'No kidding! We knew that! Please tell me, Sister, how do you propose we do that, since we do not have any more spears or arrows?'

"Celeris landed on the ground; before dismounting, Larentina yelled, with agitation in her voice, 'Brother, stop being a donkey's ass!'

"Androcles and Lucius laughed heartily at the brother and sister's flippant behavior. Lucius looked over and asked Androcles, who was trying to stifle his laughter, 'Do you have to deal with this all the time?'

"Androcles chuckled as he answered, 'My entire life.'

"Larentina commanded Androcles, 'Husband, stop diddling!' She threw her spear to him and yelled, 'Mount Celeris and kill this nasty beast! Its breath even smells of death. I think I'm going to be sick.'

"Androcles mounted Celeris and scolded Larentina, 'We have not even been married a day, and you are already acting like a nagging wife!'

"Larentina retorted, 'Be thankful you have me!'

"Androcles snickered as Celeris took off into the air once again.

"They all watched with anticipation; Larentina's spear was all they had, so Androcles only had one chance. Androcles rubbed Celeris's neck and softly said, 'Easy, boy; easy, boy. Keep it steady.'

"Androcles threw the spear and hit the Cyclops dead center in his eye. Pleased with himself, Androcles threw his fists above his head and yelled, 'Yes!'

"Everyone on the ground cheered as they watched the Cyclops snarl and growl like a wounded animal. It pulled the spear from its eye and dropped down to its knees. Within moments, the creature swayed from side to side, and then it fell to the ground and died.

"Androcles dismounted Celeris, and Larentina ran up to him, giving him a victory kiss and hugging him with pride. Lycurgus patted Androcles on his back as he shook his hand; with pride in his voice, he said, 'Well done, Brother!'

"Lucius, in turn, shook his hand and said, 'Yes, well done, Spartan, well done indeed!'

"The surviving Roman soldiers congratulated Androcles and thanked him for saving their lives.

"Larentina mounted Celeris and playfully said, 'Well, gentleman, could one of you retrieve my spear? Try not to get into any more fights with a Cyclops, and try to stay out of trouble before we are discovered. Whatever you did to anger the Goddess Athena, please do not do it again. I'll meet you all back at the Amazon camp.'

"Every single man gave Larentina a puzzled look, but Lycurgus voiced what they all were thinking: 'What? We did nothing to anger the Goddess Athena, it was you, and we received her wrath for it!'

"Larentina giggled as she playfully said, 'That is right, Brother, go ahead and blame it on your sister; you always have. Have you not learned anything from me?' She laughed as Celeris began to take off into the air, but they were stopped by Athena.

"Athena frightened Celeris, and he reared up on his back legs. Larentina was not expecting this and fell, landing hard on her back. She was dazed from the fall and shook her head to regain her bearings as she stood up. She quickly pulled her sword from its sheath.

"Athena stood there defiantly and screeched, 'You are an abomination to all that is natural! Mortal man and the gods should possess physical strength; not you! How dare you think you can be anything like them; you act as if you are my equal—a goddess and daughter of Zeus! You compare yourself to Hercules or Perseus. You disgust me! I will slowly torture you as well as the Spartans who worship you instead of me and the gods!'

"Larentina's eyes had already changed as winds, lightning bolts, and objects swirled into the air and began hitting Athena with strong force. Athena fought the objects with her own magic, repelling many of them, but there were too many objects flying toward her from different directions. The lightning bolts were so strong and powerful, they began to drain Athena's powers. Athena thought for just a moment that Larentina was becoming stronger; she was almost as powerful as Zeus.

"Larentina was enraged by this being who thought she was better than mortal man. Larentina's voice resonated throughout the forest as she bellowed, 'You are the abomination! You are in my realm, not yours; and I am stronger! My energy is all natural because I come from man, not the heavens. You came from the same creator I did! I would have fought for you as well, Athena, even though you are the one who is vile, for what you had done to Medusa!

"'You could have been treated as an equal and been freed of the chains that bound you to Mount Olympus, but you chose this. So be it! You are either with me, Sister, or against me! You made your choice, and I want you to die for what you did to Medusa! To spite you, I will find a way to break the curse that you have placed upon her! I will have vengeance, and I will fulfill the wishes of Agape, the sister of my Queen mother! If I should die fighting for freedom against those like you, then so be it! I will know with my dying breath that I died free, and I did my very best to try to change my beloved Sparta and free those who wished for it!'

"Athena had all her focus on Larentina, and she did not realize that Larentina's companions had encircled her, trapping her between them and Larentina. Athena watched as Larentina furiously charged toward her with her sword in one hand and her shield in the other.

"Athena was surprised that Larentina had the audacity to use her powers against her. Athena threw her spear and used her power to turn it into a large python. When the python hit Larentina, it instantly wrapped itself around her from head to toe. Athena then turned her attention toward the foolish mortal men, who had dared to think they could fight her. She put her hands on her hips with her legs spread apart and screamed, 'How dare you—you arrogant mortals!'

"The Spartans and Romans completely surrounded Athena, but they were at least fifteen feet from her. The men were all in guarded positions, preparing to fight Athena. The moment before they began their attack, beautiful women emerged from the ground. The women had roots for hair, and their skin was green. Leaves from the surrounding trees covered their entire bodies. They all carried a sharp, pointed tree branch like a spear. Before the men could back away, vines seeped out of the ground and started entwining around their feet.

"Lucius was the first to break free from the growing vines. He used his sword and chopped them off his feet. He was behind Athena and charged toward her, but he was stopped by one of the tree women who stood in his way, and he found himself fighting for his own life. All the other men followed suit and found themselves fighting against the tree women, who moved so quickly that the men could barely see them. They were like a swarm of flies buzzing all around them.

"Androcles received a blow to his side that broke two of his ribs. Lycurgus became careless and received a blow from the tree branch of one of the green women in his face. He was hit so fast and hard that it knocked him out for several minutes.

"Athena turned quickly toward Larentina after hearing a loud popping noise. She looked down, and parts of her python's flesh covered her body. Larentina had used her mind's energy to blow the python to pieces. All that remained of the giant snake was the tail, which was still wrapped around Larentina's legs.

"As Larentina freed herself from what was left of the python's tail, Athena's face flushed with anger because Larentina had created chaos all around them once more. Larentina's lightning bolts struck the tree women, causing them to catch on fire. Athena became angrier as she yelled at Larentina, 'You are now becoming a bother! Since you love Medusa so much, you shall join her!'

"Athena's eyes became complete bright energy; she tried to put the wicked curse upon Larentina, but Larentina's irises were full of electric static. It was the mortal woman's energy versus the Olympian goddess's energy, and Athena was losing. Athena tried for at least ten full minutes when she began to tire.

"Larentina chuckled as she triumphantly announced, 'Vain little goddess, so vain. I warned you—you are in my realm.'

"Before Athena knew it, Lucius's sword stabbed her in the midsection. She dropped to her knees as she put her hand on the wound to stop it from bleeding.

"Larentina came closer to Athena with her sword raised high to strike a deadly blow, but instead she lowered her sword. 'Very peculiar; you bleed. I thought a god did not bleed.' All the men who witnessed this came closer to Athena to see this for themselves.

"Athena now feared Larentina, and she quickly disappeared into thin air."

* * *

"Athena breathed in the fresh air of Mount Olympus. As she stood at the great doors of Zeus's palace, she looked at all the beautiful palaces and magnificent buildings of her beloved city nestled on mountaintops above the clouds. The buildings were all made of white shiny marble with veins of gray sprinkled in them. She could smell the sweet scent of wildflowers that grew throughout the city. She looked down and the wound that had been inflicted on her flesh was completely healed.

"Athena thought, *How can I bleed? I am a goddess. I have never bled before.* She put her thoughts aside as she walked through the threshold of her father's palace; Hera ran to her and grabbed her by the forearm.

"Hera commanded, 'Athena, come quickly. Zeus is becoming stronger. I need to poison him again. I cannot believe you failed.'

"Hera, as well as many of the gods who were part of this conspiracy, had been watching what had happened to Athena from Zeus's own throne chamber.

"If the gods did not fear Larentina and the Spartans before, they did now.

"As Athena walked into Zeus's throne chamber, he was still caged, chained and held in place with the magic of many of the other Olympian deities. Athena grew stronger again from being in her own realm. She became angry with her father. As Zeus lay there, she grabbed his chin and jerked it, so she could look into his eyes as she commanded, 'Tell me, Father, how do we kill the dog you created? For she is the only one who would bother to try to save you. Why do I bleed when I am in the mortal's realm now?'

"Zeus did not answer her for a few moments. He viciously laughed at his daughter before answering her, "You bleed, Daughter, because the mortals now love and believe in Larentina, more than you. What makes us strong, Daughter, is the energy from a mortal's love and fear, and you do not have enough of that energy to fight Larentina. She is growing more powerful everyday. Athena took the poison from Hera and with the help of Hera's magic, they both forced Zeus's mouth open and made him swallow it.

"As Zeus faded back into unconsciousness, he slowly smiled at what he had seen Larentina and her companions do to his traitorous daughter, Athena. His last thoughts were, *If Larentina could reach my mind I might be able to reach hers.* He used what little bit of strength he had left to try to reach her before completely drifting into blackness.

"Apollo and Hera discussed whether to kill Zeus this very moment. He warned strongly, 'We are but a few gods who are part of this. You do not know how strong this wolf is. If you kill Zeus and she happens to be growing stronger and more powerful, she could destroy all of us. Zeus will be her weakness; we do not have Zeus's brothers' allegiance on his destruction. Zeus must live so that we can use him as bait to entrap his pet. Remember, Hera, She Wolf is Spartan, and she has the strongest military force in the entire mortal world. They now worship her, not us;

that is what makes her stronger. She is a force to be reckoned with, and Zeus has discovered this.'

"Aphrodite chimed in, 'Let me try and destroy this She Wolf. Her flesh smells very familiar to me. I believe I can kill her as well as destroy her beloved Sparta.'

"Hera ignored Aphrodite as she asked Apollo, 'Did you not give her the wolf spirit? Why can you not just take this part from her?'

"Apollo contemplated for just a moment and then answered with a lie: 'The wolf is part of her now, and she has grown stronger. If I could separate the two, I would have already done so. It belongs to her soul. The only way you can destroy that part of her soul is to destroy her completely and prevent her from separating into two parts.'

"Aphrodite interrupted again, saying impatiently, 'As I said, I can do that.'

"All the gods looked at each other as well as Hera when she agreed. 'Aphrodite, you must not fail us. I want this abomination that Zeus has created destroyed.'"

* * *

"Larentina and her companions looked up toward the heavens as a storm formed. They heard thunder and could see small lightning bursts in the clouds.

"Larentina began to sob as she continued to look at the storm clouds above her. 'Father! Something is wrong. I just do not know what it is. I must go. Brother and my husband, please hurry. I will meet you back at the Amazons' camp.' She did not realize that Androcles and Lycurgus were hurt, nor did they know Larentina had a dislocated shoulder because of the python's crushing grip.

"Larentina hugged Lucius and gave him a kiss on both cheeks and also kissed him fully on his mouth. She looked into his eyes and said, 'You will truly be a great king. I thank you this day, and I understand you must live to rule your people. I hope to see you once again, Lucius.' She hugged her brother and kissed her husband. Larentina ran and jumped onto Celeris. All the men watched as Celeris ran, leaving fiery hoofprints, and leaped into the sky. They watched until Celeris and Larentina could no longer be seen.

"Lucius shook his head and sarcastically said to all that were present to lift everyone's spirits, 'I think our fathers are right: "Give a woman an inch, and she always takes a mile." Androcles, you had better retrieve her spear. This battle you Spartans have gotten yourselves into is not worth my life. Rome needs me, so I will say my good-byes. I hope to see you all once again.'

"Lycurgus and Androcles watched as Lucius and the two Roman soldiers rode away in the opposite direction. Lycurgus shook his head in disappointment as he said, 'That Roman is a coward. I should have let you kill him, Androcles. I guess he has forgotten the vow he made to my sister and Sparta.'

"Androcles replied, 'I do not believe him to be a coward, but smarter than we are. Larentina already knew that Lucius would not stay and fight beside us.'

"Lycurgus playfully chuckled as he agreed, 'Yes, Androcles, I believe you are right. We must be fools to follow my sister, even though we just witnessed another gift she possesses—the sight of the future.'

"They both laughed, as Androcles shared his thoughts. 'But he was right, we have all the glory because we follow our She Wolf into the mounds of Hades if need be. Our destinies are our own, and the gods can kiss our asses.'

"Lycurgus nodded his head in agreement, with an arrogant smile on his face. 'If we are fools, then we are fools for following my sister instead of following our kings.'

"They painfully mounted their horses and galloped as fast as they could to the Amazons' camp."

Chapter LXV

"Larentina and Celeris flew back to the Amazon camp. As soon as she dismounted Celeris, she asked Almez, 'Almez, could you please pull my shoulder and put it back into place? I have hurt myself.'

"She quickly grabbed Larentina's hand and pulled her arm and felt to be sure she set it back into place.

"Larentina moved her arm back and forth. Gratefully, she said, 'Thank you, Almez. That feels much better. Is everything ready to go? We do not have much time. I fear my father's enemies are already wise to us.'

"Almez frantically replied, 'We are almost ready to depart.'

"Poulxeria asked, 'Where are the Spartan princes?'

"Larentina answered, 'They are on their way and will be here within two hours.'

"Almez asked, 'How do you know the Olympian deities know of our plans?'

"Larentina answered, 'Because our Spartan princes just fought a Cyclops brought to them by Athena; I fought the goddess and found that she bleeds.'

"Poulxeria gasped, as she asked, 'Lycurgus?'

"Larentina answered, 'Both he and my husband are well.'

"Almez and Poulxeria in unison asked, 'What do you mean, "she bleeds"?'

"The three women looked at Corinna for the answer. Corinna simply answered, 'I do not know the answer. I will pray for guidance.' No one said a word, they simply nodded their heads in agreement with Corinna's response.

"As predicted, within two hours, Androcles and Lycurgus rode into the Amazon camp. Larentina looked up at Androcles as he was still mounted upon his horse. She held the bridle of the horse and said solemnly, 'I was unable to speak with you earlier during your battle with the Cyclops.

"'My brother's thoughts told me he told you the truth of our birth and our life. I will completely understand, my husband, if you want to return to your home and family, for I have deceived you. This plan we are undertaking is an act of treason against Sparta; there is no turning back.'

"When Androcles spoke after he dismounted his horse, his voice reflected the emotional weight he was bearing. 'What you say is true, I am very angry and disappointed in both of you, but the lie of your births was not your doing. By leaving Sparta and Greece you have done the noble thing, for Lycurgus is not the heir to the throne of the Agiad house, but what is true is you are the daughter of Zeus and the ruler of my heart.'

"Androcles let out a heavy sigh as he took Larentina's hands in his and spoke again. This time his tone was laced with the love that filled his heart. 'I made a vow to you last night, and I made a vow to Lycurgus before that. I am a man of honor, and I will honor both promises. No matter what or who you really are, Larentina, you will always remain my queen, my goddess, and my love, for you have conquered my heart and soul. I will give my dying breath to you to help keep you strong. I made that vow to you, and I will never go back on my word. If we live through this great battle in which we are nothing but pawns, we will find our own lands and rule as one. I am tired of suffering for another and a cause that is not my doing. I want peace and love, and I want to have children with you and no other.'

"Tears of love flowed down Larentina's cheeks as she kissed Androcles slowly and passionately. She looked up at her new husband and lovingly vowed, 'May the God of the Israelites bless you, keep you safe, and give you peace. I always will love you, my king, my husband, my love. You are hurt. Let me try and heal you.'

"Androcles took Larentina's hands in his and kissed her passionately and softly spoke, 'It is nothing more than a scratch.'

"Larentina smiled at her husband as her eyes changed. She touched the wound as she spoke, 'No matter, I will heal it.'

"Lycurgus playfully laughed as he broke in on the moment; he commanded, 'Enough, you two, there will be plenty of time for making babies after we get through this. We must leave, now!'

"Larentina saw her brother's blood and she quickly went to him as she commanded with love laced in her voice, 'Be still, Brother, and let me heal you as well.'

"Lycurgus laughed, but he allowed his sister to mend him.

"Everyone else had already boarded the Amazon ship, and they were waiting on the remaining four Amazon warriors, Almez, Poulxeria, Lycurgus, Androcles, Corinna, Lambda, and Larentina, who were all standing on the shoreline. As they were about to board the rowboats that would transport them to the ship, Aphrodite appeared out of thin air and walked toward them.

"She giggled as she seductively walked toward Lycurgus. Lambda was growling and barking at her. Aphrodite kissed Lycurgus passionately, and he wiped his mouth in disgust, as if he had tasted something bad. Poulxeria glared at Aphrodite, but she said nothing. She was not surprised that a great prince, such as Lycurgus, would have goddesses longing for him. She hoped that he would truly love her someday; she craved to have Lycurgus look at her the way Androcles looked at Larentina.

"Aphrodite glibly laughed again before she spoke to Larentina. 'Bad little wolf, bad—for I know your plot at hand. I knew I recognized the smell of your flesh. I know your bloodline, and I will enjoy your body soon.' The small group instinctively backed away from Aphrodite and moved in front of Larentina to protect her from the goddess.

"Larentina pushed her way in between Lycurgus and Androcles and stepped forward to confront the goddess. As she stood defiantly before Aphrodite with hatred-filled eyes, she sarcastically asked, 'Please tell me, oh, great Aphrodite, how have I been a bad pet to you?'

"Aphrodite once again giggled viciously before answering Larentina, 'This is so delicious to see you defiant before me, totally unaware that I will watch with pleasure as all your companions are destroyed. You will lose everything you hold dear, and once I have broken your spirit and consumed it, I will wear your flesh as I did with one of your ancestors, ages ago.

"'I will cherish sucking every drop of your beauty, strength, and soul from you. I will enjoy watching Spartan blood spill by Apollo's own hand because you love the Spartans so much, and chose a mortal Spartan over Apollo, who is so beautiful and perfect. But before he does that, I will also enjoy you groveling and suffering before your own kings of Sparta. To make sure you stay put, I have a surprise for you.' She commanded Poseidon, 'God of the seas, I summon you to destroy the Amazon ship!'

"Within moments, Poseidon rose from the sea in full glory. He grew more than one hundred feet tall, a giant of all giants. He was half man and half fish, a merman. He pointed his trident to the cloudless sky and lightning bolts shot from it to the heavens. The sky instantly became cloudy.

Vicious winds whipped the sea until high waves formed and battered the Amazon ship. Lightning flashed throughout the sky, and rain cascaded harshly upon the beach. Poseidon bent over and blew the ship out to sea, and the ship vanished from sight. He then turned to face Aphrodite and nodded his head once. Aphrodite blew him a kiss as he sank back under the waves and disappeared into the sea.

"Aphrodite now focused all her attention on the small party standing on the shore. She giggled with delight as she trapped the small group before her. Aphrodite spoke her evil scheme aloud. 'Now how do I keep you here until I return with the Spartan kings? It should not take me very long. Oh, I know. I will keep you entertained so you will not leave this spot.' She simply clutched the green crystal pendant attached to a golden chain around her neck and commanded, "Rise, anubi, my jackal guardians of the dead.' From the sand arose fifty Egyptian anubi holding golden spears.

"The anubi had faces like Doberman pinschers but their bodies were human. They completely circled the group, preventing them from leaving the beach. All of the anubi growled and snarled at Larentina and her companions. Lambda fearlessly barked and snarled right back at them.

"The small party began to fight for their very lives against the anubi.

"As Larentina battled one of the anubi, she asked Aphrodite, 'Please, my goddess, tell me why you do not fear the wrath of Zeus upon you? Why are you so bold as to cage me like the wild wolf that I am?'

"Aphrodite once again facetiously giggled as she answered, 'Because, silly little dog, Hera has made a pact with all the deities, and we plan to cage Zeus as I have done with you. Hera has promised you to Apollo, and before Hera kills Zeus, she will force him to watch as Apollo takes you savagely. Once Apollo grows tired of you, I will enjoy you begging me to take your soul, and then I will take your flesh and wear it until the beauty dries up.' Aphrodite licked her lips and giggled seductively as she continued, 'I haven't had so much fun in over a millennium. This is so yummy.'

"Larentina knew this would be her one and only chance, because Aphrodite did not fear her; therefore, Aphrodite's guard was down. The only way to escape was to fight their way out, so Larentina yelled out Aphrodite's real name, 'Semiramis! Lucifer's whore!'

"Aphrodite was walking toward the water and naturally responded to her real name. 'I haven't heard my real—' she started to say as she slowly turned around.

"Before Aphrodite could finish her sentence, Larentina used her power to turn the anubi back into sand, and then she charged straight toward the goddess with her sword drawn. With one strong swing, she decapitated her.

"Before Semiramis's head touched the sand, all the Egyptian anubi turned back to lumps of sand. Even though Semiramis's head was separated from her body, she was still alive. She tried to talk but could only make gurgling noises.

"Larentina bent down and picked up Semiramis's head by the hair. As Semiramis's head was looking at Larentina, Larentina laughed. 'What did you think? I was like all other mortals? I already knew you are a witch and not a god. Just as I know the Olympian deities are no gods either; they are nothing but fallen angels of the one true God, the creator of all. The God whose name is so powerful, you do not dare say it aloud. You should have taken my ancestor's threats more seriously. What? You want this crystal necklace?'

"Larentina was looking at the necklace as it dangled on her sword, and then she looked at Semiramis's head and laughed again, before saying, 'I do not believe so, for I plan on destroying it and sending you to your hell for all eternity.'

"Larentina turned to Lycurgus and politely asked, 'Brother, please make me a fire.'

"There was complete silence as Lycurgus started the fire. Larentina then asked politely, 'Androcles, could you please throw her body into the fire?'

"Larentina glared once more into Semiramis's scared eyes as Androcles did as she commanded; she said with no emotion in her voice, 'Now you have no body, like you planned to do to me; instead I took your body from you. I guess you didn't think one of God's mortal children would be the one who sent you to the pit of hell, did you? Yes, I know of your hell.'

"Larentina then dropped the head onto the beach. She walked to the edge of the woods and found a large branch, which she used to make a torch. She lit the torch using the fire that was still turning Semiramis's body to ash and set the head on fire.

"As Larentina clutched the crystal pendent in her hand, everyone looked at her in shock. Lycurgus was the first to speak. 'What have you done? We could have fought our way out of this. Once Aphrodite is discovered missing by the Olympian deities, we will suffer a miserable death or worse. We could be turned into hideous monsters for all eternity.'

"Larentina said nothing but silently sat watching the head burn. She casually walked to a large rock on the edge of the woods that was halfway buried in the sand. She picked up another rock and laid the crystal pendant on the larger rock. Before she had the chance to crush it, Poulxeria grabbed Larentina's wrist and commanded, 'Stop! You will need the magic that is contained in this crystal.'

"Larentina jerked her wrist away from Poulxeria's grip and announced, 'I looked deep into this crystal and the magic that it contains is thousands of damned souls. I must set them free. I do not know why, but I must destroy this crystal, which is what made Lycurgus and me.'

"Poulxeria let out a soft sigh before speaking and in an understanding tone explained, 'Larentina, after seeing with my own eyes a mortal woman destroy a goddess, I believe you possess some type of magic, strength, an unknown truth of these beings, and the world that surrounds you. I cannot see what you can see, but I believe you.

"'You are a unique being, for no one else would have taken me to the brink of death and then healed me. Instead of enslaving me as any other great conqueror would do, you freed me. You have given me a new life that consists of freedom, free will, respect, and leadership, and you allowed me to discover what love really is. For this alone, I will follow you to end of the world, as my queen and my friend, not my conqueror.

"'Something or someone more powerful than the Olympian gods is protecting you. Whether you believe this or not, this powerful being has always protected you. It is now clear to me why you have been protected. It is the Israelite's God you pray to, and I cast all other gods I have worshipped to the side, and from this moment forward, I will follow you because you follow this great God.'

"Larentina put her hand on Poulxeria's shoulder as she spoke softly to Poulxeria. 'This is what you do not understand, my ally. I did not give you these gifts. The one true God gave you these gifts for being one of his children. He has given us all freedom of choice, love, and so much more. It is up to us as beings with free will to fight the evil enemies of our spirit father, God. You must follow God and his design, not mine. But you are right; I must use this crystal, but the purpose is unclear to me now.'

"Almez put her hand on Larentina's shoulder and wisely commented, 'When the time comes, you will know when to use this. Whatever you do, do not succumb to its evil.'

"Corinna boldly suggested, 'Let us all pray to God.'

"Everyone in the group kneeled and bowed their heads in silence. Corinna began to pray, 'Great God of the universe who created each of us, we come before you to thank you for our freedom and to ask for your guidance and protection for the journey on which we are about to embark. We know that you have led us to each other to serve your divine purpose, and we dedicate our lives to you. Our only desire is to serve you and follow your guidance. I thank you that you are in control of the universe and that you have already defeated the evil one. May our service to you serve as a beacon to bring others to you, the one true God. So be it, Amen.'

"Everyone repeated in unison, 'Amen.'

"Androcles felt a tingling sensation in his very soul. He had never felt like this before in his life, and he was the first to speak aloud these feelings, as a new revelation overwhelmed him. 'I feel your God within me, and he has given me the insight for the crystal. The crystal will take us to the ferryman, who in turn will take us to Medusa. Medusa is the key to destroying Poseidon, and releasing Zeus from Hera's cage, as well as returning the seas to nature.'

"Lycurgus was the next to speak his feelings and revelations that God had given him. 'Androcles speaks truth; I feel the same sensation. Your God does not live outside, but within each and everyone one of us. The crystal will lead Larentina to Zeus to save him. God still has hope for Zeus, as well as all of mankind.'

"Larentina questioned, 'But how?'

"Almez answered confidently, 'Because it is within you, Larentina; you must reach into your very soul for it, to seek the truth, and the truth will set us all free.'

"Poulxeria chimed in, speaking her insight regarding the matter, 'Larentina, you are the chosen one, because you are the first amongst us to choose to follow God, the light, and creator of all. I also feel him inside me.'

"Corinna had tears flowing down her cheeks as she, in turn, spoke. 'You all have found God; we have become a nation under him as all his children. He is pleased you have chosen him over all others. Blessed are those who believe without being touched by him. Larentina, you must beware, for all magic is evil. Always remember this! I fear we do wrong by using it.'

"Larentina ignored Corinna's last statement said with conviction, 'And blessed are those who fight for God, when he commands it, for freedom and liberty. I vow that I, as well as my bloodline for all of eternity, will fight against tyranny and those who take the free will and freedom of others. I, as well as my bloodline, will stand by whoever fights for God's greatest gifts. I will do everything in my power to help God's children choose him without hindrance.'

"Everyone in the group yelled joyfully, 'Hear! Hear!'

"Lycurgus then spoke with conviction as a natural leader. 'Then let this war against evil begin! We will stay here and prepare for it!'

"Larentina began her life with the belief that her destiny was to give more freedom and equality to Spartan women; she learned that she was destined to start a war between the gods and seek justice for her birth mother. That was not her total destiny, but instead, it was just the beginning of it. This was why Zeus could not understand what her purpose was, nor could anyone else. Larentina now knew her destiny was to provide freedom to all who desire it, to right wrongs that have been done, to seek truth and justice, and to fulfill vengeance for her mother, Agape."

Chapter LXVI

"A few hours after Larentina and her friends left the Olympian palace, the Spartan entourage discovered they were missing, along with six horses. They were extremely angry that their children had committed such treason against their beloved Sparta. They not only took a large amount of food, which King Archimedes complained about, they had also stolen a slave. The queens were naturally more concerned with the fact that their children had left without saying good-bye; they were distraught with the fear that they might never see them again. King Karpos and King Alcaeus were just angry. The future of Sparta had left without explanation.

"An impromptu meeting, which included the queens, was promptly called. Bion was the first to speak his thoughts aloud. 'There is no, and I mean *no*, justification for this traitorous act. All three of them should be executed for this act against the state. There is no way, my kings, you can make excuses to get your children out of this one! The state has invested too much money and time in them. It has all been a wasted effort, especially the She Wolf. It is her nature to be wild and disobedient. We should have realized that she could not be tamed. She no longer has the protection of Zeus. I'm sure he has grown tired of her.'

"King Alcaeus was incredibly angry with his own children for their disobedience, but he still defended them. 'Zeus has already made his commands clear regarding Larentina. You know what will happen if you harm one hair on her head, as well as her brother's. Not to mention part our own military legions will go against you because they consider our sons as the future kings of Sparta; after all, they are our firstborn. They have both proven themselves loyal soldiers repeatedly, just as Karpos and I have done throughout our lives. You will not execute my flesh. I am still king, and my commands will be obeyed.'

"King Karpos angrily threatened to all who were present, 'I will kill you where you stand if you try to carry out your threats against my firstborn. Granted, what they have done looks like treason, but I'm sure they have an explanation. Be very careful, Bion, for this matter may cause a great civil unrest between our Spartan people.

"'You know the prophesies about Larentina from the Oracle. No matter how hard we have tried to prevent these prophesies from happening, they still have come true. So how can you call them traitors to the state, when I believe they are trying to protect us from being destroyed as a nation?

"'I admit, I have been skeptical since the birth of this She Wolf, but she has proven herself in more ways than I can count; I have said this numerous times. Do not forget, Bion, this She Wolf is a gift from Zeus himself. She is loved by all the Spartan people, including the perioikoi and our helots. Many helots took lashings for not performing their duties, because they were looking for Larentina when she disappeared. Remember?

"'When I think back, there hasn't been a revolt from the helots since the moment Larentina was born. They all worship her as their goddess.'

"Bion angrily retorted, 'Come! Come! She is no goddess; she admitted this in her own words to Zeus. Granted, the royal twins possess some magical connection to one another; we have seen this with our very own eyes, but that is all she possesses, nothing more.'

"At this point in the intense argument, Bion looked around him at the other members of the gerousia council. Bion saw that the kings' military escort—thirty or more soldiers—had surrounded them. He realized he needed to watch his tongue.

"There were two Spartan generals, one on either side of the kings. All the soldiers, including the generals, gripped their swords, ready to pull them out of their sheaths upon command. Each soldier had a serious, deadly expression, but they remained silent and calm.

"General Nikephoros solemnly asked, 'My kings, may I have permission to speak?'

"Both the kings looked at General Nikephoros and nodded their heads yes.

"General Nikephoros looked at the members of the gerousia, and he spoke his concerns through the eyes of a military man. 'Members of the gerousia council, let us make it perfectly clear, the Spartan military only takes commands from our kings, for they are the highest rank of our legions. The wisdom of our kings regarding this matter is true and correct. You would have parts of our military follow you, and parts of it will follow our kings, causing a civil war among us. It will be Spartans killing Spartans, instead of fighting against our common enemies. The

Spartan people will ultimately be the losers in this matter, because we will destroy ourselves within.

"'I too have been skeptical of our She Wolf since her experimental training began, but instead of failing, she has proven herself as a formidable soldier. You have not seen her on the battlefield as I have. She has saved many lives not just with her sword and other weapons, but also with her healing herbs and potions. You all are wrong; she does possess many of the Olympian gods' powers. You did not see the divine powers that I have seen. You were not there when Zeus came when she had fallen.

"'Often, when I have praised one of my commanders for a victorious battle and their actions on the battlefield, the praise truly belonged to Larentina for whispering what the enemy was about to do, giving an insight to our commanders on the field, giving them leverage.

"'I have also experienced firsthand that she can read men's minds. She will look at me from a distance right before I give a command; she nods her head as if she understands my thoughts and yells to everyone around her my commands before I speak them. This has on many occasions saved time and gave our armies more speed in attacking.

"'Remember, gentleman, our future kings and our one and only She Wolf have fought on the battlefield in many great campaigns since they were no more than fifteen years of age; they were not even finished their training. All three of them have been trusted on the battlefield with experienced soldiers, and they proved themselves as great soldiers even though they were just children. We all consider Larentina a good luck charm on the battlefield. Both our kings know this because they have been on the battlefield with me, not the gerousia council!'

"General Nikephoros only said what he knew the kings wanted to hear; after all, his total allegiance was to his kings, especially King Karpos. He regretted what he had done to Agape, but it was that whore Aphrodite who had made him do it. He had been paying for it ever since. Agape was dead, and he felt his debt of allegiance to Bion died with her. He wanted his honor restored.

"Granted, Larentina had proven herself and had proven to the general that Spartan women can protect Sparta when need be, but he really still felt a mortal woman's place was beneath a man.

"Bion commanded, 'Enough! This is getting us nowhere. I believe we should seek the knowledge of the Oracle here in Olympia.'

"King Archimedes immediately protested, "My kingdom's Pythia nor my people will have any involvement in your civil unrest! I will not put

Olympia in harm's way, nor will I provoke the gods' anger toward me or my people. Is that understood?'

"King Draco quickly responded, because King Archimedes had opened the door, 'I will help you, if you return my daughter to me.'

"King Alcaeus responded to King Draco, 'You have no say in the matter, for you have nothing to bargain with. You have already lost the wager, and your allegiance has already been won. The return of your daughter is up to my son and my son only.'

"King Draco knew that the Spartan kings were correct, but he greatly feared Poulxeria would expose his true nature before he had a chance to kill her.

"King Draco humbly agreed, 'This is true; my allegiance is with Sparta. I gave my word to both kings, and I will honor it.'

"Bion protested, 'Your allegiance is to the Spartan state not just our kings.'

"King Draco was careful but still defiantly announced, 'My allegiance is to the two kings of Sparta, not the state.'

"Both Spartan kings nodded their heads, acknowledging the correct answer of King Draco.

"King Draco was in the door; now he took it further as he said, 'King Archimedes, I completely understand your concern; a delicate matter has been set before us, but your Oracle is the closest, and time is of the essence, for if these Spartan kings are not given correct and decisive advice, you could anger the gods by not helping at all. You have no other choice but to help the Spartans discover what the gods want them to do in this matter.'

"King Archimedes nodded and vocalized his agreement. 'Yes, I fear you may be correct. I will take us all there now, so we know what to do, but you will not get any further help from Olympia.'"

Chapter LXVII

"Larentina yelled out, "Wait! Our fathers—our kings—and many others are walking into great harm. The Olympian Oracle: I see Apollo. He is going to kill them all. Brother, I must reach our father's thoughts. Give me your hand; I need your mind to help me reach him.'

"Androcles, horrified, yelled out, 'My father! Our people!'

"Larentina took his hand as she calmly spoke. 'I believe your mind can help me as well to reach them all.'"

* * *

"King Alcaeus, King Karpos, King Archimedes, King Draco, the two Spartan generals, a Mycenaean general, and the soldiers of all three armies stood back as the large doors of the Olympian Oracle's temple opened.

"With the kings leading the way, the entire group marched into the main room of the temple. The commotion caused the three priests of Pythia to run down the stairs as fast as they could. The head priest angrily asked, 'What is the meaning of this intrusion, King Archimedes?'

"King Archimedes abruptly commanded, 'Bring me Pythia now!'

"In fear of being killed, the priests obeyed King Archimedes's command and ran back up the stairs to retrieve Pythia.

"The beautiful priestess slowly walked down the stairs. She stood on the bottom step and asked calmly, 'My king, what is the urgency?'

"King Archimedes quickly told Pythia what they sought and explained the urgency of their request.

"Before Pythia could respond, the life-sized marble statue of Apollo started cracking before their eyes. King Archimedes dropped to his knees in fear, as did Pythia, the entire Spartan gerousia council members, and everyone else except the Spartan soldiers and their two kings, who stood strong.

"King Alcaeus became rigid, for he heard his daughter's voice in his mind saying, 'Father, it is me, Larentina. Do not fight me, for I must warn you. If King Karpos is beside you, grab his hand. I do not know if this will work because I never mastered this very well.'

"King Alcaeus instinctively reached over, grabbed King Karpos by the wrist, and gripped it tightly. King Karpos also became rigid as Larentina spoke to him as well.

"She continued, 'Apollo is going to destroy all of us. The war has already begun. When he is in human form, he is the most vulnerable. This is the only time he can be killed. Please do exactly as I say! The only way you can kill him is to completely sever his head from his body and then burn his head separate from his body. Both parts must be burned separately. You must do this. Please, Father, no matter what half-truths he tells you, you must be my champion. This is the only way mankind will be completely free of these fallen angels who have rejected the one true God. Queen Alexis will tell you, my father, the truth of Lycurgus and my birth. Please forgive her, Father, for you must, because in the future she will give you the true royal heir of the Agiad house.

"'Please, King Karpos, the father of my husband, forgive us for our deceit. I swear I will bear many strong and great warriors. You must unite with the Agiad house and fight together as one, as one wolf pack. Hurry, my kings, protect yourselves and your people. You both are the greatest warriors of the world. Do not allow this evil being to defeat us! Do not believe him, and do not fear him, because it will give him strength if you do! We are trying to figure this magic crystal out, and we will fight and die by your side if we can get there.'

"The Spartan kings said nothing as they gazed into each other's eyes. They both nodded their heads in an unspoken agreement. The Spartan soldiers carefully watched their kings, so they could immediately follow their lead in whatever action they took.

"Apollo now stood with his hands on his hips and angrily asked, 'Where is the She Wolf? She belongs to me!'

"Apollo was indeed a very handsome god. All the stories of his physical beauty and masculine perfection were true. He stood seven feet tall, and his hair was sandy blond. It was curly as well as short, and you could see his earlobes beneath the curls. He had a clean-shaven face and a manly nose with a full, rounded face. His eyes were a soft gray, just like Zeus's, and his body was like Hercules's. His dark maroon tunic had black trim and gold embroidery and fell to his knees. His shiny, golden chest armor had an etching of a lion's head carved into it, and he wore leather sandals laced up to his knees.

"King Archimedes kneeled before Apollo and answered, 'Great Apollo, please forgive us, for we were just seeking her whereabouts. She has run off!'

"Apollo angrily said, 'How dare you speak to me, you cowardly imbecile?'

"Everyone watched as Apollo just waved his hand and, with some unknown force, lifted King Archimedes into the air and pulled all four of his limbs from his body. King Alcaeus was the first to draw his sword, then King Karpos, as well as every one of the Spartan soldiers.

"Apollo bellowed, with complete contempt at these mortal beings, 'How dare you defy me? Zeus will not come to your rescue this time, nor will he come to save your precious She Wolf! You better fear me, or I will destroy you and all of your people.'

"King Karpos was filled with hatred toward this being and yelled back, 'Go ahead and try!'

"King Karpos was shocked at Apollo's vanity. He now wished he had never worshiped this arrogant deity. He would have to find another god to worship.

"The kings and their soldiers prepared themselves to fight Apollo. To their surprise, Apollo viciously guffawed at them. Then, he glared directly at King Alcaeus and bellowed, 'You are willing to die for Lycurgus and Larentina, when neither of them are your offspring; you foolish, foolish little man.'

"Apollo arrogantly laughed even harder. 'Little man, they did not even come from your woman's womb, but from her sister's. The only truth of these twins is just maybe Larentina is the seed of Zeus, but I do not believe that either.'

"King Alcaeus was completely shocked and confused, like everyone in the room who heard Apollo's statements. King Alcaeus became livid and was ready to strike at Apollo as he yelled, 'You lie!'

"Before Alcaeus had a chance to attack Apollo, King Karpos grabbed his wrist and calmly warned him, 'Remember her warning, Brother.'

"King Alcaeus lowered his arm, still gripping his sword tightly.

"As the white marble walls that surrounded them started shaking, dozens of human faces pushed their way through the now-rubbery walls. The faces and their bodies continued pushing themselves out of the walls; they were the damned souls of long-forgotten soldiers, who had been beckoned by Apollo from the underworld of Hades. Everyone watched in disgust and awe as the rotting corpses of the fallen soldiers came to life and surrounded them.

"The rotting corpses then began to attack, and Apollo doubled over guffawing as the Spartans began fighting for their very lives against these soldiers who were dead, yet now functioned as if they were alive.

"As King Alcaeus and King Karpos battled these skeletal remains with rotten flesh still clinging to their bones, Larentina appeared on the scene, with a prince of Sparta on either side of her and Lambda between them. She walked through the room, sword in her hand, toward the battle with Lambda barking and growling by her side. One of the Spartan soldiers announced to all who were present, 'Our She Wolf has arrived!' The Spartans fought harder to prove to their goddess they were fearless and brave.

"Apollo laughed and asked Larentina, as everyone else continued fighting around them, 'Well, my She Wolf, how can it be that you have this divine power?'

"Lambda showed her fangs as she continued snarling and growling at Apollo. She stood fearlessly beside her mistress.

"Larentina snickered back at Apollo before she answered him with a question: 'Well, since you are supposedly a god, half Brother, why do you not tell me?'

"King Alcaeus and King Karpos took advantage of this moment and approached Apollo, who had his attention completely focused on Larentina and nothing else in the large room. Apollo seemed to be totally oblivious of the heated battle that surrounded him.

"Apollo then wickedly snickered as he asked Larentina, 'Please, my mortal delicacy, tell me how you think you can destroy me. You may have little tricks up your sleeve, but they are nothing more than tricks. If by some small chance you do have divine powers, I am a stronger and more powerful god than you are.'

"Larentina factitiously laughed as she answered the pompous ass deity standing within inches of her. 'You are no god, we both know this. You are nothing more than an offspring of an offspring of a fallen angel who rejected the one true God, as am I. Or could I be a direct descendant of the Titans? Maybe that is why you fear me so.'

"While Larentina spoke, King Karpos walked unnoticed behind Apollo and stabbed him in his side. Larentina chuckled again, and then she completed her answer as Apollo dropped quickly to his knees. 'Your death will not be by my hand; it will instead be by my father, King Alcaeus.' As soon as Larentina said his name, King Alcaeus swung his sword and decapitated Apollo. In that split second, the dead soldiers collapsed into heaps of bones and rotting flesh.

"King Karpos quickly grabbed several nearby torches and set Apollo's body on fire. King Alcaeus followed suit by grabbing another torch and setting Apollo's head on fire as well.

"Everyone in the room began cheering and chanting the names of both Spartan kings. As Androcles hugged his father and Lycurgus hugged his father, Larentina watched them, smiling, overcome with joy and gratitude that this part of the war was over.

"King Draco approached the five and demanded of the Spartan kings, 'Where is my daughter? I want to see her!'

"At that very moment, the large doors opened and Celeris walked into the room with Poulxeria on his back. Poulxeria was wearing the Amazon belt because Almez proclaimed her as the Amazon queen and returned the belt to Poulxeria. She dismounted the horse and walked quickly toward King Draco, sword in hand. Everyone moved away from the pair.

"Without saying a word, Poulxeria thrust her sword into King Draco's midsection, just above his navel. As his intestines began spilling out of his body, he dropped to his knees. With his face contorted in pain, he took a shallow breath and weakly asked her, 'What have you done?'

"With hate-filled eyes, Poulxeria answered, 'For killing my mother, imprisoning me like a caged animal, taking away my childhood innocence, and murdering my child. Vengeance is what I have done!'

"Draco took one more shallow, raspy, agonizing breath, fell over, and died.

"Poulxeria then turned and faced Larentina. There were tears streaming down her cheeks as she struggled to speak. 'My queen, I know that you commanded me to stay on the shores, but I had to kill him, for he would have hunted me down and killed me as he had done to my mother.'

"Larentina hugged Poulxeria and whispered in her ear, 'I understand.'

"As King Alcaeus hugged Larentina, he asked, 'Was what Apollo said true?'

"Larentina returned his embrace and dutifully whispered in his ear, 'It is not my place to speak the truth to you, for it was not our lie; but know this, Father: Agape gave us to you for your forgiveness, and to thank you for her life. We were the greatest gift she could give you. The truth you seek must come from Queen Alexis. Lycurgus and I both love you as our king and our father, for we have known no other.'

"Larentina kissed King Alcaeus on the cheek.

"Poulxeria mounted Celeris. Everyone watched as the horse's wings appeared and they flew away.

"King Karpos put his hand on his son's shoulder and asked him, 'Son, why must you go? You are part of Sparta. You are the next ruler after me.'

"Androcles looked at his father and calmly answered, 'I belong with my queen. My home is where my heart is, with the woman I love.

"'You must go home, to our Sparta, for she will need you. This war has just begun, and we will do everything in our power to protect Sparta from these beings; that is why you must go and protect your people. If I live, and Larentina returns to Sparta, I will return with her.'

"The kings continued asking questions for at least another two hours when Lycurgus then commanded Larentina, and Androcles, 'We must go!' Androcles and Lycurgus took Larentina's hands and simply disappeared from view."

Chapter LXVIII

"The three young Spartans reappeared on the shoreline. Lambda started sniffing the sand all around them. They looked all around, searching for Poulxeria, Corinna, Almez, and the Amazon warriors, but they were nowhere to be found. All that remained of their camp was Celeris along with Androcles and Lycurgus's horses and smoldering ashes of the campfire.

"Naturally, the Spartans were expert trackers, and Lycurgus was the first to speak his observations. 'They went in that direction,' he said, pointing into the wooded landscape. 'These small footprints show at least nine people have taken our friends.'

"Androcles spoke his observations of the footprints in the sand as well. 'These footprints were made by very small people. It does not appear that there was any struggle. My guess is they spoke with these strangers, and they all left willingly. Almez must not have considered them a threat.'

"Lambda started barking toward the wooded area. Larentina commanded, 'Then we must follow them, for we need them to continue this fight. They must have had good reason to leave instead of waiting for our return.'

"The young Spartans mounted the three remaining horses and rode off at a slow pace, following the footprints and Lambda. Periodically they would stop and observe broken branches and other signs that would keep them heading in the right direction toward Poulxeria and her companions.

"After several hours of tracking, Larentina, Lycurgus, and Androcles heard beautiful singing in the distance. Although they could barely hear it, Larentina excitedly announced, 'The Muses! My sisters have them.'

"Androcles asked, 'How do you know for sure that these beings are Muses?'

"Lycurgus answered, 'No mortal could sing as beautifully as that.'

"Larentina suggested, 'Let us follow the sound and we will soon see.'

"When they were almost to the source of the beautiful singing, they cautiously crept silently to the edge of the forest; they quietly peeked through the foliage and saw a large lake. Poulxeria, Corinna, Almez and her warriors were swimming and singing with nine beautiful, petite women.

"Almez was the first to see Larentina. By this time, Larentina was standing on the shoreline with her hands on her hips, legs spread apart, and she appeared to be very angry. She let all the women swimming in the lake know her feelings: 'Shame on all of you! I commanded you all to wait for us! I find you here singing and having a merry old time! We thought you had been swept away by another angry Olympian deity!' Larentina then laughed, took off her clothing, and jumped into the lake.

"Lycurgus and Androcles looked at each other, confused; they shrugged their shoulders, laughed, and began taking their clothes off to join the women. Lycurgus smiled and said, 'This is better than heaven.'

"Androcles chuckled as he shook his head in disbelief; he teased, 'Only your sister.' Both men joined the beautiful women in the water.

"Almez swam close to Larentina and said, 'I thought you were angry with us. We had to have a little fun.'

"Larentina sadly smiled at her friend as she answered, 'I was, but it is good to clean the smell of death from our bodies; to remind us we are still among the living.'

"Larentina turned her attention to one of the petite women and asked, to be sure her suspicions were correct regarding who these creatures were, 'Are you the daughters of Zeus?'

"The woman answered, 'Yes, Zeus was our father, and our mother was Mnemosyne, a Titan goddess. We are known as muses. I am Clio.' She then proceeded to point at each of her sisters as she said their names, 'This is Urania, Melpomene, Thalia, Terpsichore, Calliope, Erato, Polyhymnia, and this is Euterpe.' As each woman was introduced to Larentina, she nodded her head.

"Clio continued to speak. 'We are not only here because you are our sister, but to help you destroy Athena. We do not like her and detest her constant meddling in everything. We have heard rumors that she plans to help Hera destroy our father, Zeus. It is time for you to know the real history of the Olympian deities. After you know our history, we will tell you how to find the underworld. Your friends have told us your plan and we believe it will work, but we will not intervene any further, for although we do not like Athena, we fear what she can do to us.'

"The muses, Larentina, and Larentina's companions made camp. Lycurgus and Androcles hunted for meat as the women made bread, cut cheese, and drank wine from the supplies that Lycurgus and Androcles had stolen from King Archimedes.

"They camped by the lake for two months as Clio told the history of the Titans, explained how the Olympian deities came into power over the earth, and described the Olympian deities as nothing but fallen angels of the true God, creator of all. Clio showed Larentina how to use the magic crystal to take them to the edge of the underworld.

"On the last night, Clio took Larentina aside after everyone had fallen asleep. She held Larentina's helmet in her hand. As she passed it to Larentina, she instructed, 'Put this helmet of your past on, and I will enhance its magic to show you the truth of your mother Agape's past.' Larentina did what was requested of her. She gasped in shock as the truth was completely revealed to her. Larentina already suspected most of this, but she was now sure of the truth. As Larentina removed the helmet, she ran to the edge of the lake and threw it into the water as tears of disappointment rolled down her cheeks. She walked back to Clio and asked, 'Do you know what I saw?'

"Clio whispered, 'No, only you know what the truth is from your own bloodline. No one else can see what the wearer of this helmet sees.'

"Larentina could not sleep; the images kept replaying over and over again in her mind. She was glad she had thrown away the helmet that had shown her the past. She knew that Lycurgus must never know the truth. In fact, no one must ever know the truth. She wished Clio had never revealed the truth of her ancestors as well as her true parents. Larentina felt it was better to have suspicions than to have those suspicions proven correct.

"The following morning they said their good-byes to all the muses and thanked them for their knowledge of history to help them destroy some of these wicked beings.

"They retraced their steps and returned to the shoreline where they had originally met up with Almez and her ship. They had hoped that the Amazon ship would find its way back to them. They all agreed in the event that Almez' crew did manage to find their way back, it was better to keep the base camp at this location."

Chapter LXIX

"The crystal took Larentina and her entourage from the shores of Greece to the edge of a world that exists between the living and the dead. Larentina was very grateful the muses showed her how to use this magic to her benefit. They now stood on the shoreline of the River Styx, a river of hate, awaiting Charon, a ferryman, to take just the women, which included Lambda, to the home of Medusa, or for lack of better words, Medusa's prison.

"It was all agreed that Lycurgus and Androcles should wait for the women to return, because just one glance from the Gorgons would turn the men into stone. While the women waited for Charon, Almez shared her strong reservations about entering the underworld. 'I know the world we are about to enter is pure evil, and I feel very strongly that we need to pray for protection, not only for our physical safety, but to help prevent the evil from creeping into our souls.'

"Everyone agreed, so Larentina began, 'All-powerful God of the universe, you know our mission, and our desire to defeat the evil ones. Give us the strength and the wisdom we need. Protect our bodies, minds, and spirits as we travel through the hatred. Bring us out victorious, so that we may give the glory to you. So be it.'

"After the rowboat arrived, the women boarded the boat and Androcles put a coin in Charon's hand. In Charon's other hand was a long wooden pole that he used to guide the boat through the shallow river.

"Androcles cringed at the sight of Charon's hideous face. He was wearing a torn and faded maroon cloak, and his slanted green eyes glowed from beneath the hood. He had clawed feet and hands, and his skin was the color of sage green. Even though Androcles could not see his ears, he knew from stories they were as pointy as his teeth. Lycurgus and Androcles watched the boat disappear into the fog-covered waters.

"Every single woman, including Larentina herself, was overcome with fear, for they were going into the unknown. They all silently prayed to God to protect them.

"The Styx River was blood red and smelled of death. The water seemed to bubble, but the bubbles were the heads of lost souls screaming to be released from their prison of torture as they bobbed up and down in the river.

"Larentina saw a small light burst up from the water for just a moment, and she heard her name faintly as the light breeze brought the voice closer to her: 'Larentina, please help me!' Larentina could have sworn it was the voice of her mother, Agape. She forced the thought from her mind.

"As they continued crossing the river, a feeling of hatred overwhelmed the women. They started bickering with each other until Corinna asked, 'What is the matter with us? This river is affecting us. We must stick together. We cannot be divided.'

"Larentina realized Corinna was correct. She scolded everyone on the small boat, 'We are all acting like a bunch of old hags. Corinna speaks the truth. United we stand, divided we fall.

"'This river is filled with souls of the damned, who are full of hatred toward the living, and the hatred is overpowering. We must fight it by talking about good things in our lives and the love that you feel toward one another.'

"Everyone became completely silent; no one could think of anything good to say. Then Corinna started softly singing a hymn of praise she remembered from her childhood. Instantly, the women began to remember good things about each other and spent the remainder of the voyage talking about each other's good qualities.

"The voyage passed swiftly, and after disembarking the rowboat, they walked cautiously toward the ruins of the island they knew as Hyperborean. They paid close attention to their surroundings as they came closer to the great civilization's ruins, which had thrived long ago. As with ruins of all great ancient cities, much remained. The women were amazed at the beautiful temples, buildings, and statues that now surrounded them. The hair on the backs of their necks stood on end; they all felt something was watching them.

"Almez was the first to speak her suspicions. 'Something is watching us, and I feel it is evil.'

"Poulxeria pointed out, 'I am wearing the belt of strength, and if it is a beast, I can destroy it.'

"Larentina warned Poulxeria, 'I do know this for sure, Poulxeria, we are in a land that is made from magic of the deities.'

"Lambda started barking and growling at something that no one else could see. Larentina pointed out a temple that was still intact; she said, 'Look! Over there! There are fires and torches burning. Medusa must be there.'

"Lambda ran to the building, which had suffered very little damage over the years. Larentina commanded, 'Lambda, come back!' It was too late, for the wolf had disappeared into the building, and everyone could hear her barking and growling, and then they heard Lambda cry out in pain. Lambda started growling and barking once again, and then she ran out of the building at full speed toward her mistress, Larentina.

"Larentina instantly drew her sword and tightly clutched her shield, as she watched Cerberus, Hades's giant three-headed hound, run full speed toward the women warriors. The She Wolf's eyes had already changed; if she was fearful, she did not show it. Instead, her actions showed courage.

"Larentina ran straight toward Cerberus and leaped into the air, landing astride the giant dog's middle neck. She plunged her sword into the spot where his middle head joined with the neck and gave her sword a twist. The middle head howled in pain as it completely died between the other two heads. Larentina continued stabbing the giant beast with all her strength.

"As the other two heads were snarling and nipping at Larentina's companions, Almez threw her long spear into one of the other necks. Her warriors followed suit as they threw their spears with all their might into the same neck, killing that head as well.

"Poulxeria followed suit and jumped onto Cerberus's third neck. She took her sword and plunged it deep in the remaining head. The beast fell toward the ground, with Poulxeria and Larentina still astride two of its large necks. As he fell, the warriors jumped off before the body slammed to the ground.

"As all the women poked the giant beast to be sure it was dead, Lambda sniffed it as well. Larentina looked up at the temple and saw Hades walking out. He looked exactly the way Lycurgus described him from a dream he had during training many years ago. Larentina realized at that moment that her brother had not been dreaming at all, but his spirit really was in the underworld of Hades.

"Hades stood there with his hands on hips and, in a scolding parent's voice, yelled at Larentina, 'Damn it, Child! You are just as bad as your brother Perseus was and almost as bad as Hercules as well. I am sick and tired of Zeus letting his favorite children roam this earth, entering into my domain anytime they please and killing anything they choose.

"'I had just created my favorite pet again, no more than a few hundred years ago.' As Hades sadly rubbed the fur of his now-dead hound, he continued scolding Larentina. 'This Cerberus was no more than a pup, and here you come along and kill it when it was only protecting my domain. Now look at it. You just wait until my brother finds out about this, young lady. I'd punish you myself, but you are Zeus's problem; he will have to deal with you himself.'

"Larentina was bewildered because she expected Hades to either turn her into something hideous or, worse, kill her and her companions. With a confused tone, she simply asked, 'Uncle, where is my father now?'

"Hades shrugged indifferently and answered, 'I do not know, nor do I really care. Hera and Zeus are always fighting about something.

"'I have too many other important things going on here to stick my nose into Zeus's problems. If it's not his children, it is his wife, or one of his lovers. They were fighting long before you were born, and they will probably be fighting long after you have turned to ash.

"'Perseus didn't kill Medusa, although I know you will feel sorry for her too. I'm the only god who knows how he tricked Athena by faking her death. Or he could have just been a silly little fool, since Medusa's sisters look identical to her, and killed the wrong Gorgon. I do not know, and I do not care.

"'Now whatever your destiny is, go and fulfill it now, before I kick you out of my domain. Just be quick about it. You have caused enough problems. Wait a minute; how did you get here to begin with?'

"Larentina stumbled for words, but before she could speak, Hades waved his hand as if to shoo her away and commanded, 'Just go. I do not want to know. You are in enough trouble as it is. What is that around your neck, Larentina? Where did you get that necklace? Is that not Aphrodite's? What have you done?'

"Larentina once again stumbled for words as she answered, 'Aphrodite's name is really Semiramis, Uncle, and she tried to kill me. She tricked all of you. She never was a deity, and she was not conceived by any of you. I defended myself and did what had to be done. If you are going to kill me for this, then so be it.'

"Hades arrogantly guffawed at his niece as he spoke. 'It will not be I, but Zeus himself. Aphrodite was one of his favorites; you know this. While he is fighting with Hera, Child, my advice is that you get what you have come for and get out. I will not be dragged into Zeus's family problems again. I do not want any part of this.'

"Larentina nodded her head, acknowledging she would do as Hades advised. The women started running toward the large temple. As they ran, Larentina realized that all the statues that they had been seeing all over the island were men who had been turned to stone by the Gorgon sisters. She prayed that her belief that the Gorgons' magic did not work on women was correct. The statues were clustered even more thickly as they got closer and closer to Athena's temple.

"Larentina and her companions stopped before entering this magnificent marble palace. As they momentarily stood outside the doors, Larentina again heard her name being called; someone whispered, 'Larentina, please come over here.'

"Larentina looked around, and in the shadows of one of the columns outside the palace, she saw a young woman. Larentina told her companions to wait and ran over to the young woman. She asked, 'Who are you? What do you want?'

"The young woman quickly grabbed Larentina's upper arm and pulled her into the shadows behind the pillar before answering, 'I am Persephone, the daughter of Zeus and Demeter. I want to leave this place with you. I can help.'

"Persephone was beautiful. She had long, flowing black hair and beautiful green eyes like Larentina's mothers. Her skin was pale, but her lips were full and the color of a deep red rose. She was several inches shorter than Larentina. She was slender, and her fingernails as well as her toenails were painted the same color as her lips.

"Larentina asked, 'Another sister? How many do I have? How did you come to be here? Wait, I heard your name from a story told to me long ago.'

"Persephone quickly answered, 'You have a lot of sisters, Larentina. I was abducted by Hades, and because he starved me, I ate here. Zeus tried to retrieve me, but once I ate my first supper with Hades, I belonged to him. Hades claimed me as his wife. My father made a deal with Hades. I am allowed to go home to my mother for six months out of the year, but then I'm forced to return here. I want my freedom from all of this, and I will do anything to be free from both Zeus and Hades.'"

PERSEPHONE, THE DAUGHTER OF ZEUS AND WIFE OF HADES

"Larentina contemplated Persephone's request before speaking; she then asked, 'Pray, tell me, how do I take you from Hades's underworld without him finding out? And how do I know this is not a trick?'

"Persephone answered quickly again, 'This is no trick. I swear it on everything that is holy. I'll simply transform into an Amazon warrior and walk out with you. He may not even notice. I will follow wherever you go, so he never finds me. I would rather die than spend another minute in this world. Every time he touches me, I want to vomit. I hate him and the cruelties that he inflicts on me.'

"Larentina let out a heavyhearted sigh as she thought of the seriousness of Persephone's request. Larentina spoke her mind: 'Very well, I will do it, but there is a price for this risk.'

"Persephone said, 'Whatever it is, I shall pay it. But aren't you a being who frees anyone who asks for your help?'

"Larentina answered, 'I am, but the payment is this: I want my birth mother to escape from here as well.'

"Persephone fearfully commented, 'Larentina, that is impossible. Your mother died. She has no body.'

"Larentina asked, 'If you can easily leave this place, why can't my mother? Hera killed her, and in my realm, that was unnatural as well. I saw a light of energy as we crossed the Styx River, and I am sure I heard my mother's voice calling me. My mother is from the energy of the light, and her soul does not belong here.'

"Persephone contemplated before answering. 'The truth is, Larentina, you are the daughter of both light and dark energy. That is why you can free me, because you are the key that opens and closes the door between the realms. I only know this because I live in the darkness and feel that part of you. Why do think Hades did nothing to you for killing his hound? He fears you, as do many of the other gods. I know he felt the dark energy that is coursing through your soul.'

"Larentina became impatient. 'Just answer me, Persephone. Can you do this?'

"Persephone hesitated before answering. 'I believe I can. I have the power to do this, but you must be willing to enter the river to retrieve her. If you can do that, I can give her body back to her with the help of your energy. It might work.'

"Larentina agreed with confidence. 'Fair enough; I agree. Now you must stay hidden until we have retrieved Medusa.'

"Persephone smiled with joy and hugged Larentina tightly because she was so grateful. 'Larentina, thank you. Now go and complete your quest. I pray that the God you worship will protect you and keep you safe so you may rescue me from this eternal prison.'"

Medusa, Athena's Virgin Priestess

Chapter LXX

"They all quietly entered the palace. They hid behind the large columns that supported the heavy weight of the ceiling. Larentina heard a loud hissing as well as slithering noises, like a large snake moving across the marble flooring.

"Just then, one of the Amazon warriors was shot by an arrow. Larentina quickly started running, as did everyone else. They heard the Gorgon's movements, but feared to turn and face her.

"As they ran, leaping over objects and pushing aside statues that were once men, Larentina looked to her side and saw another Amazon lifted up into the air by a large snake's tail. The Amazon screamed in pain; as Larentina looked up toward the ceiling, another Gorgon crush the warrior to death with her snake tail. She watched as the Gorgon's shadow slithered back down to the floor from one of the columns and disappeared from sight, but Larentina did not know if this was Medusa or not. She only saw parts of it because it was mostly hidden in the shadows; the temple was dimly lit by hearths that burned all around it.

"Larentina quickly hid behind a column before the Gorgon saw her. She boldly peeked from behind the large pillar and saw another shadow, but she was not sure if it was Medusa or not, so she called out, 'Medusa, is that you?'

"The creature responded, 'Ssssss. Who issss it that knowssss my name? Are you a woman ssss?'

"Larentina let out a relieved sigh; she still hid behind the column because she had not seen the creature who spoke. She answered, 'I am Larentina, the She Wolf of the Spartans, and daughter of Zeus. I have come to free you from this curse, if I can. I know the truth of your fate. Please, lower you bow and arrow so that we may talk before your magic kills me.'

"The hissing voice spoke again with irritation. 'I have killed no one; they all tried to kill me; the curssse that hassss been put upon me hassss killed them, not I.'

"Larentina now knew it was indeed Medusa, so she lowered her sword. She waved at Corinna to walk beside her to face the creature while she spoke to it. Larentina and Corinna cringed when they saw the hideous creature that Medusa had been turned into.

"Medusa had red, black, and white striped coral snakes as her hair. Her irises were solid black with no pupils. Her head and torso were that of a woman, but she was covered in fish scales. Below her waist, she had the body of a large snake with a rattle at the tip of it. She held her bow loosely at her side, and there was a large quiver of arrows strapped to her back.

"Larentina and Corinna could not stop the tears that flowed down their cheeks in sorrow and anguish for this poor creature. Medusa saw their tears and became angry. 'I too wassss beautiful oncessss upon a time ssss. You are the firsssst women ssss to vissssit me sincessss I was exssssiled to this curssssed and forgotten land ssss. The other Gorgon doesssss not possessss ssssspeech or language, ssss sincessss ssssshe was born like thisssss. Perseusssss, your brother, spoke with me a few timesssss, even though he would not look directly at me ssss.'

"Larentina boldly asked, 'Medusa, I must be sure of the story that has been told to me. I believe it is the truth. I was told Poseidon savagely assaulted you in the temple where you were a virgin high priestess to the Goddess Athena. Is this true?'

"Medusa answered, 'Yessss, I wassss. I wassss impregnated by thissss sssssavage act of Poseidon'ssss, and Athena, insssstead of sssseeking justicessss on my behalf, punished me for hisssss actionsssss.'

"Larentina brazenly touched Medusa's cheek and sadly announced, 'That is why we are here: to right the wrong that has been done to you, but it must be your choice.' Larentina looked at Corinna and commanded, 'Corinna, tell her of the one true God, and explain what these creatures are who proclaim themselves as gods.' She then motioned for the others to join them.

"All the Amazon women formed a circle with Corinna, Poulxeria, Larentina, and Medusa. They sat for several hours as Corinna told Medusa about the one true God, the true creator of all, as well as telling Medusa the truth about the false gods.

"Larentina then sadly spoke. 'Medusa, you must make a choice now, for the one true God cannot help you until you let him into your heart; you must truly believe.'

"Medusa started crying as she heard the truth unfold before her. Everyone stood up and joined hands, including Medusa. They all bowed their heads and closed their eyes as Corinna said a prayer, and in that moment, Medusa let God into her heart. When everyone opened their eyes, a bright light appeared from the ceiling of the temple and shone brightly on Medusa; she turned back into the beautiful woman she once was.

"Larentina's heart was filled with love and understanding; as she gazed at Medusa, she proclaimed, 'Wow! You are more beautiful than I had heard.'

"Medusa smiled as she curiously asked, 'What has happened? Let me gaze upon myself.'

"Larentina turned her shield around so that Medusa could see her own reflection.

"Medusa sadly announced, 'The curse is still upon me, for my eyes are still pitch black, but I know what I must do to change that.'

"They all returned to Charon's boat. Persephone was waiting in full view, disguised as a dark-skinned Amazon.

"Almez commanded, 'Wait! Who are you?'

"Larentina grabbed Almez's arm and murmured in her ear, 'Be silent. There are ears and eyes all around us. I will explain who she is when it is safe to do so. Please, Almez, trust me.'

"Almez looked all around her and nodded her head in agreement.

Before Charon allowed them to board, he slowly put out his hand. Princess Poulxeria placed another coin in his hand so he would transport them out of the underworld.

"Once they were in the middle of the river, Persephone changed herself back into her own likeness for a moment, as she commanded, 'Stop, Charon, I command you!' She put her hand forward, gesturing at him to stop. Charon obeyed his queen immediately, stopping the small boat in the water.

"Persephone slowly turned to face Larentina. 'She Wolf, see the flicker of bright light?' She pointed her index finger toward it. 'That is your mother's energy of light, and there you will find her, but you must swim the waters of the damned to free her and bring her back here.

"'Reach deep into your soul, She Wolf, and use just the energy of light that is part of you. Do not tap into the dark side that is also part of you. You must wrap your energy of light around your mother's soul to give her your strength. Do not fear what you see. The moment you allow fear within you, the souls of the damned will consume both of you.'

"Within moments, Larentina's irises turned to a powerful bright white energy.

"In unison, Almez, Poulxeria, and Corinna grabbed Larentina before she dove into the water. Almez turned and grabbed Persephone by both arms and shook her like a rag doll, screaming, 'Who are you? I will kill you if you do not remove the spell you have put upon my friend. Let her go!'

"Persephone quickly removed her hood and transformed herself back into her own physical beauty, just for a moment, so the women could see who she was, and then she shape-shifted back into an Amazon before she whispered, 'I am Persephone, queen of the underworld. This is my payment to your She Wolf for helping to free me from this prison. Let her go before it is too late!'

"Larentina quickly broke free from Corinna and Poulxeria and dove into the blood water and swam toward her mother's soul.

"Corinna and Poulxeria knelt down as they reached as far as they could without overturning the boat, trying to catch Larentina before she was out of reach. Their eyes were wide with fear.

"Persephone solemnly remarked, 'You all should pray to the god you worship for your She Wolf's safe return, because if she does not survive, none of us will. No living being, not even I, has ever done this before.'

"Corinna cried out, 'This is an impossible quest! Her mother died! This is an abomination! It is unnatural!'

"Persephone, with a furrowed brow, spoke angrily. 'Do you consider your precious She Wolf an abomination? I do not believe so, because she is from your realm, but she is also from mine. I believe she is the key that will close and lock the doors between our realms to prevent us from entering yours. This will be her final, most challenging quest, because she will never see Zeus again. Zeus and Larentina must make this choice together. If she does this, I hope to be locked in your realm, not mine, and I will be completely free. I agreed that her mother's death was unnatural because Hera came into Larentina's realm and destroyed Agape. Larentina knows she cannot bring back her mother's entire family, because her energy is not that strong, but she is willing to sacrifice her life as well as all of yours to right a wrong for her mother, her blood. What your She Wolf does not realize is that she will have to kill the man who helped to make her and her brother in order to completely free her mother from this realm. The question will be, can she do this without giving up part of her soul? Because the hand of justice and vengeance combined must be paid in full.'

"The boat started rocking from side to side, as the souls of the damned tried to climb aboard to somehow free themselves from the river. All the women started fighting these creatures, pushing them back into the blood-red water. The souls of the damned were once men and women. They still had their bodies, but they had no skin upon their flesh and bones.

"Corinna screamed as she was being pulled overboard. Persephone waved her hand into the air and used her powers to control their wills, saying, 'Stop! I command you.' The souls sunk back down into the water and their screams stopped as well.

"Persephone frantically commented, 'My powers are not as strong as Hades's. I do not know how much longer I can keep the river from consuming us. I hope Larentina returns soon.'"

* * *

"Larentina felt like she was swimming in mud. It took so much of her strength and energy to swim through the Styx River. The only thing that kept her going was the thought of bringing her mother back to life. For the first few moments, she did not meet any obstacles, because her bright energy seemed to repel the souls of the damned, but they soon grew bolder and started attacking her. Their screams were deafening, and Larentina often found herself lost among them.

"The souls of the damned kept pulling her down as they tried to suck her energy. She fought and broke free. She almost drowned several times, but she did not fear death; she refused to let fear in because her mother would be lost forever. She lost her bearings struggling to the surface for precious air, but she kept swimming toward her mother.

"After fighting for so long, Larentina was slowly pulled deeper under the water by the souls of the damned. She began to drown and almost gave up fighting; she did not have the strength to continue, but she still had a flicker of her will to survive. She struggled again to the surface for air after hearing her mother's voice: 'Larentina, be calm, Daughter; I am here.'

"Even though her mother was a hideous sight to see, because she had no skin on her rotting body, Larentina joyfully grabbed Agape and hugged her tightly. To Larentina, Agape was the most beautiful sight to see.

"Larentina's irises became solid bright white energy once again, but this time the white energy glowed from her entire body. Agape instinctively wrapped herself around her daughter as the energy consumed her. Larentina swam with great strength to the surface, and then Agape wrapped her arms around Larentina's neck as her daughter swam fearlessly to Charon's boat with Agape clinging to her back."

* * *

"The women on the boat cheered as they saw the white glow grow closer and closer to them. The white glow seemed to disperse the heavy fog as Larentina approached the boat. She had survived, but the women were still angry with her because she had put their lives in danger. They gasped at the sight of Agape, but no one dared to say a word about her hideous appearance.

"As Charon continued their journey to the other side of the river, Almez gave Larentina a tongue lashing. 'She Wolf of the Spartans, how could you be so selfish? You put our lives at risk without asking! If you had failed, we all would have been damned here for all of eternity!'

"Larentina answered, with passion in her voice, 'You would not have allowed me to do this. It had to be done. Please forgive me for being so selfish, but you know this has always been a part of me.'

"Corinna offered Larentina a cloak, and she wrapped it around Agape, who was shivering. Larentina looked over to Persephone and remarked, 'Your debt is not yet paid in full.'

"Persephone calmly replied, 'Neither is yours.'

"Larentina became angry. 'Persephone, I swear I will keep my part of the bargain. She will not survive in my realm without her body. Please?'

"Persephone, agitated, answered, 'She Wolf, I told you, it will take both of us to do this. It still may not work, but if you break your word, you will have a new enemy.'

"Larentina solemnly replied, 'Fair enough; let us try.'

"Larentina and Persephone knelt down beside Agape as the rest of the women watched from the bow of the small boat.

"Persephone told Larentina, 'She Wolf of the Spartans and daughter of Agape, you must now use all of your energy, and I will do the same.'

"Larentina's irises became dark maroon as the lightning bolts started flowing within them. Persephone's irises became pitch black with lightning bolts charging through them, and she commanded, 'She Wolf, concentrate on the image of your mother when she was among the living; connect all fleshly manners of her flesh.'

"Electric static started to randomly appear all around the three women. Bursts of bright light emerged. Within moments, the other women saw nothing but white energy around Agape. Then, it became a mist that floated away as everyone looked at Agape. She was a complete woman once again.

"Agape reached over and hugged Larentina tightly, kissing her all over her face gratefully. 'Thank you, Daughter. Thank you, Persephone, the queen of the underworld. Thank you all.'"

Chapter LXXI

"When they reached the shores of the living, Androcles and Lycurgus were waiting impatiently. What seemed to be one day to the women, was actually one month since they left the two Spartan princes.

"Androcles kissed Larentina, and even Lycurgus greeted Poulxeria with a kiss. She savored her first kiss from the Spartan prince. When Lycurgus broke the kiss, he looked at Poulxeria differently; she softly smiled at him, and that was the moment when Lycurgus realized that—for no decipherable reason—he loved her. He had never really loved any of the women he had been with, because he always seemed to compare them to his sister; he did not want a weak woman. Poulxeria possessed strength and courage similar to that of his sister, and maybe that was the reason he looked upon her beauty differently now.

"Androcles voiced his increased impatience. 'Had you not returned at this moment, we were prepared to cross into the underworld to retrieve you.'

"Larentina was puzzled as she spoke, 'But husband we have only been gone for one day. I could have understood your impatience if we had been gone longer.'

"Androcles was confused as well now, 'Larentina, what do you speak of? You have been gone for a month.'

"Larentina just shrugged it off as she spoke her thoughts on the matter, 'I, guess, it does not matter now for we are here in our own time.'

"Lycurgus gazed upon Medusa's beauty; she had her head lowered to the ground so that he could not look into her eyes. He asked, 'So you are Medusa? You are truly beautiful.'

"Medusa continued to look at the ground and commanded, 'Do not gaze into my eyes, for the curse is still within me.'

"Androcles realized that there was an extra Amazon warrior with them, and he asked, 'And who are you? You were not with our party.'

"Larentina warned, 'Not so loud, for there are ears everywhere.'

"Persephone removed her hood so all could see her face as she turned back into herself.

"Androcles asked again, 'Who are you?'

"She answered, 'I am Persephone, daughter of Zeus and Demeter and sister of Larentina.' She transformed herself back into an Amazon.

"Lycurgus and Androcles became annoyed at this bit of information. Androcles did not hesitate and complained, 'Larentina, you have gone too far. If we keep freeing all the deities' children that are your siblings, the gods will realize what we are doing sooner rather than later. You must send her back.'

"Larentina stubbornly commented, 'I have given my word, and I will honor it.'

"Persephone quickly, quietly moved to Larentina and wrapped her arms around her arm, clutching the She Wolf's arm as if her life depended on it. Larentina continued speaking as Androcles and Lycurgus noticed the scared expression on Persephone's face. 'I am truly sorry, Husband, but she wanted freedom and liberty, just as we do. The more people we have, the larger our army is.' She winked, batted her eyelashes at her husband, and gave him a pleading look until his face cracked into a smile.

"Lycurgus, who did not see his sister's wink, simply responded, 'Androcles, she is right. We can use all the bodies we can get to help us defeat these creatures.'

"Androcles, with a sigh, commented, 'I hope you are right.'

"Lycurgus turned his attention to another figure hidden under a hooded cloak, as he voiced his increased annoyance. 'Larentina! Who is this? Did you think we would not notice you have another among you?'

"Agape slowly removed the hood that hid her face. 'Lycurgus, it is I, your mother.'

"Lycurgus could not believe his eyes. He quickly walked to his mother, picked her up, and hugged her tightly as her feet dangled above the ground. He kissed her cheek as he joyfully said, 'Praise God, for returning you to us. How can this be, Mother?'

"Agape smiled because she now had the love of her son. As Lycurgus gently put her down, Agape lightly said, 'And I had to die for you to realize I am your mother.'

"Lycurgus felt remorse as he asked, 'Mother, please, can you forgive me? I should have believed my sister.'

"Larentina interrupted the reunion and announced impatiently, 'It is time to return to Greece.'

"The small group joined hands, linking each other to Larentina so the crystal would return all of them to the shores of Greece. Suddenly, they all became aware of Hades standing in the shallow waters of the River Styx. He stood there with his hands on his hips and angrily said, 'How dare you take my wife? You have gone too far this time, Larentina. It is bad enough you killed my pet, but to take my wife? Who do you think you are? What—how did you retrieve one of my souls from the river? I am so angry with you!'

"Before Hades could say anything else, they vanished from his sight. Hades lost complete control of his temper. He was filled with an uncontrollable rage and was determined to punish Larentina and anyone else around her. He wanted his wife back.

"Hades simply snapped his fingers, and Larentina's entire entourage reappeared before him. He bellowed at Larentina, 'Did you actually think it would be that easy to run from my wrath? Aphrodite's magic is no match to mine!'

"Larentina yelled back, 'You told me to get what I came for, and to get out!'

"Hades shook his head in disappointment and responded, 'I did not mean you could take my wife, silly girl!'

"Persephone was scared to death of Hades, because he was a very strong god. She knew she was no match against him. Her voiced quivered as she chimed in, 'You are the most vile cretin in the universe. I asked Larentina to be my champion. She did not take me against my will. I wanted her to free me. I am not a child any longer; you will not trick me again!'

"Larentina frantically looked around her trying to figure out how to get them out of this one, but Androcles came to the rescue this time. As Hades began to grow, Androcles and Lycurgus ran full speed and jumped on his back, stabbing the god before he grew too big. Everyone followed suit as they, too, thrust their swords into Hades's flesh. Both Spartan princes stabbed him in the eyes, momentarily blinding him, but some unknown force prevented their swords from going any further.

"Hades commanded the fallen soldiers to attack them again, and the souls of the damned emerged from the river. Persephone used her magic and wrapped large roots from the nearby trees around their rotting legs; as the roots grew, they engulfed their entire remains. She even tried to tie

Hades up with the roots, but her magic was nothing compared to his, and it did not work.

"Larentina used the winds, lightning bolts, and hail to hit him. She even had the winds pick up the sand and create soldiers from the sand to attack Hades, but nothing worked.

"As Hades continued to grow, he reached down to pick up Larentina but could not find her. Compared to Hades's enormous size, they all looked like fleas. Hades plucked many of them off him, and they fell into the river.

"Medusa and Agape could do nothing but bite and scratch at his flesh. Since Hades was temporarily blind, Medusa could not even turn him into stone with her gaze.

"Hades thrashed about, waving his hands around in the water, in a futile attempt to crush each one of them in his enormous hands. After a few minutes, he gave up; he eventually found his way onto the shoreline, climbed out of the river, and shrunk to normal size. He turned his head from side to side and yelled, 'My eyes will heal, Larentina, and I will crush you for this.'

"Larentina and the others swam back to shore. Androcles and Lycurgus were the first to reach the shoreline. Before Hades could disappear, Androcles thrust his sword into Hades's side. Lycurgus followed suit and thrust his sword into Hades's upper chest, just missing his heart. Larentina pulled out her sword and, with a single, swift, upward stroke, tried to decapitate Hades. Her strength was no match for his magic. Her strong blow barely pierced his skin. Larentina then thrust her sword into Hades's chest, while Androcles and Lycurgus sliced at each side of Hades's neck, finally severing his head from his body.

"Lycurgus quickly started a fire. The women searched for anything that would burn, throwing branches and other items into the fire until it blazed high. Androcles threw Hades's body into the roaring fire.

"As Larentina reached for Hades's head, Persephone grabbed it. She looked into his eyes as tears fell from her own, saying, 'I am finally free from you! And it took a woman and her champions to do it!' She threw the living head of Hades into another fire that Lycurgus had started. Persephone turned as tears of freedom cascaded down her beautiful cheeks; she hugged and kissed Larentina, saying, 'Thank you. I am grateful and will be beholden to you and your bloodline for all of eternity. I swear it.'

"Once again, everyone joined hands as Semiramis's magic crystal took them back to the shores of Greece once again, where Celeris and the other horses were waiting for them."

Chapter LXXII

"Larentina stood on the beach and gazed out to the sea, thinking about the Amazon ship that Poseidon appeared to have destroyed. As she clutched the crystal tightly in her hands, she called to mind the Amazon women on board, praying for their safe return. Suddenly, the ship reappeared in the exact spot it had been before Poseidon blew it far away. Almez jubilantly rejoiced, 'Praise God, my people have been saved!'

"Their brief moment of celebration was interrupted a few seconds later when General Nikephoros and several Spartan soldiers stepped out from the woods. They casually led their horses toward the group on the sand.

"Larentina angrily asked the general, 'What are you doing here?'

"As usual, the general completely ignored Larentina, but instead he looked at Lycurgus and Androcles as he answered, 'My princes, I am here under direct orders from both our great kings to protect you. It took us awhile to catch up to you.'

"Larentina was on the verge of losing her temper completely, but she contained it as she firmly commanded, 'You will address me, because I'm the leader of this quest, not the princes.'

"General Nikephoros arrogantly guffawed before speaking. 'Still the same old Larentina, who does not know her place. I must admit you have changed my heart to some degree regarding our women, but you still are a woman, and it appears you need to be reminded where your true place is from time to time.'

"General Nikephoros's eyes grew wide as he noticed Agape move forward to stand beside her daughter. She defiantly glared at the general, who acted as if he did not notice her.

"Larentina was filled with hatred, but still she kept her demeanor in check as she asked, 'General Nikephoros, since you are here, might I have an audience with you in complete privacy? This is of great urgency for the safety of Sparta.'

"Naturally, both princes objected to this; Lycurgus asked, 'What is this? You will address all of us regarding any matter of the state. Larentina, we have allowed you to lead this quest, but Nikephoros does have merit; you do go too far.'

"Before Androcles could protest, Larentina smiled and said diplomatically, 'Brother, Husband, fear not, for this only pertains to our great general. I must speak with him in private and allow him to make this decision. It will be up to him to discuss it with you. I do not want this important insight to leak out if Nikephoros deems it of great urgency.'

"Both princes looked at each other, bowed their heads, and spoke in unison. 'Agreed.'

"Agape had a solemn expression upon her face as she thought, *Larentina now knows the truth, and justice will be served any moment.* Nevertheless, Agape felt a twinge of remorse because her daughter had chosen to relinquish part of her soul to free Agape completely from the underworld and achieve vengeance.

"Not only did General Nikephoros still have a puzzled expression upon his face, the entire Spartan warrior party looked confused. General Nikephoros answered nonchalantly, 'Of course; come, we'll walk the shoreline, and you can tell me what troubles you. I have never doubted your intuitive insight.'

"After Larentina and General Nikephoros walked away from everyone's hearing range, she pleaded, 'Please, General, let us continue to walk, for I do not want to be seen either.' The general was still puzzled, but he simply followed Larentina into the woods.

"When Larentina was sure no one could see them, she pulled out her sword and asked, 'Do you know how I came upon this perfectly crafted sword, Nikephoros?'

"The general responded with a question: 'What does your sword have to do with the safety of Sparta? The gods gave you the sword.'

"With her sword held loosely in her hand, she seductively asked, 'May I kiss you for all that you have done for me and for Sparta, before I tell you about the future of Sparta, my future king?'

"General Nikephoros looked puzzled again and said, 'Yes, I would like that. But *I* will be the future king of our land? What about Lycurgus and Androcles?'

"As Larentina kissed the general passionately, she thrust her sword into his stomach and whispered her venom of hatred in his ear. 'This is what your future is, Father. Now you know how a woman feels when she is being assaulted and tricked by you! The only land you will be king of is the land of the damned!'

"As the general pushed her away with shock in his eyes, he grabbed for his sword, but she stabbed him again. He fell to his knees, and she answered her own question as her eyes changed; she wanted him to see what she was. 'My sword was made by mother's husband's own hand. I am truly blessed, for not only did a great mortal man claim me as his seed, but the king of the gods did as well.' Larentina wickedly snickered as she continued her confession. 'Agape thought she could lie to me because the gods gave me other gifts; she lied to me because she desperately wanted to believe it had been Zeus in her bed and not you. She lied, but I'm not so easily fooled. You brutally assaulted her when her husband was still on the battlefield. I do not give a damn if Cupid put some kind of spell upon you. You had no right. You dishonored her and she had to leave King Karpos, who she truly loved. The only man that would take her in was Erasmus, a perioikoi.

"'Agape even fooled her own sister, Alexis, into believing Lycurgus and I were the children of Erasmus, and she also suggested that I was the daughter of Zeus. She lied to me, as well as to the kings of Sparta; she used your seed of brutality to deceive all of Sparta, but what she did not expect was that I, the bastard seed from your treacherous loins, would truly give more liberties to the Spartan women. Yes, Father, I have changed our society.

"'You will die knowing that your mortal daughter deceived the entire world and the Olympian gods. Zeus himself thinks I am one of his children; deception and illusion are what I learned from Aphrodite, Agape, Alexis, and even you, but I will not become like any of you. I am much worse because Aphrodite's own dark energy somehow entered into my soul the moment I was conceived. I am an abomination. I battle every day of my life trying to stay centered between good and evil. Believe me, Father, as I confess, I have lost the battle many times throughout my life. I know I will lose it many more times. Today, I sacrificed the energy of light that is a part of me to pay the debt of vengeance to free my mother. I will walk among the damned for all eternity.

"'It was Agape herself who fed and tamed the wild wolf pack. Apollo lied, because he did not possess the power to tame the beast, but he allowed the illusion. Agape even told how a wild wolf was sleeping on her bed the night I was born. Since I was the daughter of Agape and was trained as a very young child to feed this wolf pack, I became their mistress as well.

"'The Oracle had it all wrong, Father, for when I discovered the truth I vowed to kill you, not King Karpos. Now, you will die with the feeling of being raped by your own flesh and blood, a dishonorable death indeed. There is no glory in this, is there, Father? I am a daughter of duty! To my God, my country, my family. And you are not in the future at all!'

"As she thrust her sword into General Nikephoros's flesh once more, Agape, who had followed them into the forest, appeared and grabbed Larentina's arm, yelling, 'Stop, Daughter! I will not allow you to sacrifice part of your soul for me. I am partly to blame for this, because I used you and your brother to seek vengeance on my behalf. Nikephoros did not destroy my life. I did. I foolishly listened to Bion, who played on my insecurities. I would have killed your brother and you if it were not for my sister and her destiny. Because of me, I changed everyone's true journeys through life. No matter what this man did, he will have to live with his actions for the rest of his life. He loves his kings and has lived in shame since the moment he gave in to Aphrodite.

"'Nonetheless, I am thankful he gave in, because otherwise, Sparta would not have had you and your brother in it. You have changed so much, Larentina, because you fought hard to stay within the borders of the light, and it is your nature to tap into the dark side from time to time, because that is part of you as well. You have used it for the good. Our bloodline was destined to destroy Aphrodite, and I know you already know this. You will not change everything, Daughter, so let General Nikephoros choose his own death.'

"Both women had tears streaming down their cheeks as Larentina healed Nikephoros. He grabbed Larentina and hugged her tightly as he whispered in her ear, 'Agape is true to her word, but I will not allow you or her to suffer any further. You must kill me, for I do not have the strength to do it myself. This is the only way to bring honor back to King Karpos's house. Please forgive me, Agape, for my dishonorable deed, and live in peace. Let my death be swift and noble.'

"Nikephoros dropped to his knees and waited for Larentina's blade. She hesitated as she looked down at her father and lowered her sword, saying, 'I cannot do this. There are so many shades of gray within you, Father, that I did not see before.'

"Nikephoros took Larentina's hand in both of his. 'Larentina, I do not place blame on any other, but be warned, Daughter, Bion is a venomous snake. Remember what I told you, that my discovery of the truth would set me free? You are a Spartan, Larentina, and a daughter of duty and honor.

I command you as your general and father to kill me and my soldiers so that your brother does not discover us. Do it now!'

"Larentina obeyed his order without question, quickly thrusting her sword into Nikephoros's heart, killing him instantly.

"As Larentina stood there silently, remorse crept into her heart, but it was the only way to free her mother and father. Agape quietly hugged her daughter as they both sobbed. She whispered in her daughter's ear, 'We are finally free.'

"Larentina looked into her mother's tear-filled eyes and announced with fury, 'No, Mother, we are not free, not yet!'

"Now Larentina was certain that no one would ever know the truth of her conception, except for one—but she decided to leave that for King Karpos, to see if he truly loved Agape. Larentina feared her brother would go mad if he ever knew the truth, so she ran as fast as she could to the beach. She approached the Spartan soldiers who had accompanied Nikephoros with her sword in hand. When she reached them, she did her trademark assault—she leaped onto the knees of one of the Spartan soldiers and thrust her sword down between his shoulder and neck. Before the other soldiers could strike Larentina with their swords, they were attacked by Androcles, Lycurgus, Poulxeria, and Almez. Within minutes, all the Spartan soldiers had been slain.

"With bloodthirst still in Androcles's eyes, he angrily asked Larentina, 'Why did we have to kill our Spartan brothers?'

"Larentina wiped some of the blood from her face and answered simply, 'It was necessary.'

"Androcles grabbed Larentina by both forearms and shook her angrily, saying, 'That is not good enough!'

"Lycurgus immediately pulled Androcles away from Larentina and punched him in the face. Androcles responded by hitting Lycurgus in the stomach. As a fistfight started, Larentina commanded, 'Enough! I will tell you!' Both men stopped fighting and angrily looked at Larentina.

"Everyone looked at Larentina for an explanation. She told only a small portion of the truth. 'General Nikephoros ordered me to do this because the Oracle had it wrong; it was not Karpos I would kill, but General Nikephoros. It was he who assaulted Agape, and that is why she left King Karpos, because General Nikephoros had dishonored her. Aphrodite helped him by transforming him into the likeness of King Karpos. Then Aphrodite transformed him back into himself so that Agape would know what had happened.'

"After hearing this news, Androcles solemnly said, 'My father needs to know the truth. Agape was the love of his life. He has never really recovered from this.'

"Larentina simply responded, 'Your father will be tested on what kind of king he truly is.'

"Lycurgus chimed in, 'How long have you know this, Sister? Why did you not tell me the truth?'

"Larentina answered, 'I learned this from the muse, Clio. I just did not want to believe General Nikephoros was a dishonorable man, but he died a noble one, sacrificing himself to be freed from the mistakes of his life. We all looked up to him, but someone else within our own government is truly our enemy, and it will be up to King Karpos to choose the direction Sparta shall take.'

"Both Spartan princes nodded their heads in agreement with Larentina.

"Agape finally returned to the group on the beach; out of breath, she asked, 'Larentina, did you tell them?'

"Lycurgus ran to his mother and hugged her.

"Larentina answered, 'Yes, Mother, I told them that it was the general. We cannot give them the name of the traitor, because it will be up to King Karpos to decide who it is.'

"Agape simply nodded her head in agreement."

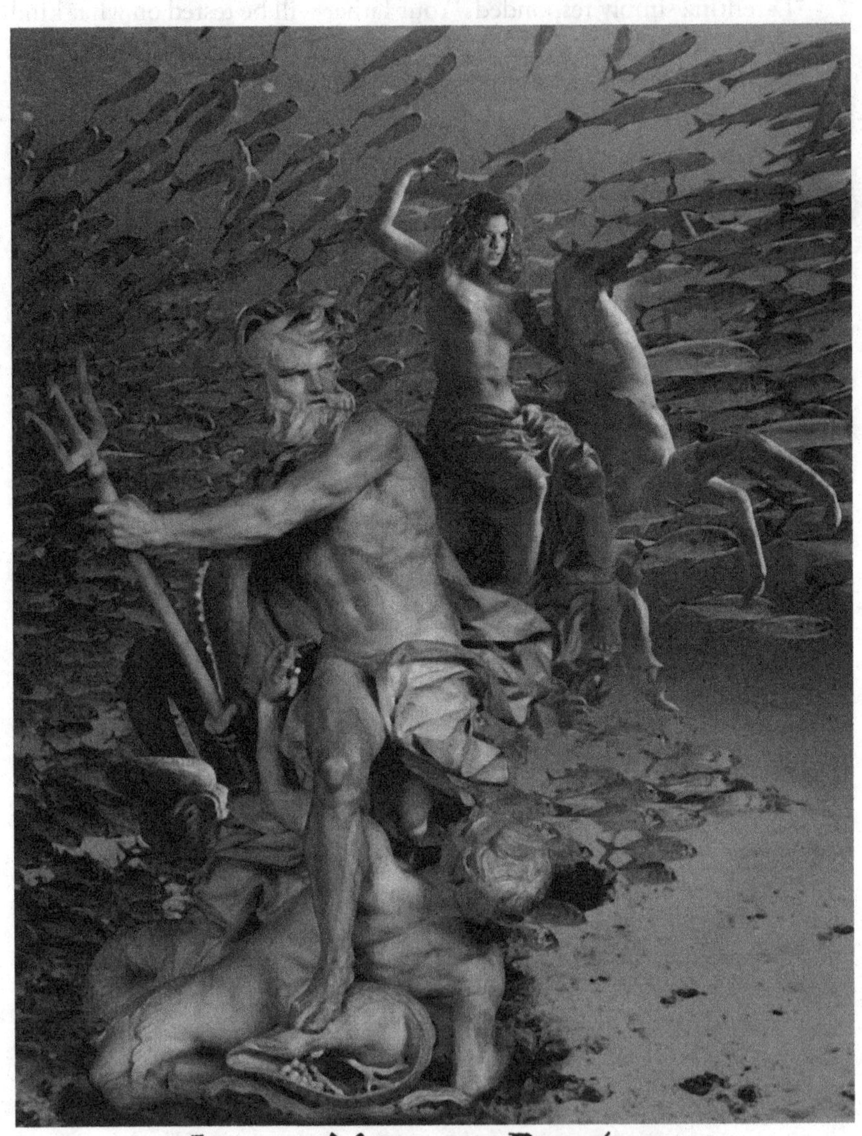

In the Wake of Poseidon

Chapter LXXIII

"As they all boarded the ship, the Amazons already on board gave them looks of confusion, but they said nothing. Almez gave the order, and they sailed into the waters of the deep sea. Almez briefly explained to her people what had happened.

"Medusa then told how Poseidon had created seahorses long ago, and she suggested that they catch a few seahorses to help them get close enough to Poseidon to speak with him.

"They sailed for many months. It was hot, and the ship was dead in the water because there was no breeze. It was a dead calm. They were running low on supplies, and they were completely out of fresh water. There was still no sign of Poseidon.

"All of a sudden, everyone heard bumping sounds against the sides of the ship. The water was still dead calm, so Larentina slowly walked to the side of the ship. She looked down, and there were green horse-faced creatures playfully butting their heads against the ship. They looked like seahorses of today, but they were as big as a full-size horse, and they even made the nickering sounds like a horse.

"Larentina smiled at one horse that pushed itself up out of the sea so that Larentina could reach down and pet its face. She yelled excitedly, 'Medusa! Medusa! Come see! You are right; they are adorable and playful too!' Medusa smiled at her new friend, knowing it was just a matter of time before Poseidon showed himself.

"Medusa kept her eyes closed to avoid the curse that still affected her; she felt the tops of the horses' faces as they bounced up and down out of the water to be petted by Larentina and the others. Medusa's eyes were closed, but she smiled as she pictured what they looked like in her mind. For a moment, she was very happy that another woman had come to her rescue. Even though it had taken hundreds of years, she could not hold that against Larentina; she was glad Larentina's God sent her and gave her mortal body back to her, even though Poseidon would soon come for her.

"Larentina excitedly shouted, 'Oh, look, beautiful mermaids and mermen.' They all came up to the ship presenting them with fresh water, oysters, shrimp, fish, and lobsters. Everyone on board eagerly excepted the gifts.

One of the mermaids asked, 'We heard rumors to look for a Amazon ship because our She Wolf is on board. Are you our She Wolf who will free us from our sea god?"

"Larentina smiled at the beautiful mermaid and simply answered, 'Me and my champions will die trying to return you and your seas back to nature.'

"The merman came up and scolded his wife, 'Noona, you are going to get us killed speaking about Poseidon in that manner. We are only here to feed these great land warriors. Now come we must leave before we are discovered.'

"As Medusa predicted, only a few moments had passed when Androcles saw Poseidon's eyes peeking up from the water, looking at them as they played with his seahorses and speaking with his mermaids and mermen. Androcles excitedly yelled, 'Poseidon! He is here!'

"The mermaids and mermen dove back into the sea and disappeared from sight.

"When she heard this, Medusa jumped overboard and climbed on the back of one of the seahorses, as everyone else watched Poseidon slowly rise out of the sea. He towered over one hundred feet above the ship; the seawaters covered him up to his belly button.

"Poseidon glared directly at Larentina and demanded, 'What magic have you come upon this time, girl? Persephone, what are you doing here? Where is my brother Hades?'

"Larentina looked up at him with no fear and yelled back, 'Where is my father, Zeus?'

"Poseidon guffawed, looked up toward the heavens, and unmercifully mocked Larentina, 'Oh, I think he's tied up at the moment.' Then he wickedly chuckled, completing his answer, 'I guess I had better rephrase that—he is chained up and probably a little drowsy from the poison that Hera served him. Do you not think you better be worrying about yourself about now?'

"Larentina bellowed up at him, ignoring his flippant comments, 'You wanted your precious Medusa back, didn't you? Well, I have brought her to you, in her complete mortal beauty—even though you assaulted her, you nasty beast!'

"Poseidon did not reply, because he was too busy looking for Medusa.

"Medusa yelled up at Poseidon, with her eyes still closed, 'God of the sea, my Poseidon, here I am!'

"Poseidon looked directly down, as he squinted his eyes, and saw the small figure beneath him. He softly said, 'Medusa, you are mortal again. How can this be? Have you decided to be with me?' He gently picked her up and held her in the palm of his gigantic hand. Medusa still kept her eyes closed and did not answer him.

"Poseidon pleaded, 'Medusa, please, won't you look at me?'

"She quickly opened her eyes, which were filled with hatred and vengeance as she transformed back into the hideous creature she had been before escaping the underworld.

"Larentina frantically yelled, 'Lycurgus, Androcles, turn your heads now!' She then looked up at the sight before her and cried, 'No, Medusa! Please, do not do this! There must be another way! Oh no, Medusa—no!'

"Although Larentina lived by the code, "Kill or be killed," she did not understand that God's code was forgiveness, not vengeance; this was a lesson she had not yet learned. It broke her heart to see her friend suffer so greatly from the bitterness and revenge that she harbored in her heart. Larentina did not realize that Medusa was sacrificing herself so the god of the sea would never hurt anyone else again.

"Larentina also believed in an eye for an eye; she believed that you must pay for the wrongs you commit, whether at the hands of God or someone else. She knew that Poseidon must die, but she also felt that this was not what God had intended. Larentina knew this, but she did not yet practice it.

"Poseidon's entire body trembled as he was slowly turned to stone by Medusa's contempt-filled gaze. He balled his hand into a fist and crushed Medusa, breaking all of her bones, but the curse of her gaze was too strong for him.

"As Medusa slowly died from Poseidon's fist, she yelled at the top of her lungs, 'Larentina, thank you for giving me the greatest gift—freedom! Thank you for being my comrade. I will always love you for this gift as a sister, even in death!'

"Larentina passionately yelled back to Medusa, 'This was not my gift. It was the one true God's gift to you. I will see you in heaven someday!'

"The powerful gaze of Medusa held strong even in death. Poseidon's body crumbled into the sea until there was nothing left of either Poseidon or Medusa.

"Larentina started weeping for the beautiful maiden who had been wrongly cursed. Poulxeria sat down beside Larentina, rubbed her back, and softly consoled her, 'Larentina, she chose to sacrifice herself for God, our children, and us, so that we may have a chance at a life without these fallen angels in it. Remember the sacrifice she has made this day.'

"Larentina looked into Poulxeria's eyes and sobbed, 'I know, but it's so unfair.'

"Almez wisely commented, 'Larentina, life is often unfair.'

"Larentina just nodded her head in agreement with Almez.

"Persephone also sat beside Larentina and gratefully hugged her. 'Larentina, I owe you so much. I am leaving you now, but I will not return to Mount Olympus. I will travel the world and mingle with the mortals. Whenever you need me,' she said, removing a ring from her finger, 'I will come to you, as well as your bloodline, for all eternity. Just turn this ring once and I will be there.' She slid the ring onto Larentina's finger, kissed her on the cheek, and simply disappeared.

"Larentina gazed at the beautiful ring on her finger, but she was puzzled by Persephone's heavy promise."

Chapter LXXIV

"It had been many months after Medusa destroyed Poseidon and the young Spartans were still sailing toward their home. There were short bursts of lightning and dark clouds appeared and disappeared. There were loud bursts of thunder and strong winds, and then seconds later, it was calm again. Larentina stumbled to her feet and called, 'Zeus! Father! I hear you!' She frantically ran around the ship retrieving her sword and shield.

"Lycurgus commanded Larentina, 'Stop, Sister! Control yourself. How do we get to him?'

"Larentina stopped running around like a wild woman and answered calmly, 'I do not know.'

"At that very moment, an odd creature appeared before them—it was an Argos, probably the only ally Zeus had left. He had many eyes and carried several dozen lambskin pouches filled with fresh water, which he silently passed out to all who were present.

"The Argos's brother was Hera's ally. He explained that he was Zeus's ally and said that he believed he had the strength to free Zeus from the chains by which he was bound. He emphatically vowed that he would not fight Hera, but he would help free Zeus. He would also carry Larentina to the realm of the Olympian gods.

"The Argos lifted Larentina above his head and carried her into the sky. They flew to the realm of the Olympian deities. Larentina stood at the front of Zeus's palace and looked around; all of Mount Olympus was in flames. Deities fought one another throughout the great streets. Chaos and spilt blood were all about.

"She quickly ran into the great palace and used her telepathy to find Zeus, who she still considered her father as well as an ally. She panicked as she ran through the large rooms, calling, 'Zeus! Father, where are you?' As she opened the great doors to his throne room, she saw him lying spread eagle on the ground. His wrists and ankles were chained. He lay there helpless as he futilely struggled to free himself.

"Larentina became livid as she saw Hera and many of the other deities arguing over who would receive what out of Zeus's domain.

"When Hera saw Larentina, she ran full speed toward Zeus; she held her sword over her head, preparing to chop off Zeus's head before Larentina and the Argos could free him. She was consumed in rage and wanted nothing more than to kill her husband for his deceit and betrayal. As Hera thrust her sword toward Zeus's neck, the sword was met by Larentina's sword, instead of Zeus's flesh. Hera was no match against Larentina, who possessed fighting skills far beyond Hera's. Hera's weapons of choice were deceit and poison.

"Hera frantically pleaded, 'Step aside, Child, I must have justice! You should understand! You are a woman; you belong on my side!'

"As Hera once again attacked Zeus, her sword was blocked by Larentina's sword. Larentina pushed Hera farther away from Zeus and said passionately, 'I know not what you speak of. Nor do I care. You have wronged my family, my people, as well as me, and you deserve to die.'

"Hera ran from Larentina and commanded the other Olympian deities, 'Be my champions! Destroy her!'

"Athena was the one who stepped forward, and she vowed, 'I hate that She Wolf! I will kill her myself! I will be your champion!' She glowered at Larentina.

"As Zeus was freed by the Argos, he became confused and asked, 'Larentina, *you* are my champion?'

"Larentina, now effortlessly fighting against Athena's sword, sounded disappointed as she answered, 'Oh, Father, shame on you. You know you have no other child left who would have the courage to go against your wife, the queen of the gods.

"'You do not love her. Why else would you break your vows to her? You should have known this would happen.'

"Zeus proudly guffawed, as he watched Larentina, his demigoddess daughter, fighting against Goddess Athena, his other daughter. As Zeus snickered, he said, 'I thought I told you I would not interfere in your life's journey. Hera and myself are not your concern.'

"Larentina teasingly replied, as she still engaged in the sword fight against Athena, 'Yes, Father, you did, but you did not command me not to interfere in yours. After all, I owe you this one. It appears to me the almighty Zeus actually needs his mortal daughter's help this time. And, yes, Father, it is my concern because your wife takes her vengeance out on the innocent instead of on you.'

"Athena was livid as she said, 'You! I should be my father's champion, not you! How could you, Father? You little bitch! I'm going to turn you into a gorgon like I did to Medusa, and no one will want you either!'

"Zeus arrogantly snickered as he grabbed Hera by the throat and commanded both his daughters, 'Enough fighting! Put down your swords. I will punish you shortly, Athena.'

"Zeus's orders were too late; Larentina had taken her sword and decapitated Athena. She held the goddess's head in her hands. To Larentina, it had to be done to honor Medusa's memory. Athena deserved death for wrongly putting a curse upon Medusa. Larentina had no other choice because Athena was planning on doing the same thing to her.

"Zeus yelled at Larentina, 'Daughter, what have you done? Put Athena's head down! No matter what she has done, she is still my daughter, as you are.'

"Larentina ignored Zeus; she took a torch and set fire to Athena's body as well as her head.

"Zeus became angry with Larentina and yelled, 'You disobeyed my command, Daughter! Why?'

"Larentina just stood and watched Athena's body turn to ash, as did her head. Zeus took his attention from Larentina as he continued to fight with Hera.

"Larentina humbly said, 'Zeus, you are not my father, but my ally. I beg you: we must close the door to our realms and allow mankind to live without interference.'

"While everyone watched Hera and Zeus, an angel appeared right beside Larentina, startling her. She asked, 'Who are you?'

"The angel smiled at her; everyone remained focused on Hera and Zeus, no one else had noticed his presence. He softly answered, 'I am Gabriel, one of the archangels of our God. You should not be in this realm, nor should these beings be in your realm. God has commanded that the doors to each of these realms be sealed shut for all eternity because of the choice that you have made. You and your bloodline will forever be the key to the doors between these two realms.

"'Remember this, Larentina: there will always be a fight between good and evil. After all, it is humankind's nature. You will always have those who will choose evil over righteousness, and the righteous will always be willing to fight against tyranny. There will always be someone who will try to stifle the greatest gift of all from God: free will. You are all God's children.

"'This means you have the choice to consume anything that God has put on this earth for you, because everything on earth belongs to you—free speech, the freedom to come and go as you please, the freedom to obey God and live by his rules, or obey the rules of the evil one, which in essence is to choose life or death for yourself. No one can make you do anything; always remember, Child, God does not force you to do anything; he only requests your love and your obedience.

"'However, I will state this more clearly: there will always be someone who will try to stifle your gifts, just because you are sentient beings created by God. They will try to stifle free thought; to tell you what is good or bad for you; to dictate how you may or may not worship God; to steal from you because they have less than you; to conquer you and enslave you; to treat you as property. All of mankind are sentient beings, and it is up to mankind to fight for their freedoms because there will always be others who choose to control and dominate, which is evil and vile.

"'You and your bloodline will always be given these gifts, but it will be your choice to use them to help others or not. Do you understand, Larentina?'

"Larentina simply answered, 'Yes, but does Zeus not have a choice in the matter?'

"Gabriel answered, 'No, for he is not from your realm. Now go and live the good and fruitful life that God has given you. Throughout mankind's future, you and your bloodline will always be there to help free those who are willing to die for it.'

"Larentina then found herself back on the beach where the battle had begun over a year ago. She looked up and saw the Amazon ship anchored in almost the same spot it was before. Two rowboats were coming to shore.

"As Androcles and Lycurgus pulled the rowboat onto the shore, she jubilantly ran up and kissed them. Lycurgus asked, as he smiled from ear to ear, 'Larentina, how did you get here? Did you use the crystal again?'

"Larentina answered, 'No, Gabriel the archangel sent me back. How did you get back here so fast?'

"Androcles chuckled as he kissed his bride and then answered, 'Zeus, with his winds—within minutes, we found ourselves here.'

"Lycurgus was still smiling and said, 'Oh, Zeus wanted me to say thank you, and you already know why you will never see him again. He said that you would understand.'

"Larentina let out an exhausted sigh. 'Yes, I will have to tell all of you the story someday."

"Larentina turned around to the large rock and crushed the crystal pendant to pieces. Then she walked slowly toward Celeris. She kissed her horse and rubbed his neck. She removed his saddle and all his equipment. She kissed him once again and then, with tears streaming down her face, commanded, 'Go home to your realm, Celeris, for you do not belong in mine. You were the greatest horse I ever had, and I will never forget you, but it is time for you to fly home and be free in your own lands.'

"Celeris looked at his mistress with sad eyes, nickered at her, nuzzled his wet nose against her face, and then he took off into the air. With sorrow, they all watched him fly into the heavens.

"Androcles stood behind Larentina and wrapped his arms around her waist. He rested his head on top of hers and whispered, 'It's time to go home to our beloved Sparta.'

"Larentina rested the back of her head on his chest as she sadly murmured, 'Sparta is not my country; it never was. Lycurgus and I will rule our own nation someday, for we can never return.'

"Androcles became angry. 'What do you mean? It does not matter to me that you are not of the house of Agiad; you still are a Spartan.'

"'Lycurgus sadly stated, 'Androcles, you are a prince and of royal blood. Your life was all truth, but ours was nothing but a lie. The gerousia council will surely execute the both of us, and there is no way the kings can stop that.'

"Poulxeria also spoke to Androcles with wisdom. 'Androcles, Lycurgus speaks the truth. We all made a vow on this very beach; we will have to create our own nation.'

"Androcles let out a heavy sigh and said sadly, 'You all are right, my home is with Larentina's heart, but I thought after this battle we would go home as heroes.'

"Lycurgus solemnly said, 'We would never be free, and I still believe they would execute Larentina and me, even though it was not our doing.'

"Androcles commanded with conviction, 'Then we will sail to Gytheiro, say our good-byes to our families, and return Agape to my father.'

"No one dared to take that from him. The following day a messenger was dispatched to Sparta."

* * *

"Larentina and Androcles casually walked the shoreline further away from their entourage until they were no longer in sight.

"Androcles picked up a sea shell and covered Larentina's ear with it.

"Larentina giggled, 'I can hear the sea from it.'

"Androcles softly smiled as he put his hands around her waist. Larentina dropped the sea shell as Androcles passionately kissed her, 'God help me, Larentina, for I love you. I love you so much, I have even given up my family and country so that I can spend the rest of my life with you.'

"Larentina lovingly gazed into Androcles's beautiful blue eyes as she confessed, 'I too love you, my husband, with all my heart. I am truly blessed to have you sacrifice so much for me.'

"They kissed passionately again. Larentina then slowly removed her clothing as Androcles's soft gaze was upon her. She blushed as she giggled, 'Too much serious talk, Husband. Instead, let us enjoy this moment between husband and wife.' She kissed him quickly and ran into the ocean still giggling.

"Androcles laughed with pure delight to her meaning, he quickly removed his clothing and joined her.

"Androcles swam all around Larentina because he was teasing her. After a few moments he let her catch him and they made love until the sun set."

Chapter LXXV

"A few days later, they arrived in the port of Gytheiro, and a messenger was immediately dispatched to Sparta. Within several hours, King Alcaeus, King Karpos, their queens, and Androcles's siblings greeted everyone who had been onboard the Amazon ship. Agape remained hidden until the news of her return was revealed because no one knew how King Karpos would react. Everyone celebrated, but no one talked about Larentina and Lycurgus returning to Sparta.

"Queen Alexis had brought Agape's youngest daughter, who broached the subject. The young girl hugged Larentina tightly and asked, 'May I go with you, Sister?'

"Larentina sadly answered, 'I'm sorry, Child, but you belong with our mother. I am a queen with no nation to rule.' Naturally, no one understood Larentina's true meaning.

"King Alcaeus put his hand on top of the young girl's head and proudly proclaimed to her, 'I will raise you as I have raised your sister; I will make you my ward. You will grow up and become a strong Spartan woman, just like your sister, Larentina.'

"Larentina rubbed Queen Alexis's tummy. Queen Alexis chuckled, 'I have only been with child a month, Larentina. The baby is not strong enough to feel him yet.'

Everyone celebrated and suggested names for the unborn child.

"Androcles spoke to his father privately and broke the news regarding Agape; he told him the entire story as he knew it.

"Queen Irene, who had been listening beside her husband, announced, 'Karpos, your heart has always been with her. I will return to my father's house, because Agape is your wife. I never was. I would rather be loved by a common man than be queen to a king whose heart belongs to another.'

"King Karpos angrily blurted out, 'Why did Agape not tell me? Where is she? I want to speak with her now!'

"Androcles told his father where she was hidden. Karpos went below the deck, yelling with excitement, 'Agape! Where are you, my love?'

"Agape opened the door and ran into Karpos's arms. Tears welled in their eyes as he lifted her into his arms. As her feet dangled above the ground, they kissed passionately for several minutes. As tears streamed down the great and powerful king's cheeks, he sobbed, 'My love, why did you not tell me? I would have been your champion, not your murderer. Did you have such little faith in my love for you? I would have died for you. I would have killed for you. I would have even started a civil war among our people for you. Instead, you allowed me to believe you betrayed me. You took my heart with you when you left. You gave no reason.

"'I knew Larentina was yours in the depths of my heart, but I just could not find myself to believe it. The wild fire that burned in our She Wolf's eyes burns in yours as well. Your fire is wild and free, whereas your sister's fire is tamed and controlled. How did you think Alcaeus and I could tell the two of you a part? You have always been a part of me. You were my reason for breathing. I have been dead since you left me.'

"With total remorse in her heart, Agape said, 'I was told that you would not have believed me, that you would have had me killed.'

"King Karpos kissed Agape passionately once more as he gently let her feet touch the ground. He showed his anger and asked, 'Who told you this? I will cut his tongue out.'

"Agape answered, 'Larentina has forbidden me to reveal who he is. She is protecting me because you must be tested by her. She says if you truly love me, then you will be willing to be tested, and the truth will reveal who the true traitor is. The choice must be yours and yours alone.'

"Karpos became annoyed. 'I do not need to be tested by your daughter, Agape. Instead of telling me the truth, you give Sparta your daughter? A She Wolf of the gods to test Spartan men's hearts? Has this been your revenge, to put a She Wolf among us to prey off of men's hearts?' Karpos guffawed as he shook his head side to side. 'Only my true queen would punish us like this, and well deserving. The chaos and mischievousness of Larentina have truly changed Sparta as well as my own heart. Very well, if I must be tested, then so be it. I know my reward will be your heart once again.'

"Agape and Karpos kissed passionately once more as Agape softly said, 'Your reward is not my heart, Karpos, because you always had that; it is a chance to show the world that you are willing to be my champion.'

"Karpos picked up Agape and carried her across the threshold of the room that Agape came from. They made passionate love for several hours.

"When Agape and Karpos emerged from below deck, Queen Alexis ran to her sister and hugged her tightly. Everyone smiled to see Karpos and Agape together once again."

* * *

"On the second day the Spartan kings and their families were visiting their children on the Amazon ship, an elderly man, who was escorted by a young beautiful woman, came onboard the ship.

"Everyone abruptly stopped their conversations as the elderly man announced, 'I am the Prophet Jeremiah from the land of Israel, and this is Princess Tamar Telphi. We have come from Egypt seeking Tamar's older sister, Corinna, who was taken away when she was just a small child.

"'We have been chosen by our God to carry the scepter of Judah and the stone of destiny to some unknown islands that are beyond the seas. I was guided to this port in hopes that she is on this strange ship because she, too, was chosen to protect the scepter of Judah and the stone of destiny.'

"Corinna quickly stepped forward and greeted her long-lost sister with hugs, kisses, and tears. All onboard praised God for the reunion.

"Corinna then told them what had happened to her mother. She explained that her mother died shortly after Larentina's birth, but before she died, she told Corinna who they really were and where they came from. As tears of joy flowed down her cheeks, Corinna told them how she had prayed every day since her mother's death that someone would someday rescue her and return her to the land of her birth, where she would once again be free. Instead it had been Larentina, the She Wolf of the Spartan people, who had freed her.

"Jeremiah told them some of the prophesies that led them to the ship. He also explained that the Spartans had been chosen as well, and they would become the rulers of this new nation and protectors of the scepter and stone as well. Their races would become mingled and ultimately create a new nation together.

"To convince the skeptical Spartans, Corinna, Jeremiah, and Princess Tamar Telphi, each in turn, told more of the legends and prophesies of their lands, until Larentina stood up and announced, 'You do not need to convince me any further, for I now know more truth of your God's design.

"'Gabriel spoke with me, and I believe this is my destiny. I will go with you to these unknown islands of which you speak. I swear my allegiance, throughout my lifespan only, to protect these objects that you speak of, but my first allegiance, as well as my bloodline, will be to protect free will, righteousness against tyranny, and good versus evil. This is the destiny of my bloodline always and forever. Do you understand?'

"Jeremiah was the only one to speak; with seriousness in his tone, he answered Larentina, 'You are a wise woman of such a young age. Yes, I completely understand your meaning, and now I understand why the Spartans were chosen for such a dangerous task that will take a lifetime to complete, but you do not understand the importance of these objects.'

"Larentina let out a heavy sigh. 'I do understand the importance to you. These objects mean nothing to me, for to me they are just objects. Understand, Jeremiah of Israel, not everyone believes in such things, and I fear they will be forgotten through the sands of time, but freedom will never be forgotten; it will always be fought for. It has always been mankind's destiny to better themselves and to fight for their God-given gifts: free will, freedom, and so much more. There will always be someone who tries to take these great gifts from us, and I, as well as my bloodline, will be there to help with others to give mankind a fighting chance, always and forever; this has been my vow to the one true God.'

"Almez became upset after hearing this discussion. After the three Spartans, with the blessing of their parents, decided to go with Jeremiah to create this new nation, she voiced her feelings. 'But Queen Poulxeria, we have just found you. You belong with your true people as our ruler.'

"Poulxeria pointed out her insight regarding this matter. 'Almez, the descendant of my ancestor's sister, you are just as deserving. I do not know your ways. I am not a leader, but you are.

"'I feel I am neither Amazon nor Mycenaean; I belong with my future husband, Lycurgus, and want to rule by his side until we are parted by death.

"'You are the rightful queen of the Amazon nation. You are the one who should rule, not me.' Poulxeria took off the belt of Ares and presented it to Almez, saying, 'You are the true queen and should be the wearer of this belt. Please take this; use it to rule wisely and fairly.' Almez took the belt and put it on. She then hugged and kissed Poulxeria on each of her cheeks and simply said, 'Thank you. I swear I will rule wisely and fairly.'

"Almez, in turn, hugged and kissed Larentina on both cheeks. Almez simply made a vow to Larentina. 'I did not pay you back for saving my life as well as several of my warriors. I vow that someday, someone in my bloodline will honor my vow to one of your descendants.'

"Larentina chuckled as she teasingly responded to this vow. 'Fair enough; I expect your descendants to honor it also.' Everyone laughed.

"King Alcaeus spoke, and everyone became silent as they listened to the great Spartan king. 'This has been a wise decision for both my children, and I will miss both of you. Even though the truth has been revealed to me, I still consider you my children, and I love you as such.

"'Larentina, you have changed Spartan ways; the Spartan women will always be grateful to you for increasing their freedoms. You have our Spartan men looking at our women not as property, but as the human beings they truly are. Thank you for this gift.' King Alcaeus hugged Larentina, and he kissed her on both cheeks.

"King Alcaeus voiced his insight to Lycurgus. 'You have been a wiser man than I, and you have taught me things that I thought I already knew. You will always be my firstborn, and I want you to rule these new lands wisely and peacefully, a luxury that I as a Spartan do not have.'

"Lycurgus replied, 'Yes Father, but I will rule equally with Androcles, my sister, and my future wife, Poulxeria.' King Alcaeus nodded his head in agreement and hugged his son good-bye.

"Queen Alexis hugged both Lycurgus and Larentina and simply requested, 'Please do not forget me or your mother. Remember we always will be your family. Thank you both for giving me a new life and future.'

"Agape, with tears streaming down her cheeks, first hugged and kissed Lycurgus and then did the same with Larentina. 'I love you both for sacrificing so much for me and making my life whole again; to live and love again. I hope to see you both before I leave this earth once more.'

"King Karpos hugged Androcles, and they too said their good-byes. The Spartan kings and their family disembarked from the Amazon ship. Although they tried to remain stoic, many tears flowed because they all knew they would never see their beloved children again.

"The following day, Androcles, Lycurgus, Poulxeria, Larentina, Corinna, Tamar Telphi, and Jeremiah bid their farewells to Almez. There were not as many tears this time, although Larentina shed a few. She smiled through her tears because she knew in her heart that she might see her Amazon friends again.

"They all watched as the great Amazon ship sailed off into the sea. Larentina looked at Poulxeria and asked, 'How could you give up being ruler of your own people?'

"Poulxeria softly smiled; she put her arm around Lycurgus's waist as she answered, 'The love for a great Spartan warrior. This is what God has given me.'

"Lycurgus said nothing but kissed Poulxeria passionately. After hearing this, Larentina simply smiled as Androcles kissed her too. Larentina then looked once again at Poulxeria as she confirmed Poulxeria's answer with a sly grin. 'This is true, my sister; I understand completely.'

"After they resupplied Jeremiah's ship with food, water, and other provisions they would need, Jeremiah and his crew shared the gifts of wine, cheese, and meat that had been given by the pharaoh of Egypt. Three weeks later, they set sail to Rome."

Chapter LXXVI

"When the two Spartan kings and their families returned to Sparta a few weeks later, they found themselves being questioned in the assembly hall as if they were traitors. King Alcaeus demanded, 'What is the meaning of this? I am king of the Agiad house! How dare you arrest my wife and put me on trial as if I am a traitor to Sparta? I do not need permission from you or anyone to leave Sparta! My comings and goings are none of your damn concern! And you will release my queen immediately. I command this! She is with child and bears the heir to my throne!'

"King Karpos had found himself in similar circumstances as he voiced his confusion, 'How dare you drag me from my home like some kind of criminal? My son is not a deserter! He left with my blessing with his new queen. He is now king to his own nation! I do not know where they have gone. Queen Alexis did not murder anyone!'

"The apella decided to keep the two kings and their families under house arrest until Queen Alexis gave birth to King Alcaeus's heir. They would continue to investigate the kings and their families until the gerousia council found proof that they were traitors or not.

"This was a thorn in Bion's side because he wanted to see both houses destroyed; he planned to rebuild them himself because the kings had become weak and caused Sparta to become weak with them, by allowing women to rule them.

"King Alcaeus managed to get a secret message dispatched to Larentina, Lycurgus, and Androcles. They were their only hope, because the kings could not act against the council, but their children could.

"During the trials which will take many months, the Spartan military legions were already dividing into two camps, one for the kings and one for the gerousia council. Sparta's unrest was becoming more visible each day the trials continued, with rocks being thrown at many of the gerousia council members as well as the kings.

"One day, Bion asked King Karpos, 'Did you or did you not know that Agape was having an affair with General Nikephoros?'

"King Karpos now realized that Bion had been the traitor Larentina referred to; he answered, with hatred laced in his tone, 'It was you who told Agape I would kill her if I found out about that! You lied, and I will see you die by my own hand! You are the traitor to Sparta, not I! You knew Nikephoros assaulted Agape, and yet you kept it a secret from me! Our She Wolf just told me the truth, but she did not give me the name of the traitor and ordered Agape not to tell me either! She told me I would discover who it was, and now I know! You, sir, are a lying son of a bitch!' It took every ounce of discipline for King Karpos to control his anger and to stop himself from killing Bion where he stood.

"When the apella heard this, they began screaming for Bion's head. Before he knew it, King Karpos pointed at Bion and commanded two Spartan soldiers, 'Arrest this traitor, now!' The two soldiers followed the orders of their king, after hearing this new truth.

"King Karpos was greeted with loud cheers when he mentioned the Spartan She Wolf, who was still loved by most, and the gerousia council had no other choice but to drop the charges against him.

"The charges against King Alcaeus were also dropped, but Queen Alexis and Queen Agape remained on trial for lying to King Alcaeus and all of Sparta, as well as for murdering Andreas after Queen Alexis gave birth. Even though King Alcaeus and King Karpos gallantly argued with the gerousia council on behalf of their wives, the gerousia found them guilty and ordered them to be executed.

"There were boos and cheers throughout the assembly hall. The kings looked at each other and feared that they would not be able to control the increasing civil unrest. They both prayed to Larentina's God in secret, to give them strength to keep their country together.

"King Karpos went to see Bion, who was now imprisoned. He looked at Bion with disgust and asked, 'Why did you not tell me? I trusted you. I thought you were my friend. I even loved you as a brother. My friend, Nikephoros, must have hated me so, to destroy the love of my life.'

"Bion arrogantly snickered as he said, 'You silly fool, she makes you weak, just as Alexis makes Alcaeus weak. I made Agape hate all of you. Sparta has been destroyed because of these ambitious whores.'

"King Karpos grabbed Bion by the throat and started choking him, but he was interrupted by King Alcaeus, who grabbed his friend and yelled, 'Stop, Karpos, you will soon have your revenge!'

"Bion rubbed his neck and sarcastically laughed, saying, 'You are both fools, for Lycurgus and Larentina are the seed of Nikephoros. Your precious She Wolf knows this, and I already discovered she killed him for it. I will die laughing at you, Karpos, because your son married your traitor's daughter.'

"Now King Alcaeus became enraged, as he gritted his teeth and said with contempt, 'You lie, because Lycurgus and Larentina were born the same night Alexis gave birth to lifeless children. I did not even know Alexis was with child until I received word on the battlefield. I was the one who relieved Karpos from the battlefield; there is no way Nikephoros could have assaulted Agape during that time because I checked on her before I left. She said nothing.'

"Bion insincerely chuckled as he arrogantly confessed, 'You are a fool. Remember Nikephoros came back before Karpos to escort you to the battlefield. Nikephoros had been lusting over the twins for years. He prayed to Aphrodite and she helped him. Nikephoros did not care which twin he got because he lusted for both of them, like most men, and when the opportunity presented itself, with Aphrodite's powers of seduction, he simply took Agape behind Karpos's back. Aphrodite changed him into the likeness of Karpos. I even thought it was Karpos who had returned.

"'Agape came to me soon after, because she believed that Karpos would avenge her. I convinced her otherwise because she had given herself to Nikephoros willingly. Soon after the deed, Aphrodite turned Nikephoros back into his own likeness. Aphrodite watched in delight as fear and shame flooded over Agape's face when she realized what had happened.

"'Agape ran to her sister for help and, instead, was somehow helped by Erasmus. How Agape fooled him, only the gods know.

"'Nikephoros vowed his allegiance to me to keep the secret, and he broke his vow the day he threatened me in Olympia. I never thought Larentina would survive agoge; who would have known? Larentina even had me fooled for some time. She even fooled Zeus himself. I do admit Nikephoros's children possess some type of magical power, but she is gone, and it's time to clean house, because even if she is Zeus's daughter, she does not have his protection any longer. She will never return in fear of being executed.'

"Both kings drew their swords and stabbed Bion together. As Bion was dying, Karpos bent down and said in a low, deadly tone, 'You are wrong, Bion, for Larentina is the daughter of Zeus, and that has been your downfall. You forget that she is my wife's daughter. She Wolf herself retrieved my true love from the dead and brought her back to me. Only a powerful goddess who came from the king of the gods could accomplish such a feat. As you die, know this: it will be Alcaeus and I who reunite Sparta once again.'

"Alcaeus bent down to Bion's other ear and defiantly murmured, 'All that you speak of does not matter, because Larentina and Lycurgus have been, and always will be, my children.' Both kings in unison thrust their swords into Bion's body once more. The kings looked at each other and nodded their heads in an unspoken agreement.

"Early the following morning, long before the sun rose, Queen Alexis gave birth to a strong, healthy boy. Her fate was already sealed, and King Alcaeus kissed his queen. The gerousia council, with several Spartan soldiers, allowed her to clean herself and dress soon after she gave birth.

"King Alcaeus washed Alexis himself. As he slowly washed her with a warm cloth from the basin of water, tears trickled down his face. Alexis put her hand on Alcaeus's cheek and kissed him ever so lightly, as tears streamed down her cheeks as well. She sadly confessed to King Alcaeus, 'I did it for you, my husband, and for Sparta. If I had not, we would not have had the honor and privilege of having Larentina and Lycurgus in our lives. I fear Larentina will not be able to save me this time.

"'They have done so much for Sparta, and I wish I was not being punished for it. Know this, my husband, my king: I have always loved you. Death cannot keep us apart because our love is so strong; we will be reunited someday. I want you to love and have many more children; something that I could not give you except for this one time.'

"Alcaeus kissed Alexis passionately and looked into her eyes; as tears still streamed down his face, he said, 'How will I live without you, my love, my queen, my life? I cannot love any other, for I only know of you; nor do I want any other.'

"King Alcaeus had his arms around his wife as she held their newborn son. One of the gerousia members walked into the king and queen's bedroom and, with a twinge of empathy, simply said, 'We will do this at first light, so my king, you may spend one more night with her.'

"King Karpos found himself in the same position and pampered Agape on their last night together."

Chapter LXXVII

"When Larentina and her companions arrived in Rome, they completely were unaware that Agape and Queen Alexis were about to be executed.

"In Rome, Lucius, now king of the Roman Kingdom, greeted them with a great celebration; Larentina was honored for her wit and cleverness in destroying the tyrannical King Servius and freeing Rome from his cruelties almost two years ago.

"Lucius's wife, Queen Tullia, had given birth prematurely and died afterward before the Spartans arrival; the baby, however, was still strong and healthy. Larentina was recently with child, and Lucius asked Larentina if she would be his wet nurse so his son would have the strength of the She Wolf. Larentina happily obliged, even though her child was not due for many months. She was blessed with plenty of milk, and no matter how hungry the infant was, she never ran dry.

"The Spartan soldiers who had been sent as messengers by King Alcaeus arrived at Lucius's palace. After giving the king's message to Larentina, they explained everything that was happening in Sparta.

"Travel arrangements were made immediately. Lucius provided Larentina with his fastest ship. He also provided her with a military escort of thirty of his strongest and bravest soldiers.

"The two young Spartan princes did not want any other outsiders coming to Sparta, so they decided to have Poulxeria and the others wait for their safe return under the protection of King Lucius.

"Poulxeria protested, 'But Lycurgus, I belong with you and Larentina. Larentina, is with child; I must be there to protect her. She is my queen!'

"Lycurgus gently hugged Poulxeria and kissed her forehead as he whispered in her ear, 'It is better that you stay here, my love. I fear for your safety because of the turmoil awaiting us in Sparta. Trust me when I say, Larentina is quite capable of not only protecting herself, but her unborn child as well. There must be one left behind to tell our story.'"

* * *

"As they sailed toward Sparta, Larentina confessed to Lycurgus and Androcles in private, 'I did not expect this. I thought it was over.'

"Lycurgus said, "Why has Bion stooped so low? Does he not even care that he is causing the destruction of Sparta?'

"Androcles voiced his concerns. 'None of us knew it would go this far, but we must stop this before both kings lose all control.'

"Lycurgus stated, 'I pray it is not too late.'

"Larentina wept, as she said, 'All our sacrifices to keep Sparta safe have been for naught. To give the desired freedoms to our women, and now Bion and the gerousia are setting us back in time. I feel I have lost the battle.'

"Lycurgus proclaimed, 'We will seek justice!'"

Chapter LXXVIII

"A strong wind sped Larentina, her brother, and her husband toward Sparta. Larentina knew that if Queen Alexis had not given birth yet, she soon would.

"Larentina was crying as the wind blew through her hair, and she watched the rough waters in front of them. Androcles came up behind her and wrapped his arms around her waist. Lycurgus stood beside her with a solemn expression.

"Larentina, still crying, leaned her head back onto Androcles's chest as she angrily confessed her emotions. 'What good am I as a She Wolf of Sparta, if we can't save our mothers and fathers? I have been given these great gifts; for what? If Alexis and Agape had not done what they did, Lycurgus and I would not exist. I swear that if they harm one hair on their heads, I will kill them all! Alexis only acted for King Alcaeus and for Spartan women, and Agape acted for justice and vengeance. They do not deserve this dishonorable death. My father will be brokenhearted and will not want to live, if they do not kill him. I swear on everything that is holy, if they destroy my blood, they will pay a heavy price!'

"Androcles vocalized his emotions. 'My father is a great and powerful man; he will die defending Agape.'

"Before they knew it, the ship was traveling down the Eurotas River and was just moments away from Sparta. Before it even dropped anchor, Larentina jumped off the boat onto the dock. Androcles and Lycurgus were right behind her. It was shortly after midnight; all of Sparta was asleep.

"Larentina, Androcles, and Lycurgus went directly to the small jail, expecting to find their fathers. Instead, they discovered Bion's body still lying in the cell. It was a recent kill, and they realized their fathers must have killed him earlier in the evening; the bodies of several soldiers were scattered in the jail from a heated sword fight. The other prisoners pleaded to be set free, but the young Spartans ignored them.

"Larentina commanded frantically, 'Our parents must be still alive! We will go and save them now!'

"Androcles forcefully grabbed Larentina's forearm and softly spoke, 'Larentina, stop. We are cloaked in darkness and have the edge of surprise. Let us first seek justice and punish the traitors. We must kill all our fathers' enemies now. Do you know who the others are?'

"Lycurgus acknowledged this, 'Larentina, Androcles is right, we have the element of surprise at this moment. We do not know for sure if our parents are still alive.'

"Larentina said nothing but nodded her head in agreement with the two princes. She calmly walked back to Bion's body as her eyes changed. She kneeled beside his body and took his lifeless hand in hers. She put her open hand on his forehead and she intensely stared into his open eyes.

"Androcles puzzled, asked, 'What are you doing Larentina? He is dead; he cannot give you the names of the other traitors now.'

"Larentina looked up at her husband as she answered, 'Shuuu, my husband. Yes, he can. His mind is slowly dieing, but it is still alive. I will get the answers from him.'

"As Larentina continued staring into Bion's lifeless eyes she spoke out all the names of the traitors to Androcles and Lycurgus; which ephors and gerousia members were involved in spying and reporting to Bion. The three Spartans headed off with equal amounts of Roman soldiers, so they could round up the traitors involved more quickly, and they planned to meet at the assembly hall.

"After a couple of hours, they had gathered all who were involved. They were each gagged with an apple in their mouth.

"As the ephors and council members, still in their night garments, looked at Larentina in fear, she whispered with contempt in her voice, 'You will die this night as the swine you all are.'

"They took each prisoner and shoved their spears through their hearts, killing them instantly. They impaled each and every one of them, with their bodies dangling from their long spears in front of the assembly hall for all to see.

"After they completed their bloody task, Lycurgus commanded the Roman soldiers to return to Gytheiro and wait for them. Larentina dipped her finger into the dead men's blood and wrote on the wall of the assembly hall, 'All who see this, know this: if you act like a swine, then you will die like one!' Then she signed it, 'She Wolf of the Spartans.'

"The sun was now beginning to rise; when Larentina saw the hangman's noose, she gasped as tears began streaming down her cheeks.

"Lycurgus saw it as well; he hugged her and soothingly whispered, 'Fear not, Sister, for I do not think they have been hung yet.'

"Androcles commanded, 'Come, Larentina and Lycurgus, we are closer to my father's home. We will go there and find out what has happened.'

"The three young Spartans ran as fast as their legs could take them before the sun had completely risen above the summit. They were met by King Karpos's coach, which was on its way to deliver Agape to the gallows, escorted by several Spartan warriors.

"When the three young Spartans stopped the coach, King Karpos emerged and wielded his sword to fight the guards. Androcles, Larentina, and Lycurgus joined in the fight, and it was over within minutes. Agape ran into her daughter's arms as Karpos and the two princes discussed how they could save King Alcaeus and Queen Alexis."

* * *

"When morning dawned, two Spartan soldiers entered the bedroom of Queen Alexis and King Alcaeus. Alcaeus went for his sword, but the soldiers stopped him. They held tightly to Alcaeus's forearms as he struggled to be free.

"Alexis handed her baby to her helot and slowly walked to Alcaeus; she softly put her hand on his face and sadly murmured, 'This is the will of the gods, my husband; not even our She Wolf will be able to save me this time. I must die so you may be free. Rule your kingdom wisely, and reunite Sparta; this is the only way. Be at peace, my king, my love.' She kissed Alcaeus once more.

"Alcaeus slumped to the floor, a broken king. The soldiers escorted them to the king's coach, which took them to the great assembly hall. As they approached the center of Sparta, they could hear a great commotion. Alcaeus heard his queen gasp, and he looked up to see dozens of Spartan citizens screaming in the streets and fleeing from the grounds of the assembly hall. Then he saw the bodies of the gerousia council members and the ephors impaled on spears outside the great hall. Alcaeus smiled with delight as he realized his daughter and son had returned to seek justice for his house. He immediately regained his strength and will to live.

"King Alcaeus had wept for his beloved queen just a few hours prior, but he now knew his daughter and son would seek justice on his behalf.

It was just a matter of time before his children returned power to the two kings of Sparta.

"Instead of Spartan citizens awaking in the morning hours to see their queens executed for treason, they beheld the bodies of their gerousia council members dangling from spears in the street.

"All of Sparta now knew their She Wolf had returned to demand justice against the dishonorable ones who tried to execute the Spartan queens, and there was panic and chaos in the streets because of this unholy sight.

"King Alcaeus jumped out of the carriage and then helped his wife out. He looked over and saw King Karpos, who winked at him and threw him a sword. King Alcaeus turned and killed the gerousia council member before he even stepped out of the carriage. As he prepared to fight the Spartan soldiers, the soldiers dropped on one knee and bowed before their king. One soldier looked up at King Alcaeus and vowed, 'My king, we pledge our allegiance to you and to Sparta. Please have mercy upon us.'

"King Alcaeus commanded, 'Rise, soldiers of Sparta, for you were doing your duty.'

"Larentina ran to her father and hugged him and her mother. King Alcaeus chuckled as he said, 'It's about damn time the three of you showed up to protect your houses's honor.'

"King Karpos proudly patted Androcles on the back as they all laughed at Alcaeus's joke.

"King Alcaeus commanded his daughter, 'Now instill fear among our people, so that Karpos and I can control them once again. Go, Larentina, now!'

"Larentina drew her sword and ran to the top step of the assembly hall.

"A nasty storm had moved in quickly, and Larentina looked at the sky and decided to use nature to her advantage. With sword in hand, she raised her arms to the heavens; she yelled in a thunderous voice, 'Spartan people, hear me well this day, for my wrath is strong and powerful!'

"The winds became stronger, thunder and lightning bolts began to cascade from the sky. Larentina's irises turned from a hazel brown to a deep dark maroon, with small lightning bolts showing in her irises. Lambda, by Larentina's side, growled and snarled as all the Spartans witnessing this dropped to their knees in fear.

"Larentina used the superstitious nature of the Spartan people to her advantage as she bellowed, 'I, whom you have claimed as your She Wolf demigoddess, command you to reunite with your kings' houses! Fear not, for I am the daughter of the house of Agiad and no other! You will continue to respect your Spartan women and honor your kings' laws. If any of you touches one hair on either queen's head, I will return with Zeus himself to destroy all of you! Live well, my fellow Spartans, and always remember to cherish your women! Now rise and honor your kings and your queens!'

"The crowd rose and cried out, 'She Wolf! She Wolf!' They lifted the kings and queens into the air. Larentina looked at King Alcaeus, who nodded his head, approving her speech.

"Larentina glanced into the future for just a moment as a small smile appeared on her lips. She truly had changed Sparta; not much, but it was a small step for the women of Sparta. She had changed the world, because there were no Olympian deities in her realm. Mankind would no longer be able to blame its wickedness on the fallen angels. She remembered her mother's words, 'Larentina, you cannot change everything.' Larentina arrogantly laughed aloud to the heavens as she looked at her mothers and cried out, 'At least I can try!'

"She ran toward Androcles and Lycurgus with her faithful Lambda by her side, and to the crowd's amazement, the three young Spartans disappeared. The storm disappeared as quickly as they did. They were never seen again by the Spartan people.

"For years to come, the Spartan men did not dare abuse their women in fear that the She Wolf would return in the night to seek justice.

"It was ruled that the names of Larentina and Lycurgus would never be mentioned again, and they were removed from all the stories, but Larentina could not be so easily removed from Spartan military history. The soldiers were forbidden to carry her face upon their shields, so they transformed her image into a wolf, which they displayed with pride. This image reminded them that Sparta really did have a She Wolf, who had been given to them by Zeus himself.

"The life of Larentina was rooted deeply into Spartan society, for what few freedoms and liberties that she had gained for the Spartan women would remain across the known world. Larentina, as a living breathing woman, would be forgotten, but her legacy would always remain.

"Little did Lucius know the Roman kingdom would turn into an empire; he was one of the last kings to rule Rome.

"Lucius had started the myth of the she wolf himself, stating, 'My son was nursed by a She Wolf, and he was transformed into a demigod by the milk that he suckled from the She Wolf's breasts.'

"A few generations later, an unwed virgin became pregnant and gave birth to twin boys. Her father, who was of Roman royalty, knew of the myth of She Wolf, and to protect his daughter, he announced that her twin sons, Romulus and Remus, suckled from the She Wolf's breasts; they grew up to become the founders of the Roman Empire.

"This is all that remained of Larentina's name, but her bloodline remembers who she truly was, and with their memory, she descended into immortality."

* * *

Mom-mom looked at everyone who was listening and calmly announced, "The end."

Christina excitably shouted out, "No, Mom-mom, that can't be the end! What happens when they arrive in Ireland?"

I cried out too, "But Mom-mom, you can't end the story there. I too want to know what happens next. What became of Persephone? Is she trapped for all eternity in the mortal realm?"

Teresa joined in, "Mom-mom, what about the other sister? The little girl who survived the fire—what happened to her?"

Mom-mom slyly grinned. "The tale of the younger sister is a tale all of its own for when our bloodlines are reunited once again. You are right, Belinda; Persephone is trapped in our realm. She even appeared in the lives of a few of our other ancestors. These tales are for another time. You are all correct, my children: this is not the end of the story, but just the beginning of another story, but that is another tale to tell indeed. The stories of our bloodline will never end, because your stories have just begun.

"Before you go off to bed, I want to give Belinda all of Larentina's possessions that have been passed down from generation to generation. Belinda, I know the She Wolf spirit is in you. We have all witnessed your abilities and strengths since your birth. Always remember, daughters of my blood, you must always protect the secret of Belinda's gifts, for if it's discovered, man could turn her into a lab rat and persecute her, because she possesses something they cannot comprehend. It has happened with many of our ancestors who were born with these gifts. Belinda, I pray the stories of our lineage trigger the memory in your blood of the true beginnings of these great gifts that you have inherited. Where did it all really start before Noah? The stories of our ancestors before Larentina are embedded in your genes; several ancestors wrote down the memories of Larentina's ancestors. But we still do not know the origins of how a girl child was born sporadically throughout the ages, leading to you, Belinda.

"Don't worry, children, for after I finish each tale of your ancestors, who made a difference in the world by simply following their calling, I will pass on their possessions to you. Belinda is the oldest and strongest, which is why she inherits the belongings of Larentina. Christina, you will be next."

1979

BELINDA REFLECTS ON LARENTINA

EN ROUTE TO FORT JACKSON, SOUTH CAROLINA

Chapter LXXIX

I continued looking out the train window, proudly smiling at the memory of Mom-mom's story. Of course, I thought it had been more myth than anything else, until she gave me Larentina's helmet, armor, sword, shield, and spear. I knew Larentina must have been given another helmet, because she threw the first one into the lake where she swam with the muses. I smile to myself because the helmet represented Larentina's ability of telepathy; she did not understand how to use it, but I do.

Mom-mom even gave me the scrolls on which Larentina had written her life story and its translation into old English from another ancestor of mine. Of course, Larentina's writings were different from the story Mom-mom told us, but the essence of truth was the same, no matter how much of a savage Larentina truly was. I must admit, Mom-mom's version was better than the original.

The train is slowing down, and I am ready to face the unknown, just as my ancestor did. I feel strong and scared at the same time. I wonder if I will be able to survive this man's army or, better yet, will this man's army be able to survive me, an American She Wolf? I guess I should feel sorry for them; after all, they have no idea I will be among them. I chuckle softly to myself after that thought.

I am more cunning, more clever, more educated, smarter, and nobler than all who came before me, and probably more arrogant as well. My generation knows what I am, and we understand the human mind, unlike my predecessors. I know how to control it and have been trained in how to use it, something that my ancestors did not have. One thing I'm most grateful for is that they all wrote about what they were able to do, even though most did not understand it.

It took my bloodline over two millennia to create me; my ancestors were part of the history of this great country, which was built on the very foundations of human rights and the belief in the one true God. My bloodline still has hope for mankind, sentient beings, who will finally understand what true freedom and personal liberty means. We are almost there, but have a long way to go. Mankind has a bad habit of reverting back to tyranny, and there have always been tyrants who use false promises to taint what human freedom is all about. As long as there are these types of bullies in the world, there will always be a she wolf with her pack lurking in the shadows to attack the vile beasts of men when they least expect it.

Mom-mom's great stories taught me to be strong; to stand up for what I believe in; to fight against anyone who tries to take my God-given liberties from me; to fight for truth, justice, and the American dream. You must fight for it, against both domestic and outside forces. Use the pen of ideas for greatness as your weapon, then the sword. Always have God by your side and in your heart, for then nothing will take the gifts of God from you.

The train stopped, and for one moment, I deliberately let my irises turn from a hazel brown to a deep dark maroon; just a flicker of electrical static charges flowed within them. I had a broad smile on my face as I stepped off the train as I too descend into immortality, feeling proud to be an American woman and proud to serve my country!

Author's Notes

This novel was fun and intriguing to write—it was fascinating to explore so many resources and learn about so many different faiths, biblical theology, and Greek mythology.

I had written a previous story in which I used the name "She Wolf," thinking I had made this name up, but during my research my mother reminded me of the myth of the She Wolf, who nursed the twin founders of the Roman empire when they were just babes. I realized that I had read this myth when I was a child, but that still did not stop me, as this story started to take on a life of its own. The ancient tale of She Wolf was not complete, and she had several different names. Historians over the ages even speculated whether the She Wolf was a woman or a beast.

As I was writing this story, I remembered talking with my father several decades ago when I was deployed overseas; I had called him one Easter to check in and keep him posted on my life.

The conversation transformed into a discussion on ancient mythology; I asked my father how the egg became part of our Easter traditions. He told me about a pagan story of an egg that dropped from the heavens into the sea. That story stuck with me through the years.

While writing this story, I called my father and asked for more information regarding this myth. I wanted to create a villain that my readers would never suspect. My father and I did extensive research and discovered many theories about the Goddess Aphrodite, and thus a nasty little villain was revealed.

My story took an entire different direction and came to life upon the pages as I wrote it. Thus this story, *Larentina: Myth, Legend, Legacy*, was born.

About the Author

Linda D. Coker was born and raised in the surrounding valley of the Appalachian Mountains of Virginia and currently resides in the beautiful state of Colorado.

She is an honorably discharged veteran of the United States Army and has a degree in business management.

Linda was one of the first women recruited after the Women's Army Corps (WAC) was disassembled and integrated into the Army.

After Linda married another soldier, it became harder for the two of them to stay stationed together; she gave up her military career so she could be by her man's side. She still played an active role throughout her husband's military career by volunteering her time to support the spouses and family members of her husband's fellow soldiers during many hardship deployments.

Linda was blessed during her travels with her husband, and she had the opportunity to work with many major contractors that support the troops. With these opportunities, she was still able to be part of the Army in the background and support her husband and his units in some capacity.

After her husband retired, Linda nearly died from the stress of her job; she took a three-year break from daily working and started writing stories. She considers herself a pretty good storyteller.

About the Artist

Howard David Johnson is a visual artist with a background in the natural sciences and history. He works in a wide variety of media ranging from traditional oils to digital media. After a lifetime of drawing and painting, his art was exhibited in the British Museum in London in 1996, as well as many other museums, including the Metropolitan Museum of Art. His work has appeared in major bookstores in America as well as magazines and educational texts. As an illustrator he has not only used the computer but has been involved in developing and marketing of software for Adobe Photoshop.